CRYPTOZOOLOGY FOR BEGINNERS

BOOK II
OF THE
CODEX ARCANUM

BY

EUPHEMIA WHITMORE, PH.D., M.L.S., D.D.S.

WITH MATT HARRY

ILLUSTRATIONS BY JULIANE CRUMP

Published by Inkshares, Inc., San Francisco, California
www.inkshares.com

Edited by Staton Rabin & Adam Gomolin
Cover design and illustrations by Juliane Crump
Interior design by Kevin G. Summers

ISBN: 9781947848825
e-ISBN: 9781947848597
LCCN: 2018943990

First edition

Printed in the United States of America

For Juliane, who knows all my secrets

WARNING!

This is no ordinary book.

Before reading further, it is recommended that you purchase and study the first text in this series, *Sorcery for Beginners*. Only when you have memorized its contents, completed your Level One Final Examination, and applied for your Sorcery Learner's Permit will you truly be able to appreciate the lessons contained in this volume. Go on. Cryptozoology will wait.

All finished?

Are you sure? Remember, this is a magic book; it's capable of sensing whether or not its owner is fibbing. Oh, very well. Even if you haven't completed those tasks, you are cleared to continue. The important thing is the study and protection of cryptids—magical creatures whose existence, until recently, has remained hidden from the world at large. If you are ready to shoulder that responsibility, and agree to absolve the Codex Arcanum, Euphemia Whitmore, and all associates, subsidiaries, underlings, and familiars of any wrongdoing or injury that may

befall you during your interactions with cryptids, then simply place your hand on the cover of this book and read aloud the following words:

"I [INSERT YOUR NAME] solemnly swear to learn cryptozoology and to protect all cryptids, living and deceased, from threats foreign, domestic, and extradimensional."

No, no, no. Where it says [INSERT YOUR NAME], you actually need to speak your own name. Please try again.

Excellent. Your identity has been registered with the Council Arcanum, and you are clear to proceed with your study of cryptozoology. As in *Sorcery for Beginners*, the lessons imparted in this volume will be presented in a narrative format. Readers will follow the adventures of several young sorcerers, many of whom you will recognize from the first book in the Codex Arcanum series. Their story will also be accompanied by facts, profiles, and additional information in four delightful categories:

THE CODEX ARCANUM

One's knowledge of sorcery should always be expanding, and these sidebars will help accomplish that.

CRYPTID CORNER

These sections will spotlight the various characteristics of magical creatures throughout the world, including their habitats, abilities, and favorite foods.

ENCHANTING
DETAILS

If there's a relevant non-magical fact or detail to explore, this is where you'll find it. Please do not use this information in school papers, as learning to do your own research is one of the most important aspects of writing.

BEWARE THE
EUCLIDEANS

Finally, space will be devoted to identifying and defeating sorcery's greatest enemies. They are devious, evil, and worst of all, well funded. You shall need all the help you can get.

This book will also instruct you on how to care for highly unique creatures, how to use magic to protect cryptids, and how to stay motivated in an ongoing conflict with a merciless foe. Having a team of skilled spell casters is recommended.

Are you ready? Then let us begin.

PROLOGUE

DAWN IN DRUMNADROCHIT

Fergus Brown had a secret.

It buzzed and thumped within him, like a cricket trapped inside a shoebox. It kept him awake at night, chewing at the edges of his mind. It woke him early in the morning, when everything outside was still the color of a week-old bruise. But worst of all, it forced him to lie.

Lying was something new for the young man. He fibbed, of course, like most fourteen-year-olds, but those false statements were about inconsequential things—things like whether or not he'd done his homework, or if he'd binned his mother's bland porridge, or if he'd snuck into his older brother Corin's room to read his comics. The young man had done all those things and more, but the actions themselves—and the lying about them— were relatively harmless.

Not so with the lies his secret demanded of him. Those lies—lies that were growing with each passing day—were decidedly harmful.

Or at least, they had the potential to be. Fergus was mature enough to recognize that. A couple years ago, he would have simply done as he liked and not even considered the possible consequences. But certain events in the last year made him grow up a bit. He knew now that the actions he was taking in service to his secret could see his brother fired, ruin the livelihood of his village, DRUMNADROCHIT, or even result in his own death.

But even knowing all of that, Fergus kept his secret to himself. And it, in return, kept him. For the last three days, it had sustained him, granting him energy and skills and a dedication he hadn't realized he possessed. For example, like most teenagers, he had never been an early riser. Nearly every day, it took a combination of his screeching alarm clock, his parents' yells, and Corin's callused hands to roust him from his bed. Not so after the discovery of his secret. Each day since then, the young Scot had sprung awake before dawn, eager to see what the day would bring. This morning was no different.

ENCHANTING DETAILS

DRUMNADROCHIT is located on the western shore of a loch in northern Scotland. It has a population of slightly over 1,000 residents, lovely hiking trails, and a considerable amount of rain.

Fergus's eyes snapped open at three thirty. He was alert and excited. He dressed quietly, made himself a lunch for school, and left a note for his parents (complete with the half-truth that he had gone running).

He did run—down through the dark, dewy grass toward the loch, his backpack bumping in time with his beating heart. But he wasn't training for the cross-country league or attempting to start an exercise regimen, although both those lies would have fit. Fergus was tall and lanky, with a crown of curly blond hair that topped his thin pale face and his warm olive eyes. His fair, freckled skin grew blotchy with the smallest exertions, but he wasn't morose or embarrassed about it. The way Fergus felt, it made little sense to fuss over things out of your control. Better to stay under the radar and accept what came your way—whether it was grades, mates, or Corin's dingy hand-me-downs. "Don't rock the boat and ye won't tip over," his dad was fond of saying, and Fergus had always agreed.

But that had all changed last Saturday. On that day, his mother had roused him out of bed at three thirty and informed him Corin had forgotten his lunch. It being the weekend, Fergus was tasked with delivering it to him. His older brother worked the graveyard shift on an oil rig in the loch, a shift that ran from eleven at night until seven in the morning. His lunch break was around four, and so Fergus had taken Corin's brown paper bag and thermos in hand without complaint and trudged through the still-sleeping village of Drumnadrochit. Although Fergus's hometown was small, boasting fewer than five restaurants and a tiny town square, it was the center of a bustling tourist trade. Thankfully, it was mid-May and there weren't many tour buses around in the wee hours. Fergus had been able to walk down the middle of the A82 main road, past stone cottages and dark grassy fields, yawning with nearly every step. He turned down a side street and soon emerged from the trees to see the lights of Corin's oil rig several hundred meters offshore. It jutted out of the mist-covered loch like a hulking metal spider.

The oil rig was the first of its kind in this particular loch. Offshore drilling had dried up several years ago, and for a while Scotland had hoped to ban all fracking and oil extraction. But a downturn in the local economy led energy companies to seek crude in more scenic, untouched spots. One such spot was the body of water next to which Fergus had lived his entire life. It was also the source of Drumnadrochit's tourists—Loch Ness.

Of course, there had been protests. In fact, Fergus could still see a few camping tents up the shore, the makeshift homes of a dozen or so protestors who still spent their days shouting at the oil rig through megaphones and waving signs at the workers. They thought the drilling was bad for the environment, but others said the rig would disturb **NESSIE**, the cryptid for

CRYPTID CORNER

Reports of NESSIE go back as early as 565 CE, but the mythology surrounding the creature was popularized with a photograph taken by a London surgeon in 1934. Though the photo was later proven to be a fake, hundreds of other sightings have since been reported.

BEWARE THE EUCLIDEANS

Readers of *Sorcery for Beginners* will recognize this LOGO, which represents the anti-magic organization that has sought to control sorcery for over 500 years.

which the loch was famous. But the offer from the energy company was so lucrative that the rig was approved and installed in a matter of months. Fergus knew his older brother felt a bit guilty about his new job, but the work paid well and it kept him close to home.

And so, on that Saturday at four in the morning, Fergus Brown had arrived at the small docked tug used to shuttle the oil rig workers back and forth to shore. The boat was sleek and high tech, with the energy company's LOGO emblazoned on the side—a cross bisected by a compass and sword. The teenager had knocked on the shiny hull, startling the napping captain awake. After he had explained his errand, the grizzled gray-haired man had grudgingly agreed to ferry Fergus to the drilling platform.

As they chugged across the misty water, they heard it. A sonorous, otherworldly bellow, high pitched like a siren but clearly organic. It made the hairs on Fergus's arms stand at attention and set his heart beating.

The Call Of The Cryptid

"What is that?" he asked the captain.

"Ach, you never heard the bellow o' Nessie?" The old man leered at him. His breath stank of cheap whiskey.

"Nessie's a thing for wee babs," replied Fergus, though there was a slight waver in his voice.

"Ye so sure about that? More 'n' more folks been spyin' the beastie o' late."

"My brother says they're pranksters," said Fergus stoutly. "People tryin' to shut down the rig with a lot of fairy-tale nonsense. I'm guessing it's a moose."

The captain snorted and spat over the side of the boat. "Time was, you wee barras were more open-minded. That Google has ruined yer sense o' wonder."

Fergus rolled his eyes in the way only a teenager can. They heard no more bellows, and spoke no further of the sound until they reached the oil rig. The captain agreed to wait for Fergus, and the teenager was directed by a **ROUGHNECK** to the back side of the platform, where his twenty-year-old brother was welding newly installed catwalks. The chorus of thumping drill pipes and chugging electrical generators made conversation difficult, so Fergus simply gave Corin his lunch and headed back to the boat.

Halfway there, he heard it again. A high-pitched bellow that somehow cut through the noise of the oil rig machines and set his heart a-gallop. Fergus looked all around, but this side of

ENCHANTING DETAILS

Not an actual "rough and uncouth person," which is the primary definition of ROUGHNECK, but an oil rig worker, which is the secondary definition. One would think oil rig workers would be miffed that their occupation has been appropriated in this way, but no. Most take it as a mark of pride.

the platform was deserted. Hoping to record the strange sound, he took out his mobile phone and opened the camera app. He panned around the dark, misty lake, his pulse thumping a paradiddle in his neck.

A shape coalesced in the mist. It was long necked and easily ten meters tall, moving at a speed of thirty or forty knots. Unlike a motorboat, however, it was completely silent. Also unlike a boat, it had eyes.

The creature—there was no other word for it—came to a stop a few meters from the oil rig and looked down at Fergus. Its head was the size of a small car, and its body was covered in brownish-green leathery skin, like a seal's. Its eyes glowed yellow in the mist. The creature sized up the teenager, and then charmingly sneezed.

"Nessie," said Fergus in awe. "Is it really you, then?"

The creature stared back at him, cocking her head to the side as if she could understand. She—for some reason it felt like a female—blinked her glowing eyes. Fergus stretched a trembling hand toward the cryptid—

And a mud pump kicked on behind him, startling both boy and beast. Nessie's eyes went wide and she gave another teeth-rattling cry. The sound was so loud, it knocked Fergus backward. The phone slipped from his hand, clattering on the metal grating of the oil platform. Instinctively, he reached for it, his eyes dropping from the massive dark shape before him. By the time he'd recovered his phone and looked up again, the creature had vanished.

Fergus got to his feet, looking up and down the length of the oil rig, but there was no more sign of the animal. Disappointment and relief fought for control of him. His heart thumping louder than the mud pump behind him, Fergus checked his recording. The footage was dark and grainy. He could see a discernible shape, but it could easily be mistaken for a boat instead of a mythical water creature. The teenager spoke, and the animal's responding bellow overloaded the camera's tiny microphone. Then the video cut out.

Disappointment won, filling his guts like cold **HAGGIS**. Fergus knew no one would believe what he'd seen. His friends, his family, even Corin, would be as suspicious of his encounter as he himself had been of the boat captain mere minutes ago. He needed proof, something more than a grainy shadow and a sound effect.

And so for three days, he'd begun to rock the vessel that was his usually placid life. He'd told no one his secret, every day rising before the sun, running down to the loch, and begging the captain to ferry him over to the oil rig. There he'd spend the next two or three hours scouring the misty water, waiting for Nessie to return. He'd even posted his video (anonymously,

---

ENCHANTING DETAILS

HAGGIS is a Scottish delicacy consisting of a calf or sheep's intestines, chopped up and mixed with oatmeal, suet, and seasoning, then boiled in the animal's stomach. It is almost universally loathed.

CRYPTID
CORNER

While it is not considered a "legitimate" science, hundreds of thousands of people worldwide believe in CRYPTOZOOLOGY. The cryptids don't care either way.

of course) on a few **CRYPTOZOOLOGY** message boards, hoping someone might give him an idea of how to contact the beast. He'd received a few suggestions, such as casting a spell of summoning or using a sonar gun to draw the creature out, but none he could actually undertake himself. He gloomily supposed it didn't matter because, as of yet, he'd seen no more evidence of the animal.

Today would be different, however. Today he had a plan.

Netting Nessie

Fergus had spent nearly all his waking hours over the last three days researching what type of creature the "monster" of Loch Ness might be. Her long neck and massive size made him guess that **NESSIE** was some kind of plesiosaur, even though they'd supposedly been extinct for sixty-five million years. But the dinosaur sketches he found online looked fairly close to the

CRYPTID
CORNER

People have also speculated that NESSIE is an oversized eel, a catfish, a Greenland shark, and even an elephant. They are all incorrect.

animal he'd seen near the oil rig. And the accompanying articles said plesiosaurs most likely ate shellfish, so he'd spent two afternoons scrubbing dishes at the nearby Craigdarroch Inn in exchange for two full bin bags' worth of shucked clams, mussels, and discarded salmon skin. It had been hard, finger-scalding work, but for the first time in his adolescence, Fergus had found something that was worth taking a little risk for. Something, finally, for himself.

His "pay bags," overflowing with their stinky contents, had been left behind the inn and were now bouncing against Fergus's legs as he made his way down to the pre-dawn loch. The bearded captain was there as always, only this morning he was polishing the hull of the company boat.

"Again wit ye?" he said as Fergus drew closer. "Research shows teenagers need more sleep 'n anyone."

"Can you just take me over to the rig?" Fergus replied.

"Ach, what's in them bags? Smells like the nethers o' Neptune himself."

"Bait," Fergus said half-truthfully. "The, uh, roughnecks wanna set out crab traps."

The captain grumbled that if the workers wanted to catch crustaceans, they could do so on their own bloody time, but he started the motor and piloted out toward the oil rig. Along the way, Fergus shook out the contents of one bag from the back of the boat. He hoped the fishy remains would be smelly enough to attract Nessie.

Once they reached the drilling platform, Fergus found a deserted spot and opened the second bin bag. The smell inside nearly made him retch, but he couldn't stop now. He spent the next ninety minutes tossing rank shells and fish bones into the loch. But there were no bellows, and no sign of the cryptid's signature profile.

Fergus sighed. The eastern sky was turning pink and the usual pre-dawn mist had dissipated. He was nearly at the end of his bait pile, and his hands stank of week-old shellfish. He'd have to shower before school, and he was out of ideas for how to see Nessie again. Perhaps it was best for him to forget his secret and return to his ordinary, drama-free life. Probably that was all someone like him deserved, anyway. He'd never been special or smart or particularly hardworking—why try to change that now? Let someone else rock the boat. His eyes stinging, Fergus balled up the bin bag and turned away from the foggy loch.

There was a sneeze behind him, exactly like he'd heard on Saturday. Fergus slowly turned his head to see a long-necked creature floating in the water beside the oil rig. Her head—it seemed obvious now that the beastie was female—rose at least ten meters above the platform. The creature's eyes weren't glowing, he saw now; they were just a very bright shade of yellow and reflective, like a cat's. Fergus peered over the edge of the oil platform and saw two flat fins jutting from her oblong body, which was similar in size to the boat he'd taken to get here. Several plastic bags were stuck to her flank. The animal shook them off, gyrating her body like a wet dog.

CRYPTOZOOLOGY FOR BEGINNERS

Nessie bent her head forward, sniffing the remaining pile of fish skin and shucked clam shells in the bin bag. She gave a pleased chirrup, then slurped down the whole mess in one gulp. Fergus could hear her teeth crunching the shells as if they were no tougher than celery. The creature moved her head forward, sniffing Fergus insistently.

"Must be my hands," he said, lifting them to show the animal they were empty. "Sorry, girl, but I'm clear out o' fish bits."

Nessie furrowed her brow, almost seeming to frown. She sneezed again, spraying Fergus with a fine mist. *Evidence*, he suddenly remembered. *I came here to get evidence.*

Quickly wiping his hands on his jeans, he took out his phone and opened the camera. It was much easier to see the creature in the growing light of dawn. "Hello, girl," he said softly. It was thrilling to see her loom over him, to know she was real. "What's your best side, then, eh?"

Suddenly, a metal bolt whizzed from beneath the platform and struck the massive creature in the neck. It bellowed in pain as blue electricity crackled down a metal line attached to the bolt. Nessie shuddered, her whole body turning to see-through mist for a moment. More electricity pulsed, and she solidified again. Her agonized cry shook the struts of the oil rig, making Fergus's heart squeeze in sympathy.

But before he could do anything, a dozen soldiers came swarming out from hidden spots all over the drilling platform. At least, Fergus thought they looked like soldiers—they carried automatic rifles and wore military-style outfits. But the insignia on their shoulders didn't indicate the flag of Scotland or even the Union Jack of Great Britain. Instead, it showed the same logo Fergus had seen on the shuttle boat—a squat cross bisected by a sword and compass.

They were **EUCLIDEANS**.

BEWARE THE EUCLIDEANS

It is estimated there are over 1 million EUCLIDEANS worldwide, with representatives from every country. Only a third of those are trained soldiers, but that's still a greater number than every active military in the world, save those of China, North Korea, and the United States.

MEMORY WIPES

Now, readers of *Sorcery for Beginners* will know how chilling that word is. Every member of that secret society is a cold-blooded villain, dedicated to the control and eradication of sorcery. The Euclideans are sworn enemies of not only sorcerers but magical creatures as well.

Fergus, of course, knew none of this. He only saw that these people were causing pain to a peaceable creature who had done nothing wrong. A creature he himself had lured there. Guiltily, he ran forward to stand in front of Nessie, holding out his arms as if that could stop any bullets the soldiers fired.

"Stop!" he cried. "You're hurting her; stop it!"

"Keep the current going," spoke a cold voice from the darkness. "Otherwise the beast will phase-shift and escape."

BEWARE THE EUCLIDEANS

As early adopters of technology, Euclideans are at the forefront of using BIONIC devices to replace and improve natural body parts. Some members install mechanical replacements even if there is no need. One hopes they have an extended warranty.

A man stepped out of the shadows of a mud pump. Unlike the soldiers, he wore an elegant dark suit. He was tall and thin, with slicked-back hair so blond it was almost white. The left side of his hollow-cheeked face was mottled with discolored skin grafts, like a patchwork quilt. But most unsettling of all, in his left eye socket there was a BIONIC replacement. The iris of the unnatural appendage glowed an icy blue. His presence was far more intimidating than the massive cryptid beside them.

"Stand aside, boy," the man continued with a crisp accent Fergus could not place. "You are swimming in waters you cannot fathom."

"I found her," Fergus said defiantly. "You can't just show up and take her. She's mine."

"On the contrary," replied the man with the bionic eye. "We own this oil rig, as well as the rights to any and all BIOLOGICAL DISCOVERIES in its immediate vicinity."

BEWARE THE EUCLIDEANS

This practice of "owning" and naming BIOLOGICAL DISCOVERIES actually goes back thousands of years. Humankind will leave its mark on anything if given the chance.

At a small gesture from the man, one of the soldiers came forward and snatched Fergus's phone. The Euclidean crushed the device beneath his boot. Behind them, Nessie gave a plaintive moan.

Fergus scanned the drilling platform, seeing the soldiers had rounded up the two dozen graveyard-shift roughnecks and were holding them at gunpoint. His brother Corin stared up at the creature from Loch Ness in slack-jawed shock.

"See to it that the workers are injected with neural inhibitors," said the man brusquely. Several of the Euclideans broke out syringes and filled them with a swirly gray substance. "Tiny robots," he explained to Fergus with a creepy smile. "They go into a subject's brain and destroy all neural pathways formed in the last twenty-four hours. A memory wipe for the modern age."

He advanced slowly toward the teenager. "But that shall not be your fate," he continued. "Because you have known about this creature for several days. Haven't you, Fergus Brown?" His bionic eye whirred, the blue iris expanding and contracting like an autofocusing lens.

Fergus made a move to bolt, but one of the soldiers grabbed him from behind, forcing him to his knees. The man with the bionic eye stood over him.

"Who are you?" Fergus said.

"Apologies for my impoliteness," said the man, giving a small bow of his head. "Especially since we are about to know each other so very well. I am Samson Kiraz."

CHAPTER I

TESTING TRISH

Those unoriginal jerks, Trish Kim thought angrily. *They did it again.*

She could see it from all the way down the middle school hallway. A green plastic rectangle taped to the outside of her locker. Like a road sign glowing at night. As she moved closer, the rectangle came into focus. It was an empty bag of frozen vegetables. Peas this time. The plastic bag featured a cartoon giant on the front, but some enterprising student had printed out Trish's frowning yearbook photo and glued it over the giant's face. *HO HO HO! BIG TRISH!* was scrawled on the bag in red Sharpie. *Brilliant,* she thought as she ripped it off. *Doesn't even match the jingle.*

She opened her locker, adding the crumpled vegetable bag to a not-insignificant pile of similar bags. She put away her books and slammed the locker door closed. Then she opened it and

slammed it shut thrice more for good measure. A few kids in the emptying hallway giggled at her actions, but when she turned to growl at them, they quickly looked away.

They know I won't hurt them. I can't. Trish was well aware that her presence could be intimidating. Straight black hair clung to her skull like a rugby helmet. Her dark eyes and small mouth seemed to be set in a permanent scowl. But most noticeably, the broad-shouldered thirteen-year-old stood at least a head taller than every other student at Henderson Middle School. Unfortunately, she had sworn not to make use of her size and skills while at school, not even in self-defense. She had to pretend she was an ordinary—albeit oversized—eighth grader. Which meant she had to endure insults, jokes, and targeted pranks— pranks such as the recent vegetable-bag-giant craze—in silence.

She got it; she stood out. And most people didn't like those who stood out. Usually she could shrug it off, but on this Wednesday afternoon, it was too much to bear. Even though eighth grade would be finished on Friday, and Trish was look- ing forward to high school in the fall, her excitement for sum- mer vacation had just been torpedoed. Worse than that—it had been vaporized by an atom bomb, covered in smelly garbage, and dumped inside a flowery pink trash bin. Trish hated flowers; she despised the color pink, and plastic was, in her opinion, the most wasteful invention ever.

All thanks to Julie, she thought darkly. Julie Alvarez had been Trish's best friend since fifth grade. They were both members of the local **SOCIETY FOR CREATIVE ANACHRONISM** chapter, they took karate together, and they often camped out in each other's backyards. Two months ago, Trish had broken her leg (due to an incident you can read about in *Sorcery for Beginners*), and Julie was the first one to sign her cast. Said cast had finally been removed last week, and Trish was looking forward to attending karate camp with Julie in June. Eight whole days of sharing a cabin with her best friend, without any parents or siblings or other kids bothering them.

Then today at lunch, Julie had suddenly announced that she would no longer be going.

"What?" Trish had exclaimed, unintentionally slamming her fork on the table. Two nearby sixth graders laughed, imitating her big movements. Trish tried to ignore them. "Camp starts in a month. Why are you wussing out?"

Julie's cheeks turned red. "I'm not 'wussing out,'" she replied icily. "I just don't wanna spend eight days in a sweaty *GI*. In fact, I'm thinking of quitting karate altogether."

Trish was astonished. "Since when? We've been in karate together for three years. You're almost a red belt."

"Yeah, well, maybe it's not for me, okay? You gotta admit, all that punching and wrestling and dirty feet, it's kinda . . . boyish."

The word made Trish stiffen. "Karate is for warriors! Samurai, ninja, not . . ." Even though they were sitting at the end of a table by themselves, she looked around to make sure no one else was listening. "Is this because of the other night?"

Julie shook her hands. "No. No, no, no, no. I just realized I wasn't as . . . into martial arts as you are. People change, okay? I'm not a . . . tomboy like you." She stood, gave an apologetic shrug, then went to throw out the remains of her chicken salad.

Now in front of her locker, Trish was positive Julie's decision was less about martial arts and more about her. Specifically, what Trish had confided to her friend the other night. The thing no one else—not her parents, her friends, not even a doctor—knew about. The thing Trish hadn't even fully articulated to herself yet.

Her secret.

Since she was small, Trish had been interested in girls. She didn't dislike boys—in fact, she often felt more comfortable around them than her own gender—but boys didn't hold the same fascination for her as females. When she entered puberty, that fascination had bloomed into full-flowered attraction. But she couldn't be sure if the feelings she was having were real, she reasoned, unless she acted on them.

And so, after stewing it over and considering it and second-guessing herself for several weeks, Trish had tried to kiss her best friend.

She and Julie had been hanging out in Julie's basement, as they had many times over the last five years. They were discussing the latest song from a female musician they both liked. Julie was talking about how good-looking the musician was, how much she admired her style, and Trish suddenly found herself grasping her friend's shoulders. Julie looked startled, but by then it was too late for Trish to turn back. She closed her eyes, pursed her lips, leaned forward—

And Julie had *leaned away*.

Recoiled might be a better word.

Trish had opened her eyes and seen that the expression on her friend's face was one of shock and even mild disgust. Trish was crushed. For the last three months, she had thought Julie was signaling her, silently confirming the two of them were the same, but in reality she had felt the complete opposite. In reality, she was horrified.

Trish thumped her locker with her fist. *Well, who needs her?* she thought bitterly. *Not me. I'm a warrior, and the only thing warriors need is someone to fight. Love is lame, anyway.*

"What's wrong, dude? You forget your combination?"

Case in point. Trish turned to see her friends Owen and Perry approach. They were both thirteen as well, but physically quite different from each other. Owen was a rangy eighth grader with tousled brown hair and a laid-back attitude, while Perry was petite, bespectacled, and had the earnest, excitable energy of a know-it-all squirrel. The two of them were holding hands, but upon seeing Trish's scowl, they separated.

"Is it stuck?" said Perry, adjusting her funky purple eyeglasses to peer at Trish's locker. "If so, we could cast a Spell for Unlocking once the hallway empties out."

She was not being sarcastic. Eight weeks prior, the three teenagers had discovered a working spell book called *Sorcery for Beginners* and had been forced to defend it from Euclideans. In the process, they had learned over a hundred different enchantments. A Spell for Unlocking was one of the Twelve Basic Incantations, but they had sworn to keep their magical talents a SECRET.

"It's not stuck," Trish said. "It's . . . forget it. Let's get outta here."

A VERY WHITMORE WELCOME

Though it was only May, the Mojave Desert surrounding Las Vegas, Nevada, had already made temperatures quite hot. Trish trudged down the LAS VEGAS STRIP a bit behind Owen

THE CODEX
ARCANUM

Keeping sorcery a SECRET is one of the core tenets of the Codex Arcanum. If humanity were to learn that magic still existed, sorcerers would be inundated by endless requests for spells, potions, and all manner of magical fix-its.

ENCHANTING
DETAILS

The LAS VEGAS STRIP is one of the most iconic and garish displays of architecture in the world. As of this writing, there are 45 massive casinos, hundreds of stores, and dozens of amusement park rides crammed into a 6.8-kilometer strip of road. It is a quintessential American creation.

and Perry. Even though it was a weekday afternoon, the streets were clogged with cars and the sidewalks teemed with gawking tourists. Massive casino hotels and flashing video signs loomed above them, nearly blotting out the sky. Since Trish and her friends lived in the nearby suburb of Henderson, they almost never came to the Strip. But today was a special occasion. Today, they were waiting to hear about the fate of Virgil Ferretti, an evil casino owner who had tried (and failed) to steal the teenagers' guide to magic two months prior. To pass the time while they waited, Owen had suggested they take a ride-share vehicle to the Strip to get ice cream. Eating junk food was one of his favorite ways to kill time.

High above them, a lone hawk circled, buoyed by the warm air currents. Trish envied its ability to take off and be alone at a moment's notice. Especially at this moment. Her friends were holding hands again, which for some reason made Trish feel awkward and angry. She was happy they were dating, of course, even if their "relationship" had so far involved only a couple of movie dates and some tentative kisses. She supposed it was the brazen display of their affections for each other that irked her. *So they like each other*, she thought. *They don't gotta brag about it to the whole world. Especially when some of us can't—*

But her train of thought was interrupted as Owen's phone chimed. He took it out and read a news alert. "This is it," he crowed, showing the screen to Perry and Trish.

"'Virgil Ferretti pleads guilty to grand larceny and attempted murder,'" Perry read with satisfaction. "'Receives twenty-five-year prison sentence.'"

"Sayonara!" Owen clapped his hands. "Told you we wouldn't have to worry about him anymore."

"I only hope Bryan doesn't try to seek revenge," Perry said nervously. She was referring to Ferretti's son, a fifteen-year-old bully who had also learned sorcery. "He looked angrier than a seasick kraken at the trial."

Trish wasn't concerned. In fact, she felt better than she had all day. "Dude, he's on lockdown, too. House arrest until he turns eighteen." She and Owen executed a multipart high five.

"But they both know magic exists," Perry reminded them. "What if they endeavor to tell someone? Or actually use it?"

Owen shrugged. "Without the spell book, the best they'll be able to conjure up are a few expensive-looking tricks. Come on, sundaes are on me."

Perry was about to respond when a crisp, melodious voice spoke behind them: "Ice cream, I fear, may have to wait."

The three teenagers turned. On the sidewalk before the broad lagoon of the BELLAGIO hotel, as if conjured from the desert air, stood an elegant British woman. Her hair was silver and swept artfully atop her head, but her age was difficult to pinpoint. She wore a dark-blue blouse and a long skirt, seemingly unfazed by the Vegas heat. It should also be mentioned that she was breathtakingly—one could even say unfairly—attractive.

Euphemia Whitmore looked at the eighth graders over the top of her silver spectacles. "Mr. Macready, Ms. Spring, and Ms. Kim. I'm afraid there's an urgent matter to which we must attend. Due to the actions of a young man in Scotland, the cryptid known as **NESSIE** has been captured. Both of them require rescue."

Since Whitmore had been responsible for giving them the book that had taught them all sorcery, the teenagers had been expecting a visit like this for the last eight weeks. But her appearances were always abrupt, and as usual, Perry was the quickest to recover.

"**CRYPTID**? As in 'mythological creature not confirmed by science'? You're talking about the Loch Ness *Monster*??"

The librarian inclined her head. "Not only mythical, but magical as well. There are, of course, many such creatures all over the globe, but wrangling

Loch Ness Monster

HABITAT:
SCOTLAND

THE **SHY CELEBRITY**

(Also Known As: **NESSIE**)

WEIGHT:
2,700 kg

LENGTH:
10 m

HEIGHT:
25 m

MAGICAL PROPERTIES:
phase-shifting, enhanced healing

Sightings of the Loch Ness Monster, probably the **most well-known cryptid** on earth, go back **thousands of years.** Because of its **physical similarities to prehistoric plesiosaurs,** people have speculated the creature is a leftover dinosaur, but this is impossible because **the lake** in which it lives is **only 10,000 years old.**

Nessie's famous **reputation for avoiding detection** is due to its **ability to magically phase-shift into any state of water-based matter** — rain, ice, even mist. It uses this power to **move back and forth between** Scotland's more than 31,000 lochs.

— DID YOU KNOW? —

Millions of dollars have been spent on books, television shows, and films about the cryptid, but **none of them have actually obtained a legitimate photograph of Nessie.**

them is difficult for those without the ability to cast spells. Letting even one of them fall into the hands of our enemies would be disastrous. Seeing as you three are now Level One sorcerers, I was hoping you could assist in this matter."

She held up a paperback book titled *Cryptozoology for Beginners*. Like *Sorcery for Beginners*, it was covered in runes and mysterious drawings. She handed it to Trish. "You may begin your studies once we have accomplished our mission and reported back to the Council."

"Council?" echoed Owen.

Trish and Perry sighed. Technically, Owen had been the one to discover *Sorcery for Beginners*, but he didn't remember half of the magical facts they had learned. Sometimes Trish wondered why he was regarded as the leader of their group.

"The COUNCIL ARCANUM, dingus," Trish replied.

Owen nodded in understanding, taking the cryptozoology text from Trish and flipping through it. There were pictures of fantastic animals and maps, but no booming voices or magically appearing words. "So, this book, it's not like *Sorcery*? You know, ensorcer-ified or whatever?" He sounded disappointed.

THE CODEX ARCANUM

The COUNCIL ARCANUM is a seven-member team of experts dedicated to the preservation of sorcery. Their library, dubbed the Codex Arcanum, is managed by Euphemia Whitmore and functions as a repository for all their collected learning, including magical manuscripts, artifacts, and even creatures.

Perry placed a hand on her boyfriend's shoulder in a gesture that meant *please stop embarrassing us.* "He means ensorcelled," she explained to Whitmore.

The librarian lifted an elegant eyebrow. "The Codex Arcanum may be a repository for magical knowledge, but not every item inside it is enchanted. Could you imagine the upkeep?" She shook her head as if they'd asked for their own personal genie. "Now, shall we depart?"

The three teenagers looked at each other. Perry's face expressed her characteristic worries about physical confrontation, while Owen was practically rubbing his hands in excitement.

Trish was likewise itching to use sorcery again, but she had concerns. "Whoa, you want us to go to Scotland now? My mom'll freak if I miss dinner."

"It does seem a bit . . . abrupt," agreed Perry. "And won't it take at least ten hours to fly there? I don't even possess a passport."

"We have no need of such tiresome trappings when sorcery is involved," replied Whitmore. "I can whisk us to Scotland instantly, but time is of the essence. The Euclideans are analyzing the cryptid of Loch Ness as we speak, and their methods are not gentle."

"Come on, guys," Owen said to his friends. "You want Nessie to be tortured?"

Trish was affronted. "Of course not, but if my mom calls the cops, it's gonna create a lot more problems. You know how long it took me to convince her to let me go to karate camp?" The reminder that Julie would no longer be joining her at camp sent a twinge of pain through Trish's chest, but she did her best to ignore it. "Unless you've got some kind of magical **DOPPELGÄNGER** that can take my place?" she said to Whitmore.

"I'm afraid not," admitted the librarian. "Such enchantments take rather a long time to create if they are to be believable." She tapped her lips in thought. "Though the idea has merit for future excursions."

"I propose we delay our departure until seven p.m.," suggested Perry. "It's only a few extra hours, and it will give us time to prepare."

Whitmore flipped open an old-fashioned brass pocket watch. Trish craned her head forward, seeing that the face of the device had at least a dozen hands, all pointing to different spots on a facsimile of the Earth. One quivering red hand was fixed on the British Isles.

"I suppose that may work for the better," the older woman mused. "It will be three in the morning Scottish time. Ideal for a stealthy approach." She snapped the watch closed. "Very well. We shall convene at the playground near Mr. Macready's home at seven of the clock local time. Bring protective gear."

THE CODEX ARCANUM

In common parlance, a DOPPELGÄNGER is someone who merely looks and/or sounds like someone else. In sorcery, a conjured doppelgänger can be imbued with aspects of the copied individual's personality as well.

HOME STENCH HOME

The smell inside the Kims' garage was horrible.

If Trish had to describe it, she would say a dead rat had been wrapped in a sweaty jock strap and then buried inside a rotten egg. It was an odor with an agenda, like it wanted to slap Trish's nose right off her face.

She shut the plastic bin of sports equipment, dropping it next to a shelf filled with similar boxes. Hopefully the next one wouldn't stink as bad.

"Knock, knock," Trish's mom sang out from the garage doorway. Her voice was bright but tinged with nervousness. For the last year or so, her parents had taken to walking on eggshells around their temperamental daughter. One never knew what would set her off these days.

Trish grunted and opened a second tub of sports gear. Nope. Just as smelly as the first box. She waved her hand around to clear the stench, an action her mother interpreted as a cue to step inside the garage. Trish's mom was a pleasantly plump woman with bobbed black hair and round glasses. She looked and smelled like a human jar of cookies.

"Julie's mom called," she began haltingly. "She wanted to let me know—"

"I heard," said Trish shortly, pulling out her karate sparring gear. She only had an hour to air it out before meeting Whitmore. She set aside a helmet and elbow and knee pads. Now she just needed some kind of chest protection.

"You must be . . . disappointed?" her mother tried.

"Nope," Trish lied, opening another box of sports equipment. She wrinkled her nose at the scent of sweat-stained leather. "People change. So what?"

"I only thought . . . Well, she's your best friend."

"Not anymore." Trish grunted as she heaved the third box aside and opened a fourth. The odor from this one was the worst yet. Holding her breath, she dug through crusty baseball gloves and stinky soccer shin guards.

"Oh, honey," her mother said sympathetically. She stepped forward to touch her daughter on the shoulder. "Maybe it's just a fight. You can't—oh my, that's rank. Whew." She pinched her nose, making her voice nasal. "You can't keep things locked up inside you. It's unhealthy. Your father and I, we support you, no matter what—"

Trish shoved aside the fourth equipment box, making her mother jump back. After Julie's reaction, the teenager was terrified her mother might respond in a similar way if she told the truth. And so she deflected: "I'm not unhealthy, I'm . . . pissed, okay? Pissed that no one in this house can put things back in the proper place!"

Trish's mom blinked. "There's no need for language. If you tell me what you're looking for, we can both—"

"My catcher's vest. From last summer. It's missing."

"Oh, honey, even if it's still here, I doubt that will fit you anymore. You've gotten so—"

"Big?" The word was bitter poison in her mouth. "Yeah, I know what a freak I am, Mom. You know why? Because everyone keeps TALKING about it!" She kicked one of the boxes angrily.

Trish's mom held up her hands in a calming gesture. "You know I didn't mean it that way. Why don't we look for the vest together? Easy-peasy." Her mom bent down, moving aside boxes and blowing at cobwebs.

Trish sighed. She knew her mom didn't deserve to be yelled at. But the teenager couldn't seem to control her emotions recently. Her brain felt like a rickety carnival ride—one moment she was calm, high above the world and able to see everything around her; the next moment she was hurtling toward the ground in a death spiral, with no idea why she was yelling.

"Here we are," said her mother, lifting out a black baseball catcher's vest and knocking the dust from it. "Fell behind the shelf, that's all."

"Thanks." Trish pulled the stiff protective vest over her head. It stopped a good ten centimeters above her waist, five for each size she'd grown since last year. Both she and her mom broke into laughter. It felt wonderful to feel something other than frustration.

It was nearly half a minute until their chuckles finally subsided. "Well, we can't have you be seen like that," her mom said, pulling off the far-too-small chest protector. "Best borrow your brother's hockey gear instead." She opened a box and shook out a larger vest. "Good thing we never get rid of anything."

Trish pulled it over her head. Her brother was two years older than her, but since Trish was taller, it was an excellent fit.

"Sure you don't want to tell me what all this is about?" her mom said tentatively.

Trish shook her head, the smile fading from her face. There was nothing to discuss. She and love were finished. From now on she would be a non-romantic person, a warrior monk—or whatever the female version of a warrior monk was. "Warrior nun" sounded dumb. "Just SCA stuff. Going over to Owen's after dinner to practice."

Her mother sighed again, but she didn't push. "Okay. Back by ten for bed."

Trish nodded, then grabbed her mom in a bear hug. She couldn't tell her that if things in Scotland went poorly, being late for bedtime would be the least of her worries.

SLIP-SLIDING AWAY

Whitmore, Perry, and Owen were waiting as Trish rode her bike into the playground. It was dusk, and the setting sun backlit the distant desert hills in shades of red and orange. The playground was only a few years old and composed of colorful recycled plastic. It contained a set of three swings, a sand pit, and a play structure with a twisty tube slide.

Trish could see that her friends had also outfitted themselves in do-it-yourself protective gear, though they'd had far less equipment to choose from. Perry wore some of her secondhand SCA training gear while Owen had wrapped his arms and legs in soccer shin guards. Both of them wore their bike helmets. Whitmore, however, was in the same skirt and blouse as before.

"You're coming with us, aren't you?" Trish asked the librarian.

"Naturally. I would never send Level One sorcerers to face the Euclideans without supervision."

"Uh, you did two months ago," she pointed out. "When we got the book back from Ferretti?"

Whitmore waved a hand in dismissal. "That was for the purposes of your Final Examination, and you were all under close watch during the entire encounter. Had any life-threatening actions occurred, we would have stepped in immediately."

"Ferretti shooting me wasn't life-threatening?" Owen asked incredulously.

Whitmore stretched out an elegant finger, tapping the bone amulet that hung from his neck. A single rune of protection was carved into its surface. Owen had been given the magical artifact by their former trainer, and it had saved his life. "You survived, did you not?"

"What about tonight?" Perry asked nervously. "We only have one magic amulet."

"Tonight I shall be with you," she assured them. "Trust your instincts, remember your spell craft, and follow my directions. Do this and everyone will survive."

The thought that anyone might die was unnerving, but the librarian held out a hand toward the plastic play structure. "Now, if you will please enter the slide."

Torn between curiosity and nervousness, the teenagers trooped up the steps to the tube slide's entrance. The inside of it was dark and echoey. They looked questioningly at Whitmore, but she gestured for them to go in. "Go on, go on. The portal I've cast will only last another minute or two."

Owen sat down first. He squeezed Perry's hand, then pushed himself downward. He gave a yell of surprise, which seemed to reverberate over a great distance. He did not come out the bottom. Once Whitmore assured them this was normal, Perry went next, squeaking in distress when she reached whatever was at the bottom of the slide.

Then it was Trish's turn. She lowered herself gingerly, as her left leg was still a bit stiff from where the cast had been. She tightened her backpack, which held *Cryptozoology for Beginners*, a sheaf of hand-copied spell pages, and a few enchanted defense items. Whitmore scanned the perimeter of the playground, then nodded to Trish to go down the slide.

The teenager pushed off, sliding around the turns of the tight plastic tube. A round circle of purple fire glowed at the bottom. Cold air and the scent of wet grass wafted upward. Trish's feet entered the flames and there was a bright flash of purple energy. She suddenly felt as if her body were a piece of chewing gum stretched between two infinitely long fingertips. The nighttime sounds of the playground slowed down to a deep, drawn-out pitch. Just when it felt like her muscles and bones could not be pulled any further, her body snapped back together. She dropped a few centimeters, landing in a patch of dewy grass, immediately soaking her bottom.

She got to her feet, then doubled over, her head swimming from disorientation. It felt as if the ground beneath her were spinning like an out-of-control billiards ball. It took every ounce of her will to keep from vomiting.

Behind her, there was another purple flash and Whitmore stepped lightly down to the grass. The librarian regarded the teenagers with amusement. "Apologies for the travel sickness," she said. "Crossing eight time zones instantaneously can make people a bit ill. It shall pass."

"You mean . . . we're not dead?" Trish said queasily, her head still between her legs. "I feel dead."

"Don't be ridiculous," replied the librarian. "You have merely journeyed ten thousand miles in the breadth of a blink. Behold." She held out her hands, indicating the dark forested hills that surrounded them and the fog-covered body of water before them. It was the middle of the night and the sliver of moon had set hours ago. "That, my young sorcerers, is Loch Ness."

Chapter 2

Loch And Loaded

"Whoa, whoa, whoa," said Owen, lifting his head and then promptly lowering it again due to nausea. "You expect us to take on a bunch of Euclideans in this condition? I can't even stand."

"I concur," Perry said in a quavery voice.

"As I said, the disorientation will pass," replied Whitmore, moving her fingers in a complex pattern. "In the meantime, we may occupy ourselves with battle plans."

Trish raised her head to see the librarian make a square out of her thumbs and forefingers. She spoke a word in ICELANDIC, and a golden square of light appeared between her fingers. She

THE CODEX
ARCANUM

The Spell to See in Darkness was developed in ICELAND because half the year, the country is cloaked in near-constant night. Even if one can't feel the sun, remembering that it will return is important to one's mental health.

stretched her hands apart, creating a rectangular window suspended in the air. She moved it back and forth, revealing that anything seen through the floating rectangle appeared as if lit by the midday sun. The effect was so cool, it made Trish momentarily forget her own nausea.

Whitmore centered the rectangle on a structure several hundred meters across the loch. An oil rig. She turned her right hand, magnifying the illuminated image. One end of the structure had been draped in thick white rubber sheeting of the sort exterminators use when tenting a house for fumigation. Armed soldiers with the Euclidean logo on their shoulders could be seen patrolling the edges of the platform. Trish gritted her teeth at the sight of them.

"That is our objective," said the older woman, indicating the white-tented area. "I have no doubt Nessie is being held within." She formed a few runes and tapped each soldier she saw. Every place her finger touched, a glowing luminescence was left behind. She zoomed out, revealing at least a dozen Euclideans to contend with.

"You want us to take on all of them?" Owen gagged, but he managed to keep down his dinner. "That's double the amount we fought off at **DRAGONRIDGE ROCKS**, and we had way more kids helping us."

THE CODEX
ARCANUM

The Battle of DRAGONRIDGE ROCKS took place on the outskirts of Henderson, Nevada, and serves as the climax to *Sorcery for Beginners*. It also illustrates how dangerous fighting with magic can be.

"True, but you did not have me," replied Whitmore. "However, since our enemies have no qualms about killing children, I suggest we adopt a stealthy, nonlethal approach."

"Uh, definitely," said Trish. She tried to stand, but her legs felt like wet spaghetti. "I'm all for protecting animals, but I'm not committing murder to do it."

"What if we make ourselves invisible?" suggested Perry. She managed to rise to a sitting position. "That way we can sneak past and won't even have to fight."

"A worthy idea, but I'm afraid they are prepared for that." Whitmore zoomed in on one of the Euclidean soldiers, indicating a device strapped to his face. "Infrared goggles. Renders our invisibility enchantments moot."

Owen pointed to a docking platform on the rear side of the oil rig. "If we enter from that side, we only have to get past three guards."

Whitmore surveyed the path of his finger and nodded. "It would appear to be our best approach." With a few finger positions and a gesture, she swept aside the magical viewing window. The tiny dots of luminescence remained, highlighting the position of each soldier on the far-off drilling platform. "Once we begin our attack, I urge you to stay together and remain silent. If the whole platform is alerted, our odds of success will be greatly decreased. Are you ready?"

Trish got gingerly to her feet, happy to discover her nausea seemed to be abating. She yanked Owen and Perry up as well.

Whitmore swept her hands through the air, fierce determination etched across her face as she formed a few familiar rune shapes. Then she spread her fingers at both herself and the young sorcerers, speaking a single word in Welsh: *"Hedfan."*

FLIGHT AND FIGHT

The four of them rose off the ground, as weightless as soap bubbles. Of them all, only Trish had experienced the Spell for Flight before. She could see now what a clumsy job she'd made of the casting. Her enchantment had been solely focused on her feet, which left her body dangling upside down and her weight supported solely by her ankles. It had been rather painful, and Trish had not been terribly eager to try the spell again.

Whitmore's casting, however, was completely different. The whole of their bodies felt light and fleet, as if they were floating in outer space. It was thrilling and unearthly, reminding Trish why she loved magic so much. It had been weeks since they'd been able to cast any of the spells they'd learned, and she was eager to flex her mystical muscles. She assumed an attack position, but a gesture from the librarian made them all rotate FORWARD so they were parallel with the ground and facing the oil rig.

THE CODEX
ARCANUM

Of course, the Spell for Flight allows for the caster to fly in any position—standing, backward, even upside-down if one chooses. But facing FORWARD cuts down on wind drag and allows the sorcerer to see where she is going.

"Remember, keep quiet," the older woman reminded them. "No matter how enjoyable this might be." Then she flicked her fingers forward, and the group shot across the misty loch. They flew about three meters above the water, close enough that their speed left a wake on the surface behind them.

It was exhilarating to move so quickly and so silently. *This is how that hawk must have felt*, Trish thought as they curved around the loch to approach the rear of the drilling platform. *I can't believe that was only a few hours ago.* She restrained herself from whooping with pleasure. She stretched her fingers down in an attempt to brush the water, when Whitmore's voice broke through her reverie:

"We've been spotted. Attack!"

Trish looked up from the loch to see a soldier staring at them from the drilling platform twenty meters away. His astonishment at seeing four flying people froze him for a moment. Then he remembered his training and spoke into the radio receiver attached to his shoulder.

Trish and the others hastily began conjuring spells. "You spotted him. Why didn't you attack?" Owen complained to Whitmore.

"Because I am currently keeping us from dropping head-first into the loch," the librarian responded calmly, making a few slight finger adjustments. "Hurry, he is taking aim."

The Euclidean had indeed leveled his M5 rifle at them, but he was too late. Trish finished the movements for her enchantment and thrust a hand toward the soldier.

"Fulgur venire!" she whisper-shouted. A bolt of lightning arced from her palm, briefly illuminating the loch and striking the soldier directly in the chest. He convulsed, collapsing into an unconscious lump. Trish's hands tingled with magical energy and her heart pounded. It felt great to be casting spells again, but even stunning the soldier made her feel slightly guilty. *It was us or him*, she reassured herself. *Dude shouldn't have brought a gun to a spell fight.*

Whitmore curled her fingers toward her palms, making the four of them rise upward. Then she brought her hands down, setting them all upright on the metal catwalk of the drilling platform. A few more hand motions cast off the flying spell. Gravity gripped them all once more.

"Nicely done," the librarian murmured to Trish. She lifted the Euclidean's infrared goggles and placed a hand over his face, murmuring a long string of words in some Middle Eastern language. The young man inhaled sharply, then breathed deeply. "A **SPELL TO INDUCE SLUMBER**," she explained to the teenagers. "Not even the apocalypse could rouse him now." She toed the soldier's assault rifle into the loch and indicated the luminescent blobs that stood between them and the white-tented area of the

---

THE CODEX
ARCANUM

A **SPELL TO INDUCE SLUMBER** was not included in *Sorcery for Beginners* because casting it can be quite tricky. One must properly execute the runes to induce sleep without succumbing to them. More often than not, the sorcerer nods off before he or she can finish the enchantment.

oil rig. "Only two Euclideans stand in our path, provided we remain stealthy."

Suddenly, the man's shoulder radio crackled and a rough voice issued from it: "Oi, 782-Gamma. You still got eyes on that incoming?"

The four sorcerers looked at one another, unsure how to proceed. Whitmore pulled off the radio receiver and held it out to Owen. He pushed it back toward her, shaking his head.

Whitmore held it out more insistently. "They are expecting a man's voice," she whispered.

"Yeah, and I'm still a teenager!" he whispered back.

With a sound of frustration, Trish grabbed the receiver from the librarian's hand and pressed the button. She dropped her voice a couple octaves and adopted a British Cockney ACCENT: "Negative, mate. False alarm."

The other three were impressed. "Mimicry level: goddess," said Perry.

Trish shrugged modestly. "A few weeks hanging with Alec Incanto had its advantages," she replied, referring to their original magic trainer (who quite sadly ended up betraying them to Virgil Ferretti—why he did this can be read about in *Sorcery for Beginners*). "I'm good at voices."

THE CODEX ARCANUM

Of course, a sorcerer could use a glamour to alter his or her ACCENT, but such a casting takes time. Often the non-magical solution is the most expedient.

Perhaps she should have left well enough alone. The radio crackled to life again. "Why didn't you use the communique code?" The Euclidean commander asked suspiciously. "I'm sending a guard."

Whitmore held out the radio receiver again, gesturing for Trish to continue. "Uh," she said in her regular voice before remembering to speak in a lower register. "Uh, bad idea, matey. There's some kind of slippery substance here—whoa! Ahhh!" She clunked the receiver against the metal grating of the platform a few times, then clicked off the button.

The others weren't looking so pleased now. "What?" Trish whispered defensively.

"'Slippery substance'?" Owen whispered sarcastically. "You just guaranteed the Euclideans'll come investigate."

Trish's face burned in embarrassment. "Well, at least they won't be looking for us," she said huffily. "Next time you have a bright idea, feel free to take the wheel."

"If I do, you can bet I'll be a better improviser," he shot back.

"What's done is done," said Whitmore softly. "I suggest we find Nessie."

Release The Cryptid

Quietly, the sorcerers made their way across the drilling platform, crouching behind supply containers and ducking past still-operating mud pumps. Whitmore's incandescent tags made it easy for them to avoid most of the patrolling guards. One suddenly turned onto their path, but Owen quickly stunned him with a thunderclap spell to the face. Luckily, they were standing next to a chugging electrical generator at the time, and the booming sound went unnoticed.

A few meters later they came across a guard posted at the center of the drilling platform. Perry whispered a few words and thrust out a hand, encasing him in a column of ice. Trish patted the frozen prison as they crept past, but the Euclidean could only make a few muffled sounds in response.

Within moments, they reached the southern corner of the structure. From behind a large mud pump, the four of them peered at the white rubber tent shielding one whole corner of the drilling platform. Two guards were posted at its entrance, but a call on their radio sent them toward the spot where Trish's "slippery substance" was supposedly located. The pathway to the white tent was now clear, but they could see the entrance had been fitted with a security airlock sealed by an electronic keypad.

"Blocked at every turn," Perry fretted. "And of course the Spell for Unlocking has no effect on electronics."

"Worry not," said Whitmore. She removed a foldable hunting KNIFE from her blouse pocket and opened it, revealing a

---

THE CODEX
ARCANUM

While spells are useful, ordinary human tools can have their own benefits. KNIVES, for example, work in any condition, regardless of weather, spell components, or the sorcerer's level of hunger.

sharp four-inch blade. "We are not beset by the same frivolous fears of contamination as our enemies."

She jabbed the knife into the white rubber of the tent, slicing an opening large enough for them all to step through. Once they were all inside, the librarian formed four finger positions and placed her hand on the open tear. *"Exsarcio,"* she said. The edges of the seam glowed purple and then sealed themselves closed. The wall of the tent was as smooth as if the cut had never occurred.

They turned to inspect the inside of the quarantined area. A tower of science equipment had kept them from being spotted by anyone inside the tent. The teenagers peered around the edge of it, seeing that the parts of the drilling platform that couldn't be moved had been covered in clear plastic sheeting. That, plus the white walls, made Trish feel like they'd stepped into a hollowed-out iceberg. High-tech scientific equipment and computers had been arranged all over the space. Strong klieg lights, the sort used on film sets, had been set up at the corners of the tent, illuminating the work area at the center with harsh beams. Ten scientist types in thick white hazmat suits moved under the lights, checking monitors and collecting data. It reminded Trish of the cold hospital room where the doctors had set her broken leg. The sort of room in which things died.

Thankfully, the subject in this room was still alive. Nessie floated in the water of the loch, her dark body surrounded by four metal mesh walls that crackled with electric current. Her glowing, expressive eyes locked onto Trish's. The cryptid's body shimmered, briefly becoming see-through, but an electric burst from the metal mesh caused her to solidify again. A tear ran down her leathery muzzle and she gave a plaintive moan, begging for someone to free her. The plea made Trish's heart squeeze in agony. How the scientists milling around the magnificent creature could ignore such pain, she had no idea.

Her fingers moved without thinking and she spoke a word in Latin. A purple fireball appeared in each of her palms. She lifted her hands, ready to rain down righteous hellfire—

But Whitmore grabbed her shoulder, dispelling Trish's incantation with a gesture. "Your anger is justified, but shortsighted," she whispered firmly. "If we attack, there would be a protracted fight. Nessie might be injured in the process."

She indicated two Euclidean guards patrolling the edges of the work area. Like the scientists, they wore thick hazmat suits. Unlike the scientists, they carried automatic rifles. And unlike their outdoor counterparts, they were without infrared goggles. "I propose we clear the area in a more stealthy manner."

They scanned the tent for a way to accomplish this. Perry pointed to an "In Case of Emergency" alarm button halfway across the tent. Unfortunately, it stood apart from any cover, in full view of the Euclideans.

"Easy as **FERMAT'S LAST THEOREM**," the small girl whispered lightly. She took a moonstone from her pocket and tucked it into the laces of her left sneaker. Then she ran her palms up the

ENCHANTING
DETAILS

FERMAT'S LAST THEOREM was for many years considered the most difficult problem in all of mathematics. The equation was posited by Pierre de Fermat in 1637, who claimed there was an easy solution, but it was not actually solved until 1994. Because the eventual proof was so complicated, it's speculated that Fermat was simply pranking everyone.

side of the tent, wetting them with the condensation that had collected there. Her hands moved gracefully through the air, her fingers forming runes and then enclosing them in a circle. She brought her palms together over her head, letting the drops of water trickle down to her scalp, and then whispered a word in Icelandic: *"Ósýnileika."*

The drops of water on her head expanded, unfurling into shimmering see-through ribbons that wrapped themselves all over her body. Within seconds, the teenager was completely transparent. Whitmore conjured up her magical viewing window, illuminating Perry's body so they could observe her progress.

"Be right back," the invisible teen murmured nervously, then made her way quietly over to the alarm button. Her passage rustled the plastic sheeting as she went by, but the guards didn't seem to notice. She reached the edge of the work area, on the other side of which stood the alarm button. Unfortunately, there were about four Euclidean scientists in between the girl and her objective.

"This looks promising," one scientist said, calling a Euclidean who was clearly in charge over to his microscope. "Analysis indicates the cellular transformation reacts to external stimuli."

"I don't want promising," the supervisor said in an accented voice that sounded familiar. "I want results. We must learn how it controls the phase-shift."

Chastened, the scientist bent over his microscope again. Perry began to move past him, then hesitated. As Whitmore had continually reminded them, being transparent did not prevent one from being heard, felt, or smelled.

"Come on, P. It's just like dancing," Owen muttered.

"Dude, she hates dancing," Trish reminded him.

There was a suspenseful moment during which Perry stood motionless, mere centimeters from several Euclideans who might notice her presence. Trish silently gestured for her friend to get going. Finally the tiny teenager made her move. With the grace of a ballet dancer, she ducked around the first scientist, stutter-stepped around another, and swept past the third. But the fourth scientist surprised her. She stood suddenly, making Perry lunge backward and bump into a table covered in lab equipment. A glass Erlenmeyer flask tipped over, rolling off the edge of the table—

But Perry crouched and caught it with her hand. The sound made the scientist turn to the table, but by then Perry had gently lowered the flask to the floor. The scientist picked it up, shrugged, and placed it back where it belonged. Whitmore, Owen, and Trish all exhaled in relief.

Perry continued past the scientist and slammed her hand against the alarm button. The sudden blaring of the siren made the scientist spin around, knocking several glass flasks to the ground. Yellow emergency lights flashed inside the tent.

"Remember the protocol," spoke the familiar-sounding supervisor. "Do not remove your garments until you are outside the airlock. Quickly, people."

The scientists followed the man's orders, quickly filing out of the tent. But their leader stayed behind, indicating for the two guards to check the space. They clicked on the infrared scopes attached to their M5 rifles and held the weapons to their face-plates, scanning the interior of the tent.

"Hurry," Whitmore whispered. "We must subdue them before they spot Ms. Spring."

Owen and Trish both began to charge up attack spells, but they weren't fast enough. "Contact!" shouted one of the guards, tucking his rifle to his shoulder and preparing to fire.

"*Frysta maxima!*" shouted Owen, extending a hand toward the Euclidean. A funnel of ice crystals sprayed from the teen-ager's fingers, encasing both the soldier and his weapon in an eight-centimeter layer of ice.

The other Euclidean spun toward them and squeezed off two shots. Trish flung an arm over her face, and the tranquil-izer darts impacted her enchanted chest protector. Gold rings of energy spread out from their point of contact, like ripples in a pond. The darts clattered to the metal grillwork of the floor, their needles bent flat.

Capitalizing on her attacker's surprise, Trish formed a few runes and stretched her hands toward the guard. She felt like a bird that had been caged for weeks and was finally allowed to fly again. *"Kasirga!"* she cried.

A cyclone burst from her fingers, knocking the rifle from the Euclidean's hands. She reached into her backpack, pulling out a sand-filled board game timer and tossing it at the Euclidean soldier in a single smooth motion. *Boo-yah*, she thought in satisfaction as she watched the timer tumble across the room. *That's what you get for takin' on a warrior mage, son.*

The hourglass landed at the soldier's feet, and a shimmery bubble encased him. He attempted to grab the timer, but his body seemed to be stuck in extreme slow motion. Whitmore turned to the teenager, arching a curious eyebrow.

"I tweaked the Spell to Stop Time," Trish explained. "Figured if you inverted it to affect the user instead of everyone else, it could work as a temporary **PRISON**. Wears off in about an hour."

"Ingenious," Whitmore said approvingly. Trish grinned, feeling a glow of pride in her chest. "But stay at the ready—this last one is wilier than most."

THE CODEX ARCANUM

Time PRISONS are but one of many creative uses of the Spell to Stop Time. Sorcerers have used the enchantment to slow down floods, speed up their own attacks, and bake cakes in seconds.

The Euclidean leader lifted his hands in surrender. A hand motion and a word from Whitmore knocked off his hazmat suit helmet, revealing a thin, hollow-cheeked face, slick white-blond hair, and a glowing blue bionic left eye. The teenagers immediately recognized Samson Kiraz, as he had nearly killed them only two months prior. He had partnered with Ferretti to steal *Sorcery for Beginners*, but the teenagers had managed to get it back and defeat a whole team of Euclidean mercenaries in the process.

Still, he smiled at them like a wolf debating how to eat a rabbit. "Hello, children. I see you've joined forces with an international terrorist. What a pity."

Whitmore stepped forward, her elegant fingers crackling with purple energy. "And I see your last encounter with cryptids didn't teach you to give them a wider berth. At least you managed to replace your eye."

"Actually, I owe that SALAMANDER a debt of thanks," the man said, tracing the pattern of skin grafts on the left side of his face. "My . . . replacement parts have many more useful applications."

"What's the matter with you?" Trish demanded. Her voice shook as she lifted a handful of purple fire. "Nessie didn't do anything to you. She's just trying to live her life, and you stick her in a cage and torture her? You deserve to be a cyclops, Cyclops."

"You may think me a monster," said Kiraz, moving to a table and dropping his hand to a dial, "but I'd be careful with your spell casting, child. If I'm injured, my hand may turn this dial,

SALAMANDER

HABITAT: VOLCANOES

A FIERY FELLOW

WEIGHT:
250 - 900 g

LENGTH:
10 - 20 cm

HEIGHT:
1 - 3 cm

MAGICAL PROPERTIES:

impervious to heat, can generate **any type of fire**,
able to **breathe lava**

One of four "elemental" **cryptids** (along with the slyph, nymph, and gnome, all of which are extinct), the salamander is **small in stature** but **quite powerful**. It can **harness any aspect of fire** at will, and can **withstand temperatures up to 6,000 degrees Kelvin** (which is hotter than the surface of our sun). It is a **mild-mannered creature**, but if it perceives a **threat, it will destroy all in its path**.

It has a **fondness for chocolate**.

— DID YOU KNOW? —

Most salamanders **live in volcanoes** or **lava vents**, but one or two have made their **homes in nuclear power plants** due to the extreme heat.

sending one hundred thousand volts into your animal friend's enclosure. And I fear not even a magical cryptid can survive such electrocution."

"You wouldn't!" Perry cried, casting off her invisibility spell. A few finger movements, and her hands were sparking with electricity. "You couldn't murder an endangered species simply out of spite."

"Of course not. I wish to preserve this creature's life. To learn all that it can teach us. But if the recklessness of Euphemia Whitmore kills a defenseless endangered cryptid, that also benefits our cause." Kiraz raised his head high. "So. Since it appears we have a stalemate, you will dispel your enchantments, surrender yourselves to me, and reveal the locations of all magical creatures—"

WHAM! A metal toolbox collided with the back of Kiraz's head. He looked around blearily, his bionic eye spitting sparks, then he slumped to the ground. Behind him stood a tall teenage boy of fourteen, with a crown of curly blond hair and a sprinkling of freckles over his pale face.

Fergus Brown grinned. "Bloody hell, he does go on, don't he?" he said, then shielded his face when the sorcerers stepped forward to attack. "Oi. I'm on your side. Or hers, anyway." He jutted his head back toward the Loch Ness Monster.

"Then you have our gratitude," said Whitmore, letting the magical energy dissipate from her fingers. She walked quickly to Kiraz's body, formed a few runes, and placed a hand on his back. *"Immobiles."* The man's limbs **LOCKED TOGETHER** and he went stiff as a board. "I assume you are the young man who found her," she said to Fergus. "The Euclideans imprisoned you as well?"

"For the last day or so, yeah. That alarm gave me the chance to bust out." He blushed, rubbing a hand on the back of his head. "Are youse all like her, then? Magic and whatnot? 'Cause, um . . . it's kinda my fault she got pinched. I, uh, posted a wee video of the bonny beastie online."

"An honest mistake," said the librarian. "But we shan't hold it against you. Quickly, children, let us free the poor creature before our enemies return."

They killed the power to the mesh cage and dismantled the walls with a few aimed spells. Realizing she was free, Nessie chirruped gratefully. She shook herself all over, briefly going transparent and then solidifying again. The great creature sneezed, then gazed suspiciously down at the sorcerers. But after they held out their hands and spoke gently, she bent her head forward, snuffling each of them in turn. Fergus received an extra-long head bump.

Trish stroked the cryptid's damp, leathery muzzle, feeling a purr rumble deep in the animal's throat. Looking deeply into its

THE CODEX ARCANUM

Because it is meant for inanimate objects, using the **LOCKING** spell on humans can be fairly dangerous. Surgery has occasionally been needed to separate fused body parts.

warm, trusting eyes, she could tell this was a being who didn't give a fig how tall she was, what she looked like, or whom she liked. *If only I could learn the Spell to Breathe Underwater and live down here with you*, she thought, patting Nessie's neck.

There was a hiss from the front of the tent. Euclideans were massing at the airlock, their backlit shadows staining the white fabric wall like ink. Owen sent a thunderclap toward a tool cabinet, which tipped over in front of the entrance.

"Clever, but it will delay them only briefly," said Whitmore. "Everyone place your hands upon Nessie. You as well, young man." She gestured to Fergus, who quickly obeyed.

There was a small explosion, and the tool cabinet spun away from the airlock door. A dozen Euclidean soldiers in hazmat suits streamed into the quarantine tent, each of them pointing an assault rifle. Trish forced herself to keep her hands on the damp cryptid.

"Deep breaths," Whitmore advised the teenagers. "Whatever happens next, hold on to Nessie."

The teenagers did as she asked. Owen wrinkled his nose. "Ugh, she kinda stinks."

"Deal with it," Trish told him.

The Euclideans encircled the Loch Ness Monster, tucking their rifles into their shoulders. The sorcerers were trapped.

But Whitmore looked up at the creature's yellow eyes. "Now."

Nessie bellowed. Her cry shook the scientific equipment and caused the battle-hardened soldiers to take a step back. The teenagers felt a strange tingling under their hands, then all of them—kids, cryptid, and quixotic librarian—were enveloped in water and pulled into the loch.

CHAPTER 3

SHORE LEAVE

An instant later the sorcerers were hurtling through the dark water, suspended in a warm bullet-shaped orb of liquid, like pieces of fruit in a Jell-O mold. The teenagers swung their arms, instinctively trying to swim, but it made no difference in the warm plasma.

Trish had been glad of her hooded sweatshirt in the cool Scottish mist, but now it and her chest protector clung to her like a cement vest. A band of pressure began to tighten around her lungs. *I forgot to take a deep breath*, she realized in a panic. *How much longer are we gonna be under here? And where did Nessie go?* Within moments, she would have to breathe, and she didn't want to inhale whatever was surrounding them. The two glowing yellow orbs ahead of them made her think that somehow the cryptid had absorbed them.

Thankfully, their speed came to a halt and the plasma disbanded, leaving them floating in the much colder waters of the loch. Trish's feet quickly found the squishy bottom of the lake and she stood, taking large gulps of air in relief. She looked around to get her bearings. The drilling platform was little more than a few twinkling lights in the distance. Fog shrouded a line of trees just up the shore. Nessie solidified behind them, shaking herself all over and sneezing like a wet collie.

"Good girl," Fergus said, laying a hand on the cryptid's flank. "Don't know how you got us outta there, but we're much obliged."

"She **PHASE-SHIFTED** of course," said Whitmore, wiping off her glasses and settling them back on her aquiline nose. "Magically switched between different states of matter. Nessie and her family are old pros at it. It's how she was able to bring us with her just now." Her fingers formed a few rune shapes and she began walking to the grassy shore, her clothes steaming as they dried.

The four teenagers followed her, shivering. "That must be why no one's been able to confirm her existence," said Perry, looking back at the cryptid in admiration. "Think about it. Anytime someone tried to document her, she

CRYPTID CORNER

PHASE-SHIFTING is a magical skill that only elemental creatures such as water nymphs and ifrits possess. A shame, because it makes games of hide-and-seek far more interesting.

simply turned into water or fog or some other type of sorcerous camouflage."

They were all on the shore now, facing the large mythological creature. "What's gonna happen to her now that the Euclideans know she exists?" Trish asked worriedly.

"She will be fine," Whitmore assured her. "There are over thirty thousand freshwater lochs in Scotland, and Nessie has shifted to most of them during her long life. She and her KIN are quite adept at avoiding capture. Given what we've seen of the Euclideans' operation, I'm more concerned about the world's other cryptids."

"What do you mean? How many of them are still alive?" asked Owen.

Whitmore's expression became troubled. "At one point there were thousands of magical species on this planet, each with their own unique abilities. But I'm afraid human expansion, climate change, and various other factors have reduced that number to just over **ONE HUNDRED**."

Whitmore bowed to the animal. "We apologize for the treatment you were given by our species. I'd advise you and your family to stay out of sight for a while."

CRYPTID
CORNER

Nessie's KIN can be found all over the world, but they have been given different names depending on their location. The ogopogo lives in British Columbia, "Champ" resides in Lake Champlain, and the Mokele-mbembe calls the Congo River Basin home. All are the same species.

CRYPTID CORNER

The actual number of cryptids is difficult to determine, as some of them are reclusive and others are invisible. So while we're fairly confident there are more than ONE HUNDRED left in the world, the verified number of living magical creatures is eighty-three.

Before they could wonder if Nessie understood her, the cryptid also inclined her head.

Trish stepped back into the loch, holding out her hand. "Take care of yourself, okay, girl?"

Nessie rumbled affectionately, stretching out her long neck and bumping the teen's hand with her head. Then she turned back toward the water. Her dark body transformed into a cloud of mist, which curled around them once then spiraled off into the distance.

Owen waved a hand before his mouth. "Ugh. Hope we didn't swallow any of her."

HELP WANTED

Whitmore cast the drying spell on each of the teenagers. They sighed in relief as the water was wicked away from their cold, sodden clothes and protective gear.

The librarian inclined her head to Fergus. "Your assistance is appreciated, young man. In future, if you happen to discover anything magical, best keep it off the internet."

She turned to leave, but the Scottish teen stepped forward. "Wait a tick, miss. I know, uh, what I did was wrong like, but as you said, honest mistake. If there's more o' these beasties out there, well . . . I'd like to help."

She looked him up and down. There was a long moment of silence as Fergus shifted uncomfortably under her gaze. *Poor guy*, Trish thought wryly. *I know what it's like to be on the receiving end of that look.* She stepped forward. "Geez, just let him come already. I know from experience we can use all the help we can get."

The older woman looked at her over the top of her spectacles. "Taking on a candidate without proper magical training is dangerous for both the individual and our organization. No, it's better to wipe his memory." She formed a series of complicated finger positions, her motions leaving golden trails in the air.

"Whoa, whoa, whoa." Owen pulled the librarian's wrist, making whatever spell she was conjuring dissipate. "You're just gonna zap him and leave him on his own? The Euclideans know who he is. We had a spell book in that situation, and trust me, it still wasn't easy."

Whitmore frowned at him, taking out her strange pocket watch. "You have a suggestion, Mr. Macready?"

Owen reached into his backpack, taking out a battered chemistry textbook. A few muttered words and a hand motion, and it became a red-and-white paperback titled *Sorcery for Beginners*. He gave it a long, lingering gaze, as if saying goodbye to an old friend, then held it out to Fergus. "Guess you could use this more 'n me," he said gruffly. "We're not beginners anymore, anyway." Perry placed a consoling arm around him. "Word of advice, though," Owen said, still holding on to the spell book. "Certain things you can't rush. Do what it tells you, and, uh . . . take good care of it, okay?"

Finally Owen let it go. Trish thumped her friend on the shoulder, impressed by his maturity. The Owen she'd met three months ago wouldn't have parted with such a treasure so easily. Even Whitmore gave a subtle smile of approval.

Fergus flipped through the pages, eyes widening as his name magically appeared in the dedication. He grinned as if it were Christmas morning. "Aye, that I will. Cheers, mate."

Whitmore tucked away her watch. "By accepting this volume, do you swear to learn and protect its contents from all enemies of the arcane arts, including the Euclideans, on pain of death?" Fergus nodded eagerly, and she tapped the book with her index finger. "Until we meet again, Candidate Brown. The rest of you, with me, please."

Trish gave a wave to Fergus, then she, Perry, and Owen followed Whitmore into the dark woods surrounding Loch Ness. "So you're leaving him to deal with the Euclideans by himself?" Perry asked in a timid tone. "Isn't that . . . dangerous?"

"No more so than what you three dealt with. And the book shall monitor his well-being." Whitmore began sizing up trees in the vicinity, occasionally pressing on their trunks with her fingers. "Unfortunately, this encounter has revealed more pressing matters. Matters that must be discussed with the entire Council. Ah-ha."

She stopped before a Norway spruce with a trunk roughly two meters wide. The librarian removed a key ring from the pocket of her skirt. It had over a dozen old-fashioned keys on it, of various shapes and sizes. Some were made of simple brass while others were encrusted with jewels. One, Trish noticed, seemed to be made of smoke.

Whitmore selected a key made of hammered gold, with movable rings embedded in its BOW. Finding a cleft in the spruce bark, Whitmore inserted the golden key into the tree trunk. It went in as smoothly as a hot knife through butter. The rings on the key spun, then snapped together with a *click*.

Whitmore turned the key. Lines of golden light broke through the spruce tree. They moved and connected, quickly forming the outline of what could only be a door. Trish had seen plenty of magical displays before, but this one was particularly charming. Whitmore pushed on the tree, and the newly formed door swung inward.

Golden lamplight spilled into the dark forest. Inside the tree was an impossible sight: rows of bookshelves stretched well beyond the limits of the spruce, rising ten stories and extending for at least the length of a city block. Statues and paintings

ENCHANTING
DETAILS

A typical key is made up of two parts: the blade, which slides into the lock, and the BOW, which is the part one turns. Magical keys may have a few other parts, some even located in other dimensions.

adorned various bits of wall space. Strange artifacts spun and smoked in display cases. The floors above shifted, and a handful of bookshelves revolved lazily. Outside each level's windows it appeared to be a different time of day. Perry and Owen immediately recognized the space, having been there before. But Trish knew of it only by description, and so posed the question in a voice of awe:

"Is that . . . the Codex Arcanum?"

A warm smile curled Whitmore's lips. She held out a hand, and the three teenagers stepped through the magic doorway.

MIND SPLINTERS

What immediately struck Trish was the smell. It was the olfactory equivalent of a cozy quilt or a mug of hot cocoa over flowing with marshmallows. It was the **AROMA OF BOOKS**. She closed her eyes to better enjoy the scent, but a puff of air made her turn.

Whitmore pulled a section of the bookshelf shut, and the darkened trees of the Scottish Highlands vanished. There was no seam or hinge in the wall; it was as if the door to Loch Ness had never existed.

ENCHANTING
DETAILS

Because books are composed of organic materials such as wood pulp, and organic materials go through chemical decomposition, the AROMA OF BOOKS actually changes over time. Some people prefer old, some prefer new— librarians simply prefer that they exist.

"Dude, how'd you do that?" asked Trish. "Are there, like, portals to every country somewhere in here?"

"The secret lies in the key," said Whitmore, spinning her key ring once before returning it to her skirt pocket. "No matter where you are in the world, it can create a doorway that leads you straight back to the Codex Arcanum. No complex portals required, and it saves quite a penny on plane tickets."

Welcome back, a voice intoned in all their heads. The teenagers winced, feeling as if a large bell had been rung in the depths of their brains. They looked up to see a strange creature galloping silently down the side of a bookshelf. It was about the size of a bulldog, though that was all it had in common with an ordinary canine. The creature had four stumpy cloven-hoofed legs, a long cowlike tail, and its body was covered in gold and purple scales. Its adorable face was like a cross between a hippo and a dragon, and it had sparkly, intelligent eyes. Two curled horns extended straight back from the top of its skull. Trish couldn't help but smile at the sight of it. The animal was a **KIRIN**, and its name was Kyle.

"Has everyone assembled?" asked Whitmore, leading Kyle and the teenagers into the center of the Codex Arcanum.

Not yet, intoned the kirin. Now that they were expecting it, the cryptid's voice in their heads was less off-putting. *Several participants had to be roused from their slumber.*

"One of the drawbacks of maintaining a worldwide membership," the librarian informed the teenagers. "If you all don't

KIRIN

Qilin, Kỳ lân Trung Hoa,
Girin, Kirin,
Gilen

A WALKING LIE DETECTOR

(Also Known As:
The UNICORN of CHINA)

WEIGHT:
60 - 80 kg

LENGTH:
140 cm

HEIGHT:
70 cm

HABITAT:
EAST ASIA

MAGICAL PROPERTIES:

telepathy, able to **walk on any surface,**
uses **psychic attacks** when angered

Known by several names, the **kirin** can be found **all over Asia.**
This cryptid is greatly admired for its **power, wisdom,** and
propensity for **bringing good fortune.**

A kirin can live to be **a thousand years old** and only appears
in **places ruled by a wise and benevolent leader**
(even if those places are as small as a bookstore).

It can **walk on any surface** — snow, water,
grass — **without leaving a mark.**

All in all, the **ideal house pet.**

——— DID YOU KNOW? ———

Because it can **read human thoughts,**
the kirin **will only attack** those who **wish it
harm** — often **before they act.**

mind, I'm going to freshen up before our meeting. Feel free to do the same and look around—but please, touch nothing without first consulting Kyle." She pushed aside a counter with an old-fashioned cash register on top of it. A brass spiral staircase descended into the floor below. Whitmore hurried down the secret passage, and the counter swung back into place.

Owen took Perry's hand in his. "What do you say, wanna go explore a bit?"

Perry blushed, but then looked back apologetically at Trish. The teenager shrugged in a *do whatever you want* manner. The smaller girl grinned, then she and Owen disappeared around a corner.

Trish pulled off her chest protector and pads and turned to inspect the Codex Arcanum. It was as cool and mysterious as Owen and Perry had described it. She wondered if every display case held some sort of magical object. The one closest to her merely seemed to contain a pair of tattered brown leather shoes. "**SEVEN-LEAGUE BOOTS**," she read off a golden plaque beneath the case. *That's not even a real unit of distance.* She straightened and nearly yelped out loud when she found herself face-to-face with Kyle. Somehow, he had soundlessly appeared on top of the case.

THE CODEX
ARCANUM

Since a league is roughly equal to three miles, the famed SEVEN-LEAGUE BOOTS are able to walk twenty-one miles with a single stride. Since it's difficult to go anywhere closer while wearing them, they are not recommended for walks around the neighborhood.

You have a secret, he spoke into her mind. His adorable, strange head tilted to one side, curious. *I can feel it.*

"Dude, can you turn down the psychic volume?" she replied, stepping backward as if more distance between the two of them could prevent his mental snooping. "And what do you care? Everyone has secrets."

Perhaps, the creature mused, tilting its horned head to examine her. *But this one causes you pain each time your thoughts draw near it. Like a splinter in your mind.*

"That's not . . . My brain's splinter-free, buddy." She walked over to inspect another display case and, more importantly, change the subject. This one held a long silver broadsword with a channel of ruby running down the blade and a hilt made of blue ice. "'JOKULSNAUT'?" she read off the case's plaque. "Sounds like a made-up word."

Be warned, said the kirin, walking down the front of the display case and fixing her with his wise liquid eyes. *Splinters such as the one you hide have a tendency to force their way out. The process, if not done properly, can be painful. You will feel better once you admit the truth.*

The squat creature turned suddenly and galloped up the sides of the bookshelves, vanishing into the shadows as quickly

---

ENCHANTING DETAILS

JOKULSNAUT is actually a very famous magical sword once wielded by the Icelandic warrior Grettir. The modern-day finding of it is detailed in the Codex Arcanum case file *Seeking the Salamander*.

and quietly as a breeze. Trish stood alone in the quiet library, feeling small in spite of her height. *The truth? Fat chance. Not after Julie's reaction. Who is he to judge what I keep secret, anyway?* she thought fiercely. *He doesn't understand the emotional crap we humans have to go through. I'll "process" when I'm good and—*

A *click* interrupted her thought spiral. Euphemia Whitmore emerged from the staircase beneath the library counter, smoothing out a new scarlet vest and a cerulean skirt. Trish thought it a bit unfair that the librarian got to change clothes while her own sneakers were still damp with lake water, but she was glad to be distracted from her inner monologue.

"Much better," said Whitmore, adjusting her silver spectacles. "And where are the other two? Not touching anything, I hope."

Before Trish could make a wisecrack, there was a *clunk* as some books fell from a nearby shelf, and a scuffling of feet. Perry and Owen emerged from the bookshelves, looking simultaneously embarrassed and pleased with themselves. Trish forced a smile.

"We were just, ah, brushing up," Owen said unnecessarily. "On our skills." Perry actually giggled, then cleared her throat.

"Capital," said the librarian. "If you three could follow me, please. Stay close together."

The Council Arcanum

She led them up two flights of brass-banister stairs and down an aisle, taking one turn and then another. Trish glanced back, feeling as if the bookshelves were rearranging themselves once they were past. She certainly couldn't see the rest of the library anymore. But before she could get too nervous about it, Whitmore stopped at a large wall of books. She scanned the shelves, locating a volume with an emerald-green cover and placing it in an empty slot on the fourth row from the bottom. There was a *click*, and the wall before them split apart to reveal a wide, curving stone staircase lit by flaming torches.

"I love this place," Trish murmured happily. Owen and Perry joined hands and practically skipped up the steps together. Whitmore gestured for Trish to follow. The librarian came after her, pulling the secret door shut. It blended perfectly into the stone wall.

The spiral staircase ascended for a few stories. It was colder here, and they could hear waves crashing somewhere nearby. Smells of salt and seaweed wafted their way down the stairwell. Finally they reached the top and found themselves atop the open parapet of a stone fortress. A dark body of water surrounded them on three sides, lit only by the stars. Waves broke against the wall a hundred meters below, and the sea was so vast they couldn't see the other side. Behind them was a medieval fortress built directly into the rocky promontory.

"Where are we?" said Perry.

"DUBROVNIK, CROATIA," replied Whitmore. "One of the Council's many meeting places throughout the world."

"How come we didn't have to portal?" asked Trish.

ENCHANTING
DETAILS

DUBROVNIK is a lovely city on the Adriatic Sea. It is ringed by two kilometers of well-preserved sixteenth-century walls, and includes several castles and forts such as the Tvrđava Bokar, seen here. Fort Bokar also composes the second exterior level of the Codex Arcanum.

"The Codex Arcanum has ten permanent entrances across the world, one for each level of the building," said the librarian. "No spell is required to enter them, only a knowledge of where they are and how to open them."

She continued onward, her heels clicking on the six-hundred-year-old flagstones. She pushed open a heavy set of wooden doors in the stone wall, beckoning the teenagers toward a central keep. Torchlight flickered inside. They entered to see an open three-story space with a central raised platform surrounded by circular stone risers. The stage area was lit by flaming wood torches. It reminded Trish of the theaters-in-the-round she had seen during a family trip to **STRATFORD-UPON-AVON** in England.

On the central platform sat seven of the most unusual adults Trish had ever seen. They were of various ethnicities, sizes, and ages, though none of them appeared to be under fifty. One of them was bearded and had a lower half made of red smoke, while

ENCHANTING
DETAILS

STRATFORD-UPON-AVON is the birthplace of renowned playwright and poet William Shakespeare. Several Elizabethan-style theaters still exist there today and serve as stages for the Bard's excellent works.

another was tall and ashy gray, like a birch sapling come to life. A third had the head and wings of a bird and wore an elegant silk kimono. A fourth was transparent.

Before Trish could take in all their faces, Whitmore indicated for the teenagers to sit on one of the risers. Several of the rows were already filled with what looked to be three or four dozen teenagers of varying ethnicities. She, Perry, and Owen took a seat in the first available spot, unable to see most of the others due to the dim torchlight.

Whitmore stepped onto the central platform, moving her arms in a series of coordinated gestures. She stretched out her fingers, and a purple wave of energy spread through the room. It made the eardrums of each person it connected with vibrate in a not-unpleasant manner, then it disappeared.

"Welcome," said the librarian. "Hopefully, my **SPELL TO UNDERSTAND OTHERS** will make it easier for us to converse. We have much to discuss."

"I hope so," said a round-faced Saudi man in a white smock and gold keffiyeh headdress. "These meetings of yours always seem to take place in the dead of night, Euphemia."

"My apologies, Dr. Ahura. But unfortunately,

THE CODEX ARCANUM

While the SPELL TO UNDERSTAND OTHERS can overcome language barriers, it is still incumbent on the spell caster to convey his or her intentions concisely and clearly. No amount of magic can help if one is confusing.

CRYPTID CORNER

There are several types of magical BIRD-PEOPLE, from the Slavic sirin to the Filipino ekek. This particular Council member is a tengu, a Japanese protector of the mountains with bird and human qualities.

the Euclideans don't use business hours to plan their cryptid-poaching operations."

There was an intake of breath from the Council members, and murmurs spread among the teenagers in the room. The BIRD-PERSON raised a hand, speaking in the wise tones of an older woman. "So it is true, then? They abducted the cryptid of Loch Ness?"

Trish was still processing the fact that the bird-lady could talk, but Whitmore nodded. "Thankfully, I was able to rescue the beast with some assistance from our newest Level One sorcerers." She indicated Perry, Owen, and Trish, who was irked to be thought of as the librarian's "assistant." "But we have a greater problem."

She moved her hands in an elegant pattern and muttered a string of words in French. Sprays of brightly colored light sprang from her fingertips, forming a life-size three-dimensional re-creation of the Euclideans' work area in the Loch Ness quarantine tent. There were scattered gasps from some of the younger sorcerers. Using her hands, the librarian made the image partly translucent and adjusted the angle of the scene so everyone could see.

Owen leaned over to Trish and Perry. "Wouldn't a photograph be easier than casting such a complicated GLAMOUR?"

THE CODEX
ARCANUM

Since GLAMOURS are created in the imagination, they can be easily manipulated to fit the spell caster's needs. However, a keen attention to detail is required for any kind of quality presentation to others.

Before Trish could make a joke, someone in the row behind shushed them.

"As you can see," Whitmore continued, zooming in on the image of Samson Kiraz with a gesture, "the Euclideans are now assigning their most senior operatives to the matter of cryptids." There were more worried murmurs through the room; clearly Kiraz's reputation was well known. "But I'm afraid I have worse news."

Whitmore spun the three-dimensional image and zoomed in on a monitor behind Kiraz. One screen showed a map of the world, with dozens of marked locations, complete with global positioning coordinates. Next to the map was a list of names and accompanying pictures. A handful jumped out at Trish:

Batutut - hominid, EXPIRED
Bunyip - magically resistant mammal, CAPTURED
Chupacabra - vampiric canid, SIGHTED
Jackalope - horned jackrabbit, SIGHTED
Jersey Devil, aka Leeds Devil - winged bipedal horse, SIGHTED
Kirin, aka Qilin - psychic chimera, UNCONFIRMED
Kongamato - giant flying mammal, CAPTURED
Loch Ness Monster, aka "Nessie" - phase-shifting plesiosaur, CAPTURED
Sasquatch, aka "Bigfoot" - primate/hominid, CAPTURED
Salamander - fire elemental, EXPIRED
Thunderbird - electro-productive giant bird, SIGHTED
Unicorn - magical horse, UNCONFIRMED

Wow, Trish thought to herself. *All these magical creatures are actually* alive *out there? The Earth's a whole lot more magical than I realized.* And indeed, there were dozens more listed, many of which had "Expired" or "Captured" next to their names. It was both exciting and overwhelming to realize there was so much magic in the world. But before Trish could even picture what a hundred cryptids looked like, Whitmore continued speaking.

"The Euclideans are hunting magical creatures," she declared. "From our encounter with Nessie, it seems they are particularly focused on their abilities. Why, we do not know, but it's clear their goal is to capture as many as they can, even if the creatures perish in the process."

Concerned whispers spread among the risers. A bald man with dark skin rose from his Council seat. His deep voice immediately quieted the room.

"We cannot let this atrocity continue. Our cousins require protection."

There were several sounds of agreement. The gray-skinned man also stood, smoothing his smart tweed suit. He spoke with a German accent: "Mr. Mutwa speaks rightly. But there are less than fifty of us present, and scores of Euclideans. How can we protect the whole world?"

Dismay settled on the crowd. Even if each of them were assigned to keep watch over one cryptid, there would still be dozens left unmonitored in the wild, and sorcerers would be scattered all over the globe. Perry and Trish looked at each other with concern. Was there no way to prevent these other creatures from being captured and tortured like Nessie?

"Herr Stromberg is correct," Whitmore admitted. "We will never be able to compete with the Euclideans on a numbers basis. That is why we must take the initiative." She looked evenly at her assembled audience. "Sorcerers, Council members, ladies and gentleman all: I propose we create a magical zoo."

Chapter 4

Animal Rights

Immediately, there were shouts of dissent from several Council members. Trish and her friends were surprised at the force of the response. There were plenty of zoos in America, and they frequently kept endangered animals safe from predators, hunters, and environmental issues.

The bearded man with the red smoke legs raised his voice above the others: "Unacceptable! The jailing of wild animals goes against millennia of cryptid preservation efforts. To do so means adopting the methods of our enemies."

ENCHANTING DETAILS

zoos have been around for at least 3,000 years, but only in the last few decades have they focused on providing the animals with enclosures that resemble their natural habitats. Not coincidentally, the life expectancy of zoo animals has also increased.

Whitmore lifted her elegant hands and the hubbub subsided. "It is unorthodox, I know. Goodness knows we'd prefer all magical creatures to stay in their natural habitats. But such action is doomed for failure." She ticked off the reasons on her fingers: "First, the advance of high-resolution satellite imaging and the expansion of human civilization have exposed cryptids all over the world. Most can no longer hide from the Euclideans in nature. Second, we cannot ensure their safety when we are spread so thin. According to this list, at least a half dozen cryptids have already perished in Euclidean captivity. We need to house them in a protected, secret location, at least temporarily. A zoo is the only logical answer, Arghan Div."

The bearded man's eyes glowed red with anger, while fire seemed to smolder within the pillar of smoke that made up his lower half. One or two other Council members folded their arms in agreement. The bird-woman raised her hand, however. "Say we agree to this plan, Euphemia. How do you propose we care for these creatures?"

"We have the whole of the Codex Arcanum to draw upon for knowledge," answered Whitmore. "I nominate our resident **IFRIT** and cryptozoology expert to spearhead the effort." She

CRYPTID
CORNER

IFRITS are fire-spirits and a subclass of the powerful djinn. While they cannot grant wishes, they are able to transform into smoke, flame, or other fire-related elements. They prefer to shelter in small spaces and are highly susceptible to water magic.

inclined her silver head toward the glowering man with the smoke legs.

"Seconded," said Herr Stromberg mildly.

"All in favor?" asked Whitmore. Five of the Council members and Whitmore raised their hands. Only the transparent woman and the ifrit were opposed.

"Very clever, Euphemia," rumbled Div. "Forcing me to take part in your scheme even though I am clearly against it."

"I merely believe in supporting those most qualified for the given job," she responded with a placid smile.

The transparent Council member stepped forward for the first time. She was sunken-eyed and long-faced, with a head of undulating black hair and a pencil-thin nose. Every movement and vocalization on her part clearly required an effort of concentration.

"Is that a ghost?" Trish whispered to the dark-haired teenager next to her.

"No, she is alive," replied the girl. "But her physical form is elsewhere. We are seeing her astral spirit."

"ASTRAL PROJECTION?" asked Perry excitedly. "How long did it take her to perfect that skill? Can Level One sorcerers do

THE CODEX
ARCANUM

ASTRAL PROJECTION is the ability to magically detach the spirit from the body and send it far afield. No one knows who first invented the practice, but it probably occurred during a boring business meeting.

it? How many planes—?" But the teenager held a finger to her lips, cutting off Perry's flood of questions.

The astrally projected woman began to speak. Her voice was tinny and distant, as if they were hearing her from an old-fashioned radio. "As the only Council member who is not there in person, allow me to advocate for the other hidden creatures. If humanity were to become aware of their existence, the consequences could be devastating. The cryptids might never return to their natural habitats."

A few Council members nodded in agreement. The bird-woman spoke: "But the age of technology advances, and keeping the arcane arts secret grows more difficult every day."

"We have seen the human reaction to magic many times in the past," the ash gray German reminded them, dabbing his upper lip with a handkerchief. "The Spanish Inquisition, Salem . . . usually it ends quite badly for us."

"I thank you for all your viewpoints, Council members," said Whitmore. "But such debates are, for the moment, moot. Our enemies have a target list. And so must we."

"Agreed," said Dr. Ahura. "Our first priority must be to locate and secure these animals before the Euclideans. I assume you have a plan for this, Euphemia?"

"Not as such," the librarian replied. "But I believe we can cobble one together quickly enough. Sorcerers," she said to the audience, "you may converse amongst yourselves." Then she and the other Council members huddled together.

Meet And Greet

Owen and Perry immediately put their heads together to start conferring over everything they had heard, leaving Trish once again outside the clubhouse without the secret password. Fuming, she pulled *Cryptozoology for Beginners* from her backpack and began to flip through it as loudly as possible. She had a vague plan to look up some of the animal names she'd seen on the Euclideans' list, but a hand tapped her on the shoulder. It was the dark-haired girl sitting next to her. Behind her, the rest of the audience nervously mingled. They ranged in ages from their teens to their early twenties, and were congregating in small groups of three or four. The girl stuck out a hand to introduce herself.

"I am Inez, and this is Rodrigo," she said. A skinny teenager with dark curls gave Trish a jaunty wave. Trish shook Inez's hand. "We come from Mexico. You are the Level One Americans Ms. Whitmore spoke of, yes?"

"How'd you guess?" Trish replied.

"We met your other friend from Las Vegas earlier," she said. "The handsome boy in the hood? He is quite knowledgeable about sorcery."

Trish blinked in confusion. "You mean Owen?"

"No, the other one." She nodded to the far side of the rotunda. "He is just there."

Trish squinted, trying to see into the far shadows. A young man in a black hoodie stood there, obscured by the crowd. There was something familiar about him. A careless confidence that she recognized, but from where?

Rodrigo tapped the book in her lap. "We finished that one about six months ago. Much less tricky than *Sorcery for Beginners*, don't you find?"

"I, uh, I haven't really started it yet," Trish admitted, still trying to get a look at the young man's face. Who else could be here from Vegas? Had Whitmore invited Ravi and not told them? She thought her friend had sworn off magic after he'd been nearly suffocated by magically multiplying apples. Besides, whoever was in the hoodie was much taller than Ravi.

"Don't worry, you are not far behind," Inez assured her. She jerked her head to the rest of the crowd. "Most of us here are Level One or Two."

This reminded Trish of a question she'd been meaning to ask for a while. "How many levels are there?"

Rodrigo shrugged. "Nobody knows. From what we've heard, all the Council members are Level Six or Seven. Nobody knows **WHITMORE'S LEVEL**, though."

Trish inspected the cover of *Cryptozoology for Beginners*. "So you go up a level each time you finish a book?"

THE CODEX ARCANUM

No one knows **WHITMORE'S LEVEL** because no one has thought to ask. But we'll let you in on a secret: she's Level Nine. As for how many levels there are? That must wait for another sidebar.

"You must pass a Final Examination as well," Inez said. "It is different for everyone. We had to chase a QUETZALCOATL around Chichen Itza and tag it with magic."

"It pooped on me," offered Rodrigo.

Over his shoulder, Trish saw the young man in the hoodie disappear back into the shadows of the castle keep. "'Scuse me," she said, and stood. She made her way across the room, dodging groups of teenage sorcerers, anxiously feeling she had to confirm the mystery person's identity. But by the time she reached the other side of the room, the young man had vanished. Had he seen her approaching? She scanned the crowd, but saw no sign of him. Before she could look further, Whitmore clapped her hands together once. All conversation in the room ceased.

"Thank you for your patience, sorcerers," she said. "If you could please return to your seats, the Council and I have formulated a plan."

MARCHING ORDERS

The librarian conjured a large glamour of the Earth. Dozens of location markers glowed on its slightly translucent, slowly rotating surface. "Our goal is to locate and secure as many of the world's cryptids as possible before the Euclideans can capture them. To achieve this, we must divide our resources."

She made a hand gesture, and the surface of the globe unrolled to a flat two-dimensional rectangle. Areas were highlighted in various colors. "The Earth shall be split into eight

Quetzalcoatl

HABITAT:
JUNGLES IN CENTRAL AND SOUTH AMERICA

A FAIR· AND FOUL· WEATHER FRIEND

WEIGHT:

50 - 150 kg

LENGTH:

4 - 15 m

HEIGHT:

2 - 3 m

MAGICAL PROPERTIES:

can generate **wind, rain,** and **lightning** by flapping its wings;
its **screech** can **knock prey unconscious**

Worshipped by **many groups** in ancient **Central** and **South America,** the **Quetzalcoatl** was thought to **engineer the seasons** and was even **credited by the Aztecs for creating humankind.** Many sacrifices were made to the animal to guarantee a good crop. In reality this cryptid can only control **some aspects** of the **weather,** and it usually does so **to subdue its prey.**

DID YOU KNOW?

The **temple** at **Chichen Itza,** Mexico, which functions as a calendar, was also **built to cast a Quetzalcoatl-shaped shadow** at **sunset** on the **summer solstice.**

sectors. One Council member will supervise operations in each of the sectors you see here. Sorcerers will be grouped into teams and tasked with collecting as many cryptids as possible. Each team will be led by the most senior sorcerer, but all will report to their supervising Council member."

Perry raised her hand.

"Yes, Ms. Spring?" asked Whitmore.

She stood shyly. "These collecting trips. How long do you imagine they will be?"

"However long it takes. A few weeks, a month possibly. It rather depends on your success in securing the animals. Some of them, you'll find, are quite adept at evading capture." At this, Rodrigo and Inez nodded emphatically.

"Don't worry about your families," Whitmore continued. "We'll find some way of covering for your absences." The librarian clapped her hands again. "Now we shall assign teams. After you hear your name, please come up front to coordinate with your supervising Council member."

As the librarian began to call out names, Trish's thoughts drifted to the hooded person she'd spotted. *I know I've seen him before, I know it.* Could the person be a Euclidean spy that no one else had noticed? Or maybe some teenage celebrity she'd seen on television? Trish assumed Whitmore wasn't above recruiting **FAMOUS SORCERERS**, so long as they were capable spell casters.

Before Trish could ponder the hooded person's identity further, Whitmore turned her attention to her and her friends.

THE CODEX ARCANUM

It's true, a FAMOUS SORCERER may be just as skilled as an unknown one. But it's difficult to roam the world protecting the arcane arts in secret when everyone wants a selfie.

"And finally, we come to my team. These five will be in charge of securing the cryptids of North America. Your team leader will be Jacinda Greyeyes. The others will be Perry Spring, Owen Macready, Trisha Kim . . . and Bryan Ferretti."

The name hit Trish like a fire spell to the gut. *He* was the person in the black hoodie. The same person who had tormented her and her friends for the last three years at Henderson Middle School. The son of Virgil Ferretti, who had recently gone to prison because of them. The bully whom they had defeated two months ago, and who was supposed to be under house arrest until he turned eighteen. *I must have misheard her.*

But as she saw him descend the risers and lazily throw back his hood, revealing that familiar smug half-smile and the orange Mohawk and icy blue eyes, Trish recognized him instantly. She felt like the air had been sucked from her lungs. She stood without knowing she was doing so, her blood roaring in her ears. "What," she said, surprise and anger making her voice shake, "is *he* doing here?"

"Yeah, he's a Euclidean," Owen added, also getting to his feet. "He tried to kill us two months ago!"

There were murmurs of surprise from the gallery. Whitmore lifted her hands to quiet everyone. "It is true, young Mr. Ferretti fell in with the wrong people. But our enemies did his family no favors by leaving them to be arrested. He has expressed regret for his past crimes, and an eagerness to fight for the proper side going forward."

Trish scoffed. "He's lying! That's what he does. Like father, like son."

"I am not. Like my father," Bryan replied icily. "For starters, he's doing twenty-five to thirty in a federal prison, while I'm walking free in a Croatian castle."

Whitmore looked at him sternly over the top of her silver spectacles. "A fact conditional on your behavior. The moment you use magic improperly, you will find yourself back under house arrest before you can say 'presto.'" Bryan folded his arms, but kept his mouth closed.

Perry stepped forward timidly. "If I may—perhaps it would be best if Bryan were on another team. Given our . . . shared history, emotions will be running high. You said yourself, good sorcery relies on a clear head and calm demeanor."

Trish felt a grudging appreciation for Perry. *She and Owen's face-sucking might be annoying, but girlfriend can be killer clever when she applies herself. Using Whitmore's own guidelines against her? Genius.*

The librarian, however, was not swayed. "I know it's not ideal, but we need teams who are familiar with the customs and language of their search territories." The other Council members nodded in agreement. "It will be difficult enough to locate the cryptids. I'm afraid you'll have to be good soldiers and work together. Bryan is an accomplished Level One sorcerer, and our task requires all the help we can get."

"Hold on, he's Level One too?" said Trish. "When did he pass his Final Exam? I know it wasn't at Dragonridge Rocks, 'cause that's where we kicked his ass."

Bryan gave her that smug half-smile, refusing to take the bait. "Anytime you wanna have a rematch, Big Trish, you let me know the time and place."

Big Trish? The old insult made her step forward. Her hands moved without thinking—

But before she could finish her spell, a translucent purple disc bloomed between her and Bryan. Trish thumped it with her fist, but it was as solid as a steel wall. Whoever cast the shield spell had a considerable force of will.

"So these are the kids you're sticking me with," a cool voice said behind Trish.

They all turned to the speaker. A sixteen-year-old girl stepped up onto the dais. The magic shield dissipated as she lowered her hands. Her face was highlighted by naturally arched eyebrows, full lips, and prominent cheekbones. Long raven-colored hair was swept to one side of her head, spilling in soft waterfalls and revealing the other side of her skull was shaved to stubble. Her black leather jacket and ripped jeans fit her well but seemed selected for comfort, not fashion.

But her most arresting feature was her eyes. They were gray as a knife blade, and just as sharp. One wouldn't want to be on the receiving end of a glare from those eyes, as Trish currently was. She blushed, dropping her own gaze to the floor. For some reason, her pulse had quickened.

"No offense, Ms. Whitmore," the new girl said, raising an unimpressed eyebrow, "but how come I get stuck babysitting the noobs?"

"I assure you, they are more than capable," said the librarian mildly. "Despite their current lack of decorum. Sorcerers, please resume your plans," she said to the group at large. They separated into their teams and Whitmore stepped forward, frowning. "As for you four," she said to Owen, Perry, Trish, and Bryan, her voice severe, "allow me to introduce your team leader. A Level Three sorcerer from **FLYING DUST FIRST NATIONS** in Saskatchewan, Canada. This is Jacinda Greyeyes."

MEET THE NEW BOSS

Trish felt the blood rising to her cheeks again. This girl was their *boss*? She was barely older than they were!

ENCHANTING
DETAILS

The tribe of FLYING DUST FIRST NATIONS belongs to the Cree Nation, which has over 200,000 members living in North America. They are further divided into eight subgroups based on dialect and region. Flying Dust governs six reserves in Saskatchewan.

Jacinda surveyed them coolly. "What's it gonna be, noobs? You ready to be good little soldiers, or do I gotta keep casting shield spells?"

Trish glanced at Owen and Bryan, who were both staring at Jacinda, slack-jawed. *Guess I'm not the only one who noticed her looks.*

Perry cleared her throat pointedly, making Owen regain his train of thought. "Uh, sure. Yes. Aye, aye, *capitan*." He blushed furiously, and received a whack on the shoulder from Perry for his trouble. "What?"

"How 'bout you two?" Jacinda said to Trish and Bryan. "You ready to play nice?" Her steely gaze swiveled between the two of them. Ignoring the thump of her heart, Trish folded her arms and stared back, refusing to be the first one to crack.

A long moment passed. Finally Bryan grinned and lifted his hands. "Hey, I'm just happy to be out of the house, boo. I'm cool."

Jacinda turned back to Trish. The team leader's eyes were intense and unblinking. Despite her resolve, Trish broke her gaze and gave a noncommittal grunt.

Taking this as a yes, Whitmore drew her group over to the back of the castle keep, where Jacinda bent to put the finishing touches on a portal diagram drawn in chalk. On the back of her leather jacket was a First Nations–style drawing of a great bird called the **PIYESIW**.

"Hey, sorry we got off on the wrong foot back there," said Owen. Trish noticed both he and Bryan were checking out

CRYPTID
CORNER

Also known as a thunderbird, the PIYESIW (pronounced pee-yah-syoo) can be found throughout the northern United States and Canada. Thunder is created by the beating of their enormous wings, but they rarely bother humans.

Jacinda's crouching form. She resolved to never look so stupid. "None of these guys knew about sorcery before they met me," Owen blurted. Affronted, Perry nudged him in the ribs. "It's true," he said defensively.

"Maybe you wanna tell her about how easily you lost the book, too, Macready," said Bryan, giving Jacinda a jaunty head nod. "I'm the one who took it from him, FYI."

She ignored them both. "I don't care what any of you did before this," she said, chalking runes into the portal diagram. "I don't care how many spells you know or how many books you've read. I care how you handle yourselves." Her eyes slid to Trish, who stuck out her chin defiantly. "Once we're out in the field, we'll be dealing with wild animals, all of them magical. They will not hesitate to attack and even kill someone they perceive to be a threat." Jacinda moved her eyes to Perry. "And I don't want four dead kids on my conscience."

"We're not kids," Trish heard herself saying hotly. Enough was enough; they had fought over two dozen Euclideans and single-handedly rescued the Loch Ness Monster. It was time this gray-eyed girl showed them some respect.

"Can you drive a car? Drink a beer? Vote?" Jacinda asked. Trish opened her mouth to respond, but found no sound came out. "Then you're a kid, kid." Trish felt herself blushing again, hating that her body was betraying her so. "But don't worry," Jacinda continued in a slightly gentler tone. "You'll all get a chance to prove how awesome you are in a couple days. We leave first thing Saturday morning."

She chalked a final rune in the diagram and stood. Her fingers quickly formed a few runes, and she held a hand over the enchantment. *"Ignis."* The lines of the diagram flared with purple flames, then died down to a pulsing glow.

Whitmore turned to the teenagers and gave a slight bow. "My thanks for your assistance in Scotland. Study your crypto-zoology book, prepare your best protective enchantments, rest, and I shall see you again shortly." Then she turned on her heel and went to speak with the other Council members.

"This portal will take you back to the playground in Henderson," Jacinda said crisply. "Try not to get in trouble over the next couple days."

"Whoa, we gotta go back to Vegas?" Bryan didn't look pleased at the prospect. "I thought I was done with that house arrest bullshit."

"Like Ms. Whitmore said," Jacinda replied evenly, "we need a couple days to prepare. Use the time to study and practice your spell work." The team leader gestured to the portal. "Bedtime, kiddos."

The repetition of the word made Trish's stomach churn. *Well, I'm not gonna let her see she's getting to me*, she thought furiously. *I can be just as detached and cool as she is.* Shoving Owen and Bryan aside, she strode into the enchanted circle. A cylinder of purple energy rose around her, and the castle keep, the sound of the waves outside, even the smell of wet Croatian stone—all of it—vanished like the flare of a shooting star.

CHAPTER 5

SOMETHING'S FISHY

Trish stared moodily at the fish in her aquarium.

Since she was little, she had loved all kinds of animals. She didn't know whether it was their lack of petty emotions, or their easy acceptance, or simply the fact that they looked cool. She only knew that it was soothing to be around them. She had begged for years for a puppy or a kitten or a hammerhead shark, but the fish were the only pets she had ever been allowed. So for every birthday and Christmas the last four years, she had asked for more.

Now her aquarium was nearly half the size of the big living room couch and contained over two dozen species of fish. There was the instantly recognizable blue tang and clownfish, of course, but also several types of tetra, a sailfin molly, some rainbow kribs, and her favorite—a magnificent red lionfish she had named Simba.

She tapped more flakes into the top of the aquarium. Normally, caring for her fish was a calming, meditative activity, one that made her forget the stresses outside her house. But on this Saturday morning, looking at her pets reminded her of all the cryptids out in the world. The magical creatures who had no idea they were being hunted by Euclideans. Whose lives were now her responsibility. The only problem was, taking care of the cryptids was going to be a lot more difficult than tapping some flakes into an aquarium. Trish would never admit it out loud, but she wasn't entirely sure she was up for the challenge. Taking on a few non-magical human soldiers was one thing, but facing off against a chupacabra, or a thunderbird, or a Jersey Devil was another matter entirely. She'd read all the North American creature pages in *Cryptozoology for Beginners*, and nearly each one had a **DANGER LEVEL** of three or above.

At least no one could say she hadn't tried to ready herself for the task. Despite Whitmore's entreaties to rest, the last two days had been exhausting. Upon their return from Croatia, she, Owen, and Perry had spent nearly all their waking hours preparing for their mission and pretending to pay attention to their final hours of eighth grade. They had placed **SPELLS OF**

CRYPTID CORNER

A cryptid's DANGER LEVEL is calculated by how powerful it is, how much magic it possesses, and how likely it is to attack humans. Of course, this tendency can also be affected by how well a sorcerer treats the beast.

THE CODEX
ARCANUM

While a spell of protection can keep out one's enemies, SPELLS OF DETECTION can secretly alert a sorcerer if someone has interacted with their possessions. Both have useful applications when it comes to home security.

DETECTION and Protection around each of their homes, in case the Euclideans tried anything in their absence. They had also enchanted several items to assist them in capturing cryptids: timepieces to slow or increase speed, warded objects to defend them from various types of damage, and clothing items that were so magically shielded they could stop bullets. The two days of near-constant sorcery had left Trish's hands stiff and her head swimming with rune marks. Every time she closed her eyes, she saw spell patterns.

"Honey!" her mom called from the kitchen. "Breakfast." Trish said a quick goodbye to her fish, making sure the feeding instructions she'd left for her fifteen-year-old brother, Alex, were in plain sight. Then she went to the back of the house where her mom and dad were waiting with a special meal of bagels, scrambled eggs, and bacon.

"We are so proud of you," her mother gushed, coming over to peck Trish on the cheek. She had to stand on her tiptoes to do so. "Your first overnight trip without us. To think, we didn't even know you had applied to this program!"

Trish gave a weak smile, then quickly turned away to butter a bagel. Whitmore had sent a very official-looking email to

Trish's parents on Thursday morning, informing them that she, Owen, and Perry had been selected for an all-expenses-paid, very prestigious animal conservation internship. As far as her mom and dad knew, their daughter was going to spend the next two weeks cataloguing and tracking endangered animals, under the best of care. It wasn't a complete falsehood, but Trish disliked lying to her parents. Not telling them what had really happened with Julie had been eating at her all week, and now another lie had been added to her tower of guilt. She knew it was far safer than informing them that magical creatures were real and their sorcerer daughter was battling against a well-armed foe to protect them, but that knowledge did not make her feel better.

"Got everything you need, Person?" her father said from the table. The nickname was a leftover from her toddler days, but she couldn't hold it against her dad. Donald Kim was a skinny, balding accountant with a goofball demeanor. He looked over his glasses at her. "Toothbrush, dental floss? Underpants?"

"Ugh, Dad. Yes." Trish shoved half the bagel in her mouth so she wouldn't have to confirm every item she had packed.

"And, uh, this is what you're wearing?" said her mother, adjusting Trish's dragon-themed tank top so it hung more evenly over the T-shirt underneath. She cast her eyes critically downward to Trish's oversized basketball shorts. "Honey, it's your first day. Surely you don't want something more . . . photogenic? Like a dress? First impressions, you know."

Trish brushed her mother's hands away. "We're doing fieldwork, Mom. They said to be comfortable."

Her mom sighed. Their arguments over clothing had begun two years ago, and by now it was clear that they had very different ideas of what was "comfortable." She moved behind the kitchen island, stuffing the rest of the bagel into her mouth.

"How 'bout we give you a little spending moola just in case?" her dad suggested. He stood up from the table and took out his wallet, counting out five twenties. "You never know what sort of fancy events might rear their ugly heads."

"Thanks, Dad," Trish mumbled, pocketing the money. He also had to stand on his tiptoes to kiss her goodbye. She embraced him, giving their so-standard-it-was-now-a-joke three pats on the back. He chuckled, then took off his glasses to brush at his eyes.

"You know we're behind you no matter what, right?" he said. Trish nodded.

"And anytime you need to talk, you can call us," her mom added. "In fact, call us anyway. Once a day. Or even twice."

She hugged her daughter, barely able to wrap her arms all the way around. Trish wished she could shrink down to the size of a speck so they'd stop gazing at her. Thankfully, the doorbell rang, saving her from further scrutiny. She extracted herself from her mother's viselike grip, popped a strip of bacon in her mouth, grabbed her bag, and went to the front door, shouting goodbye to Alex on the way.

Trish opened the door to see Jacinda on her front step. Her aviator sunglasses, leather jacket, and usual stone-faced expression all combined to make her mysterious and stunning. Her long hair had been carefully tied back to hide the shaved part of her scalp. Jacinda brightened upon seeing Trish's parents, removing her sunglasses and holding out her hand to introduce herself.

"So delightful to meet you both." Her voice sounded completely different from the rough growl Trish had encountered in Croatia. "I'll be Trisha's supervisor while we're in the field."

"Oh my goodness," Trish's mom said, reacting to the strength of Jacinda's grip. "And the, um, work you'll be doing, it's completely safe?"

"Oh, absolutely," Jacinda assured them. "It's mostly cataloguing and photography. Very low impact." She smiled in a manner that was so charming and professional, Trish had to restrain herself from doing a double take.

"Make sure she checks in with us, huh?" Trish's dad asked.

Jacinda inclined her head politely. "I'll make it a top priority, Mr. Kim."

Trish was enfolded in more hugs and peppered with more kisses and then Jacinda took her by the elbow, gently steering her down the path to the street. Trish turned to give one more awkward wave to her crying parents.

"Nice folks," Jacinda said, the smile dropping off her face as she slid her sunglasses back on. "Hopefully all that stuff I told 'em doesn't turn out to be lies."

"Look, I don't know what your deal is," Trish said, turning away from her house, "but maybe you're the one who should learn to 'play nice.'"

"I'm not here to play, kid," Jacinda replied. "And I'm not here to be your bestie. My job is to make sure you survive. That's it."

Trish opened her mouth to respond, but an eager voice cut her off.

"Top o' the morning!" called Perry, bounding out of a brand-new thirty-foot-long recreational vehicle parked across the street. It was a huge oblong block of metal painted in black and purple, with tinted black windows that obscured the inside.

"Isn't it tremendous?" Perry said, practically hopping around Trish like a jackrabbit. "Our first official mission, in our own traveling domicile. Aloha, Mr. and Mrs. Kim!" she called to Trish's parents, who were still sniffling on the front steps.

"This is our mission vehicle?" Trish was unimpressed. "Aren't we gonna be portaling everywhere?"

"The four of you aren't advanced enough," Jacinda replied crisply. "Portal magic is tricky and dangerous. Besides, *KANA'TI* here provides us with cover, a place to sleep, and plenty of room for supplies."

"Jacinda named her after the Cherokee guardian of the hunt." Perry loved to spout off bits of trivia like this.

ENCHANTING DETAILS

In Cherokee myth, *KANA'TI* was also the first man. His wife, Selu, is credited with giving people corn.

"Great. But shouldn't we have, like, a military-grade mobile base? Or a tank?"

"Wouldn't be very incognito, now would it?" replied Jacinda. "*Kana'ti's* perfect for our needs. I'm gonna tell Ms. Whitmore we're leaving."

As she walked off to make the call on her satellite phone, Perry tugged on Trish's hand. "Come on, I'll give you the grand tour." Trish gave one last wave to her parents, then stepped inside.

Close Quarters

The inside of the RV resembled more of a tiny apartment than a vehicle. Across from the entrance was a couch, upon which Owen sprawled while he thumbed through a stack of hand-copied spells. Seeing Trish, he got to his feet and gave her a fist bump.

"Pretty sweet, huh?" he said, indicating the surroundings. "Fridge, microwave, satellite TV—it's, like, nicer than my whole house."

"I was getting to all that," Perry said a little testily. Owen lifted his hands in surrender, plopping back on the couch. The tiny girl guided Trish through the rest of the vehicle. "As I was saying before I was man-terrupted, there's a fully functional kitchen with an expandable eating area. Behold." She indicated a small table with booth seating, then pulled out a table leaf to provide more room. There was also a tiny two-burner electric range and a sink.

Perry opened a small door just past the kitchen to reveal a cramped toilet and shower stall barely big enough for Owen, let alone Trish. "Bathroom and shower, obviously. Everything feeds off a freshwater tank, but we can also connect the RV to city water lines."

Across from the bathroom, Perry slid back a partition to reveal two small single-sized bunk beds. "Sleeping quarters. Each one has two-by-four-foot cabinet storage."

"Did you memorize the owner's manual or something?" Trish asked.

"Naturally." Perry pulled back an accordion door made of faux wood to reveal a back room with a queen-sized bed, two windows, and a wardrobe. "You can store your bag in here for now," Perry said. "We, um, haven't decided on who's sleeping where yet."

"You mean you and your boy toy aren't sharing the honey-moon suite?" came a sarcastic drawl. Two black military boots swung down from the sleeping niche above the driver's and passenger seats. They were followed by black workout pants, a shirtless but impressively muscled torso, and the grinning face of Bryan Ferretti. A complicated glamour of the United States hovered above his right palm, but it disappeared as he closed his hand. He winked at Perry. "I thought you lovebirds would want some unsupervised snuggle time."

Perry and Owen turned bright red at his words. But Jacinda responded first, entering on the driver's side and slamming the door shut. "I'll be assigning the bunks," she said firmly. "We don't want any distractions on this mission."

"So you admit it, these guns are too distracting for you." Bryan flexed his biceps.

"That's right," Jacinda said, arching one eyebrow. "You're so pale, it's a driving hazard."

Trish stifled a laugh, but Bryan scowled. "Well, this sure is starting off lame. I mean, is this a magical rescue mission or a Bible camp?"

The team leader held his gaze. Trish admired her steeliness. "You don't like your spot, we've got tents and sleeping bags too."

"Oh, I'm good." Bryan jumped down, landing on the floor of the RV with a *thud*. "I was just looking forward to hearing Macready try to figure out the female anatomy."

"I know all about the female anatomy!" Owen shot back.

"Ugh, TMI," said Trish.

"What's the matter?" Bryan now sauntered over to her, his eyes roving up and down her figure. He smelled of sweat and some sort of spicy aftershave. "Talking about bodies make you feel uncomfortable, Big Trish?"

"It makes everyone uncomfortable," said Jacinda firmly. "Now sit down."

Bryan shrugged and flopped into the kitchen table booth. He wiggled both his eyebrows at Trish as if to say *I know something she doesn't*. Trish quickly turned to see if Jacinda had seen the exchange, but the team leader was already behind the wheel.

Bryan laced his hands behind his head, clearly pleased with the discomfort he'd caused. "You need any help driving, *kemosabe*, you let me know. Been a wheelman for almost a year now."

"Well, I've been driving since age ten, white boy," she replied, turning out of the neighborhood. "Benefits of growing up on a caribou farm. And it's Jace."

Trish took a seat on the couch beside Owen and Perry. "What about Whitmore?" she asked as the RV drove through suburban Henderson. "Will she be meeting us somewhere?"

"Maybe later on. Right now, she's busy dealing with other sorcery-related issues. We five are the front line of North American cryptid collection."

Jacinda merged the RV onto the 15 freeway and began driving northeast. The GPS display in the center console showed them heading to a spot in southern Wyoming.

"So what's our first target?" said Bryan, again conjuring his United States map glamour. It was impressively detailed, with a different color for each state. Dots glowed as he listed off cryptids: "Bear Lake Monster? Thunderbird? SHUNKA WARAKIN?" The others looked at him, surprised that he could rattle off so many cryptids. "I've been on house arrest for two days," he reminded them. "Plenty of time to bone up."

CRYPTID CORNER

Known for its bright-red pelt and unusual size, the SHUNKA WARAKIN is thought to be a magical cousin of the prehistoric dire wolf. Its power is limited, but its howl can carry for hundreds of kilometers.

"We're starting off a bit easier than that," said Jacinda. "Ms. Whitmore heard a few Euclideans were sniffing around Wyoming. Our first task is to find and capture a jackalope."

Fearsome Critters

Trish pulled her copy of *Cryptozoology for Beginners* from her backpack. She flipped to the North America section to remind herself what a jackalope was. The book was laid out like an encyclopedia and organized by zones: all the cryptids of Europe were grouped together, as were the magical creatures of northern Africa, Scandinavia, Southeast Asia, and so on. There were illustrations for each animal and maps of their habitats, but the cryptids themselves were unlike any Trish had seen in an ordinary reference guide. There were phoenixes, Minotaurs, satyrs, and a hundred more besides. She had been disappointed to learn, however, that there were no DRAGONS.

She flipped to the section they were currently driving through: western North America. According to Whitmore's book, the region spanned from New Mexico to California and went all the way up to Alaska, the Yukon Territory, and the Northwest Territories. As she looked at the map, the territory lines magically shifted and relabeled themselves to indicate the

CRYPTID CORNER

This is because DRAGONS do not exist. Ironically, they have been written about more than any other cryptid in history.

passage of time, until it mirrored a present-day America. *The places might change*, she thought, *but the cryptids remain the same.* She read along as words appeared on the opposite page:

While there are overlaps with Central America, the section began, *the western United States boasts several cryptids unique to the region, such as the thunderbird, the wampus cat, and the once-widespread jackalope.*

Trish sighed. Despite their repeated suggestions to perk up her style, Whitmore's writing was still as dry as ever. Trish finally located the page that detailed the object of their first mission:

"'Jackalope,'" she read aloud to the other sorcerers as *Kana'ti* continued up the 15 freeway. "'The Master Mimic. One of many so-called fearsome critters to inhabit the United States.'"

"That's the bunny with antlers?" asked Bryan, leaning over her to peer at the illustration in *Cryptozoology for Beginners*. He had thankfully pulled on a tank top, but it did nothing to mask his adolescent scent. "Doesn't look very scary to me."

"The 'fearsome critters' were just tall tales," Perry informed him. "Animal stories made up by lumberjacks to haze newbies." She sat back next to Owen on the couch and adjusted her glasses primly. "Bryan's not the only one who did the homework."

"Some of those tall tales were based in reality, though," Jacinda said from the front seat. "The Jersey Devil, wampus cat, and snallygaster are all still alive and kicking. Biting too. You guys might even get to meet them, provided you don't get killed."

"Upbeat as always," said Trish under her breath. Then, louder: "Why are you so worried that we can't handle ourselves?"

"Experience," replied their team leader shortly. "When it comes to cryptids, I've learned to expect the unexpected."

When the young woman didn't want to explain any further, Trish shook her head and read the rest of the jackalope page aloud.

"Piece of cake," said Owen. "Can I go take a nap now?"

Trish noticed that he seemed more irritable than usual this morning. *I hope he and Perry aren't fighting. The two of them might be annoying sometimes, but if he screws things up with her, he's an idiot.*

"Uh, how are we supposed to buy whiskey for this thing?" Bryan asked. "I left my fake ID at home."

"It's been taken care of," Jacinda replied. "Whitmore doesn't want any of you breaking laws unnecessarily."

"Super sweet of her," said Bryan sarcastically. "Especially since I'm breaking house arrest by being here."

"No one will see through the **DOPPELGÄNGER** we created," Jacinda assured him. "You should all study and rest up while you can. **JACKALOPES** are nocturnal. We'll be working late tonight."

THE CODEX ARCANUM

While DOPPELGÄNGERS are capable of speech, they're limited to a handful of phrases and have a limited emotional range. In other words, they make excellent stand-ins for teenage boys.

JACKALOPE

THE **MASTER MIMIC**

WEIGHT:
3 - 4 kg

LENGTH:
75 cm

HEIGHT:
50 cm

MAGICAL PROPERTIES:
perfect pitch, ability to imitate any sound
or human voice, can speak any language

The **jackalope once roamed** all over the **western United States.**
Human expansion and **trophy hunting** have led to only a **handful**
remaining on the entire continent. While similar creatures have
been spotted all over the world historically (the wolpertinger in Europe,
and the Al-mi'raj in the Middle East) the jackalope is the **only living**
horned rabbit.

The jackalope can flawlessly **imitate any human voice** or **language,**
and frequently uses this ability to escape capture. They are
suspicious of people, but **fiercely loyal** if one can
win their trust.

Jackalopes have a preference for **single-malt aged**
whiskey.

DID YOU KNOW?

In the town of Douglas, Wyoming,
it's **legal to hunt the jackalope** for
only **one day of the year** — June 31.
A day, appropriately enough,
that **does not exist.**

Dinner And A Show

Nine hours later, they reached their destination outside of Bear River, Wyoming. They had stopped twice to fill up on gasoline and snacks, but otherwise it was a tedious, mind-numbing wall of driving. The teenagers spent the time poring over *Cryptozoology for Beginners* and attempting to ignore Bryan's antagonistic remarks. Some (Perry) were better at these tasks than others (Trish). Owen retreated to the master bedroom and spent most of the time brooding alone, despite several attempts by Perry to include him. And Jacinda stayed mostly silent, listening to classic rock on satellite radio and rebuffing any attempts at friendly conversation. This included Bryan's grotesque displays of flirting, for which Trish was thankful. She might still be committed to her warrior monk status, but she didn't think she could handle being the fifth wheel to two lovesick couples.

The sun now hung low in the west, bathing the clouds in golden-red light and making the rolling hills of Wyoming resemble a picture postcard. Jacinda pulled *Kana'ti* off the road and parked next to a pebble-lined stream. Undulating light-green grassland stretched out in all directions like a whispering sea. There were a few ranch-style homes here and there, but it was mostly wide-open space. Their team leader got out and stretched, telling them to set up for a quick dinner.

"Pretty rando spot you picked here," said Bryan as he used a Spell to Manipulate Objects to unfold the legs of a card table and cover it with a tablecloth. "Pretty, but rando."

"The Euclideans' last reported location was a quarter mile from here," Jacinda explained, going into a downward dog yoga pose.

"And what's our approach if they're still nearby?" said Perry nervously, opening a cooler of hot dogs and condiments.

"Fight them, subdue them, find and extract the cryptids." Jacinda raised her arms above her head. Trish forced herself to keep her eyes on the green camping stove she was unpacking. "But we have the advantage. The Euclideans don't know what to look for. Most **CRYPTID SIGHTINGS** are based on flimsy or mistaken evidence. Since we know what the animals really look and sound like, hopefully we can get to them first."

Trish studied the butane fuel canister, trying to figure out how it locked into the camping stove. "So how many of these capture missions have you gone on?"

"Captures? None," said Jacinda, arching her back like a cobra and tilting her head upward. Bryan openly gaped at her figure, but Trish refused to sink to his level. *Warrior monk*, she reminded herself. *You're an ice-cold warrior monk.* "The policy of Codex Arcanum has always been to leave these creatures in the wild. But I've been on five or six cryptid research trips in the last six months. I helped Ms. Whitmore heal a wounded **JERSEY DEVIL**

CRYPTID CORNER

In fact, there are over 15,000 **CRYPTID SIGHTINGS** reported every year in North America alone. Most are due to overactive imaginations and intoxication.

a few weeks back, and before that I, um . . . I was sent to capture a salamander. That was my Level Two Final Exam." She jumped to her feet, looking right at Bryan. "Eyes front, Ferretti."

He jolted, botching his casting of a Spell of Attraction on some folding chairs. They clanged together and collapsed in the dirt, making Trish laugh. He glared at her as he bent to pick them up.

"So how are we to go about bagging our big game, then?" Perry asked with clearly faked confidence. She seemed to be in awe or fear of their team leader—Trish couldn't decide which.

"We'll go over all that after dinner," said Jacinda, lifting her arms over her head and rolling her neck. "How do you guys like your veggie dogs?"

"*Veggie* dogs?" said Bryan, wrinkling his nose. "You trying to poison us, Injun Josephine?"

"I am Flying Dust First Nations,'" said Jacinda coldly. "Not Native American, not Indian, and definitely not 'Injun.' I am also a vegetarian. So if you city kids want factory-farmed, cruel-to-animals, processed meat products, we can stop somewhere and you can buy 'em yourself."

CRYPTID CORNER

The **JERSEY DEVIL** is a kangaroo-like cryptid with the head of a goat, the wings of a bat, and the legs of a horse. It lives in the Pine Barrens area of southern New Jersey, and its scream can momentarily render people unconscious. Which can be a good thing, considering how unattractive it looks.

No one else complained after that. The meal was simple—vegetarian hot dogs, chips, potato salad—but there was something about eating outside in the Wyoming air, Trish thought, that made the food extra tasty. She barely noticed the lack of meat. The sun went down while they ate, streaking the big prairie sky in swaths of red, orange, and amber.

Once they were done, Jacinda ordered them to quickly pack up. Trish sidled up to Owen, who was shoving the food in the rear of the RV. "You okay, dude?" she asked him quietly. His dark, silent mood had continued all through dinner and she was growing tired of it.

"Yeah. No," he replied, trying to cram the cooler underneath a stack of camping tents. "I, um . . . saw my mom last night."

"Whoa." Owen's parents had separated nine months ago, and because of her work travel, he'd only seen her in person a handful of days since then. "Did she just show up?"

"Kind of. She was in town on business." He gave a dry laugh that was completely devoid of humor. "Of course, she missed our graduation for 'work reasons.'" He finally shoved the cooler into place. "She took me and Perry out to dinner last night. She wanted to hang out today, too, but I told her I was coming with you guys. Then she asked if I could postpone it one day, 'cause what's more important?" He gave another bitter laugh. "You believe that? She ditches her only kid for whatever top-secret garbage she's working on, then guilts me for wanting to do something that I think is important."

"Did you . . . tell her what we're actually doing here?" Trish asked carefully.

"Dude, of course not. She thinks it's some animal conservation internship, like we told your parents. My dad backed me up, said it was a big opportunity, but she wasn't happy about it." Owen sighed, sitting on the back bumper of the RV. "Perry doesn't get it. She thinks I should have stayed back for a day too. She says I'm being 'unnecessarily petty.'"

Trish sat next to him. "I know you guys are . . . a thing or whatever, but you haven't known her as long as I have. Yeah, she's super smart, but not about everything. Got kind of a blind spot when it comes to parent stuff."

"Because of her dad?"

Trish nodded. Perry's father had died when she was ten years old. She told everyone he was an explorer and that he'd disappeared while on a dangerous journey, but Trish wasn't so sure. She'd heard her own parents sigh about Perry's mom, and how hard it must be for her, working two jobs to take care of her daughter. Trish had never mentioned this to Perry herself, because what was the point? Her father had been gone for almost four years. Questioning why he'd died would only make her friend feel worse.

"Parents are dumb," she finally said. "You live with 'em for years, but they barely know anything about you. I mean, my own mom still thinks she's gonna get me in some girly-girl dress one day. She doesn't get that I'm . . ." She hesitated, kicking a pebble toward the stream. "That I'm never gonna be into that stuff."

"Yeah." Owen looked out at the setting sun. "You think we'll ever be able to tell 'em the full truth about us? You know, about sorcery and what we've been doing?"

"Probably **BETTER THEY DON'T KNOW**. Then they don't have to worry."

"I guess. Hey, thanks for . . . checking in and stuff." He nudged her with his shoulder. "The last few weeks, Perry and I have been spending so much time together . . . I know the three of us haven't . . ."

"It's cool," she said, nudging him back. "You guys make a good couple." It was true. She hadn't said it before, but Owen grinned bashfully.

"Yeah? I don't really know what I'm doing," he confided.

"Nobody does, dude. My dad told me once that in relationships, all you can do is have fun and try to be nice to each other."

Perry came around the side of the RV. "Ahoy, mateys," she said timidly. "Everything shipshape?"

"Aye, aye, me hearty," Owen replied fondly, giving her a squeeze with one arm.

THE CODEX ARCANUM

As a matter of fact, "BETTER THEY DON'T KNOW" is the unofficial policy of the Codex Arcanum. We even considered putting it on the storefront sign, but it was too unwieldy.

Trish could see how relieved Perry was that Owen was no longer mad at her. But before Trish could bring her up to speed on what they'd discussed, a Jeep turned off the road and stopped near their campsite. Its halogen headlights illuminated the teenagers, making it difficult to see anything else. A trim man in a wide-brimmed hat and a tan uniform stepped out of the vehicle. Painted on the door next to the police crest was a logo—a cross bisected by a flaming sword and a compass.

The symbol of the Euclideans.

CHAPTER 6

COP TO IT

Trish's pulse immediately quickened. She shook out her fingers, nervous about the prospect of having to fight an actual police officer.

"Evenin'," the uniformed man said pleasantly. "I'm Lieutenant Doyle with the local PD. You kids got a permit to camp here?"

Bryan also looked nervous, but Jacinda strolled past him and raised a calm hand in greeting. "Do not. Attack," she said softly to the others through a charming smile. "I thought this might happen."

She turned away from the officer, making a few hand motions. Then she spun back around, stretching out a hand and whispering in **FRENCH**, *"Vous nous verrez comme des agents fédéraux pour le gouvernement Américain."*

THE CODEX
ARCANUM

While memorizing a few helpful phrases can help with the casting of glamours, speaking fluent FRENCH makes using such enchantments far easier. It also looks good on a college application.

A blob of light sprang from her hand, wrapping around Lieutenant Doyle's eyes. He shook his head as if momentarily blinded, then peered at the teenagers. To him, they now looked like adults of varying ages: Jacinda was a tough woman in her thirties; Bryan was an overweight, balding man in his forties; Owen had a beard; and Perry was nearly two feet taller. Trish had been glamoured to have light-gray hair and glasses. All the teenagers now appeared to wear the bland dark suits favored by U.S. federal agents.

"My apologies," he said. "Huh. For a second there, I thought you all was younger."

"No worries," said Jacinda in a deeper, more mature voice that was not part of the GLAMOUR she'd cast. She flipped open a hot dog bun, which the Euclidean perceived to be a federal ID. "Homeland Security, investigating reports of a possible terror plot involving wild animals."

THE CODEX
ARCANUM

Auditory GLAMOURS are much more difficult to cast, as the range of human hearing is far more discerning than the visual spectrum. Listen to any auto-tuned song if you want proof of this.

"I see," said Lieutenant Doyle, peering intently at the featureless white bun. Trish bit her lips to keep from laughing at how silly he looked. "Thing is, none of you feds contacted local law enforcement. That there's the usual procedure."

Trish saw Bryan conjure a ball of lightning behind his back. She was impressed he could do it without looking, but he looked jittery, ready to attack at any moment.

Jacinda kept her cool, though, pocketing the hot dog bun. "I'm well aware of the procedure, **OFFICER**. This is a classified operation."

"Really? Well then, surely you can show me some kinda proof o' that so's I can alert my compadres in the area."

Trish and Perry glanced at each other. Where there was one Euclidean, there were bound to be more. Trish only hoped their enemies hadn't already rounded up every jackalope in Wyoming. "Your, uh—" she began, then remembered to drop her voice and speak like a bureaucratic gray-haired adult. "Your companions. Are they nearby?"

"Hither and yon." Lieutenant Doyle smiled. "We like to cast a wide net. Now how 'bout that there proof?"

Trish saw his hand rest on the revolver in his hip holster. If he pulled it, there was no way they'd get out of this situation

BEWARE THE EUCLIDEANS

Our enemies often look to law enforcement **OFFICERS** and career soldiers when searching for new recruits. Their penchant for rules and proficiency with weapons are an ideal match for the Euclidean lifestyle.

without alerting the other Euclideans. They had to subdue him before then. She angled her body, beginning to form the runes for an elemental spell. A column of earth silently rose behind the police officer, ready to envelop him if need be—

But Jacinda stepped forward, pointing her hand toward the Euclidean and muttering under her breath.

A look of desperate realization suddenly came over the officer's face. "Oh, shoot. Sorry. I just remembered—the oven!"

He scrambled back into his cruiser. Trish dropped her hands, and the pile of dirt crumbled back into the ground just before the officer reversed into it. He gave them a small wave, then drove off like his pants were on fire. Jacinda's glamour disappeared when he was out of sight.

"I thought I told you both *not* to attack," the team leader remarked.

Bryan let the ball of electricity in his hand fizzle out, and Trish colored with embarrassment. Out of all the people to be lumped in with. They'd both been eager to fight, but Jacinda's **CLEVER SPELL CASTING** had thankfully defused the whole situation. Trish mentally kicked herself for not listening.

BEWARE THE EUCLIDEANS

CLEVER SPELL CASTING is almost always more beneficial when combating enemies than blasting away with elemental attacks. These books will hopefully give you plenty of examples of how to do that.

"The last thing we need," Jacinda continued, "is for the Euclideans to discover one of their operatives was zapped by magical lightning or smothered in dirt. Do you two agree?"

"Of course," Trish said defensively. "I just thought—"

"I didn't ask you to think. I asked you to follow my lead."

"What was that spell you used on him?" Owen asked, clearly trying to change the subject.

"I cast a Spell of Suggestion to make him think he left his oven on," Jacinda said lightly. "You all would do well to learn it."

"Hey, I know my spells backward and forward, Sacagawea," Bryan replied acidly. "But if a Euclidean cop tells someone he spotted me, I go from house arrest to wanted fugitive."

Perry stepped between them. "Jacinda dispatched him, so it's a moot point. But I gather that we no longer have much time to locate these jackalopes."

"We do not," their team leader said grimly. "I only hope the Euclideans left us something to find. But before we start, we need to go over the rules."

RULE OF THREES

Jacinda went into the RV and pulled out several large reinforced plastic cases as she spoke. "First, no magic unless absolutely necessary. Sorcery has a tendency to spook animals."

She opened one of the cases to reveal six sets of night vision goggles with attached headsets. The goggles looked like a small pair of binoculars that could be raised and lowered if necessary.

"Second, we work in pairs. Stay in contact, no lone-wolfing it when we're out in the field. That's how people get impaled by unicorns."

While they secured the night vision rigs to their heads, Jacinda unlocked a second case. Inside it, resting on form-cut foam, were four strangely shaped pistols with long barrels. TRANQUILIZER GUNS, Trish realized.

"Now we're talking," said Bryan, lifting one from the case without asking.

"Third rule," Jacinda said, taking it out of his hand. "Weapons are not toys. I will be in charge of administering all tranquilizers, and they will only be used at my command. The wrong dosage or combination of chemicals can kill a cryptid."

She showed them one of the darts, which was about the length of an ordinary syringe, with a tuft of fibrous material at the end to keep it balanced in flight. Jacinda demonstrated how to pull back the slide on the pistol, load the dart, then raise or lower the velocity if need be. Once she was satisfied that each of them could handle the weapon, she assigned them into teams.

"Perry and Owen, you'll take the northern section," she said, indicating the dark line of rolling hills. The moon hadn't yet risen, and the clear evening sky was beginning to

ENCHANTING DETAILS

While tranquilizers have been used in animal capture for thousands of years, the modern TRANQUILIZER GUN was invented in the 1950s by Colin Murdoch.

show a brilliant tapestry of stars, far more than Trish usually saw in Henderson. "Trish, you're with me," their team leader continued, briefly making eye contact. The team leader's electric gray gaze once again made Trish's heart beat faster. She nodded quickly, forcing herself to stay focused. "And Bryan—you stay here with *Kana'ti*. Let us know if more Euclideans show up."

"You're friggin' benching me?" he said in disbelief. "I have multiple hunting licenses. I've killed and skinned my own game. I'm way more useful than these wimps." He looked pointedly at Perry, who dropped her tranquilizer gun as if it were a lit stick of dynamite.

"Once you prove you can follow orders—like when I tell you to put on a shirt or not use magic—you're welcome to join us."

"This is bullshit." His freckled face was blotchy with anger. "I'm risking prison time to be here. I'm traveling with people who hate me. I ain't going through all this to wait in the car like some kid."

Had he been speaking to her, Trish would have attacked Bryan several sentences ago. She was impressed that Jacinda merely raised an eyebrow. The team leader slowly stepped toward him, her voice low and firm. "These are the rules of this mission. You don't wanna follow 'em, I can draw up a portal to Henderson anytime. So what's it gonna be?"

The other three held their breath as Bryan glared at the team leader. The former bully clenched his jaw, seeming to decide between responding with words or a spell. Finally he did neither, breaking her gaze and kicking up a cloud of dirt. Without a word, he walked back to the RV and went inside, making sure to slam the door.

"Same goes for the rest of you too," said Jacinda, fixing her steely gaze on each of them in turn. "Are you all ready to do what I say, when I say it?" Once they'd all nodded, the team leader placed a night vision rig on her head and smiled genuinely for the first time since they'd met her. "Then let's go catch a cryptid."

Discussions In The Dark

Trish and Jacinda walked through the whispering Wyoming grass, listening to crickets chirp as they scanned the dark horizon. Their night vision goggles made everything shades of muddy green, but more than once they prevented them from stepping into prairie dog burrows and turning an ankle. Perry and Owen were already out of sight, having set off in the opposite direction. Jacinda had told them to stay in touch over their headsets. As they walked, the team leader occasionally poured out a few glugs from a very expensive bottle of **WHISKEY**. Even from several feet away, the smell burned Trish's throat.

ENCHANTING
DETAILS

WHISKEY is a strong alcoholic beverage made from fermented grain. If it's made in Scotland, it must be referred to as Scotch whiskey. In Gaelic it's called usquebaugh, or "water of life," which tells you the extent to which Scots value their liquor.

This might actually be kinda nice, she thought, *if I wasn't stuck with Major General Serious.* She couldn't figure Jacinda out. She was clearly tough and skilled, but something was keeping her cold and distant from everyone. Trish didn't know if it was the weight of her responsibilities or simply her natural demeanor. Still, they couldn't spend the next however many weeks alternating between arguing with each other and enduring awkward silences like this one. Maybe Jacinda just didn't realize that Trish respected her. After another excruciating minute of silence, she cleared her throat.

"Nice, uh, nice work back there with the Euclidean," Trish said. "The way you used that Spell of Suggestion? I probably just would have let Bryan zap him."

It was half meant as a joke, but Jacinda nodded soberly. "That's because you and Bryan have a lot in common."

"What?" *I try to be nice, and she compares me to a legit criminal?* "I am nothing like him," Trish said hotly. "Nothing. I should tell you some of the things he did to people before we got him put on house arrest. Things I would never do, I'll tell you that."

"You both attack without planning," Jacinda responded, pouring out more whiskey. "And you speak without thinking. Neither of you is very good with trust."

Ugh, that word again. "I'm not—I trust people. I trust . . . Perry and Owen."

"Only to a point. Do they know everything about you? About who you really are?"

Trish felt her cheeks burning, and was glad for the surrounding darkness. "I don't know what you're talking about," she said as calmly as possible.

"Please. Anyone can see you're hiding something." She turned to look at Trish, lifting the night vision goggles to her forehead. The infrared light of Trish's goggles made the team leader's normally striking irises look black and eerie. "Let me guess. You feel like you can't tell anyone about it. Not even your parents, right? Like if you do, it'll change their perception of you. That for the rest of your life, you'll be defined by that one thing."

How does she know all this? Did she cast some kind of mind-reading spell on me? Trish's palms began to sweat at the thought of Jacinda looking inside her head. "Nobody is just one thing," she said defiantly. "And it's nobody's business, anyway."

"If you say so. But until you open up to someone—until you *trust* them—you won't get them to trust you. People can tell when they're being lied to. Can't be part of a team if you're holding back, doll."

"Don't call me that," Trish snapped.

"Fair enough." Jacinda flipped down her night vision goggles again, now looking like an owl with empty round circles for eyes. "But the longer you wait, the harder it is. Believe me, I know." Without another word, she walked past Trish into the prairie.

The teenager stayed behind, her heart thumping against her ribs. Thoughts swirled inside her head like bats in an attic. *She knows? Does that mean she had a similar secret? That she's . . .*

like me? Her stomach flip-flopped at the notion. But then that feeling was crushed by the immediately following thought—*So what if she is, Big Trish? You think she's gonna take you under her wing? You're an oversized, unlovable monster, while Jacinda—* Trish shook her head to stop her internal tirade, but the facts remained: Jacinda was sixteen, she was a Level Three sorcerer, she had traveled the world. She was exotic, experienced, alluring. *What could someone like her have in common with* you?

But before Trish could answer that question, a voice cried out for help. It echoed across the prairie, barely on this side of adolescence and cracked with pain.

Owen.

SNIPE HUNT

"Help!" the teenage boy repeated from somewhere to the northeast. "I'm stuck, and it's a-comin' after me. Help."

Trish cranked up the velocity on her tranquilizer pistol and ran forward, making sure to keep her finger off the trigger. The last thing she needed was to accidentally fire a dart into her own foot. She made it to where the team leader was waiting, her pistol also in hand.

ENCHANTING DETAILS

A SNIPE is a well-known fictitious creature said to reside all over North America. The time-honored method of hunting snipe is to send someone out at night with an empty bag, and inform them the creature will run into it. Since the animal does not exist, the victim of this prank is literally "left holding the bag."

Jacinda pressed the "Talk" button on her headset. "Perry, Owen, can you hear me? Over." A fuzz of static in their ears was the only response. She repeated her query, her voice cracking anxiously, but to no avail.

"Maybe they're too far away," whispered Trish.

"The range should be good for at least two miles," Jacinda replied. "Unless the mics were switched off or broken somehow. Perry, Owen—" she began, but Owen's voice cut her off again. It sounded closer.

"Help!" he called, real desperation in his voice. "Somebody get this varmint. Ow!"

Varmint? Trish thought. *What is he, an old-timey prospector now?* But people said all kinds of strange things when they were in pain. When her broken leg was being set, she herself had fretted that a suit of armor wouldn't fit over her cast. She was just about to go after him, but Jacinda held her back.

"Wait. Something's wrong," she said, scanning the horizon.

To Trish's eye, it looked like nothing but windblown grass. "He's hurt, that's what's wrong," she said. "It's gotta be the Euclideans."

"Then why didn't Perry radio in?"

"I don't know, maybe she's hurt too. Maybe they got captured."

As if to confirm her words, another voice piped up out of the darkness, immediately recognizable in its earnestness:

"Please help!" Perry called, sounding even closer than Owen. "We can't move, and they're a-coming back!"

"I have an idea. We can use—wait!" Jacinda called, but Trish was already running in the direction of her friends' voices. She jumped over soccer ball–sized rocks and narrowly avoided a prairie dog hole. Thankfully, her increased heart rate flooded her body with adrenaline, making her senses heightened.

"This way!" called Owen again, much closer now but veering off to the south. "They're right behind me!" Trish looked around as she ran, but the only person she could see was Jacinda. The team leader wasn't even following her. Instead she was digging through her backpack for something. Was it possible the Euclideans had caught Owen in some kind of camouflage net? Or had he been dragged into an underground trap? And what had happened to Perry?

"Over here!" called the tiny girl, even closer than Owen had been. "The villains are gonna get us!"

Her friends were only a few meters away now. Trish put on another burst of speed, ready to lift her pistol—

But Jacinda cut in front of her, her speed magically increased by the enchanted timer in her hand. Trish's feet stuttered to a stop. *Right*, she thought as the blood rose to her cheeks. *Forgot all about the enchanted items we had with us.*

Her team leader's blurry form resolved itself until she looked like a human being again. Both she and Trish lifted their night vision goggles. Trish opened her mouth to apologize, but Jacinda cut her off, her gray eyes blazing in the dark.

"This is exactly what I'm talking about," she hissed, the cold disappointment in her voice making Trish feel like she'd been stabbed in the gut with an icicle. Jacinda stepped forward, holding out her hand. "You can't be trusted to follow orders, and you certainly can't be trusted with a tranquilizer—"

She was cut off by a metallic *thwick*. Jacinda looked down at her left ankle in surprise, then her entire body was yanked backward through the prairie grass, feet first, by some unseen powerful force.

"Jacinda!" Trish yelled, pulling her night vision goggles back down. There were a few motionless lumps in her muddy green vision, but whether they were boulders or an unconscious teenage sorcerer was impossible to tell.

Which meant Trish was alone on the prairie with an unseen enemy.

Alone On The Range

Screw the rules, she thought. *Time to do what I do best.* She began to form runes to conjure flame, thinking a small prairie fire might flush out whatever was attacking them, when a voice spoke up out of the darkness.

"Help me, Trish."

It was Jacinda, though the usual hard edge was gone from her voice. Instead, she sounded mournful and even scared. There was desperation in her words, a raw begging that tugged Trish's feet forward.

"Where are you?" she called out to the empty prairie.

"They done got us," came the reply, tantalizingly close and dripping with heartache. "Outsmarted each and every one of us. All except you. Please, doll. Help me."

She was about to do just that, to run pell-mell toward the pained voice, when she saw two glowing specks appear in her field of vision.

The specks were just a dozen millimeters apart, and hovered about half a meter off the ground. Then they blinked, revealing themselves to be oversized eyes. The head in which they rested was almost entirely obscured by prairie grass, but as Trish peered at it, a shape began to resolve itself in the muddy green of her night vision. A shape they had been seeking all along.

It was a jackalope.

The cryptid had long twitching ears easily the length of its body, and a constantly quivering nose. Its scruffy coat was thick with fur, and its long back legs looked ready to spring away at a moment's notice. But its most prominent feature was the completely ridiculous, delicate set of antlers sprouting from the crown of its adorable head. Trish resisted the temptation to say "awww" out loud. There was no way this cute little critter could be a danger.

Then it spoke.

"I'm just over here," said the jackalope in a **PERFECT IMITATION** of Jacinda's voice. "Hurry, they're a-coming back."

CRYPTID CORNER

A jackalope only needs to hear a voice once to render a PERFECT IMITATION of it. Because of this, it also possesses a lovely singing voice.

Seeing the team leader's voice come from the cryptid's mouth was surreal. But it did explain why Jacinda and her friends had been talking like old-fashioned cowboys: it hadn't been them talking at all. The jackalope had used its gift for mimicry to send them running all over the prairie in an effort to protect itself. Even though she still didn't know where Owen and Perry were, Trish decided to adopt a new approach.

"Hey there," she said, tucking the tranquilizer pistol into her waistband behind her back. "Hey, little buddy. I'm not gonna hurt you."

"They're a-coming!" said the jackalope in Owen's voice. "Better run, they're evil!"

"You're not fooling anyone with your big talk," Trish said. "Come here." She crouched down to make herself smaller. Reaching into her backpack, she again scanned the prairie. Still no sign of Jacinda or the others. Trish hoped the animal hadn't somehow swallowed them.

She took a small flask of whiskey out of her pack and uncapped it. She poured some into her hand, her nose crinkling at the smell. "Want some?" she said to the cryptid. "It's single malt, aged twenty years."

The jackalope twitched its nose and took a tentative hop toward her. Trish could see that it was favoring its right hind leg as it moved. There was a deep red gouge along its foot, like it had been burned with a hot wire. "I don't know, missy," it said in Perry's voice. "Might be better to run."

"You can't run on that injured foot," Trish said soothingly. "Why don't you have a drink and let me look at it?"

The animal hopped even closer. Its nostrils flared, clearly smelling the whiskey. Trish could reach out and touch it, but she stayed still. "I told you, these beasts cannot be trusted," the jackalope said in a voice Trish hadn't heard it use yet. But she recognized it immediately.

It was the voice of Samson Kiraz.

"You saw the Euclideans, didn't you?" Trish whispered. "That cop said they were in the area. You must've seen them and escaped, huh?"

"Leave the snares," said the cryptid in Kiraz's accented voice. "We'll capture any leftover vermin and return for them."

"Leftover—they got some of your friends?"

The jackalope switched back to Owen's voice. "I told ya to run," it said mournfully. "I told ya they were a-com—"

Before it could finish the word, a tranquilizer dart came zipping out of the darkness. It struck the jackalope in the neck. "Run!" it screamed in Jacinda's voice. It sprang away from Trish, shouting in a series of different voices as it bolted: "Run, run, run, run!"

But the cryptid only hopped a few meters before it keeled over into the prairie grass, unconscious.

ENTRAPMENT

Trish sprang to her feet, quickly conjuring a ball of purple fire. But it was Owen who limped out of the darkness, tranquilizer pistol in hand. Perry was several meters behind him, also favoring one leg.

"Chill, T," he said, wincing as he put weight on his left foot. "It's just us."

She closed her hand, extinguishing the magic flame. "Why did you do that?" Trish said angrily. "It wasn't gonna hurt me!" She ran over to the jackalope, gently lifting its small antlered head. The creature gave a teeth-rattling snore.

"Are you nuts? It took out me and Perry in, like, two minutes. Led us right into these metal snares by making us think you were in trouble."

"Yeah, it did the same to us," said Trish, standing up and lifting her night vision goggles. "But it was just using its voice mimicry to protect itself. The Euclideans already caught a bunch of its friends."

"I thought these retractable devices were their handiwork," Perry said, limping up beside Owen. She held up a scorched high-tech chrome metal box with a broken wire dangling from it. "They placed them all over the prairie, for any animal to step into. Unconscionably irresponsible."

"And that tricky thing used 'em against us," said Owen, pointing to the unconscious jackalope. "Gotta say, I'm kinda impressed. Where's Jacinda?"

"Ugh. Over here," came the pained voice of their team leader. They went toward her voice to find her left leg had also been caught in one of the Euclideans' retractable snares. She gingerly prodded a lump on her head. Owen formed the runes for a lightning spell and stretched his hand toward the snare, but Perry stopped him.

"One moment. It might behoove us to inspect the box before destroying it. May I?" she said to Jacinda.

The team leader nodded, and Perry bent down to study the contraption. It had the look of an expensive laptop computer, featureless and slick. A blue light blinked at the base of the device.

"As I suspected," Perry said, tapping the tiny light. "The devices are outfitted with Wi-Fi. Possibly even a camera. *Et voilà*." She located a pinhole on the front of the trap and smushed a bit of mud over it. "Impressive engineering, but we must assume the Euclideans have seen us."

"Which means we need to leave," said Jacinda, wincing as she got to her feet. She formed a few runes with her fingers, muttered two activation words in Latin, and blasted the spring snare box with a bolt of lightning. The contraption fizzed, and the metal wire around her ankle went slack.

When she saw the unconscious jackalope, she turned apologetically to Trish. "Nice work," she said sincerely. "If it hadn't been for you, this little guy would have taken us all out and escaped."

"Hey, I'm the one who tranq'd him," Owen complained. Perry elbowed him. "What? It's true," he whispered to her.

Jacinda looked away in embarrassment. "I, uh . . . I owe you all an apology." She bit her lip, then looked up to make eye contact with each of them. "This is, well . . . it's my first time, okay? Leading a team like this. I may have been . . . possibly . . ." She growled, then spread her hands defensively. "A bit too harsh. But it was all to keep everyone safe."

"Oh my God, enough already," Trish said, giving the older girl a bump on the shoulder. "Don't wanna see you pull a muscle trying to apologize. It's fine."

"Indubitably so," Perry said consolingly. "Besides, it's our first time too."

Jacinda gave them a grateful half-grin. "Okay, then. Can everyone make it back to *Kana'ti*? It'll be easier to cast healing spells if I can see."

The others nodded and began to limp through the swishing prairie grass. "After that," Jacinda groaned, favoring her sprained ankle, "we better strike camp and get back on the road. Looks like the Euclideans are already way ahead of us."

CHAPTER 7

DRIVEN TO DISTRACTIONS

"There is a wonderful American phrase for situations such as this," Whitmore mused, her face filling the video screen in *Kana'ti*'s front console. "But I cannot bring it to mind."

The North American sorcerers were three hundred and seventy miles from where they'd captured the jackalope. Once they'd gotten the animal back to the RV and quickly packed up camp, Jacinda and Bryan had driven through the night until they reached Fort Collins, Colorado. The team leader had wanted to put as much distance between them and the Euclideans as she could before calling Whitmore.

Just as the sun was beginning to rise in the east, they pulled *Kana'ti* into the parking lot of a fast-food establishment. The other teenagers stirred, having dozed off in their clothes. Once everyone had freshened up in the restaurant bathroom, they gathered around the front of the RV while Jacinda video-called

ENCHANTING DETAILS

IDIOMS are colloquial phrases that metaphorically describe a situation. Depending on the country of origin, similar situations can be expressed by very different idioms. For example, the American idiom "killing two birds with one stone" is expressed as "while diving, drink water" in Indonesian.

the Codex Arcanum librarian. She quickly explained everything that had transpired in Wyoming. But rather than scold them or offer solutions, Whitmore was now discussing **IDIOMS**.

"Help me out, Yanks," she chided them. "It's that phrase one employs when things look bleak but there's still some minuscule chance of success?"

"'Snowball's chance in hell'?" said Owen.

"'Darkest before the dawn'?" suggested Perry.

"'Totally and completely boned,'" drawled Bryan.

"No, no, no. It's much cleverer than that. Something to do with nine pins, or billiards . . . 'Behind the eight ball!' That's it." Whitmore looked off into the distance. "Wonderful visual."

"Great," said Trish, trying to maintain her patience. "Now that we can perfectly picture our crappy situation, what do we do about it?"

"What one does in the game of billiards," replied the librarian. "We circumvent the obstacle."

Jacinda wrinkled her forehead. "I'm . . . not sure I follow."

Whitmore sighed at the slowness of her charges. Readjusting her silver spectacles, she muttered a few words and conjured a transparent three-dimensional **GLAMOUR** of the planet Earth.

**THE CODEX
ARCANUM**

There are two types of GLAMOURS: those that alter the vision of a single subject (such as the hallucination Jacinda cast on the Wyoming police officer) and those that use nearby light particles to create a mirage that can be seen by anyone. This glamour is an example of the latter.

The video screen flickered, momentarily confounded by the magical energy it was relaying. The librarian crooked a finger, and dozens of glowing green dots appeared on the globe.

"Clearly, the incident at Loch Ness caused the Euclideans to ramp up their efforts," the older woman explained. "Since then, dozens of their teams have been spotted all over the globe, attempting to capture cryptids. These are the targets they've acquired in just the last five days." Over a third of the glowing dots—including one in the southwestern corner of Wyoming where the jackalope's friends had been abducted—became covered by red X's. "Since we cannot hope to compete with their numbers, we must regain the advantage by doing something they will not expect." She dispelled the glamour with a wave of her fingers.

"And? What is it?" Trish asked impatiently. The idea that the Euclideans might capture every cryptid on the planet before they even had a chance to stop them was galling.

"I don't know," Whitmore responded mildly. "I was merely stating the problem we face. It's the first step to solving anything."

The teenagers looked at each other uneasily. As long as they'd known her, Whitmore had always had an answer ready for their

BEWARE THE EUCLIDEANS

MAGICAL ENERGY DETECTORS work by searching for spikes in expended spell power. Since every enchantment expels a bit of magical energy, more than one or two castings in the same location is enough to draw the attention of our enemies.

questions. To be privy to her decision-making process and see she was just as unsure and confused as them was more than sobering—it was scary.

"Haven't you been fightin' these guys for, like, a hundred years?" said Bryan, voicing each of their internal thoughts. "How could you not have a plan B?"

Whitmore pursed her lips. "One of the disadvantages of a highly technological foe is that their resources and methods keep evolving. Global positioning systems, worldwide satellite feeds, and MAGICAL ENERGY DETECTORS have made it quite easy for them to locate cryptids. If you have any ideas on how to counteract all that, allow me to employ another idiom: I'm all ears."

ENCHANTING DETAILS

Rabbits are the second-most commonly used animal in MEDICAL TESTING and research. Their relatively large size, docile nature, and inexpensive cost all make them ideal subjects. The rabbits, I'm sure, see it otherwise.

There was an uncomfortable silence. "What about getting the media involved?" said Jacinda with the air of someone who had brought this up multiple times before. "Tell people these creatures exist. I mean, they go nuts when a regular bunny gets taken for MEDICAL TESTING. Imagine what they'll do when they find out the Euclideans are snaring jackalopes for who knows what."

Trish thought the idea had merit, but Whitmore firmly shook her head. "We have tilled this row before, Ms. Greyeyes. One of Codex Arcanum's core beliefs is to keep magical knowledge a secret. We cannot trust humanity to use sorcery wisely, or to treat these animals with compassion. One only needs to visit Sea World to see that."

"But if people saw how special they are—" Jacinda insisted, but the librarian raised a hand.

"The Council has spoken. We must find another way."

There was a long moment of silence as they pondered. Then Perry's face lit up. "Ooh! The Euclideans may possess better tech, but they're still at the mercy of space and time. Sorcerers are not."

Owen said, "You're not suggesting we use the SPELL TO REWRITE HISTORY, are you? Bad idea."

Perry hated it when people underestimated her intelligence. "Of course not. I'm suggesting we focus on our strengths." She patted a stack of hand-copied spell pages.

"Portal-hopping," Owen realized. "You wanna get us to the cryptid locations before the Euclideans can reach 'em."

THE CODEX ARCANUM

While there are several enchantments that affect the flow of time, REWRITING HISTORY is incredibly dangerous. Anything altered can change the present and create paradoxes that not even Level Nine sorcerers can undo.

"I like it," said Bryan. "No offense to *Kana'ti*, sweetheart, but the drive time is killing us."

"It's Jace," the team leader reminded him coldly. "And you wanna pack all this equipment on your back?"

They all lapsed into thought once more. Trish's brain felt simultaneously exhausted by the previous day's events and electrified by her anxiety for the future. Every minute they didn't come up with a solution, the Euclideans got closer to capturing or killing another cryptid. She had to hope that the animals' inborn abilities were enough to keep them safe at the moment. After all, the jackalope had managed to evade the Euclideans merely by pretending to be something it was not.

Something it was not.

"How 'bout we create a distraction?" Trish said.

"You mean, like, you in a bikini?" Bryan snarked. "Hard pass."

Owen hit him on the shoulder. Bryan shoved him back. Trish took a breath to prevent herself from hexing him, then continued. "I mean a magical distraction. You said the Euclideans know when there's been a cryptid sighting. What if we created a bunch of fake ones?"

"Mass hallucinations," said Perry, warming to the idea. "Ingenious. If we cast a variety of glamours all over the country, the Euclideans won't know which one to investigate first."

"They'll waste all their time chasing ghosts," said Owen with a grin. "Nice, dude." He and Trish bumped fists.

Whitmore tapped two elegant fingers together, then came to a decision. "It runs counter to our Statute of Secrecy, but very well. On your way to collect the next cryptid, create as many fake sightings as you can. I shall instruct the other teams to do the same. Best of luck."

CRAZY ABOUT CRYPTIDS

The next two days were a blur of driving and spell casting. The team put hundreds of miles on the RV each day as they zigzagged their way toward the southern border of the United States. Jacinda wondered aloud if there was some way to bewitch *Kana'ti* to drive itself, but the others voted this idea down.

As the team leader drove, the others reread *Cryptozoology for Beginners* so they would all have a better sense of the animals they needed to create. Then they took turns casting glamours at the people they passed on the freeway and those they saw at rest stops and gas stations.

Sorcery being more of an art than a science, each teenager went about this in a different way. Perry would study and analyze the potential recipients of her glamour, calculating which person was most likely to spread the word about what he or she had seen. Owen was more lackadaisical, casting glamours at whomever crossed his field of vision first. Bryan took particular delight in startling people with visions of cryptids at awkward moments, such as when someone was peeing. And Trish tried to focus on those who were doing something mean, such as those hitting their sister or trying to break open a snack machine.

The glamours themselves were simple—a brief glimpse of a strange creature in the distance—but they were effective. People would exclaim with excitement, fumble for their camera phones, and describe what they'd seen to their companions. Several of them called the police to report their sightings. Many more posted on social media.

Bryan noticed this when he saw the tags #cryptidsighting and #cryptids were trending in the American Southwest. News outlets picked up on the story, and within twenty-four hours other sightings began popping up all over the country, even in places where they had not cast any glamours.

"It's classic **MASS HYSTERIA**," said Perry while they watched a news story cataloguing the spike in **SASQUATCH** sightings. "Think about it. We know the Euclideans already captured him, but human perception is incredibly malleable. People want to be part of the movement, so they convince themselves they've seen something too."

"Look!" said Owen, pausing the web video. He pointed to a sour-looking uniformed official behind the Sasquatch reporter. On the shoulder of his black jacket was the Euclidean symbol. "It's working. They're running all over the place!"

ENCHANTING
DETAILS

MASS HYSTERIA occurs when a group of people all believe something that is not true. Classic examples include the Salem witch trials, the dancing plague of 1518, and Black Friday doorbuster sales.

SASQUATCH

HABITAT:
**PACIFIC NORTHWEST, U.S.;
BRITISH COLUMBIA,
CANADA**

CANADA

UNITED STATES

THE
MOSTLY GENTLE
GIANT

(Also Known As: **BIGFOOT**)

WEIGHT:
110 - 130 kg

LENGTH:
n/a

HEIGHT:
210 - 250 cm

MAGICAL PROPERTIES:
its **fur** can **change color** to act as **camouflage,
supernatural strength**

A **hairy, upright-walking apelike creature** that lives in the **Pacific
Northwest**, the Sasquatch has been sighted by human beings
since back before Europeans came to the continent. Sasquatches
have been **accused of stealing cattle and sheep**, but they
are **vegetarian and very shy.**

Similar hominid-like cryptids exist in Asia (the **Yeti**),
Australia (the **Yowie**), and Florida (the **skunk ape**).

─── DID YOU KNOW? ───

The Sasquatch can **lift up to four or five
times its own weight**, enabling it to
pull full-grown trees from the ground
and throw car-sized boulders.

Being a **peaceful creature**, however,
it rarely has cause to do so.

"Just remember our other goal," Jacinda reminded them from the driver's seat. "It's more important that we find and secure the real cryptids."

Their team leader had been behind the wheel of *Kana'ti* for nearly eight hours straight, stopping only twice to fill up on gas and use the bathroom. Her striking gray eyes were blood-shot and her skin was waxy. Even so, Trish was impressed by her strength and patience. She never once complained about her responsibilities. They hadn't spoken one-on-one since the awk-ward conversation in Wyoming, and Trish was glad for that. If Jacinda brought up Trish's "secret" again, the teenager still had no idea how to respond.

Instead, she'd spent the last two days getting to know the jackalope. They'd kept him in a large wire cage for the first day, but once Jacinda had magically healed his leg wound, he was able to hop around the RV's bedroom. Trish fed him carrot sticks and celery straws along with great helpings of whiskey as she tried to get a sense of how smart he really was. He was at least as clever as a myna bird, able to repeat anything he heard with perfect mimicry. This made for some awkward conversations.

"What's wrong, lil' cowpoke?" the jackalope asked in her mom's voice when Trish entered the master bedroom with his lunch. He had overheard it during a phone call with her parents, and it startled her every time he used it.

"Nothing," she replied stiffly. "And will you quit doing that?"

"We're just concerned about ya, Person," The cryptid now said in her dad's voice. It was uncanny how the animal was able to suss out her mood and pick the perfect voice to match it.

As if sensing this, the jackalope nuzzled against her leg while she dumped vegetables into a dish. "Tain't healthy to keep things all bottled up inside," he commented, now sounding like Jacinda.

She debated telling the cryptid how she truly felt. How it seemed like she was all alone in the world, even when she was surrounded by people. How it felt like no one would ever accept her for who she was. Then she remembered she was talking to a horned rabbit.

"I'm fine," she finally replied. Outside, the RV passed a sign that read "Welcome to Texas—Drive Friendly." The sun was low on the horizon, making the yellow fields out the window glow like molten gold. "It's just been a long couple days."

"Tell me about it," the jackalope drawled in Bryan's sarcastic voice as he munched on celery sticks. "This joint smells like a barnyard."

"Ugh." She made a sour face. "Please don't use *that* voice unless you have to."

"Sorry, T," he said in Owen's voice, resting his adorable muzzle on her knee. "I'm just a-tryin' to puzzle you out. I'm a silly varmint."

"No, you're not." She sighed, scratching the jackalope on the space between his antlers. "I'm just—I dunno, it's weird. I'm in this car with four other people, but I still feel . . . alone, I guess." She looked out the window at the passing cow pastures. "Jacinda—Jace—spends all her time driving, Perry and Owen are like this nation of two, and Bryan stays in his man-cave all day, which is fine by me." She had to admit, it did feel nice to talk to someone, even if that someone was an antlered rabbit with a tendency to figure out your innermost thoughts. "I just worry that it'll always be this way. That I'll never have someone who . . . gets me."

"I get you, partner," the cryptid said sleepily, now using Perry's voice. "And you get me. Us lonesome varmints gotta . . . stick . . . together." He closed his eyes contentedly.

"You like that word, huh?" Trish shifted her hand to scratch the creature under his furry chin. "Well, I suppose we've got to call you something." She took his tiny muzzle in her hands. "Varmint. You like the sound of that?"

The jackalope snored like a chainsaw in response.

Fangs And Fury

Several hours later, Trish wished she had joined Varmint in his afternoon nap.

It was just past 2:00 a.m. and she was tromping through a foggy cow pasture outside Rusk, Texas. Jacinda had brought them to this isolated pocket of the Lone Star State to locate and capture a **CHUPACABRA**. But despite Whitmore's assurances that the animal's **MAGICAL ENERGY SIGNATURE** was somewhere nearby, they had been searching the area for two hours with no luck.

THE CODEX ARCANUM

Anything magical—be it item, place, or creature—has a unique MAGICAL ENERGY SIGNATURE. Once a sorcerer knows what it is, a Spell of Location can be used to pinpoint the subject. Capturing it, however, is a whole other matter.

Trish yawned loudly. The smell of manure was strong in her nostrils, and her jeans were streaked with what she hoped was mud but was more likely cow poop. It was impossible to tell in the dark. She had already resigned herself to destroying these clothes when the group was done with this mission.

"This is stupid," Bryan murmured over the radio. "If this thing has any sense, it's asleep in its burrow right now."

"Chupacabras are nocturnal," Jacinda whispered back. "And they're easily startled, so can it."

"I'd be startled too if I was that hideous. But you know what that's like, don't you, Big Trish?"

"Will you shut the hell up, Ferretti?" Owen hissed over the radio. "Why you gotta be such a jerk to everyone, anyway?"

"He's just lashing out," Trish said, trying to sound unruffled. Bryan's comment had stung more than she was willing to admit. "It's what weak creatures do when they're scared."

"You wanna see scared, why don't you come say that to my face?" he shot back.

"'Cause no one wants to see you crap your pants," Jacinda replied. Trish flushed with pleasure at the comment, and Owen laughed. "Now everybody zip it."

CHUPACABRA

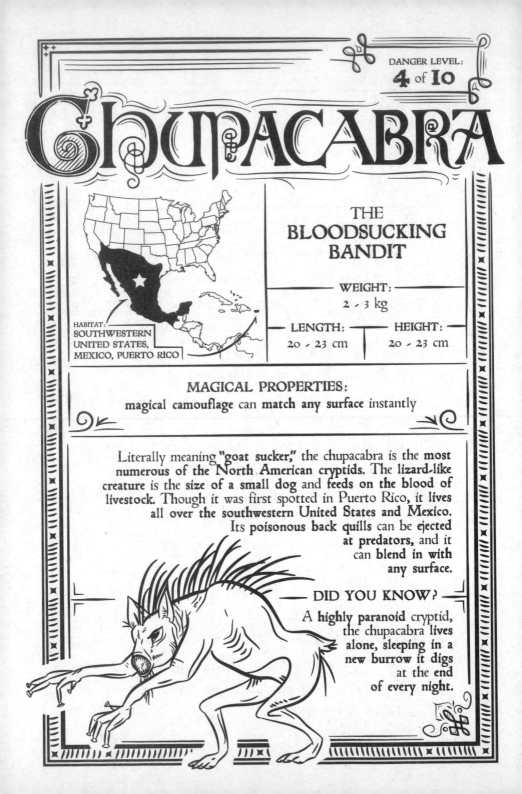

THE BLOODSUCKING BANDIT

HABITAT:
SOUTHWESTERN
UNITED STATES,
MEXICO, PUERTO RICO

WEIGHT:
2 - 3 kg

LENGTH:
20 - 23 cm

HEIGHT:
20 - 23 cm

MAGICAL PROPERTIES:
magical camouflage can **match any surface** instantly

Literally meaning **"goat sucker,"** the chupacabra is the **most numerous of the North American cryptids.** The lizard-like creature is the size of a **small dog** and **feeds on the blood of livestock.** Though it was first spotted in Puerto Rico, it lives all over the southwestern United States and Mexico. Its **poisonous back quills** can be ejected **at predators,** and it can **blend in with any surface.**

DID YOU KNOW?

A **highly paranoid** cryptid, the chupacabra lives alone, sleeping in a new burrow it digs at the end of every night.

They continued through the muddy cow pasture in silence for a moment. "Uh, guys. Guys!" Perry whispered frantically. "I believe I have pinpointed our quarry."

Quickly and quietly, they squished their way to where Perry stood like a statue. She pointed a finger toward a cluster of sleeping cows several meters away. Through their night vision goggles, they could see a disgusting, lizard-like creature attached to the neck of one of the heifers. It was about the size of a Chihuahua, its scaly hide perfectly blending with the cow to which it was attached. A row of sharp quills protruded from its back, and four suction-cup paws gripped its prey. A gross slurping sound reached their ears. Trish realized with a lurch of her stomach that the cryptid was drinking the heifer's blood.

"That is one ugly cow sucker," Bryan said.

"I'll tranq it on my mark," Jacinda said softly. "Three . . . two . . ."

Squish. Owen stepped in a large pile of manure, adding a fresh burst of poop smell to their noses. The chupacabra whipped its head toward the sound, revealing beady red eyes and a round mouth ringed by blood-dripping fangs, like a leech's. It gave a gurgling hiss at them, its scales changing to dark black. Then it bounded away, leaping from the back of one cow to the other.

"Get after it!" Jacinda told them. "Use the shield spell to block its escape!"

They ran after the cryptid, dodging cows and slipping on the muddy ground. The heifers stirred, mooing sleepily as the teenagers passed.

"There it is!" Trish called, pointing several meters to the northwest. The speed of the tiny lizard was impressive, and its camouflage scales made it very difficult to track. *Nice superpower, being able to blend in like that,* Trish thought as she ran after it. *Would definitely come in handy at school.*

Five meters to her left, Perry quickly conjured a shield, then cast a wind spell to send it soaring ahead of the chupacabra. The cryptid thumped off the magical barrier, shook its head, then turned to the south. Owen conjured another shield, which Perry sent to block its progress in that direction. Then Bryan did the same when the animal tried to go west. Within moments, the teenagers had blocked the chupacabra's exit on all sides except their own. It hissed at them again, looking quite fierce in spite of its small size.

"Sorry, gorgeous," Bryan said. "End of the pasture."

The chupacabra arched its back, sending three of its needle-sharp back quills shooting toward him. Bryan yelped, ducking behind Trish. But she stood her ground and quickly conjured a shield. The quills thumped off the purple barrier.

"Nice reflexes," Bryan breathed, toeing one of the sharp four-inch-long quills.

"Maybe think of that, next time you wanna insult me," she suggested.

Frustrated and cornered, the fierce cryptid leapt at them. Its leech-like mouth was stretched wide. Its red eyes blazed. Its

THE CODEX ARCANUM

The SPELL OF CONTAINMENT creates an impenetrable bubble around an object or person. It lasts as long as the caster can maintain his or her focus, but be warned—once the oxygen inside is used up, any living thing contained within will suffocate if not released.

suction-cup paws scrambled for purchase on Trish's shirt. She began forming runes for the SPELL OF CONTAINMENT—

But suddenly the chupacabra dropped to the grass, a tranquilizer dart embedded in its scaly hide. Jacinda stepped forward, blowing on the barrel of her tranq pistol like it was a smoking gun. "Greyeyes," she said in a James Bond voice, "Jace Greyeyes." Then she added in her normal voice: "Nice block, doll."

The word didn't anger Trish like it had back in Wyoming. In fact, she was glad that none of the others could see her furious blushing through their night vision goggles. *You're a warrior monk*, she reminded herself. *Act like it.* "No biggie," she said lightly.

The team leader holstered her pistol. "Ferretti, since you're so tough, why don't you carry our new friend back to the RV?"

Bryan slunk over to pick up the unconscious animal, whose camouflage scales had faded to a mottled greenish brown. "Ugh, it smells like butt."

"We don't smell like rosebushes either," Jacinda replied. "Soon as we get back to the RV, our next mission is to clean off this cow poop."

CHAPTER 8

SOUTHERN HOSPITALITY

After their showers and a few hours' sleep in an RV park, the team left Texas to round up the cryptids of the American Southeast. The terrifying **ROUGAROU** they immobilized in a swamp outside of New Orleans. The **WAMPUS CAT** was caught in one of Trish's time traps outside Chattanooga, Tennessee. The Florida **SKUNK APE** was incredibly polite, agreeing to leave its habitat once the situation was explained. With the exception of Varmint, each animal was sent to Codex Arcanum's secret cryptid facility via portal after it was captured for which Trish was grateful.

CRYPTID CORNER

Often compared to werewolves, **ROUGAROU** are actually humans with the head of a wolf. Like werewolves, they possess magical strength, speed, and healing abilities. Unlike werewolves, they are unable to speak or hold down a day job.

The WAMPUS CAT gets its name from the nineteenth-century American word *catawampus*, which was a term used to describe any mysterious creature. The actual wampus cat resembles a jaguar, though its pelt can render it invisible and it has bat wings.

CRYPTID CORNER

The SKUNK APE is a cousin of the Sasquatch and lives in the Florida Everglades. It is gentle, vegetarian, but incredibly foul-smelling, which leads to its isolated lifestyle. Its limited magic is entirely odor-based.

CRYPTID CORNER

So far, Varmint was the only nice-smelling animal they'd encountered, and there wasn't a lot of extra room in the RV.

Along the way, they continued casting fake cryptid sightings. It was tiring, repetitive work, but it did bring them all a bit closer. After his poor showing with the chupacabra, Bryan's attitude had mellowed quite a lot. Even Trish had to admit that he was quite a skilled spell caster. Jacinda's trust in her teammates had also increased—she no longer made them run every glamour they created by her first, and she even flashed Trish the occasional smile. Each time, Trish felt her stomach jolt in response, and each time, she chided herself for being such a wimp.

It was on their sixth day on the road that they encountered their most troublesome cryptid yet. Whitmore had tasked them with finding and securing the altamaha-ha, a horse-sized aquatic creature that haunted the waters near Darien, Georgia. Evidently the Euclideans had been searching the river for it too, but so far

they had come up short. Whitmore hoped the teenage sorcerers'
knowledge of magic would give them an edge.

But first, there was the issue of how to capture the marine
animal. Arghan Div had added a freshwater tank to the cryptid
zoo, but how they would get a transport portal into the river had
stumped the sorcerers for a bit. Finally Perry hit upon the idea of
carving the portal diagram on a block of stone, dropping it into
the water, and encouraging the cryptid to swim over it. Jacinda
approved this plan, and they drove *Kana'ti* to a secluded spot
outside Darien to help her create the spell diagram.

PERSNICKETY PORTALS

"How come you gotta draw new diagrams every time we
need a portal?" asked Bryan. "Wouldn't it be easier just to reuse
the same one?"

They stood on the grassy shore of the Altamaha River,
underneath the shade of a large mangrove tree. Varmint nib-
bled on cattails, occasionally mimicking their voices. Now that
he trusted Trish and the others, he made no more attempts to
run away.

This being Georgia in the summer, the group was bombarded by a cloud of mosquitoes. Bryan had taken to zapping
them with small electrical bursts, apparently not seeing the irony
of killing creatures while on a mission of animal conservation.
Perry offered to create a circle of protection, but Jacinda said it
was a waste of spell components. So Bryan continued firing tiny
lightning bolts at the troublesome bloodsuckers.

"Every portal enchantment is unique," said Jacinda, checking some star charts on her phone and jotting down calculations. She chewed on her lower lip when she was concentrating, a trait Trish found both adorable and highly distracting. She forced herself to look back down at the cryptozoology book. "They work by connecting two separate points on the globe. But you can't just type in a GPS address because the earth moves in FOUR DIMENSIONS. Longitude, latitude, position, and—"

"Time," breathed Perry. Her eyes were bright with excitement, as they often were when she was solving a new problem. "The earth doesn't just revolve; it rotates through the solar system. Which in turn moves through the universe. So where we are now . . ."

"Is not where we'll be an hour from now," finished Owen. "That's messed up."

"It's a lonesome way to die," agreed Varmint in his cowboy voice.

"Is that true?" asked Trish. She blushed when Jacinda looked sharply her way. "You . . . you're saying if we stepped through a portal to China or whatever, and we got the destination time wrong, we wouldn't end up in China?"

ENCHANTING DETAILS

While the first three dimensions can be easily conceived of, the FOURTH DIMENSION, commonly thought of as time, is trickier. Albert Einstein theorized that time was relative, and that the farther you lived from Earth's gravity, the faster you would age. One hundred years later, his idea was proved to be correct.

"Correct," said Jacinda, jotting down some complicated math computations. "Because China even in the near future is not where China is now. Most likely you'd end up floating in outer space. Like Varmint said, a lonesome way to die." Her gray eyes looked troubled for a moment, but then she refocused on her calculations. "In fact, Ms. Whitmore told me the first space explorers weren't astronauts but sorcerers who got their portal calculations wrong. That's why new portals have to be made every time, and why they can't be reused. A portal destination is only safe for about ten minutes."

"Damn," said Bryan. "Now I'm kinda glad we've spent the last six days in a safe, smelly car."

"Don't blame me, partner," the jackalope said to him in Perry's prim voice. "You're the one who only scrubs once in a blue moon." Trish chuckled, but turned it into a cough/shrug when Bryan spun to look at her.

Jacinda finished her calculations. "Okay," she said, getting to her feet. "Now once we locate the ALTAMAHA-HA, all we have to do is enter the current time and burn the updated coordinates into the slab." She indicated a large stone square the teenagers had pulled from the ground with an earth manipulation spell. The rest of the portal diagram had already been carved into it. Bryan cast a flying enchantment on the slab, making it rise into the air and then drop in the center of the Altamaha River. Perry conjured a globe of light to mark the spot.

ALTAMAHA-HA

SOUTHEASTERN UNITED STATES

HABITAT:
ALTAMAHA RIVER
NEAR DARIEN, GEORGIA,
UNITED STATES

THE **WATER WIZARD**

WEIGHT:
300 kg

LENGTH:	HEIGHT:
250 - 275 cm	90 - 120 cm

MAGICAL PROPERTIES:
can **manipulate any amount of water** surrounding it

This cryptid was first sighted by the **native Muscogee tribe** and was frequently **blamed** for any **river-related weather abnormalities** or **accidents**.

In reality it is a **quiet and shy creature, preferring to hide** instead of attacking. But **if cornered it can create deadly waves, waterspouts,** and **whirlpools.**

As a **water elemental,** it also has a **weakness** to both **fire** and **ice.**

DID YOU KNOW?

The altamaha-ha **reproduces** by **fertilizing its own eggs,** thus having **no need for a mate.**

One sometimes wishes the same were true for humans.

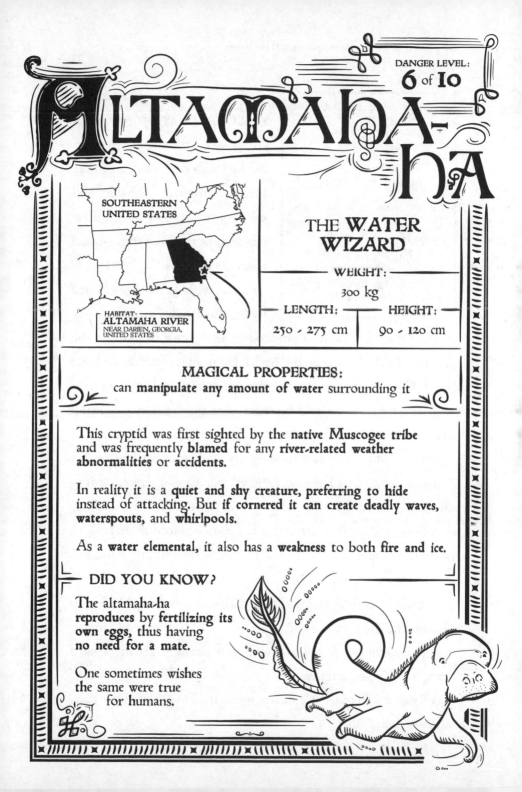

THE CODEX ARCANUM

To cast a SPELL OF LOCATION, the sorcerer needs a locating device (such as a compass or a dowsing rod), a selection of magically charged gemstones, and the energy signature of the sought-after being or object.

The trap set, they cast a SPELL OF LOCATION on several compasses. To avoid being spotted by locals or Euclideans, they made themselves invisible and split up, flying low over different parts of the brown tree-lined river. Owen stayed by Perry's side to assist with her still-awkward flying. Every few minutes, they checked their enchanted compasses, which spun to indicate the direction of the hiding altamaha-ha. Even so, it was over an hour later before one of them triangulated the cryptid's position.

"Got her," Bryan said to them over the headsets. "I think she's in some kind of cave under the riverbank."

He sent up a magical firework so they could easily find his position. The rest of the team flew over to the shore, casting off their invisibility spells. Perry had some difficulty landing, swooping and curling around a few times before managing to touch down with a *thud*. Thankfully there weren't any witnesses at this part of the river.

"Very graceful," said Bryan sarcastically. "You're lucky you didn't wake the thing up."

"I thought we were done with you giving everyone a hard time," said Owen angrily.

Bryan snickered. "What, you lovebirds can't take a little constructive criticism?"

"Perry can spell cast circles around you," Owen replied. He turned to face her. "You okay?"

She nodded, adjusting her purple glasses. "Regrettably, Bryan is correct. I do lack an affinity for flying."

"Well, get ready to do it again," said Jacinda, double-checking the altamaha-ha's entry in *Cryptozoology for Beginners*. "This cryptid can control water, and it'll use every trick it has to evade us. We need to work together." She entered the current time into her phone, and quickly translated the resulting coordinates into runes. "We have ten minutes to finish the spell and herd it toward the portal. Everyone ready?"

The others recast their flying spells, and Jacinda spun her hands in a few complicated patterns. She moved her arms apart, and the ground beneath them peeled back like the lid of a tin can.

They got a brief glimpse of a greenish-gray creature in a watery cave. It was as long as a horse, with a body like a sea lion's and a head like a manatee's. The animal blinked in sleepy confusion, saw the floating sorcerers, then slapped a geyser of water at them. The group was knocked backward, and the cryptid splashed into the Altamaha River.

"Don't let it get away!" said Jacinda, wiping water off her face. "If we lose it, we'll have to go through all this again."

The team flew out over the river, forming a rough line about three meters above the water. The undulating snake shape of the altamaha-ha could be seen corkscrewing through the river at a rapid pace. It turned back to look at them, affording Trish a glimpse of its gentle bovine face.

"Aww," she couldn't help saying. "It's like a cute little sea cow—" But she didn't finish her sentence because the altamaha-ha spit a stream of river water in her eyes. She spluttered, slowing her pursuit to rub her eyes.

Bryan laughed. "That's what you get for not keepin' your eye on the—gah!" He too got a face full of spit water.

"Evasive action!" called Jacinda as the altamaha-ha continued spitting. They bent and turned their fingers, making themselves swoop back and forth over the river, but the cryptid kept pace with them.

Perry took a hit in the shoulder, wobbled, then slammed facefirst into the river. "Perry!" called Owen.

"She can take care of herself. Stay with it!" Jacinda ordered, but Owen peeled off to help his splashing girlfriend anyway. Jacinda cursed.

Thankfully, Trish and Bryan had caught up to the cryptid. They flew this way and that to avoid getting hit by more spit. Trish would have preferred to cast a shield spell, but that required two hands. She needed one hand to maintain **FLIGHT**.

"This is stupid," Bryan called as he dodged another water loogie. "Why don't we just zap this thing with a little lightning?"

THE CODEX ARCANUM

While the Spell for FLIGHT is useful, it requires constant hand adjustments to control height and velocity. This greatly limits the enchantments that can be cast while flying.

"No! Electricity might kill it," said Jacinda as she caught up to them. "Just keep moving it toward the—Euclideans!"

Behind them, three speedboats shot down the river. Each held four Euclidean soldiers, aiming a variety of weapons. They were closing in fast.

"Seriously? How the crap did they find us?" Bryan complained.

"Probably all our spell casting," Jacinda replied. "Whitmore said they have devices that can detect spikes in magical ener— look out!"

While they'd been talking, the altamaha-ha had flicked its tail. A brown wave the size of a house rose out of the river and rolled toward them. Jacinda and Trish flew upward and over it, but Bryan went sideways. He wasn't fast enough to dodge it. The wall of water smacked into him, cancelling his flight spell and leaving him splashing in the river.

The wave continued on down the river, and the Euclidean speedboats tried to swerve around it. One got swamped and its engine died. The other two, unfortunately, kept coming.

"Bryan, you're the best flyer. Go keep 'em off us," Jacinda ordered him.

"Happy to," he growled. He recast the Spell for Flight and shot out of the river, already forming the runes for an attack spell with his free hand. The grin on his face reminded Trish that the Euclideans had left his father to take all the blame for their actions. No doubt he was looking forward to some sorcerous revenge.

Meanwhile, the altamaha-ha tried to use the distraction to disappear into a side tributary. "Oh, no you don't," said Trish. Keeping herself aloft with her left hand, she sketched out a few runes with her right. She curled her fingers upward, and a mound of mud rose in front of the tributary entrance, blocking the cryptid's escape.

"Nice one!" called Jacinda, swooping down to continue the chase.

The compliment made Trish glow, but her pleasure was short-lived. The altamaha-ha made an O with its muzzle, and a cloud of FOG spiraled from its mouth, enveloping Jacinda. No matter where the team leader flew, the fog stayed with her.

"I can't see anything!" she shouted to Trish. "Here, you'll have to herd it to the portal yourself." Her waterproof phone flew out of the fog bank, and Trish managed to catch it with her free hand. "I'll go try to help Bryan."

"You told us not to split up!" Trish called back.

"You've got this!" Jacinda replied.

Buoyed by the older girl's confidence in her, Trish zoomed back down to fly just above the river. Behind her she heard a great *crunch* as one of the Euclidean boats hit one of Bryan's

CRYPTID CORNER

The altamaha-ha can create and control nearly every aspect of water—waves, rain, even FOG. Doing so requires concentration, however, so the best defense against the altamaha-ha is to distract it.

conjured obstacles. She shook her head, refocusing her energy on catching sight of the cryptid.

But she didn't need to. The beast suddenly leapt out of the water, coiled its strong tail around her, and plunged back into the muddy Altamaha River.

Water immediately went up Trish's nose. She coughed, instinctively seeking the surface, but couldn't tell which way was up. All she could see were bubbles and coils and brown water. She knew she must not breathe, but already there were hot bands of pressure across her chest. If she didn't get some air soon, this adorable cow creature was going to kill her.

Desperately, she formed the runes for a fire spell and pressed her now-burning hand to the animal's flank. The altamaha-ha mooed, recoiling from her touch and surfacing. The ploy gave Trish the chance to take in a lungful of air. Through the water in her eyes, she saw the third Euclidean boat launch off a ramp of ice and crash on the riverbank. Bryan flew back toward Trish, chortling with glee.

"Dumb Euclideans," he said, watching in amusement as the altamaha-ha rolled Trish over and over the surface of the river. "I see you're having fun."

"How 'bout—helping!" she shouted through a face full of water. "Finish—the portal spell!" She chucked Jacinda's phone at him.

He smoothly nabbed it out of the air. "Keep your shirt on, Big T. I've got a plan."

"Is it a fast plan?" she spluttered. "'Cause this thing's—trying—to drown me!"

"Trust me," he replied. "Just keep it occupied."

Bryan gave himself a burst of speed, then canceled his flight spell and dove headfirst into the river right above the portal stone. *Pretty smooth*, Trish thought grudgingly. *But how am I supposed to keep this thing occupied?* Since she couldn't think of any better ideas, she let the magical flames streaming from her hand expire and began forming the runes for another earth manipulation spell. She had an idea that she might be able to create a ring of rock around the cryptid. But before she could complete her casting, the altamaha-ha pulled her back beneath the river.

Trish held her breath, clinging to the animal for dear life as it tumbled through the water. Where was Bryan? Within moments, she'd have to scorch it again so she could take a breath. And this time, there was no guarantee the creature would stay with her. At any second, it might let her go and vanish into a wave.

Her lungs spasmed inside her chest. Whatever Bryan had planned, she couldn't wait for it anymore. She had to surface. Her hands formed the runes for the Spell to Conjure Fire—

And a wall of ice appeared in the murky river. The altamaha-ha collided with it, shaking its head dazedly and giving a moo of surprise. It surfaced, giving Trish a chance to breathe. Then it headed in the opposite direction. Back toward the portal, which now glowed with purple flames. Bryan hovered over it, smiling in satisfaction. "Told you to trust me," he said, then thrust his free hand toward the cryptid. "*Frysta maxima.*"

More ice crystals bloomed in the summertime river, forming walls to either side of the altamaha-ha. The rock-hard barriers formed a chute leading directly to the portal Bryan had completed. Beneath the water, the cryptid first bashed its coiled body and then Trish against the frozen walls, but Bryan's enchantment held.

Trish looked ahead to see that the glowing ring marking the portal diagram was only a few meters away. She formed the fire spell again. *Sorry, girl, but this is for your own good*, she thought, placing a fireball against the creature's smooth flank.

Whether it did understand her or it was simply annoyed, Trish would never know. She only knew it finally released her. As she floated to a stop in the river, she caught one more look at its silly sea-cow face before it swam over the portal enchantment. A beam of purple energy flashed in the water, and the altamaha-ha was gone.

Trish splashed over to the grassy riverbank where the others were waiting. The fog bank encircling Jacinda had disappeared with the cryptid, and all of them were soaking wet. They looked back up the river to see Euclidean soldiers running toward them.

"We gotta lose 'em," Jacinda said. "Invisibility spells." She ran a hand down Trish's wet left arm. The touch sent tingles of electricity up and down Trish's body and short-circuited her thought process. Before she could react, the team leader gracefully formed the runes for the spell, winked at her in thanks, then clapped her hands over her head and disappeared. The others followed suit, though Trish needed a nudge from Owen to remember what spell they were casting.

Thirty minutes later, they had managed to shake their Euclidean pursuers and make it back to *Kana'ti*. It was nearly dinnertime in Georgia, and the sun hung low on the western horizon as they drove up Highway 99. Trish was hoping they could stop somewhere for barbecue and hush puppies, but Jacinda insisted they call Whitmore first to report in.

The librarian answered on the fifth ring. "Well done, sorcerers. The altamaha-ha arrived safe and sound." Behind her, they could see Arghan Div trying to feed the ornery animal a variety of vegetables. It spit a stream of water at him, forcing him to break apart in a cloud of red smoke. "Despite a fondness for **EXPECTORATING**, it appears to be enjoying its new water tank." She ducked as another loogie went over her head. "However, I'm afraid an even more pressing issue has arisen. Our European team has vanished."

CRYPTID CORNER

EXPECTORATING, or spitting, is done by animals for a variety of reasons—to catch food, to show anger, even to distract a partner during mating. Let us hope this last practice does not carry over to humans.

Chapter 9

Late-Night Teatime

The soothing aroma of Lady Grey tea permeated *Kana'ti*. Whitmore filled six china cups (she refused to drink from plastic) and sat with the North American team around the vehicle's dining table. Rain pattered gently on the roof. The local time was nearly half past two in the morning, though only four hours had passed since they'd captured the altamaha-ha. The RV was parked on the outskirts of a charming German town with the overly syllabic name of **VILLINGEN-SCHWENNINGEN**. They hadn't been in the country long, but Trish was already getting the

ENCHANTING
DETAILS

Germans do love long words, but in this case the town was originally two separate villages, VILLINGEN and SCHWENNINGEN. They merged in 1972 and, like many a progressive couple, decided to hyphenate.

sense that many German words were overly syllabic. A nearby road was named Schwarzwaldhochstrasse, the bakery was called Meisterbäckerei Schneckenburger, and even the town hall had a sign that read "Ortsverwaltung Weilersbach." She missed the simplicity of American signage.

Traveling to Germany had been surprisingly easy, once they'd figured out how to do it. They had debated several magical methods—calling up a tornado that would carry them to Europe, using a time enchantment to speed up their journey— but finally they decided to simply cast a portal. The issue was creating one big enough to encompass the length of the RV. Because of *Kana'ti*'s size, and because portals had to be circular, they ended up having to create a diagram with a circumference of over thirty meters. It took all five of them to draw the spell in an empty high school parking lot. They didn't finish until well after dinnertime, but since school was out for the summer, there was no one around to bother them. Right before they drove into it, Jacinda told everyone to move up front.

"Why?" said Owen as he and Perry squeezed into the passenger seat. Trish pressed in behind them, holding Varmint in her arms. Bryan was in his usual spot in the bed niche above them, so he didn't need to join them.

"Hopefully it's nothing," said the team leader, putting *Kana'ti* into drive. "But, um, I've never used a portal on something this big. I'm hoping it doesn't, like, start transporting the RV before the whole thing is inside. This is just a precaution."

"You mean *Kana'ti* might get cut in half?" asked Trish, trying to sound conversational about it.

"I'll try to go fast," said Jacinda.

"Better rub all four of that jackalope's feet just in case, Big Trish," said Bryan from up above.

"Shut up, Ferretti," she replied mildly. His attitude had thawed considerably since she'd saved him from the chupacabra, but he still couldn't resist razzing the others now and then. She supposed it was a hard habit to break.

Jacinda stomped on the gas. The tires squealed and then caught, launching them across the empty parking lot. The vehicle was up to fifty miles per hour when they drove over the portal enchantment. The purple beam shot upward, obscuring the windshield. Then the magical energy vanished and they found themselves speeding through a quaint village with rain-slicked cobblestone streets. Jacinda hit the brakes quickly enough, but the RV skidded for quite a while before gently crunching into the aforementioned Meisterbäckerei. Thankfully, Germany was six hours ahead of Atlanta, and even the bakers were still asleep at two in the morning.

Whitmore stepped from the shadows. "*WILKOMMEN in Villingen-Schwenningen.* A very clumsy entrance, Ms. Greyeyes."

ENCHANTING
DETAILS

For those who haven't seen *Cabaret*, WILKOMMEN simply means "welcome."

"Sorry," the team leader called, sticking her head out the window to check the rear of the vehicle. When she saw the whole thing had come with them, she breathed a sigh of relief.

Whitmore came aboard, somehow completely dry in spite of the rain outside and her lack of an umbrella. She directed them to a large turn-off just outside of town. Even in the darkness of the wee hours, they could see the jagged silhouette of the massive **BLACK FOREST** in the distance. Though it was early June, the air still had a cold bite to it. Perry told them it was because they were over two thousand feet above sea level, and the city was a ski town in the winter months. When they stared at her in wonder, she explained she'd made use of the short drive to research their environs.

"Great, I'll be sure to come back at Christmas," Bryan drawled from the upper bunk. "But in the meantime, you mind telling us why I had to break international travel rules as well as my house arrest to come here?"

The librarian ignored his tone, forming a few runes to keep her tea spoon stirring of its own accord. "As you know, we had sorcerer teams assigned to each continent. Our European team, led by Augustus Stromberg, spent the last week collecting cryptids all over the EU." She made a few gestures, conjuring

---

ENCHANTING
DETAILS

The **BLACK FOREST** is a mountainous woodland located in the southwest of Germany. While it served as a natural barrier in ancient times, today it is a popular tourist destination, offering hiking trails, water sports, and skiing.

a see-through map of Europe. Several dots were highlighted green. "Last night they were in the Black Forest, tracking a local UNICORN. One moment their magical energy signatures were there, then the next moment they were gone. Vanished, along with all their gear."

Trish raised a hand. "Can you explain what these energy signatures are, exactly?"

"Every magical creature has one," Whitmore replied, forming a few hand motions and muttering some French. A glamour of a spiky ball of rainbow-colored plasma appeared above the table. "Even Level One sorcerers like yourselves. Think of them like fingerprints. They display how much power a being has, how often it uses magic, which types of spells it prefers, and so on. Once a sorcerer knows a creature's energy signature, it can be tracked anywhere in the world."

Varmint whistled. "It's a one-size-fits-all lasso," he said in his cowboy voice.

"So, if the unicorn's signature is gone too . . . does that mean It's dead?" asked Owen. He and Trish shared a look of concern.

"Possibly," Whitmore replied, casting off both glamours with a gesture. "But our enemies may have found a way to mask

CRYPTID
CORNER

Though there are representations of UNICORNS all over the world, their habitat is confined to mountain ranges in Europe, Asia, and the Middle East. Unlike horses, they are solitary creatures, gathering to mate only once every seven years.

UNICORN

HABITAT:
WOODLANDS OF
NORTHERN EUROPE,
FERTILE CRESCENT
& CENTRAL INDIA

A HORSE OF MANY COLORS

WEIGHT:
360 – 450 kg

LENGTH:
150 – 170 cm

HEIGHT:
150 – 180 cm

MAGICAL PROPERTIES:
can **purify any poison, cure any sickness,**
and **heal light wounds**

A **regal** and highly **magical animal,** unicorns can be **found
all over central Europe.** They prefer **alpine woodlands** and will
only allow themselves to be **touched by virginal human females.**
("Maids" in the antiquated sense.)

Unicorn **horns** are **highly prized** for their **powers of purification,**
but they are useless if not
attached to the
living beast.

The creature can only be held
by **chains of ensorcelled silver.**

DID YOU KNOW?

When **angered,** the unicorn's
horn will glow.

Its **pelt** may **change colors**
depending on **its mood.**
What each **color means**
is **unique** to **every animal.**

THE CODEX
ARCANUM

Casting spells is not the only way to remove magic. If an object or being is placed under a concealment ward, their magical signature will be HIDDEN.

magical energy so that we cannot track them. It is my hope that our friends and the unicorn have been somehow **HIDDEN**."

Perry cast a small cyclone to cool off her tea. It circled around the top of her cup until she closed her hand and took a sip. "How can we assist?"

MAID TO ORDER

Whitmore moved her hands in a series of complicated patterns and muttered in French. A three-dimensional topographic map of the Black Forest appeared on the table between them. She tapped a finger on the map, illuminating a small spiky ball. "This was the last location of the unicorn Herr Stromberg and his team were tracking. I propose we start there. If we can find the cryptid, hopefully we find them."

"But if they're captured, won't the Euclideans be nearby?" Trish asked.

"Almost certainly. Which is why I suggest we take a page from your book and draw them away with a diversion."

"All over it," said Bryan. He hopped down from the bunk and jabbed a finger into the see-through town of Villingen-Schwenningen. "We'll cast a few glamours over here, then zip into the forest and lasso that unicorn."

CRYPTID CORNER

MAIDS have always been associated with unicorns. Doubtless it is because unicorns can cure any poison, and so it was imagined that only "pure" young women could entrap such beasts. Once the unicorns realized young women are far easier to work with than men, however, they made it a tradition.

"There is one small wrinkle," said Whitmore. "The unicorn will only allow itself to be captured by a **MAID**."

There was a pause. "Like . . . a professional house cleaner?" asked Owen.

Perry patted his shoulder patiently. "She's referencing the more arcane usage, obviously. As in, a young woman who hasn't . . . had relations." She blushed at the last two words.

"Correct," said Whitmore. "Which means only the female members of our team will be able to pursue this cryptid."

There was another beat as that sank in. Bryan furrowed his brow. "Hold up. Jacinda, you haven't . . . ? Seriously?" When she stared back at him stonily, he grinned. "Well, I am more than happy to show you the ropes, babe. Just say the word, and—"

He froze as she thrust a hand toward his crotch. Her fingers were sheathed in glowing blades of magical energy. "Come within two feet of me, and you'll be a maid next." Bryan raised his hands and took a step back.

"Wait, why does it only have to be girls going after the unicorn?" asked Owen. "I haven't . . . you know . . . either." His cheeks colored red.

"Big surprise," said Bryan sarcastically. "But yeah, this whole deal is sexist."

Trish snorted. "Oh, you guys are mad you can't do something 'cause of your gender? I could literally run circles around the elementary school boys' soccer team, but they refused to let us play co-ed. I say it's about time something favors us."

Whitmore arched an eyebrow. "As much as I may agree, this is not political. This cryptid simply has its preferences, and they have been such for many hundreds of years. If anyone other than a female maid gets within a quarter mile of the beast, it will attack. And platitudes about gender equality will not change its mind." Bryan folded his arms and frowned. "Take heart. Since I am also unable to assist, I shall accompany you and Mr. Macready. We will create the distraction, while our three 'maids' secure the unicorn."

They drove into the Black Forest to drop off Jacinda, Perry, and Trish. The rain was still falling, making the dark woods seem even more gloomy. After the three of them had shouldered packs containing magical items to assist with their capture, Trish bent to say goodbye to Varmint.

"Watch out for them, huh?" she said as she scratched the jackalope behind his antlers.

"All for one and one for all, partner," it replied in her mom's voice. It was still odd to hear the animal mimic other voices so perfectly, especially when they came from her family. The cryptid gave her an affectionate head bump, making sure not to poke her with its antlers.

"Give us thirty minutes to draw the Euclideans' attention," Whitmore said to the young women. She put *Kana'ti* into gear and drove back toward Villingen-Schwenningen.

THREE NOT-SO-LITTLE MAIDS

With the RV gone, the forest surrounding them seemed much more foreboding. It was a little after 4:00 a.m. and even the nocturnal animals seemed to have gone to sleep. Thankfully, Trish's body clock was still on East Coast time, so she wasn't tired.

Jacinda conjured a three-dimensional glamour of the surrounding area. It was about the size of a piece of paper and far less detailed than Whitmore's magical landscapes. The trees were tiny green triangles, and the grade of the terrain kept shifting. Still, it had the last known location of the unicorn's energy signature, and Trish supposed that was the most important part. "Let's keep our lights off and go quietly," Jacinda suggested.

They made their way into the Black Forest with only the soft glow of Jacinda's glamour to guide them. The light caught her lips in such a way that it made Trish wonder what they would feel like on hers. Then she shook her head, frustrated with herself. More and more thoughts of this nature had been springing into her mind of late. It was like her brain went fuzzy anytime her eyes landed on Jacinda. *You're better than this*, she told herself fiercely. *You're a warrior, now focus.* She forced herself to break her gaze and inspect her surroundings instead. The rain was a gray curtain that prevented them from seeing more than a few meters in any direction. It also made the ground wet and muddy.

This combined with the omnipresent deadfall made every step treacherous.

"Did you know, the **BROTHERS GRIMM** used this forest as inspiration for all their fairy tales?" Perry whispered excitedly, dropping back to walk beside Trish. "Imagine if everything they wrote about—witches, giants, goblins—was actually true. They could still be here, all around and watching us." She sounded absolutely delighted by the idea.

"I'm worried enough about the Euclideans," Trish whispered back. "I don't need to add monsters on top of that."

"Oh, I highly doubt those quote-unquote 'monsters' were as bad as they were made out to be," Perry responded. "Think about it. All the cryptids we've encountered had terrifying tales invented about them at some point. Stealing babies, being in league with the devil, et cetera. But when we actually met them, they weren't so bad. Just different."

"News flash: people hate anything that's different," Trish said sourly, kicking aside a stick. "It's why those idiots at school stick vegetable bags on my locker. It's why we have to capture these animals instead of letting 'em run free."

ENCHANTING DETAILS

The **BROTHERS GRIMM** were not sorcerers but historians, collecting many true tales of magic and cryptids and passing them off as folklore in their well-known *Children's and Household Tales* (1st ed. 1812). Whether these stories helped or hindered the cause of sorcery is a matter of much debate.

"I assure you, it's not any easier to be the shortest person in eighth grade, especially when you're valedictorian," Perry said. "I've been ruminating on this conundrum, and I believe Jace is correct. We should consider showing the cryptids to the world, rather than hiding them away. Let people see these animals as we've seen them. It may be awkward at first, but if history teaches us anything, it's that people must be aware something exists before they can accept it."

"It's a nice idea," Trish agreed as they clambered over a mossy tree stump. "Too bad it's not how the world works. Whitmore's right; if people knew unicorns were real, they'd hunt them to extinction just so they could stick a sparkly horn on their—"

She broke off as a rumble cut through the quiet pre-dawn air. Ahead of them, Jacinda dispelled her glamour and cast a wind spell, opening a tunnel through the blanket of rain. The three young women looked toward Villingen-Schwenningen to see an impressive fireball rise above the town. Then the inky mist closed about them again.

"That must be Ms. Whitmore's distraction," Jacinda whispered. "Sit tight for a moment."

The seconds seemed to pass like hours as they waited. Perry conjured a translucent shield above them so they wouldn't get soaked. "I hope they're all right," she said, nervously spinning the see-through purple disc.

Several more minutes passed. Despite her resolve, Trish kept sneaking glances at Jacinda's profile, but she looked away each time the team leader noticed. *We're here for the cryptids*, she reminded herself. *Everything else is a distraction. You're a sorcerer, not some lovesick Disney princess. Friggin' act like it.*

She had just stood to shake out her fingers when they heard the roar of rotors. Spotlights pierced the rain from less than a kilometer away. Jacinda made another magical window in the weather to reveal a CH-47 Chinook cargo helicopter lifting into the air. It had been painted black, and the Euclidean logo was printed prominently on the side.

The young women ducked behind a tree as the helicopter passed overhead. It continued down the mountain to Villingen-Schwenningen. Perry looked nervous, but Jacinda clapped her on the shoulder.

"Don't worry," she said. "They have Ms. Whitmore with them. Now let's see where that chopper came from."

THE LONE EUCLIDEAN

They reached the Euclidean encampment in less than twenty minutes. It was easy to locate, as their enemies had made no effort to conceal their presence. The entire area was illuminated by bright klieg lights running off noisy generators. A circle roughly the size of an American soccer field had been clear-cut in the spruce forest, and the massive trunks had been tossed aside like used toothpicks. The smell of fresh pine sap was strong in their nostrils. At one end of the clearing stood four white trailers, of the kind one sees at construction sites, though these were clearly more expensive and high-tech than those. Each was fitted with a satellite dish on a retractable pole. Several military-style tents had also been set up around the perimeter.

At first glance, the encampment appeared to be deserted. Then Perry pointed out a shadow moving in one of the trailers. "It appears they left behind a sentry."

They started forward, but Jacinda put a hand on Perry's arm. Trish felt an irrational stab of jealousy and pushed it away. The team leader pointed to a tree trunk above them. Their eyes followed the line of her finger to a wireless security camera drilled into a pine tree about ten meters off the ground.

"On it," said Trish, eager to take action after too much time inside her head. She moved her hands in a few choppy motions, muttered the activation words, then flung a lightning bolt at the security camera. Sparks flew from the device, and the little blue light on it went dark. Her hands tingled with the feel of magic.

They circled the perimeter, quickly dispatching several more cameras in similar fashion. "Should we kill the lights too?" Trish asked as they crouched behind a wide spruce on the edge of the clearing. The silhouette of the sentry could be seen moving back and forth inside the trailer.

"Negative. Right now they're camouflaging us." Jacinda peered at the trailer. "Let's see how our sentry reacts to losing her cameras."

As if hearing them, the speaker system on the roof of the trailer crackled to life. A voice issued from it, female and clearly trying to hide her nervousness. "Attention, trespassers. This is a private research facility. Perimeter defense drones have been activated. Leave the area now or face the consequences."

"I know that voice," Perry said. "But I don't recall speaking with any female Euclideans."

"We can play 'Guess Who?' later," said Trish. "Whoever it is wasn't kidding about those drones."

Two buzzing quadcopters the size of laptop computers streaked across the clearing toward them. They were outfitted with thermal cameras and tranquilizer dart guns. The rain didn't appear to slow them in the slightest.

"On second thought, enough hiding," said Jacinda. "Time to sideline whoever this is and find our unicorn." She pulled a plastic sand timer from her pocket and turned it upside down.

There was the usual *whoom* of silence as time froze around them. Raindrops hung like motionless diamonds in the air. Trish poked one, watching it break apart into smaller pellets of slow-moving water. "I love sorcery," she murmured happily.

"Stay close," said Jacinda. The two words were louder than a shotgun blast in the eerie quiet of stopped time. The three young women walked quickly toward the trailer, making a path through the suspended rain as if it were a beaded curtain. They passed the frozen drones, snapping off their rotors as they passed. The girls made sure to stay close together so no one dropped out of the time bubble encasing the sand timer. Soon they reached the door to the sentry's trailer. It sported an electronic keypad, but Jacinda formed a few runes and pressed her palm to the lock. *"Resigno."*

The keypad sparked, unlocking with a satisfying *click*. The three maids moved inside to see a wall of security monitors at one end of the trailer. Eight of them were dark, having been zapped by the young sorcerers, but images on the remaining screens depicted vantage points around the encampment. Clearly they had missed some of the Euclideans' security cameras.

A woman was crouched in front of the screens, her back to them. She had a small trim frame, and her wavy brown hair was pulled into a ponytail. A white doctor's coat encased her torso, and a headset was clamped to her skull. On the desk before her sat a Taser.

"Grab her gear," said Jacinda, the sudden loudness of her voice making them wince in the frozen silence. Trish and Perry stepped forward, taking up the weapon and unplugging the headset respectively. Jacinda turned the sand hourglass back to its starting position, and time resumed.

A burst of sound blared from the console before the monitors. Someone was in the middle of speaking. Their voice had the tinny, static-laced quality of a poor radio transmission.

CRYPTID CORNER

Even though DRAGONS do not exist, people's fascination with them make the creatures ideal for any kind of attention-getting distraction.

"—multiple sightings of a dragon here, repeat **DRAGON**. What is the nature of the encampment threat? Over."

"Unclear," said the woman, then she realized her headset had vanished. She reached for the Taser, but that was gone too. Slowly, keeping her hands up, she turned. Her face was etched with fear. When she saw the intruders were teenagers, she blinked with confusion.

Trish was confused as well. She had seen this woman's face, but where? It wasn't from any of the places they'd visited in their week crisscrossing the United States. It was from somewhere more familiar, like her school or her home.

Home. Trish had laid eyes on this woman multiple times before in Henderson. She'd seen her proudly holding a baby boy, running alongside a five-year-old learning to ride a bike, and standing beside a brown-haired seventh grader, both of them smiling in the same pained sort of way. She had seen the way she wrinkled her forehead whenever Owen was deep in thought. But before she could confirm the mystery woman's identity, Perry blurted out two words in shock:

"Mrs. Macready?"

Chapter 10

Eleanor Explains

The woman before them sagged. She didn't look surprised so much as . . . resigned. Like a criminal who finally realizes she's been caught.

"Macready?" said Jacinda. She peered at the Euclidean, then her eyes widened in recognition. "You're Owen's *mom*?"

Eleanor Macready sank into a chair before the console, nodding miserably. The transmission behind her continued to squawk. "902-ECHO, are you there? This is 715-Bravo. Respond, 902—" The voice was cut short as she turned off the transmitter.

BEWARE THE EUCLIDEANS

Once a person joins the Euclideans, they are given a new identity consisting of a number and a military letter, such as 902-ECHO. Only the very top officers, such as Samson Kiraz, are allowed traditional names. (Though his is almost certainly an alias.)

"Whoa, you're a Euclidean?" said Trish in disbelief. "That's why you divorced Mr. Macready and you've been traveling the world for eight months? Does Owen know?"

Eleanor's eyes went wide as she shook her head. "No, no, no. Of course not. And you can't tell him. Please. He's mad enough at me as it is."

"Why should we assist you?" Perry said defiantly. "He has a right to know his own mother's in league with the enemy."

"We're not . . . You don't understand," Eleanor began, then sighed in frustration. "I wanted to help. Do something that had an impact on the world. The Euclideans, they approached me a year ago. Said they needed qualified veterinarians to help with a classified program to preserve endangered animals. And the specimens they showed me . . . well, they were pretty far from anything I ever learned about in zoology class."

"So you signed up to torture animals," Jacinda stated with disgust.

"Torture? No, no, no. That's not what we're doing at all," she replied. She spoke with the bright energy of one who is convinced she's right. "This is preservation, humane and necessary. Many of these animals are the only ones of their species left. We take them in so we can catalogue their abilities and keep them from going extinct. It's my job to make sure they're well treated."

She seemed sincere, but Trish scoffed. "What a bunch of unicorn crap. We were at Loch Ness, lady. Your coworkers were electrocuting Nessie!"

Eleanor frowned. "I laid out specific guidelines for how all these animals should be handled. We only use restraints in extreme cases, and the creatures are never, ever supposed to be hurt."

"Well, your people lied to you," Jacinda informed her. "The Euclideans don't care about cryptids or magic. They only want to use them to become more powerful."

"On a tangential topic," Perry interjected, "how long have you known that Owen is a sorcerer?"

"Just a few days. My superiors, they have detailed files on each of you." Eleanor ran a hand through her curly hair. "I'm still . . . processing what you kids can do. I mean, it's one thing to encounter creatures with amazing abilities. But to realize that humans can cast spells, turn invisible, even fly—that takes some adjustment. I didn't even know Owen was one of you until he left for his 'internship.'" She seemed annoyed, proud, and nervous all at the same time.

"He came to stop your animal poaching!" Trish was vibrating with rage. She couldn't understand why Eleanor was pretending the Euclideans weren't evil incarnate. Was it possible that she didn't know her organization's true intentions? She certainly didn't seem like Kiraz or Bryan's dad; it honestly appeared as if she wanted to help.

"I think there's been some misinformation on both sides of this conflict," said Eleanor. "Everything we do, we do for the betterment of the human race."

"Oh, is that, like, your official slogan?" Trish snorted. "Tell that to the mercenaries who tried to kill us back in February."

"I've seen those files," Eleanor said. "All those weapons were loaded with nonlethal ammunition. Mr. Kiraz, he was trying to keep you kids safe. You should have never been allowed to run around with such an incredibly dangerous book of magic."

"The Euclideans shot your son with a gun," Perry told her. "They would have killed him if he hadn't been wearing an amulet of protection."

"That was Virgil Ferretti's doing," Eleanor insisted. "Mr. Kiraz assures me they had no knowledge that he was carrying live rounds. That's why he was expelled from the organization immediately." Eleanor tucked a bit of wavy hair behind her ear. "In fact, we were instrumental in making sure he received the maximum sentence for his crimes."

"Will you stop pretending you're one of the good guys?" Trish exploded. What was it with Owen's family and wanting to rewrite history? "Your boss watched me get almost-drowned. He threatened to electrocute the Loch Ness Monster. These are not nice people!"

Eleanor sighed. "I know there are some in my organization who believe sorcery is . . . unnatural, but I'm not one of them. I see it as a science, albeit one we can't fully understand yet. The work we're doing, it is safe, and it's incredibly important. We both want the same thing—to protect these animals. We should be working together."

Trish and Perry were too stunned to answer. But Jacinda jutted her chin at one of the monitors behind Eleanor. "You're not doing any harm to cryptids, eh? Then why is there a unicorn chained up in one of your trailers?"

Perry and Trish followed her gaze. There on one of the security monitors was the beast they sought. Its single horn glowed, and its beautiful red flank was wrapped in silver chains attached to the walls of the trailer. It bucked against its restraints, but only succeeded in leaving welts on its hide.

Eleanor closed her eyes, knowing this didn't bode well for her case. "I recognize how that must look, but that animal is the last of its kind in Germany. Possibly in all of Europe. We can't let it be shot by some ignorant hunter or hit by a semi. We need to take it in, protect it, but . . . sometimes animals don't understand what's in their best interest. We tried several times to sedate it, but somehow it keeps metabolizing the tranquilizers."

"Naturally. It's a unicorn," Perry said. "Their primary ability *is* PURIFYING POISONS."

"Okay, see, that's a good thing for us to know," said Eleanor quickly. "Perhaps you three, you can help us figure out how to better care for it."

CRYPTID CORNER

Not only can unicorn horns PURIFY POISONS, they can also heal wounds, prevent sickness, and even make spoiled milk drinkable. Unfortunately they can't fix bad cooking.

"Did you ask the other team of sorcerers to help you, too?" Trish asked. Eleanor blinked in confusion. "The ones who disappeared right around here yesterday."

Owen's mom shook her head firmly. "I was told the animal was found by a local ranger. If there had been others like you, I'm sure I would have seen them."

"Don't count on it," Trish replied. "We sorcerers can turn invisible."

"Look, all we want is to understand this creature. I promise you."

"Well, I think I've heard enough," said Jacinda icily. She bent her fingers to form a few runes, then extended her hand toward Eleanor Macready. *"Frysta."* A wall of ice a meter thick bloomed in front of Owen's mom, imprisoning her in the end of the trailer. Her blurry figure pounded on the ice, but it would take her some time to get through.

"Come on," said Jacinda, turning to leave the trailer. "Let's go rescue that unicorn."

ENSORCELLED SILVER

They found the unicorn's trailer with little trouble. The outside of it was covered with spells of concealment, which Perry said must explain why the animal's magical energy signature had vanished. The thought that the Euclideans might have a sorcerer nearby made them all nervously glance around the empty camp. Seeing they were still alone, they cast a Spell of Unlocking on the trailer door.

It opened to reveal a towering, elegant, mythical beast whose image had appeared on a million school folders. The unicorn was easily two meters tall at its **WITHERS** and possessed an impossible nobility. A curl of white hair hung down from its chin like a goatee. Its bright-red flank was wrapped in chains that were attached to the trailer walls, but still it bucked upon seeing them, lashing out with ebony hooves. Its liquid eyes were wild with fear. The animal's spiral **HORN** burned like hot silver in the dark.

Impulsively, Trish dropped to one knee. "We're sorry this was done to you," she said, looking up at the towering animal. "But we are here to help. Will you allow us to do so?"

There was a moment in which the only sound was the metal *pong* of raindrops on the trailer roof. The animal stood, quivering, then its **COAT** shimmered and faded to a calm, pure white. It whinnied, bowing its head in a regal nod.

ENCHANTING DETAILS

Since horses can bend their heads downward, their height is measured not from head to toe, but from hoof to the highest part of their backs, also known as the **WITHERS**.

CRYPTID CORNER

Though the magical properties of a unicorn's **HORN** cannot be used once it is removed, some people still value the horn more than the animal.

CRYPTID
CORNER

A unicorn's COAT changes color depending on the animal's mood. They also use this ability to camouflage themselves from predators, humans, and tiresome wildlife photographers.

"Thank you," Trish said. Jacinda nodded to her approvingly. Together, they began to form the runes for a Spell to Conjure Fire. They had just stretched out their hands to cast the enchantment when Perry stood from where she had been inspecting the chains.

"Wait!" she cried. "The restraints are—"

But before she could finish, Trish and Jacinda cast their spells. Tongues of purple fire hit the chains and were absorbed. There was a moment of quiet, then twin flame waterfalls spit from the silver links, filling the trailer with heat. The two girls would have been roasted alive had Perry not conjured a magical shield before them. Purple flames met purple mesh, dissipating into nothingness. The unicorn's pelt again turned as red as a stop sign.

Trish coughed. "Sorry, bud. Not attacking you, I swear. That was a mistake." She turned to Perry, lifting her hands in silent question.

"The chains, they're ENSORCELLED," her friend explained. "Unbreakable by magic or anything else."

"Where did the Euclideans get enchanted chains?" asked Jacinda.

THE CODEX
ARCANUM

The easiest way to use magic, in fact, is to find something magical. There are many non-magical people in history whose fortunes have changed because they stumbled across ENSORCELLED OBJECTS.

"They placed concealment spells on the trailer; it may be that they have a sorcerer in their employ," Perry replied. "Which means the thin man we encountered back in February isn't the only spell caster to whom they have . . . access."

Uh-oh, Trish thought. She once more checked the camp for approaching sorcerers. "Maybe we should free this guy before whoever cast these enchantments comes back," she suggested.

Jacinda was already inspecting the padlocks that fastened the chains together. "These just look like regular old locks. Maybe we could cast a spell on them?"

The unicorn's coat flared an even brighter red and it gave a warning whinny. "It would appear those are booby-trapped too," said Perry. "But the wall, I'll wager books to bullfrogs, is not."

"Dude, that is not a saying," Trish informed her.

Perry shrugged and conjured the fire spell again. Magical purple flames wrapped around her index finger. Slowly, she traced a circle around the mooring posts that held the chains to the wall of the trailer. The magic fire cut through the flimsy metal of the trailer walls like a sword through water. One by one, the mooring posts fell away. Perry blew on her finger to extinguish the flames.

The unicorn's coat shimmered back to white. His great back twitched, and the girls stepped forward to gently unwind the chains. As soon as they pulled them away, the red welts on the animal's hide began to vanish.

"That's better, huh, bud?" said Trish. She reached up to take the last link off the great animal's neck, but hissed as one of the metal wall pieces sliced into her hand. A thin trickle of blood ran down her wrist.

"You okay?" asked Jacinda, coming over to inspect the wound.

"Just a cut," Trish replied lightly. Actually, her palm was throbbing with pain, but she didn't want the team leader to think she was a wimp. The unicorn, however, became a shade of curious yellow. It touched the rip of its glowing horn to the slice. A cool minty feeling flowed through Trish's hand, washing away the pain and leaving behind a mild tingle.

The wound on her hand was gone. The trickle of blood remained, but there wasn't even a scar where the wound had been. Jacinda inspected Trish's palm, gently prodding the area with her fingertip. "Whoa," she said breathlessly, her striking gray eyes meeting Trish's. "Magic."

Trish's heart pounded as the team leader continued cupping her hand. It felt as if small bursts of electricity were spreading from Jacinda's fingertips into her skin.

"Didn't feel a thing," she managed to croak, not wanting to break the older girl's grip. The unicorn whickered, gently probing Trish's chest with its glowing horn. Its kind eyes blinked in concern. *What's it doing?* the teenager thought frantically. *Does it think my feelings for Jace are some kind of trauma or something?* This was apparently the case, as the animal continued to tap on her chest. *OMG, it's trying to heal me. How do I turn off this dumb thing?*

As she tried to shoulder the unicorn away, Jacinda furrowed her brow. "What's wrong? Did you get bruised or something?"

"Nope. I'm great," Trish replied, managing to keep her voice light. She shoved the unicorn's horn even harder. "I think this cryptid's broken."

Jacinda gave a dazzling grin. Trish smiled back but then felt something thump into the side of her neck. Jacinda's smile vanished. Her startling gray eyes widened. Trish reached up to see what had struck her, and her fingers met a heavy metal cylinder with a soft tuft at the end. She pulled it free, gazing at the object that rested in her palm:

A **TRANQUILIZER** dart.

THE LAST STAND OF THE UNICORN

The unicorn's pelt flared red again. Jacinda grabbed Trish by the wrist, pulling the taller teenager behind her. Purple light

---

ENCHANTING DETAILS

TRANQUILIZERS have vastly different effects based on the weight and metabolism of the animals on which they're being used. Some creatures fall immediately, while others may take up to half an hour. Best to err on the side of caution, however—too many tranquilizers can stop a subject's heart.

bloomed inside the dark trailer as she conjured a shield spell. Three more tranq darts thumped off the glowing mesh, clanging uselessly on the metal floor.

What a badass, Trish thought as the protective enchantment faded and Jacinda began to cast another spell. *Hmm. Maybe I should conjure something, too.* But her brain seemed slow and her movements were sluggish. Also, the trailer was beginning to roll under her feet like the deck of a ship. She put a hand on the wall to steady herself.

Outside, a semicircle of black-suited soldiers was converging on them. Each one pointed a military rifle. Trish knew on some level they were a threat, but she couldn't muster the energy to decide what to do about it. The edge of her vision was growing dark anyway. It took a major effort to simply keep her eyes open.

There were a few out-of-focus flashes as Jacinda dispatched one, then two, of the approaching mercenaries. "You're amazing," Trish heard herself saying, the words slurring together. "Like a warrior princess."

Perry crumpled into a ball nearby, a silver dart protruding from her chest. The peaceful expression on her face made Trish jealous. She wished she could lie down too. She was so tired.

Suddenly there was a cool pressure on her neck. Icy threads coursed through her body, bringing clarity like a pail of cold water to the face. Within moments her head was clear again. She looked over to see the unicorn's glowing horn pressed to the spot where the tranq dart had hit her.

"Thanks, bud," she said to the cryptid, then turned to face their attackers with renewed vigor. Five Euclideans were advancing, less than ten meters from the trailer. A massive cargo helicopter—the same one they'd seen lift off less than an hour earlier—hovered just over the rain-drenched encampment. More soldiers could be seen zip-lining down from the vehicle.

Time to waste these fools, Trish thought fiercely. Her fingers moved quickly but surely, each hand conjuring magical lightning. She could feel magical energy flowing through her, strong and satisfying. Bright-blue bolts of electricity leapt from her hands. Each one struck an enemy, sending them tumbling backward as if yanked by a string.

Jacinda conjured another shield, blocking more tranquilizer darts. "Hold 'em off!" she bellowed to Trish over the roar of the helicopter rotors. She pulled off her backpack, rummaging for another enchanted timer.

Trish stepped out of the trailer, racking her brain for a quick but devastating spell to cast. Invisibility, wards of protection, spells to summon animals—each one took preparation and components. All she had around her was a bunch of clear-cut tree stumps and some cold earth.

Earth. As the Euclideans pointed their weapons, Trish swept her arms through the air. Her fingers quickly traced runes. She slammed a hand into the wet forest floor and muttered a few words in Latin.

Great pillars of earth erupted from the ground before the trailer. The force of them knocked down two of the advancing mercenaries, but they didn't block them all. One Euclidean got off a shot, sinking a tranq dart into Jacinda's stomach. The team leader growled in anger, responding with a thunderclap that sent her attacker flying.

But then she dropped to one knee, her eyes rolling in her skull. "Get the . . . unicorn out," she told Trish in a slurring voice. "That's an . . . order." Then she slumped sideways in front of the trailer and lay still.

"Jace!" Trish shook the team leader, but her body was limp. She growled in anger and stood, patting the unicorn on its flaming red flank. "Enough playing defense. What do you say we take the fight to them?"

The animal seemed to understand. It tossed its mane and bent its front **FETLOCKS**, lowering its great head so Trish could clamber onto its back. "Seriously?" she said. "I thought I'd have to convince you."

The animal whinnied in a way that clearly meant *No time for jokes, get on!* Trish flung one leg over the cryptid's broad neck. She'd never ridden an ordinary horse before (unless you counted the donkey she'd once sat astride at a school fair), to say nothing of a unicorn. She was pretty sure

ENCHANTING DETAILS

FETLOCKS are the joints between a horse's lower leg and its foot. Half of all racing injuries are related in some way to the fetlock.

this guy would be insulted by the donkey comparison. Trish laced her fingers through the silver hair of his mane, trying to remember any tips she'd read about bareback riding. Something about gripping with your knees?

Before she could recall anything else, the unicorn sprang forward. Trish instinctively hung on, but nearly went tumbling anyway. The cryptid was fast. Raindrops pelted her in the face as the unicorn leapt over the five-foot-tall earthen barricade she had conjured before the trailer. Up in the air, she had a clear view of the encampment. The cargo helicopter still hovered overhead, its rotors cutting through sheets of rain. More Euclideans were zip-lining downward, while the five or six already on the ground swiveled their tranquilizer rifles toward Trish. *Geez, that thing's worse than a clown car.*

The unicorn landed with a thud. Trish quickly conjured a magical shield, but three tranquilizer darts struck the unicorn's flank. It shucked them off with a twitch of its massive muscles and galloped toward its attackers, blazing horn at the ready.

"Don't kill them!" Trish yelled. It wouldn't help their cryptid protection efforts if the animals were known to skewer humans. Thankfully, the unicorn once more seemed to understand. As he tore across the encampment, panting loudly, he merely knocked the Euclidean soldiers aside with the flat of his shining horn. The earth bounced beneath Trish and the cryptid felt as slippery as a seal, but somehow she managed to stay on his back. She moved her hands in a practiced pattern, a flower of electricity blooming in her palm. Her fingers extended, releasing a bolt of lightning that sizzled through the raindrops and struck an attacking Euclidean in the chest. The soldier fell to the muddy ground, twitching.

The unicorn cantered to a stop at the opposite end of the clear-cut circle. His flank turned a deep yellow, seemingly undecided between running for the cover of the woods and going back for another attack pass. "Get out of here," Trish urged, tugging the cryptid's silver mane toward the woods. "Run and hide somewhere they can't find you."

Again, the great beast's eyes blinked in understanding, but this time it did not obey. The unicorn snorted angrily, his flank flaring red and his horn burning like a meteor in the night. Evidently he wanted to impart another lesson to the people who had imprisoned him. She pulled harder on his mane, but moving a mountain would have done more good. The unicorn reared backward, throwing Trish to the wet forest floor. The wind was knocked from her, but she caught a glimpse of the animal, backlit by rain, as he prepared to charge his enemies. Despite her concern for the creature, there was no denying it was a magnificent sight.

Then she heard a *thwip*, and a black object streaked toward them. A **BOLA** wrapped around

ENCHANTING DETAILS

A **BOLA** is a thrown hunting weapon made from a length of rope and two weighted balls. Bolas can be used to capture running cattle, game, or even birds.

the cryptid's back fetlocks, preventing him from bolting. The unicorn planted his front legs and kicked, but the bola stayed tight. His red flanks became a fearful, sickly green as he toppled sideways. Trish rolled aside to avoid being crushed, but in her haste she didn't look where she was rolling.

Her skull cracked against a fresh-cut tree trunk. The scene before her swam, her vision blurring like a watercolor left in the rain. Tears filled her eyes, and her mouth tasted like metal. Voices approached, sounding as if they were echoing from the depths of a deep well.

A net of silver mesh draped over the wild-eyed green unicorn. He whinnied in distress, bucking his head but unable to escape. Trish reached out a hand to soothe him, but black spots were now appearing in her vision. "Stop," she pleaded with the advancing Euclideans. "Can't you see you're scaring him?"

One of them leveled a rifle at her, but an explosion of light across the camp redirected his attention. Euphemia Whitmore stepped out of the Black Forest. Her entire body burned with ethereal white flames, and her expression was terrible to behold. She stretched out her hands, looking every bit an avenging angel.

Ribbons of silver fire ripped through the encampment, darting around tree trunks and trailers like massive serpents. The Euclideans yelled as they scrambled for cover. The enchanted net that held the unicorn, however, lifted off the ground, pulling the creature toward the cargo helicopter. Trish grabbed at it, but her fingers were clumsy and heavy. The unicorn continued upward, nickering in panic. A movement caught Trish's eye, and she swiveled her head back down to see mercenaries pulling Owen's mom from a trailer. They hooked her to a dangling zip line and then they, too, were raised into the sky.

Whitmore swept her fingers through the rainy air, muttering some fiendishly complex incantation. The cargo helicopter banked away just as a globe of blue-white energy erupted from the librarian. The concussive explosion of light sent Trish backward into the mud. The head injury she had sustained finally took hold. Her eyes fluttered shut and the forest around her went black.

Chapter II

A Family Affair

Trish awoke in *Kana'ti*'s master bedroom. Varmint was nosing despondently in his cage, but he perked up and began chattering away when Trish sat up from the bed. She moved gingerly, but was surprised to find her head felt absolutely fine. There wasn't even a lump on her skull from where she'd struck the tree stump. She peered out the window, seeing the rain had finally stopped. The position of the sun seemed to indicate it was early afternoon. Ten hours had passed since she'd lost the unicorn.

She stumbled out of the bedroom to find everyone gathered around the kitchen area. They were snacking on various baked goods that Whitmore had procured at Villingen-Schwenningen's Meisterbäckerei. Through the front window, Trish saw they were parked on a hill overlooking the picturesque town.

"At last, she has arisen!" called Perry, coming over to hug her friend. "We were waiting for you to proceed with a full download."

"Not like we're on a ticking clock or anything," Bryan drawled with his usual double helping of sarcasm. He bit into a *Käsekuchen*, chewing noisily. "So long as Big Trish gets her beauty rest."

"What's your problem, Ferretti?" Trish asked, walking over to him and folding her arms.

"My problem," he said, slowly standing and licking his fingers one by one, "is I'm risking a lot to be here. And it's all wasted when you drop the ball."

"It wasn't her fault," Jacinda informed him. "The Euclideans overwhelmed us. You okay?" she asked, laying a hand on Trish's shoulder.

She nodded, swallowing an odd lump that had suddenly appeared in her throat. "How did I—" she began, but Whitmore gently interrupted.

"I brought you all back after the Euclideans absconded with the unicorn. My Spell of Healing took care of that goose egg you received during the scuffle, but sleep, I often find, is the best medicine."

Jacinda removed her hand, leaving Trish's shoulder feeling like a cold, windswept heath. Her feelings were further doused by Bryan's next words: "Plus, it looks like your one-horned pal is back under a concealment spell, so we don't even know where they took it. Thanks for that."

Trish angrily began to form a spell, but Whitmore stopped her with an elegant hand. "Infighting only helps our enemies. Now that we're all assembled, perhaps we can get a picture of everything that transpired last night."

As Trish wolfed down a sampling of pastries, Whitmore relayed their end of the evening. She and the boys had cast several glamours depicting a dragon attack, making sure to follow it up with some non-hallucinatory fire spells. As predicted, the reports drew the Euclideans with their cargo helicopter. They had fun for a while, sending their enemies running in circles, but the soldiers had suddenly broken off their investigation and headed back to the forest in their helicopter.

Jacinda and the others then recounted what had happened at the Euclidean encampment. At first, the team leader skipped over their conversation with Owen's mom, but Whitmore pressed them on the identity of the sentry they'd dispatched. The girls shared a guilty look with each other.

"It was . . . Eleanor Macready," Trish said.

There was a moment of stunned silence, then Owen laughed. "Okay. Good one, guys."

The young women looked at each other awkwardly. "Owen . . . we all saw her," Perry said, gently touching him on the wrist. "There was a Euclidean tattoo on the back of her neck. She's one of them."

He stared at his friends for a moment, waiting for them to take back what they'd said. Trish watched his face cycle through emotions, her stomach tightening more and more with each one: fear . . . anger . . . and finally denial. He pulled his hand away from Perry. "No.

BEWARE THE EUCLIDEANS

Unfortunately, our enemies do have various methods of BRAINWASHING human beings. Some involve hypnosis, some pharmaceuticals, and some nanotechnology. All of them are dangerous.

That doesn't . . . They must have captured her. **BRAINWASHED** her. Like the Thin Man."

Bryan cocked an eyebrow. "So they left a prisoner to act as sentry for their whole camp?" He made a noise like a "wrong answer" buzzer. "She went to the dark side, Macready. Suck it up."

"It could've been . . ." Owen desperately cast about for other possibilities. "I dunno, a trick, then. Someone made up to look like her. Placed there to mess with our minds!"

Jacinda shook her head. "They had no idea we were going to be there," she reminded him. "Why spend hours covering someone in latex just in case you happened by?"

"I don't know!" Owen pushed up from the dining table. He paced the small space like a cornered chupacabra. "I just know she wouldn't . . . She's not like them, okay? She wouldn't sign up for that. She loves animals more than . . ." His voice caught and he looked away. ". . . almost anything."

Perry went to put an arm around him, but he shrugged her off. After giving him a moment to collect himself, Whitmore cleared her throat. "Unfortunately, what your friends say is true. I can confirm that your mother joined the Euclideans some time ago."

A different kind of silence descended on the RV. Owen turned to look at the woman who had recruited him, his eyes dark and dancing with fury. "You *knew*? How long?"

The librarian took a sip of her tea. "She joined ten months ago at least, though the exact timeline of her **RECRUITMENT** is difficult to—"

Owen slammed a fist against the wall of *Kana'ti*, making Perry jump. "No, how long did you know she was a Euclidean and not tell me?"

Whitmore steadily held his gaze. "From the moment we met. The Codex Arcanum does not accept new candidates without fully vetting their friends and family. There was some dissent about allowing you to join our ranks, in fact, but I argued that having a relative on the opposite side might sharpen your . . . motivation."

"A relative?" Owen barked a humorless laugh. "She's my *mother*. She ditched me and

BEWARE THE EUCLIDEANS

From what we've been able to determine, the Euclidean **RECRUITMENT** process can take months or even years. Details are difficult to ascertain because rejected recruits have all memories of their time with the organization erased.

my dad to run around the world with a group of psychotic anti-magic murderers!"

"Actually, dude . . ." Trish interjected. "She wasn't acting like one of them. I don't think they've told her everything they've done."

"I concur," Perry added quickly. "She didn't even know magic existed until last week. It's probable she thought the Euclideans were her only inroad to these areas of knowledge."

Despite their attempts to console him, Owen shook his head. "I gotta . . . yeah, I gotta take a walk," he said to no one in particular. He pushed open the door of *Kana'ti* and left.

"I, um, I'll just go accompany him. Make sure he doesn't accidentally curse something," Perry said, then hurried out the door after her boyfriend.

LUNCH PLANS

Trish looked at Whitmore angrily. "Why didn't you tell him?"

"You believe he would have taken the news better two months ago?" the librarian replied.

"Of course not," said Jacinda. "But he's certainly not going to be in the best frame of mind for whatever comes next."

"Boo-hoo. Some of us have been through much worse, parent-wise," said Bryan, now grabbing a *Milchbrötchen* from the pastry tray. "So what *is* the next step now that we've lost the unicorn and a whole team of sorcerers?"

"I have been musing on that very question since last night," Whitmore said. She finished the remains of her tea, then placed it back in its saucer. "We could continue to secure the world's remaining cryptids, but it would be like putting our finger in a single crack of a rapidly crumbling dam." She looked down into her empty teacup. "No matter how we view the situation, our enemies are winning."

"Have we considered the possibility that they might not *all* be our enemies?" Jacinda suggested. "I know it sounds crazy, but maybe they're not all evil. Maybe they're just misinformed. Owen's mom, she didn't seem like Kiraz."

"I'll field this one," said Bryan. "As an expert on crappy parents, they'll say anything to get to what they want. She was scamming you guys."

"I am inclined to agree." Whitmore stood to rinse her teacup in the sink. "Even if Eleanor does not share the beliefs of her fellow Euclideans, the organization has spent centuries proving it cannot be trusted."

"So what do we do, then?" Trish demanded.

"I have a notion, but I'm afraid it's rather dangerous." Whitmore dried off her teacup and met the teenagers' eyes. "We can **ATTACK** the Euclideans head-on."

BEWARE THE EUCLIDEANS

Frontal **ATTACKS** have been launched against our enemies several times in the past. They have nearly always ended in great loss of life.

A variety of expressions crossed the young sorcerers' faces. Bryan smiled in anticipation, Jacinda was concerned, and Trish was dubious. "I thought they 'greatly outnumbered' us," she said.

"Oh, they do. By a factor of a thousand to one." The librarian busied herself with carrying the other teacups and plates to the sink. "However, we can be fairly confident they're holding the majority of the abducted cryptids in a single location. Easier to secure. If we attack that place, the element of surprise may allow us to free their captives."

"Now we're talking," said Bryan, rubbing his hands together excitedly. "Where is this soon-to-be-magically-demolished Euclidean compound?"

Whitmore began filling the sink with soapy water. "That we do not know."

"Can't we just cast a Spell of Location on it?" asked Jacinda.

"Or use a Spell of Summoning on one of the captured animals?" suggested Trish.

"All worthy ideas, all attempted and failed." Whitmore scrubbed dishes and set them on a towel to dry. "As your encounter with the unicorn proves, our enemies have at least one sorcerer on their payroll. Someone who is adept at casting spells of concealment. We must find another way to locate them."

This stumped the teenagers for a moment. Bryan snapped his fingers. "My dad always said, 'Nobody can hide forever. Especially when people are involved.' We just gotta find someone who knows where these a-hole poachers went."

Trish was surprised by his intensity. Perhaps, despite all his insults and attitude and occasional shirtlessness, he cared more for their cause than he let on.

The librarian pressed two fingers to her lips, thinking. "Someone, no. But I know of some*thing* that may provide us with their location. Such a request, however, invites enormous risk."

She lapsed into silent contemplation. After it became clear she would not be divulging her idea anytime soon, Jacinda spoke up. "Well? What is it?"

Whitmore blinked as if waking from a deep sleep. "Hmm? Ah, yes. I'm afraid there's nothing else for it. Children, I suggest we consult the SPHINX."

DANGEROUS PROPOSALS

A short while later, Trisha was bent over *Cryptozoology for Beginners*, rereading the entry on Whitmore's proposed target.

"Have you seen this?" Trish asked Jacinda. "'People who fail to answer the Sphinx's riddles are *devoured*'?"

She and the team leader were outside *Kana'ti*. Perry and Owen were still off somewhere, and Bryan had retreated to his stinky sleep cave. Whitmore had used her Codex Arcanum key to go and get a few magical items before they left for Egypt. Jacinda had decided to use the downtime to recast the defensive enchantments she'd placed on the RV, while Trish sat under a shady pine to research their upcoming cryptid encounter. Varmint nosed through the grass beside her.

Sphinx

AFRICA

HABITAT:
ABU SIMBEL
EGYPT

AN EXACTING
ORACLE

WEIGHT:
120 – 170 kg

LENGTH:
3.5 m

HEIGHT:
3 m

MAGICAL PROPERTIES:
predestination, immortality, resistance to magic

The Sphinx is a **singular, highly magical** cryptid that has **existed** for **thousands of years**. Its **long life**, great **intellect**, and uncanny **insight** make it one of the **wisest** and **most sought-after** creatures on the planet. The **ancient Egyptians worshipped** this cryptid as a **goddess**, but **advances in technology** and human **civilization** led to the animal being **hunted**. It was forced to go into **hiding** in the **Egyptian desert**.

The Sphinx can **answer any question** with magical **accuracy**, but supplicants must first **pass its tests**. Those who **fail** are usually **devoured**.

DID YOU KNOW?

The Sphinx is the world's **oldest living cryptid**, with an estimated **age** of **4,500 years**. And yet, it's still in **peak physical shape**.

Jacinda continued jotting runes on the side of the vehicle with a silver marker. "Whitmore said it would be risky." She had shucked her flannel shirt in the warm afternoon and was wearing only a black tank top now. Trish was trying her best not to stare.

"Risky, not deadly," she protested. She wanted Jacinda to think she was tough, but she didn't want to face a murderous creature to prove it. "I mean, this thing's a big step up from unicorns and jackalopes. No offense, bud," she said to Varmint, scratching him behind the antlers.

"Aw shoot, lil' filly," said the cryptid in his cowboy drawl. "I know wherefore lies your heart." He continued in a singsong voice: "Trisha and Jacinda, sitting in a—"

Trish quickly covered the jackalope's mouth before he could go on. As Varmint struggled to get free, she spoke up. "So you've dealt with animals like this before? Deadly ones, I mean?"

"Sphinx, no. Deadly creatures, yes." Finished with her runes, Jacinda stood and stretched her back. Her figure caught the afternoon light in a particularly engaging way, but Trish was just as impressed with her spell work. It was strong and precise, much like the young woman herself. Jacinda turned her head, smiling slightly when she caught Trish gazing at her.

Blushing, Trish dropped her eyes. "Oh yeah? Which ones?"

Jacinda arched an eyebrow, moving on to the wheels of the vehicle. "You remember how I told you about my Level Two Exam? Capturing the salamander?" Trish nodded. "Well, it, um . . . it didn't go well." She kicked at the grass with the toe of her boot. "I thought magic could do anything back then. But someone . . . a sorcerer friend of mine, he . . . he got killed." Her striking face clouded at the memory. "He was only fifteen." She brushed at her eyes. "And it was my fault."

Trish was stunned. *No wonder she's been such a hard-ass this whole time. To see another sorcerer die, and to blame yourself?* "I'm sorry," she said softly.

"Me too." She looked back up at Trish, her startling gray eyes shining with tears. "It all came down to trust. I didn't trust him, the salamander didn't trust us . . . that's why I've been so tough on you guys. I didn't want that to happen to you, too. These cryptids, they can tell when someone's . . . holding back."

Trish swallowed. "And you still think that's what I'm doing?"

Jacinda swept her dark hair to one side, exposing the shaved part of her scalp. Her gray eyes assessed Trish seriously. Trish swallowed, her pulse thumping in her neck. Her tongue seemed glued to the roof of her mouth. Jacinda continued softly, "I'm not gonna push you anymore, Trisha. The next step . . . that's up to you to take."

Impulsively, without stopping to second-guess herself, Trish did just that. She stepped toward the older girl. The single motion took more courage than facing a whole squad of Euclidean soldiers. She suddenly felt aware of every detail around her—the dull buzz of honeybees in the bright-green clover, the curl of yellow pollen spores on the wind, the slow, wispy undulation of the white clouds overhead. Jacinda stood, neither advancing nor retreating. Her gray eyes were a fog bank of mystery.

"I don't know how to do this," Trish mumbled.

"It's easy, doll." The word jolted through Trish like a bolt of lightning. "All you gotta do is say how you feel."

"But what if . . ." But she couldn't bring herself to finish the sentence yet. Her unspoken words hung thick between them. Somehow, the tall teenager took another step forward. If she wished, she could reach out and touch Jacinda's shoulder.

And so she did. Jacinda's pupils expanded and her lips parted slightly at Trish's touch. Her bare shoulder went bumpy with gooseflesh. For the first time, Trish could see flecks of purple in the sixteen-year-old's gray irises.

"What if . . . how I feel is . . . not returned?" Trish whispered. She felt if she spoke any louder, whatever enchantment had befallen them would be broken.

Jacinda lifted her own hand to Trish's shoulder. Her fingers were warm, but the contact still made Trish shiver. "Trust me," Jacinda murmured. "It is."

And then her eyelids closed and she leaned forward. Trish froze, her mind a tornado of conflicting desires. She had only practiced such maneuvers on the back of her hand or her pillow before. She didn't know if she should clutch Jacinda's head or place her hands on her cheeks. Did her lips need to pucker? Should her mouth be open or closed? Would dipping be required?

But then Jacinda's lips were on hers and all thought left her brain. There was only warmth and softness and the smell of her skin, like bread warm from the oven. Her arms encircled the older girl, clutching at her as if she were a life preserver in a vast, lonely ocean. Even with no experience, she discovered she knew how to kiss back, gently parting her lips and moving her hands up and down the curve of Jacinda's strong back.

She wasn't sure how long the kiss went on. It felt like decades and milliseconds at the same time. But before Trish could fully appreciate what was happening, it was over. Hearing a shout behind them, Jacinda broke away from Trish. The soft openness vanished from her face, replaced by her usual mask of grim determination.

WITH A TRACE

"What's wrong?" Jacinda called as Owen came speed-walking up the hill. Behind him, Perry was running to catch up. Owen's mobile phone was clutched in his hand, and his cheeks were red with shame.

"I urged him . . . not to do it," Perry said, trying to regain her breath. "But he's more obstinate . . . than a stubborn Minotaur."

There was a beat as Perry and Owen glared at each other.

"That doesn't actually explain what happened," Trish said impatiently.

Owen exhaled. "I . . . called my mom."

Jacinda was aghast. "Like, on your phone? You called a known Euclidean on your own *phone*?"

"I didn't know she was a Euclidean!" he shot back. "At least, I wasn't sure. Not the way you guys were. I just, I wanted to hear her say it to my face."

"And did she?" asked Trish sarcastically. "'Cause your peace of mind, that's the most important thing in this *worldwide war* we're fighting!"

"She's my mom, T. Sorry if it's hard for me to be totally objective about these things. Anyway, we only talked for a couple minutes." Owen pried the back cover off his phone and removed the SIM card. He formed a few runes over the tiny card, then muttered, *"Hedfan."* The SIM card flew out of his hand and spiraled off into the sky.

"So I'm guessing you didn't just do that for funsies," Jacinda said, nodding to the retreating card.

"It's a precaution," said Perry. "We're 80 percent positive Mrs. Macready didn't trace the call." She looked tentatively at her boyfriend. "Seventy-five, eighty."

"Unbelievable," Trish said to Owen. "We barely got away from those guys last night, and you put one of 'em on *speed dial?*"

"I just thought . . ." he said miserably. "I thought I might be able to maybe change her mind. Get her on our side."

"Well, looks like you're a real master of persuasion, Macready," Bryan said as he stepped out of *Kana'ti*. He rolled his neck and pointed to the sky above Villingen-Schwenningen. Two black dots approached, quickly revealing themselves to be twins of the military cargo helicopter they'd seen last night. "Mommy sent the Euclideans right to us."

CHAPTER 12

ESCAPE ROUTE

Owen's expression fell even further. "Inside," Jacinda ordered the teenagers. "Go, go, go. And buckle up."

Perry and Bryan immediately scrambled into *Kana'ti*, tugging a distraught Owen with them, but Trish ran to scoop up Varmint. She turned to see Jacinda forming runes and pointing at each of the vehicle's tires. She spoke a word in Welsh, and they all briefly glowed purple.

"You put a flight spell on the RV?" Trish asked, trying to keep the nervousness from her voice.

"Among other things," the team leader replied. "Hopefully it will make it easier to keep 'em off us. Now get in, get in."

She squeezed her shoulder and Trish hurried inside. The helicopters were only a few dozen meters away now. One of them banked, revealing a gun turret jutting out from the side. It opened fire—

Just as Jacinda pulled the vehicle's door closed. Bullets thumped into the metal, sending golden ripples all over the magically shielded outside surface. For the moment, Jacinda's protection wards seemed to be holding. The gunner realized this and stopped firing.

"Yeah, they seem real nonviolent to me," Bryan commented from his perch above the driver's area.

"Nonviolent, no, but nonlethal, yes." Perry peered out one of the windows at the flattened ammunition. "They're using **RUBBER BULLETS**. I think their aim is to trap us."

"You see? Maybe they're not all evil," insisted Owen.

"Which would totally explain why they're shooting at us," Bryan said sarcastically.

"Either way, Whitmore's last orders were to avoid 'em. We're leaving." Jacinda turned the key in the ignition, and *Kana'ti* practically jumped off the ground in excitement.

Trish got into the passenger seat, buckling her safety harness. One of the Euclidean helicopters hovered in the air directly before them. She could see armed soldiers already zip-lining down to the road beneath the hill on which they were parked. "How many times have you done the flying car thing?" she asked, trying to sound casual.

BEWARE THE EUCLIDEANS

RUBBER BULLETS are frequently used by our enemies to incapacitate and distract spell casters. While not intended to be lethal, they can still cause bruises, broken bones, and yes, even death.

"Before now? None." Jacinda grinned apologetically. "But the theory's solid."

"Yay, untested magic," said Bryan from above. "My favorite kind."

Jacinda put the RV into drive. "So let's test it."

She stomped on the gas, sending the vehicle straight toward the steep edge of the hill. *Kana'ti* dropped, affording them a stomach-lurching moment of weightlessness—

Then Jacinda put the car into another gear and stomped the gas again. The pedal briefly shone purple. The nose of the RV lifted, and the whole heavy vehicle shot upward, flying over the heads of the Euclidean soldiers. They nearly collided with the spire of a Gothic church, but Jacinda turned the wheel to bank right at the last moment. The car was only a few meters above the city rooftops, so she pulled down the turn indicator, causing them to rise upward.

"I had to improvise a little on the controls," she explained to Trish, turning left to avoid a rooftop billboard. "Seeing as cars don't really have ways to address 'up' and 'down.'"

"The helicopters are following us!" Owen called from the back bedroom.

"Scurvy scallywags!" said Varmint in a scratchy sailor voice Trish hadn't heard yet. "Gird yerselves and give 'em what for!"

"I agree with the pirate bunny," said Bryan, hopping down from his perch. "And I call dibs on window number two."

He opened a side window. The sudden burst of wind inside the RV cabin rattled blinds and sent a loose stack of napkins spiraling. Quickly and fluidly, his pale, freckled hands formed a series of runes. A fireball the size of a soccer ball bloomed in his hand. With deadeye accuracy, he hurled it at the closest pursuing chopper. It exploded on the hull, making an impressive display of flames, but the vehicle kept coming.

"You gonna stand there and gawk, or are you gonna help?" Bryan said to the others.

As he began to form another spell, Perry and Owen opened windows on the opposite side of the RV. Trish unbuckled herself as well, but paused when Jacinda grabbed her by the wrist.

"Be careful," the team leader said, her gray eyes shining with concern. "That's an order."

"Yes, ma'am." Trish squeezed her hand, then jogged to the kitchen, pulling a chair beneath the RV's sunroof/escape hatch. The procedure to open it was not immediately evident, so she formed the runes for the Spell to Conjure Thunderclaps and simply knocked it off the hinges. The rush of air blew her hair around her face and brought tears to her eyes. But she gripped the edge of the hatch and pulled herself out onto the roof of the RV.

The wind whipped around her like a hurricane. They were several hundred meters above the ground now, the height making the buildings of Villingen-Schwenningen look like models. Trish could see a few people on rooftops pointing their camera phones after them, but she couldn't worry about that now. Hooking her legs on the edge of the escape hatch, Trish faced the pursuing helicopters.

Ice shards and fireballs cast by the others streaked back-toward the vehicles, but they didn't seem to be doing much. Trish's instinct was to join in, but there was no guarantee they could bring down the helicopters without injuring anyone on board. She wasn't a fan of the Euclideans, but she didn't want any deaths on her hands either. *What would Jacinda do?*

Gripped by sudden inspiration, Trish took out her mobile phone and entered a phrase into an **ONLINE TRANSLATOR**. After reading it over a few times, she took a bead on the lead helicopter pilot and fixed an image in her mind. She moved her hands through the air, fingers forming runes. *"Votre hélicoptère se détraque et vous devez atterrir immédiatement,"* she read from her phone screen, then extended her hand.

Nothing happened, most likely due to her horrible pronun-ciation. She went through the spell again, taking time to pro-nounce each word slowly and in a French accent.

A blob of colored light flew through the air, wrapping around the helmet of the pursuing helicopter's pilot. Had Trish been able to see and hear as he did, she would have heard alarms go off and seen every dial and gauge go haywire on the control panel. But she didn't need to witness any of that to realize her magical hal-lucination had worked. The pilot immediately began lowering

THE CODEX
ARCANUM

In years past, a sorcerer would either need to speak fluent French to cast glamours, or carry around bulky dictionaries. Nowadays, ONLINE TRANSLATORS make casting magical hallucinations easy—provided the translation is correct.

the helicopter despite the protests of his fellow Euclideans. He set the aircraft down in a field just outside the town.

Trish smiled in satisfaction. Unless they had someone else who could fly the vehicle, the pilot wouldn't get back in until her glamour FADED. There was still the matter of the other helicopter, however. It had moved forward, and she could see an older man leaning out one side of the chopper. He had a matted gray beard and wild, shining eyes. His fingers were moving in a familiar pattern.

Runes, Trish realized. *He's forming runes. He's a—*

Whoosh! Before Trish could finish her thought, the bearded man cast his spell. A glowing projectile streaked toward the RV, leaving a trail of purple sparks in its wake. Trish winced as it impacted on one of the rear tires, scorching off several of Jacinda's flight runes.

THUNK! The tail end of the RV dropped at a steep angle. Trish tumbled forward, losing her grip on the escape hatch. Her phone fell inside the RV, and she slid down the roof of *Kana'ti,* her hands scrabbling for purchase. The branches of the Black Forest seemed to reach for her from a hundred meters below.

THE CODEX
ARCANUM

Most glamours FADE within ten to fifteen minutes. They can be held longer if the sorcerer maintains concentration. The current record for maintaining a glamour is ten days, and it only faded because of an unexpected sneeze.

She was almost off the vehicle when her right hand snagged the metal ladder attached to the back of the RV. Her body swung around, dangling in midair by one arm. Trish stared at the long drop beneath her feet, her heart pounding in her throat. She could hear Perry and Owen yelling at Jacinda to level off. Trish glanced at the still-smoking back tire. She didn't want to find out what would happen if they lost another flight spell.

But before she could tell the others there was a sorcerer pursuing them, Jacinda dropped the nose of the vehicle, causing Trish to float upward and land on the roof of the RV with a heavy *thump. At least I'm back on something solid*, she groaned inwardly.

She rolled onto her stomach, glaring at the pursuing helicopter. Already the Euclidean sorcerer was forming another spell. Owen, Perry, and Bryan were still firing off elemental attacks, but this pilot dodged them with ease. They needed to hinder the helicopter in a way he couldn't predict. Trish scanned the surroundings for anything that might help. *Kana'ti* was about a thousand meters above the alpine treetops now, nearly level with the snow-dusted mountain peaks in the distance. There was no way they'd reach them in time, but perhaps they could make use of something closer.

Trish crawled back to the open escape hatch and stuck her head down inside the RV. "Can you take us down?" she called to Jacinda. "Right above the treetops."

The team leader nodded and pulled down the turn indicator. *Kana'ti* dipped downward, but Trish was prepared this time.

She braced herself against the escape hatch, water streaming from her eyes as the Black Forest grew closer and closer. Jacinda moved up the turn indicator, leveling off just a few meters above the treetops.

Behind them, the remaining pursuit helicopter dropped as well. The course correction had caused the Euclidean sorcerer to abandon his last spell, but Trish could see his fingers were already moving once more. They had maybe a few seconds before he attacked again.

"Follow my lead!" Trish called down into the RV. She moved her fingers, choppily forming runes and pointing at the spruce trees below. *"Crescer maior!"* she commanded in PORTUGUESE.

Three treetops suddenly grew several meters skyward. The Chinook helicopter banked sideways to avoid them, and the Euclidean sorcerer's spell went wild. Inside the RV, Perry clapped with delight.

"Marvelous idea," she called. "Owen, Bryan, use the SPELL TO INCREASE PLANT GROWTH."

THE CODEX ARCANUM

Because spells were developed all over the world, their activation words are in a variety of languages, from Latin, to Icelandic, to PORTUGUESE.

With all four of them casting the spell, dozens of treetops began springing upward, forming a series of woody obstacles the Euclideans couldn't avoid. The pilot slalomed back and forth a few times, the rotors of his vehicle cutting through

THE CODEX ARCANUM

When casting the SPELL TO INCREASE PLANT GROWTH, a sorcerer should consider his or her surroundings. Several sorcerers have tried to perk up their house plants only to find them putting holes in their rooftops.

nearby branches, but soon the treetops were too dense to continue. Rather than be pummeled further, the cargo helicopter backed off and followed at a distance. Jacinda guided *Kana'ti* into an opening in the tree canopy, and soon the Euclideans were obscured from sight.

Perry and Owen whooped inside the RV. Trish dropped back down inside, and was surprised when Bryan chucked her on the shoulder with his fist.

"Hey, uh . . . that was good thinking back there," he said grudgingly.

"I know," she replied, giving him a sturdy punch back.

QUESTIONING AUTHORITY

Jacinda found a small lake deep within the Black Forest and landed the RV on a patch of its grassy shore. Excited as always to impart information, Perry told them it was fed by the Kirnach River, a tributary of the larger Brigach, which interestingly enough—but Bryan thankfully asked her to stop before she recited the entire Wikipedia page. Jacinda parked beneath a large oak, then cast a spell of invisibility on *Kana'ti* in case the Euclideans sent more helicopters to look for them. They quickly set to work drawing another ninety-foot portal, using their phones to consult rune translators and STAR CHARTS.

"What's in Egypt?" Owen asked when he saw their destination. In the excitement of the chase, the others had forgotten that he and Perry had been absent when Whitmore had suggested their next step. They quickly told their friends the plan to ask the Sphinx for the location of the Euclidean's hidden base.

"Shouldn't we wait for Ms. Whitmore to do this?" Perry said nervously. "I'm not sure it's judicious to approach such a dangerous cryptid without her expertise."

"I left her a message. She'll catch up to us," Jacinda replied, using a fire spell to carve the massive portal diagram into a damp forest clearing near *Kana'ti*. "She does this. Disappears without telling you when she'll be back, gives you spell books without letting you know how they work . . . She does things in her own time."

"That's a nice way of putting it," said Bryan, burning runes into a border of the diagram. "When we were creating that dragon distraction last night, she barely told us what to do. It's like she forgot we were even there sometimes."

"I noticed that too," Owen agreed. "The spacing out, the forgetfulness. Is she . . . mentally all there?"

THE CODEX ARCANUM

Portal spells use STAR CHARTS for positioning. They are by far the most accurate gauge of location, since the Earth is constantly moving through our solar system.

"Of course," Jacinda said crossly. "She's got a lot on her mind, that's all. You try managing a secret worldwide organization of sorcerers."

Bryan lifted his hands in defense. "It's a valid question, Tiger Lily. We're getting attacked by Euclideans everywhere we go. We deserve to know if our commander's a few bullets short of a full mag. I mean, how old is she, anyway? Eighty? Ninety? A thousand?"

"Nobody knows," Jacinda admitted. "But it doesn't matter, because she's doing fine. So drop it."

They finished drawing the portal diagram within the hour and drove *Kana'ti* through it. To immediately be transported from a lush green alpine forest to a vast yellow desert was a bit of a visual shock, but at least Egyptian time was only an hour later than German time. They had portaled so much in the last week, Trish and the others barely noticed the nausea that came with time displacement anymore.

What Trish did notice was the heat. It radiated off the ground, practically squeezing the air from her lungs. The sun hung low on the western horizon, painting the sand dunes with ever-lengthening shadows. She couldn't imagine what it was like in the blaze of midday. The town of ABU SIMBEL sat in the distance, a small collection of cream and tan buildings on the edge of Lake Nasser. The streets were lined with scrubby green desert plants. On the edge of the lake were two large trapezoidal

The village of ABU SIMBEL is located in southern Egypt, near the border of Sudan. It is best known for two temples built for Pharaoh Ramesses II in 1264 BCE.

mounds, which Perry informed them contained the famous **TEMPLES** that drew tourists to the area.

"That's not where we're going, though," said Jacinda. She turned, pointing into the empty sea of sand to the west of the town. "Whitmore said the Sphinx lives out there somewhere."

"So how do we find it?" said Bryan. "I'm guessing you don't have a Find My Sphinx app in your papoose."

"No, but I do have an Idiot Alarm," she shot back, pressing a button on her satellite phone. It buzzed repeatedly, and she brandished it in his face. "Look at that, it works."

Trish barked a laugh. Bryan rounded on her, but Owen spoke up before they could get into it. "Can't we use a Spell of Location on it, like we did with the altamaha-ha?"

"In that case, we had the creature's magical energy signature," she said. "Which we don't have for the Sphinx. We'll have to think of something else."

The two **TEMPLES** were actually moved from their original location in 1968 to make way for the Aswan Dam reservoir in Lake Nasser. Thankfully, they were not magical, because such a relocation would have destroyed any wards, enchantments, or supernatural energies contained in the site.

The teenagers looked out at the desert. It only seemed to contain sand dunes and a distinct lack of cool air.

"Are you positive Whitmore sent us to the right place?" Trish asked Jacinda tentatively. "My grandma spaces out sometimes, and she's way younger than Whitmore."

"I'm sure," Jacinda said shortly. She scanned the empty desert with a pair of high-powered binoculars.

"Ooh! Ooh!" Perry spoke up excitedly: "What if we don't search for the cryptid, but for its domicile? Think about it—the Sphinx is a highly magical creature; it stands to reason its house would be, as well."

"If it's magically camouflaged, that actually makes it harder for us to find it," Bryan pointed out.

Perry shook her head. "Not if we use —"

"—A SPELL TO REVEAL MAGIC." Owen finished. They grinned at each other and briefly kissed. Bryan made a barfing sound. Owen quickly dug through his backpack and removed two hand-copied spell pages.

THE CODEX ARCANUM

The particulars of a SPELL TO REVEAL MAGIC can, of course, be found in *Sorcery for Beginners*, which you really should read before attempting any of the actions contained in this guide.

Knock, Knock, Knocking On Sphinx's Door

"It will be stronger if we cast it together," Jacinda said. "Everybody form a line."

While the teenagers did that, she took out a toolbox filled with spell components and handed a glass marble to each of them. In unison, they rubbed the marbles with their thumbs, then formed four complicated hand movements. As it was a spell they didn't use often, it took them several tries to get the casting correct. They knew they were on the right track when their fingers left trails of purple light in the air.

Jacinda nodded, and they all intoned in Latvian: *"Atklāt visu burvju."* The team leader clicked open a silver lighter and gently blew on the flame. It detached, expanding into a translucent golden orb that spread out in all directions. Everything it passed through briefly vibrated, then *Kana'ti* began to glow as if it were phosphorescent. Several objects inside the RV also glowed, as did the stone amulet around Owen's neck.

"Super plan," Bryan commented. "Too bad it's only showing us things we already know are enchanted."

But Trish was scanning the horizon. "Hand me the binoculars," she said quickly to Jacinda. She clapped them to her eyes, locating a glowing dot about two or three kilometers in the desert northwest of them. Just behind it stood the glinting blue-gray waters of the Toshka Lakes. She pointed the dot out to Jacinda, who managed to catch sight of the glowing marker right before the spell faded.

"Nice work," she said.

The compliment made Trish flush with pleasure. Impulsively, she stepped forward to kiss Jacinda as Owen had kissed Perry, but the team leader's eyes widened. She gave an almost imperceptible head shake and turned to face the others. "We have a destination. All aboard."

Jacinda quickly walked to the driver's side of *Kanati* and got in. She didn't look back. Trish stood frozen on the sand, her heart feeling like it had been stepped on by a skunk ape. *It happened again. The pull-away. She must regret kissing me. I knew I shouldn't have told her how I felt. I knew it, I knew it, I—*

"Yo." Trish blinked, seeing Bryan was beside her. "You comin' or you gonna stand here and drool?" When she rounded on him in anger, he lifted his hands. "It's a joke, chill out. You're standing out here like you're in a coma."

Trish followed him into the RV, sitting near the kitchen and glancing in confusion toward the driver's seat. Jacinda kept her eyes focused on the desert ahead and put the vehicle in gear. They reached the place Trish had spotted in a matter of minutes, but had to cast the Spell to Reveal Magic once more to locate the exact source of the glow.

It turned out to emanate from a block of sandstone nearly buried at the base of a dune. After brushing it off, they discovered ancient, sand-blown hieroglyphics carved into its side. Beneath the carvings were three glowing runes. Then the spell faded again, and the runes disappeared from the block of sandstone.

Jacinda pulled out her **SATELLITE PHONE**, and within seconds found a hieroglyphic typewriter app. The others crowded around, but Trish stayed near *Kana'ti*, sulking.

"Good thing you brought that," Owen said as Jacinda studied the hieroglyphics. "I don't even think my primo roaming plan would get reception out here."

"Whitmore told me it's one of the best defenses magical places have," she said as she entered glyphs letter by letter. "Most of them are so far off the beaten path that they're difficult to reach without sorcery."

She hit the "Translate" button, and a message appeared:

To enter, form the signs and speak.

"Ooh, a riddle," Perry said. "I love these."

"Of course *you* do, Nerd Queen," Bryan said. "But just once, *I'd* like one of these missions to be easy."

Trish got to her feet, her fingers itching to cast an attack spell. "What is your problem, Ferretti? All week, we've had to put up with your crappy attitude, and I'm sick of it."

Bryan turned to her, scowling. "Well, maybe I'm sick of putting up with *you*."

"Can we not get into this now, guys?" asked Owen. "It's Sphinx time, remember?"

But Trish didn't take her eyes off Bryan. "No, I wanna know. Why are you so awful to everyone?" She looked him up and down critically. "Is it just how Daddy raised you? Survival of the jerkiest? Hurt them before they hurt you??"

Bryan's eyes went cold. "You mention my father again, and we're gonna have words."

"Your father," she sneered, fingertips crackling with magical energy, "is a child-torturing, murder-attempting, low-life piece of crap. And I thought you were a man of action."

Bryan shoved her. Trish shoved him back. Their hands were a blur as they both formed spells—

But Jacinda stepped between them, laying a hand on Trish's shoulder. "That's enough. We don't have time for this."

"Yeah?" Trish shouted. "Tell him that."

Perry and Owen glanced at each other in confusion. "Come here," Jacinda said, firmly taking Trish aside. Bryan spit into the desert sand and went back inside *Kana'ti*, slamming the door.

Once they were deep enough in the desert to speak privately, Jacinda gave Trish a disapproving look, one which she didn't need a translator app to understand. "What's with you?"

"You're asking me? You're the one playing . . . mind games."

"Keep your voice down," Jacinda said. "Just because we . . . you know . . . doesn't mean I'm ready for them to know it."

Trish clenched her fists until her nails bit into her palms. "What, are you embarrassed of me? You think I'm a . . . a monster or something??" Her voice was tinged with hysteria and her chest was tight with tension. She couldn't bear to meet the team leader's eye. It was like what had happened with Julia, only much worse. *Because this time*, she thought wretchedly, *you should have known better.*

But Jacinda took her gently by the shoulders. "Hey." Trish forced herself to look into the older girl's gray eyes and was relieved to see they were warm with compassion. "I like you. But we don't need any more distractions right now. Especially from Bryan."

Trish exhaled and nodded.

"Just trust me." She gave Trish's shoulders a squeeze. "Once we're done with what we have to do here, there'll be plenty of time to figure things out." She smiled. The expression was so dazzling, Trish wondered how she could keep it to herself all the time.

"I'm sorry," she said miserably. "I just—we never talked about it, so I didn't—and I've never—you were my first, okay?" She exhaled. "That's why it might have been . . . weird."

"It wasn't," Jacinda assured her. "And I'm honored."

Trish couldn't resist smiling as well. The two young women spent a few moments grinning shyly at each other before a shout from Owen reached them:

"Where are you guys? Get back here!"

They returned to *Kana'ti* to find Owen excitedly forming the three runes that had appeared on the sandstone pillar. His hands glowed purple, but then the magical energy quickly faded.

"Fascinating, isn't it?" Perry said excitedly. "We've determined it's an opening spell, but it appears to require an **ACTIVATION WORD**. We served up a few of the classics, but thus far nothing's worked."

"Maybe try them in Arabic?" Jacinda suggested.

They attempted several activation words in that language, but none of those worked either. Then Trish had an idea. She double-checked the translation app on Jacinda's satellite phone to confirm her theory. She formed the three runes, her fingers glowing with purple energy, and spoke the word "enter" in Arabic.

The sandstone pillar dropped into the desert. The ground vibrated beneath them, sending sand particles skittering across their sneakers. A door opened in the dune before the teenagers. Sand poured downward like a whispering waterfall, revealing an ornately carved set of stone stairs leading down into a dark temple. Trish grinned.

"Like Perry said, it's a riddle. Form the signs and speak 'to enter.'" She gestured to the stairs. "Who wants to go wake up a Sphinx?"

THE CODEX
ARCANUM

Adding a secret ACTIVATION WORD to unlocking or opening spells is a good secondary security measure. Think of it like placing a password on your computer, only in this case your computer is a priceless magical sanctuary for one of the world's most powerful cryptids.

CHAPTER 13

TEENS DESCENDING A STAIRCASE

Despite their excitement, the sorcerers did not immediately rush into the subterranean temple. Jacinda had Owen and Trish go into *Kana'ti* to stock up on moonstones, rhino hair, and other spell components, while she and Perry double-checked the spells of protection they'd cast on various items of clothing. Owen already had his stone amulet, of course, while Trish had recast the enchantments on her brother's chest protector and hockey pads. Bryan had opted to draw a spell of protection directly onto his hooded sweatshirt, but because the enchantment required animal milk, the garment smelled faintly of spoiled cheese.

Their spells of illumination were more creative. Owen and Bryan enchanted their belt buckles to cast light, while Perry conjured a tiny glowing globe that she could move around with the flick of her finger. Trish chose a simpler solution, creating a purple **FIREBALL** that hovered just above her open palm. There it functioned as both a light source and a potential weapon.

THE CODEX
ARCANUM

The drawback to using magic FIREBALLS as illumination is that they share the other properties of fire as well—namely, the ability to set things aflame.

"You think we should wait for Ms. Whitmore?" Jacinda muttered to Trish once everything was ready. "There's been no word from her since Germany. We could sleep here and hope she shows up in the morning."

"What if the Euclideans find us before then?" Trish replied. "Or someone else? The temple's right there. I say we ask for help while we still can."

Jacinda bit her lip nervously, but nodded in agreement. They rounded up the others and began walking down the stone steps into the Sphinx's temple. Jacinda took the lead, followed by Trish, then Perry and Owen next to each other. Finally, Bryan brought up the rear. Sand continued to pour downward in carved channels on either side of the staircase. The whispering hiss made Trish's skin crawl. Their various forms of light cast eerie shadows on the walls, illuminating carvings of mythical animals that seemed to squirm with life. Many of the carvings, Trish realized, had been scratched out.

"Hold up," she said, coming to a stop. Perry and Owen nearly collided with her.

"What is it?" Jacinda said softly. Whether it was the echoing nature of the space or its obvious solemnity, they all felt the need to speak quietly.

Trish took *Cryptozoology for Beginners* from her backpack and began flipping through it, comparing the entries to the wall carvings. After looking at a dozen or so, she still hadn't answered.

"You wanna spit it out already?" said Bryan. "Personally, I don't like standing in such an obvious spot for an ambush."

Trish flipped to the page describing the Australian BUNYIP, then found a similar carving on the wall. It had been scratched out, and the marks looked fairly recent. "From what I can tell, every creature that's crossed out on this wall is listed as 'extinct' in the book. And the unmarked ones are still alive." She turned to the jackalope page in her book and pointed to a similar carving on the wall. It was unmarred.

"So they match. What does that mean?" asked Owen.

"I don't know," Trish admitted. "Except that whatever lives inside this temple is pretty well informed."

"Well, that's why we're here," Jacinda reminded them. "Might as well get on with it."

They continued downward. The air grew cooler as they descended, and several times they had to equalize the pressure in their ears. Then, one hundred and fifty meters from the temple entrance, they reached the main room.

It was circular, with a domed ceiling that soared at least two hundred meters overhead. SEVEN great Sphinx statues were arrayed around the rotunda, each one at least five meters tall. In the floor below was a round pool filled with water the color of sapphires, no doubt fed by an underground spring. It smelled

BUNYIP

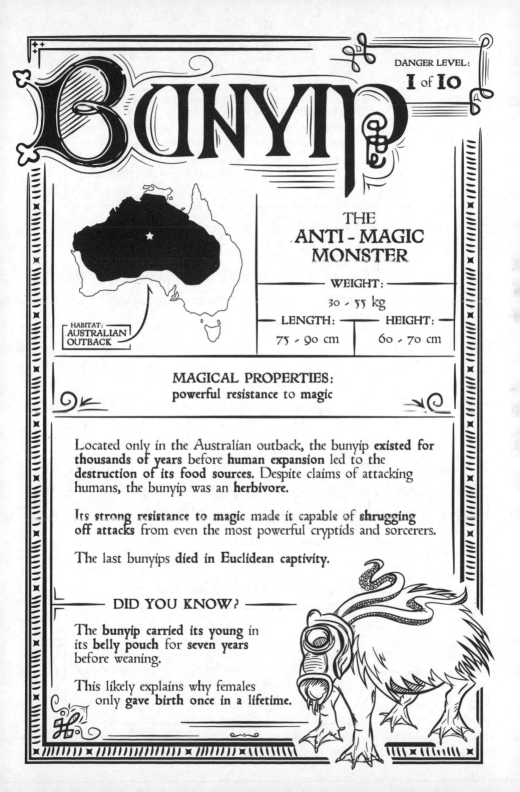

HABITAT:
AUSTRALIAN OUTBACK

THE ANTI-MAGIC MONSTER

WEIGHT:	
30 - 55 kg	

LENGTH:	HEIGHT:
75 - 90 cm	60 - 70 cm

MAGICAL PROPERTIES:
powerful resistance to magic

Located only in the Australian outback, the bunyip **existed for thousands of years** before **human expansion** led to the **destruction of its food sources.** Despite claims of attacking humans, the bunyip was an **herbivore.**

Its **strong resistance to magic** made it capable of **shrugging off attacks** from even the most powerful cryptids and sorcerers.

The last bunyips **died in Euclidean captivity.**

DID YOU KNOW?

The **bunyip carried its young** in its **belly pouch** for **seven years** before weaning.

This likely explains why females only **gave birth once** in a lifetime.

CRYPTID CORNER

Originally, there was one great Sphinx for each of the SEVEN continents. For various reasons—lack of food, environmental poisoning, foolish warrior quests—they were killed off until only the African cryptid remained. It has been the only one of its kind for over fifteen hundred years.

a bit musty, but not unpleasant. The entire chamber was lit by watery beams of late-afternoon sunlight that entered through a large square of crystal embedded in the temple ceiling. The light was reflected ingeniously throughout the room by movable panels of polished brass. The teenagers extinguished their magical forms of illumination.

Perry peered up at the ceiling through the binoculars. "The entire structure is underwater," she whispered excitedly. "I believe we're beneath some part of the TOSHKA LAKES."

"Guess that explains why no one's found it," said Trish in a similar whisper.

"Yeah, cool architecture, et cetera, but how do we find the cat lady?" asked Bryan in a normal tone of voice. The words "cat lady" echoed off the sandstone walls.

The other teenagers winced, but there was no immediate response. Jacinda fiercely held a finger to her lips.

ENCHANTING DETAILS

The TOSHKA LAKES are three bodies of water that lie to the northwest of Abu Simbel. They were formed so recently that they have yet to be given individual names.

"What?" said Bryan, taking care to lower his voice this time. "I thought we were trying to talk to it."

"We are, but I'd prefer if it didn't take us by surprise," hissed Jacinda.

Bryan raised his hands in surrender. The teenagers found another staircase down to the lowest level of the rotunda. The sapphire-colored spring bubbled quietly. The seven sphinx statues loomed over them, their eyes blankly staring into the distance. Beside each of them, a wide tunnel led off into darkness.

"This place is huge," Owen whispered. "Should we split up?"

Trish snorted. "Dude, haven't you ever seen a horror movie? We might as well sacrifice ourselves right now."

"So what, then? We just start going down the tunnels one by one?" said Bryan.

A voice spoke out of the darkness. It was feminine but sharp-edged, with a wild quality that could be heard in every syllable. The language was ancient Egyptian, but a sudden ache in their minds, like an ice shard in the cerebral cortex, made them realize they could understand the meaning behind the whispered words:

"That will not be necessary."

THE RIDDLES OF THE SPHINX

They spun toward the source of the voice, each of them forming their preferred defensive spell. One of the sphinx statues began to move. At first all they could see of it were two golden cat eyes. Then the cryptid stepped into the light, revealing a regal Egyptian face surrounded by a mane of jet-black hair. Its body was that of a golden lion, adorned with two massive walnut-colored eagle wings. The entire creature was the size of a small elephant.

The Sphinx looked down at them, its lion tail twitching silently back and forth. It sniffed the air. *"Humans,"* it said, the ice splinter in their brains again conveying the meaning. *"It has been many years since I have tasted the scent of your species. Why do you seek me now?"*

Jacinda stepped forward without hesitation. Trish felt a swell of pride and affection at her bravery. "Great Sphinx, we have been sent by Euphemia Whitmore to seek your counsel. The world's magical creatures are being taken."

"Yes. The treachery of your kind has felled many of my cousins." The golden cat eyes regarded each of them in turn. *"What would you ask of me?"*

"Ms. Whitmore was hoping you might be able to grant us some advice, O sagacious Sphinx," said Perry, bowing her head slightly. "Regarding how to find them."

The great animal stared down at them, motionless as the other six statues on its pedestal. It looked, thought Trish, like a cat selecting the mouse it wished to eat for dinner. *"Advice,"* the Sphinx repeated, a throaty purr rumbling in the back of its throat. *"Very well."* It leapt to the floor, silent on its great paws. *"But first you must answer my riddle."*

"Seriously?" said Bryan. "Your cryptid buddies are getting abducted and tortured by Euclideans, and you'd risk not helping them if we don't guess correctly?"

"Worse than that," the Sphinx replied with a smile. Its fangs were at least six inches long, and very sharp. *"Fail to answer truly, and I shall devour you. Do you wish to proceed?"*

The teenagers looked at each other nervously. *Sure would be nice to have Whitmore here with us,* Trish thought. *Especially when this kitty looks so hungry.* The Sphinx licked its chops, and Trish remembered it could probably hear what she was thinking. "We got this," she said, forcing herself to sound more confident than she felt.

Jacinda nodded. "Go ahead," she said to the cryptid. "Ask your riddle."

The Sphinx paced back and forth silently. *"Answer truly, and I shall grant you three questions."*

"What? Why does there have to be a limit?" asked Bryan.

"Three questions," repeated the Sphinx. *"But first you must answer mine: I am neither bought nor sold, yet can be valued more than gold. I am built up not by hand but can be broken by a single man. What am I?"*

Jacinda beckoned the teenagers into a huddle. "Hedge funds," said Bryan confidently. "My dad made a ton of money on 'em years ago, but they don't really exist."

"Yeah, but they're still bought or sold, dingus," Owen replied.

"As it is a riddle, I don't believe the answer will be straightforward," agreed Perry. "I recommend we think laterally. What are some unusual things that are 'built' but not bought or sold?"

"Countries," said Jacinda.

"Careers," suggested Owen.

"Sandcastles!" said Bryan. The others looked at him. "What? I'm sure there's some weirdo out there who values 'em more than gold."

Trish shook her head. "This isn't about giving any old answer. Anytime someone in a story solves a riddle, there's, like, a meaning or whatever behind it. Something they're supposed to learn. Like Oedipus realizing he needs to be a man, or Gollum figuring out he lost the ring of power."

"Good thinking," said Jacinda. Trish looked downward to hide the goofy smile that came unbidden to her face. "So what do we need to learn?"

The teenagers fell silent as they thought. *"Immortal though I may be,"* said the Sphinx, *"I shall not wait forever. Two minutes."*

"Come on," complained Bryan. "You never said anything about time limits."

"Focus," Jacinda told him. "We need to learn the value of . . . teamwork?"

"Empathy?" said Perry.

"Honesty?" said Owen, clearly thinking about his mother.

Trish reflected on her own experiences over the last ten days. How she'd been forced to rely on others, how she'd opened up, and most of all how she'd taken the leap to express her feelings to Jacinda. And suddenly she knew the answer.

"Trust," she said to the Sphinx. "The answer to your riddle is trust."

The others winced, having not agreed on this answer before she spoke. There was a long moment of silence, then the massive cryptid bowed its head.

"Very good. You may pose your questions. But remember, if you ask more than three —"

"Yeah, yeah, you'll devour us," finished Bryan. "You ask me, what you need is a big bowl of Fancy Feast."

Q & A

Jacinda pulled Trish back into the huddle. "It's a good thing you got that right," she said reproachfully. "From now on, we reach a consensus before saying anything."

Trish blushed. "Sorry. I got carried away."

Jacinda faced the others. "Okay, this is our one shot at an all-knowing ORACLE. Maybe we should write down our questions first."

For the next few minutes, they scribbled suggestions on a sheet of notebook paper. The Sphinx waited patiently behind them, its tail silently swishing back and forth. Once, it licked

CRYPTID CORNER

Actually, there are a few other ORACLE creatures still in existence. But all of them are at least as dangerous and difficult to locate as the Sphinx.

its front paw to wash a speck of invisible dust from its magnificent dark mane. Eventually, after much heated debate and crossing out then circling of ideas, the teenagers were able to agree upon three questions.

"Okay," said Jacinda, stepping forward to face the Sphinx. It blinked its golden eyes expectantly. "Ready?"

"I am."

Jacinda made sure she had the right sentence, then enunciated clearly: "Question one. Where are the Euclideans keeping the captured cryptids?"

The Sphinx closed its amber eyes, a purr rumbling deep inside its chest. Then it opened them again. *"Those whom you wish to find are scattered over the surface of the world."*

"Fantastic," said Owen sarcastically. "That doesn't help at all."

"It was too broad a question," said Jacinda, crossing out and underlining suggested phrases. "Clearly she's picky about word choice." When the others agreed to Jacinda's new selections, she looked up again.

"Okay, question two. Where exactly are the Euclideans holding the largest number of captured cryptids and . . . how do we find that place?"

Technically, it was two questions in one, but the Sphinx seemed to let it slide. Again, the cryptid looked inward before answering. *"Deep within an enchanted fortress, alone upon a sandy isle, surrounded by a vast blue sea, reside the creatures you seek. They cannot be located by magic or maps, but only through your failure."*

"Well, that's disconcerting," Perry said.

"And unhelpful," agreed Owen. "We need GPS coordinates," he enunciated loudly to the Sphinx. But the great cryptid merely blinked her golden eyes.

"I think Cat Lady never answers a straight question," Bryan commented from the side of his mouth.

"It's okay, we still have one more turn," Trish said. "Let's approach this from a different direction." She leaned forward, pointing to a query farther down the list. Jacinda shook her head, but Trish tapped the paper forcefully. The others shrugged in agreement.

"Okay, question three," the team leader said resignedly. "What are the names and current locations of the Euclideans we can trust?"

The response was so immediate, the Sphinx did not even have to close its eyes. *That is a fourth question. Per our accord, you must now be devoured.*

Jacinda stepped back, while Perry and Trish began casting defensive spells. "Whoa, whoa, whoa," said Owen. "What do you mean, a fourth question? She read them, that was clearly three."

You forget the question she posed first. The human child asked if I was ready. I replied that I was. Now, with my regrets, she must die.

And before any of them could respond, the Sphinx bared its fangs and leapt at Jacinda.

DEATH IN EGYPT

Gone was the elegant human bearing the cryptid had held throughout their interaction. As it fell upon Jacinda, cruelly raking the team leader's leather jacket with its black claws and tearing through layers of protective enchantments as if they were no more than tissue paper, the Sphinx revealed what it truly was: a wild animal.

Perry conjured a shield and flung it between Jacinda and the creature, but the Sphinx batted both her and her spell aside like cat toys. Trish heard herself shouting as she blasted the creature with a gout of purple flames. Sneezing on it would have done more damage. The cryptid spun, its tail whipping around and striking Trish in the stomach.

It was like being hit with a thick cordon of rope. Trish went sprawling across the floor of the temple, the wind knocked clean out of her. Wheezing, she raised her head to see the Sphinx clamp its jaws on to Jacinda's skull. It shook her, and the last protective enchantments on the team leader shimmered and broke apart as if they were made of water.

Owen and Bryan stepped forward to cast attack SPELLS, but the Sphinx shrugged them off like gnats. It backhanded

---

CRYPTID CORNER

One of the dangers of magical creatures is that some of them are resistant to SPELLS. The unicorn, Sphinx, and bunyip all share this ability, and it makes capturing them even more difficult.

Owen into a statue, shattering his stone amulet and knocking him unconscious. Then it turned to Bryan. Trish staggered to her feet, her chest still wrapped in bands of pain as she tried to get air back into her lungs. Sound echoed in her ears as if everything were five miles distant. The Sphinx was speaking to Bryan, something about learning respect, but she could no longer understand the Egyptian words clearly.

The creature bared its fangs, preparing to take off Bryan's head in one bite, when a burst of gunfire cracked through the temple air. The Sphinx roared in pain, stepping away from Bryan and looking toward the new threat. Five Egyptian policemen stood on the rotunda balcony, automatic rifles trained on the animal. Their eyes were wide with surprise and terror.

"Wait," Trish croaked, but her voice wasn't strong enough to carry much beyond her own ears. She began casting a shield spell, but her fingers were too clumsy to complete it.

The Sphinx reared back on its hind legs and spread its wings in challenge. Even with Jacinda's blood dripping from its muzzle, it was a magnificent sight. Powerful, magical, and deadly—a perfect representation of the world's mythic creatures. For a moment, at least. Then the cryptid flew toward its new attackers.

Terrified, the five men opened fire. BULLETS thumped into the soaring creature, spraying feathers and fur. Its golden eyes went wide with fear. The Sphinx gave a wounded, surprised mew, and it fell from the air like a stone statue. It struck the floor of the temple, cracking the painted tile beneath it. There

CRYPTID CORNER

Since iron is a powerful antidote to magic, **BULLETS** are especially effective at wounding cryptids. Especially cryptids whose defensive magic developed long before the invention of modern weapons.

the great creature lay, whimpering like a wounded house cat, brought down by a few small lumps of lead.

The policemen came barreling down the stairs, pointing their guns and yelling in Arabic. They were a variety of ages, but each was clearly scared. Only Bryan was still in any state to properly respond. He made a few elegant motions with his arms, clapped his hands over his head, then rolled into the temple pool and disappeared.

Trish crawled over to Jacinda, gently taking her hand. The team leader's face was a bloody ruin of teeth marks. She struggled to breathe, blood oozing from an open gash in her cheek. "Don't . . . let them . . . kill it . . ." she whispered as the policemen surrounded them.

Trish's vision was suddenly blurred by tears. She wanted to touch Jacinda's face, to assure her everything would be okay, but there was no part of her head that seemed intact. Instead she squeezed Jacinda's hand, then raised her other arm in surrender. One of the policemen, a twentysomething beanpole with a wisp of a mustache, roughly grabbed her wrists and handcuffed them behind her back. She was too numb to resist him.

Perry and Owen were handcuffed as well, though the two of them were barely conscious. Behind her, Trish saw an overweight policeman approach the Sphinx with his automatic rifle. She could hear the cryptid's labored breathing. Its blood was a dark stain on the sandy floor. Once the policeman was within striking distance, the Sphinx raised its magnificent head. It hissed at the man, showing its sharp, glistening fangs—

And a final gunshot shattered the stillness of the underground temple. The Sphinx fell back and went still, the golden light fading from its all-seeing eyes.

CHAPTER 14

DETENTION

The room was eerie in its lack of features. Four white walls surrounded a metal bench, a wood table, and metal chairs bolted into the floor. Harsh fluorescent lights buzzed in the ceiling. There was no two-way mirror such as Trish had seen in the interrogation rooms on TV shows, but there was a camera affixed to one corner of the ceiling. There were no clocks, no windows, no way of telling where or when they were.

Perry and Owen huddled together on one of the benches. They had returned to lucidity in the police car, and the three of them had agreed not to cast any spells until they knew where Jacinda had been taken. Trish had watched in gut-churning anxiety as their mauled team leader was loaded into an Egyptian ambulance and driven off to the north. She had pleaded to go with her, but was ignored. She had considered forcing the issue with magic, but worried that interfering with Jacinda's medical treatment might make things worse than they already were. If only she had bothered to learn a few healing spells! But such enchantments were reserved for more advanced sorcerers, and Trish hadn't forced the issue with Jacinda or Whitmore. She bitterly regretted that now.

With no other options, she had allowed herself to be escorted to the small police station in Abu Simbel and be locked in this featureless detention room. The handcuffs had been removed, but until they knew where Jacinda had been taken, she didn't see any point in trying to escape. A policeman had brought them food some time ago—stale pita bread and some kind of grayish paste—but she wasn't hungry. It seemed as if days had passed since their incarceration, but perhaps it was only hours. All Trish knew for certain was that it had been early evening when Jacinda was taken away. Perry and Owen tried to sleep, but every time Trish felt herself dozing off, anxiety about Jacinda jolted her back to wakefulness.

Rather than rest, she paced. Back and forth, like a tiger in a cage, from one blank white wall to the other. Her formerly broken leg ached, but she kept walking. No matter how much she moved, however, she couldn't escape her thoughts. Everything that had happened—the loss of their supplies, Jacinda's injuries, the death of the world's oldest cryptid—it was all her fault. She had told Jacinda they could handle the Sphinx. She had opened the door to the temple, which had caught the attention of the local police and allowed them to enter the Sphinx's lair. Who knows what they had done with poor Varmint. Hopefully he would keep his mouth shut so they wouldn't stick him in an Egyptian circus. Or worse, eat him.

Then there was the matter of Bryan. Trish had no idea where the former bully had gone. Perhaps he'd finally made good on his threats to abandon them. The idea wouldn't surprise her; he'd been talking about ditching them since Wyoming. In frustration, she kicked one of the metal chairs.

The sound startled Perry and Owen awake. "Sorry," Trish said.

"It's okay," Owen yawned. "I thought someone would've come talk to us by now."

Trish sat, jiggling her foot anxiously. "Everything is so messed up. We were supposed to be helping, but everything we did made things worse. The unicorn's captured, the Sphinx is dead, and Jacinda . . . Jacinda is . . ." Tears welled in her eyes before she could finish. Angrily, she brushed them aside. "And it's all because of me."

Perry walked over, wrapping her small arms around Trish's waist. "That is a patent falsehood. None of us could know these events would transpire as they did."

"Yeah," said Owen, also standing to place an arm around his friend. "Most of the bad things that happened were because of Euclideans. Or crappy timing."

"But we could be finding and helping her, and instead we waited. We waited and now we're stuck here. And we don't know where she is." Trish curled her fingers into fists, wanting to pound the table into a tiny metal ball. "We don't even know if she's . . . if she's still . . ." But she felt too miserable to finish. More tears filled her eyes, but she didn't bother to wipe them away this time.

Owen took a step back and inspected her. "What's going on with you guys? No offense, but I didn't even see you cry when you got hit by that car. Did you have a fight?"

Trish shook her head. "It doesn't matter."

"Of course it matters," said Perry matter-of-factly. "You're our best friend. What affects you affects us."

"Yeah, dude, we know something's been bugging you," put in Owen. "We're not blind."

Trish shrugged off Perry's arm. "Yeah? Well, you might as well be since you've both become . . . whatever you two are."

Perry ignored the attack, gently taking Trish's hand in hers. "Try us."

Trish looked away, her cheeks burning with embarrassment. It was such a small thing, she knew that. She had faced down mercenaries and monsters without hesitation, yet saying a few words gave her pause. And yet . . . who knew what the future held? *What if we don't escape? What if I never see Jacinda again? If I don't tell 'em the truth now, I might never get the chance.* That was a pain she could no longer bear. If there was anyone in the world she trusted, it was Perry and Owen. *Time to take the plunge.*

She lifted her eyes from the floor and took a steadying breath. "I . . . like girls."

Her friends blinked. "And?" said Owen.

"I *like* like them," Trish clarified. "Ever since I was a little kid." It was such a relief to finally say it out loud. She might be in a prison cell, but for the first time in her life she felt truly free. "And . . . I like Jace especially."

Perry smiled. Trish snatched away her hand. *Here it comes*, she thought. *I took the leap, finally spilled the beans, and now they're gonna pull away. Just like Julie.* She steeled herself for the reaction—but then Perry wrapped her in a warm embrace.

"Finally," she said. "I've been wondering when you would unburden yourself."

"You knew?"

"It didn't take a Sherlock Holmes–level deduction," she replied lightly. "We've been friends for six years, after all. I'm proud of you."

"Yeah, well, I had no idea," said Owen, but he too gave Trish a hug. "But it's awesome, dude. Congrats."

"But, I mean . . ." Trish was at a loss for words. "You guys don't care?"

"Why should we?" said Perry. "It doesn't change our friendship by any metric whatsoever."

"Or what we think about you," added Owen. "Actually, I might respect you even more. It's brave."

"I mean, I don't know about brave," said Trish, now blushing with pride. "I'm not, like, a crusader or anything."

"Admitting the truth is always brave," insisted Perry. "Especially when it's hard. But why did you wait so long to tell us?"

Trish kicked at the concrete floor with her sneaker. This part was harder to admit than everything else she'd said so far. "I had a . . . bad experience a few weeks back. I tried to tell Julie about . . . who I am. I showed her, actually. Ugh." Quickly, she told them what had transpired, and how she'd had similar feelings for Jacinda from the moment they met, and how she'd finally done something about it. "But now that we like each other, it's kinda scary too. Like . . ."

"Like you didn't know it was possible to feel so strongly about a person," said Perry, taking Owen by the hand and smiling up at him. "Like they fill in vectors your genome didn't know were missing." He furrowed his brow, but kissed the crown of her head.

"Something like that, yeah." Trish grinned. "Also, she's super hot."

"*Super* hot," agreed Owen.

The three of them laughed. Trish lapsed into appreciative silence. She'd been dreading this conversation for weeks, but now that they were having it, she felt relieved.

"So . . . ?" asked Owen with a grin. "How long's this been going on?"

Trish blushed again. "I mean, we're not like you guys or anything. We just kissed."

"You kissed?" Perry whacked her friend on the arm. "And when were you planning to convey this crucial information??"

"It only happened earlier today. Or yesterday, I guess." She grinned at the memory, but then an image of Jacinda's bloody, mutilated face flashed into her mind. Her anxiety came rushing back, hitting her with the force of a tidal wave. "What if she's not okay, you guys? What if she didn't . . . ?" But she couldn't bring herself to finish the sentence.

"She's tough," said Owen. "Maybe even tougher than you. Once we get some spell components, we'll cast a Spell of Location to find her, then have Whitmore or someone on the Council dial up one of those Level Seven **HEALING SPELLS**. She'll be good as new, you'll see."

Perry hugged Trish with one arm. The three of them sat on the bench, comforting each other in the harsh glare of the fluorescent lights. But soon enough, Trish stood.

"Enough of this waiting. Varmint's gotta be somewhere in this dump. I say we grab him and get out."

She was just about to start casting a Spell for Unlocking when the detention room's electronic door lock opened with a *clunk*. Owen and Perry sprang to their feet. All three teenagers readied defensive spells.

THE CODEX
ARCANUM

The efficacy of HEALING SPELLS is not determined by a sorcerer's level. Medical knowledge of the human body is far more important, as one wouldn't want to fuse internal organs together, reverse a patient's blood flow, or misplace a nose.

THE NEGOTIATOR

Eleanor Macready entered the room, wearing khaki fatigues and pulling a metal rolling suitcase behind her. She shut the door and turned to face the teenagers, her face tight with concern.

"Not a good idea," she said, nodding at their glowing hands, then gesturing to the camera in the corner. "Unless you want them to storm in here and start shooting."

Owen let his spell flicker out, and the other two followed suit. He folded his arms angrily. "What do you want, Euclidean?"

Owen's mother flinched slightly. She bent and lifted the rolling suitcase onto the table. "I don't think you kids realize how much trouble you're in. Four American minors, without valid passports or visas, caught trespassing in a previously undiscovered temple in the company of, for now, what the local authorities think is a deformed lion. 'International incident' is just the beginning. They think you might be spies."

"Where's Jacinda?" Trish demanded. "Is she still . . . is she okay?"

"She's alive," Eleanor replied. Trish and the others exhaled in relief. "But her condition is critical. She lost a lot of blood, and her face . . . If you truly want to help her, you all need to come with me. Now."

Perry and Trish looked to Owen. He scoffed. "We don't partner with liars."

Eleanor glanced at the camera and positioned herself so it couldn't see her face. "The Egyptian justice system doesn't work like it does in America. They can hold you for up to thirty days without charges while they investigate."

"Thirty days?" said Perry in shock. "What about our parents? The American government? Don't we have CERTAIN INALIENABLE RIGHTS?"

"Not in Egypt." Eleanor began to unzip the metal suitcase. "The only reason I'm here is because they think I'm with the American embassy. But if we don't leave soon, the actual embassy will get involved. And that will make things much more difficult."

"We're sorcerers," Trish reminded her. "We can magic our way out of here anytime we want."

Eleanor looked at them shrewdly. "If you planned to do that, you would have done it already. You were waiting to hear about your friend. And she, I'm sorry to say, was flown to Cairo last night after she was stabilized. Even if you were somehow able to hire a car, it's a twelve-hour drive. Plenty of time for the locals to hunt down three young American fugitives."

Anger bubbled inside Trish like tea in a boiling kettle. Once again, the Euclideans were three steps ahead of them. Owen's mom was right—without Jacinda or Whitmore, they didn't

---

ENCHANTING DETAILS

Perry's phrase "CERTAIN INALIENABLE RIGHTS" is a direct quote from Thomas Jefferson's Declaration of Independence, which defined these rights as life, liberty, and the pursuit of happiness, as well as declared that all men are created equal. Interesting viewpoints from a man who owned hundreds of slaves.

know how to portal out of the country. Part of her wanted to blast her way out of the police station and take their chances just to prove Owen's mom wrong. But there was Jacinda to consider. If they escaped, would the Euclideans take her hostage? Use her as a bargaining chip?

"Why'd they send you?" Owen asked. "Your bosses thought we wouldn't attack Mommy?"

Eleanor swallowed nervously, but her voice was steady. "You shouldn't be 'attacking' anyone, young man," she replied crisply. "The three of you, you're children, not soldiers. You should have never been allowed to run around the world wielding unchecked power like this. It's irresponsible, unsafe. Your actions—rash, illegal, and very unsupervised actions—led to the death of the world's oldest living cryptid."

"*They* killed the Sphinx!" Trish shouted. "We were trying to—"

"The Sphinx died because you entered the country illegally, parked where everyone could see you, and led the local authorities right to it. When we track down a cryptid, do you think we do so without the permission of the creature's homeland? Without informing them where we'll be? Without capture permits? We don't **BREAK LAWS**. Sorcerers do."

Her logic gave them pause. Still, Trish refused to believe that everything she'd seen the Euclideans do was in service of justice.

Eleanor took out a stack of forms and fanned them out on the table. "We made a deal with the Egyptians. In exchange for

BEWARE THE EUCLIDEANS

While it's technically true that using sorcery BREAKS LAWS, that's only because the current legislation in most countries was written by Euclidean sympathizers. Readers are highly encouraged to write to their representatives and demand more magic-friendly regulations.

a generous grant from the Euclidean Foundation, the charges against you three will be dropped and you'll be released into our custody. It's time for you to go home. All you have to do is sign."

Perry lifted one of the documents like it was radioactive. "What about the cryptids you've taken?"

"They'll be given the best care we can provide. You have my word."

Perry set the form back on the table. The three teenagers looked at one another, coming to a silent agreement.

"If Jace were here, I know what she'd say." Trish shook out her hands and began forming runes with her fingers. *"Fulgur venire!"*

Eleanor dove out of the way as a bolt of lightning sizzled from Trish's hand. It struck the door lock, short-circuiting the electronics inside. Trish pulled the door wide—

And saw the hallway was filled with at least a dozen armed Euclideans. At the head of them was the gray-bearded sorcerer she'd seen in Germany. There was a moment of stillness, then the soldiers all began shouting for the teenagers to surrender and get down on the floor. Trish closed the door again, holding it shut with her back.

"Shields!" she cried to the others.

Owen and Perry stepped forward, fingers working in unison. They stretched their arms out just as the door burst open, knocking Trish sideways. Eight or nine tranquilizer darts thumped off the glowing purple discs that appeared between the teenagers' hands. As they clattered to the linoleum floor, Trish got to her feet and formed the runes for the Spell to Conjure Ice. *If I can barricade the doorway*, she thought, *then maybe we can escape through the ceiling or back wall. There'll still be the issue of finding a car and driving it to Cairo without money, passports, or knowing how to drive, but one problem at a time.*

She was about to call out the activation word when the room burst into flames. The walls, the furniture, even her friends—everything was covered in fire. Trish was momentarily paralyzed. Should she cast the ice spell and save her friends? Or conjure a cyclone to suck the oxygen from the room? The heat coming off the walls made it difficult to breathe, much less think.

"What's wrong?" Owen shouted to her, somehow managing to conjure a shield despite his whole body being aflame. "Why are you just standing there?"

Before she could ask why he wasn't more concerned with his own predicament, another volley of tranquilizer darts flew through the mist. Two struck her in the arm and stomach. Through the smoky haze, she saw Perry had been hit as well. The small girl cast a thunderclap spell as she dropped to the floor.

The booming sound rocked the hallway, knocking their attackers to the ground. This included the bearded sorcerer.

He hit the linoleum hard, and the raging fire surrounding Trish abruptly vanished. Everything that had been consumed by flames only seconds before was now pristine and unburned, including her friends.

The fire was a glamour, she realized, anger beginning to rise inside her. *That bearded backstabber cast a* glamour *on me.* Her hands began to re-form the runes for the ice spell—

But more tranquilizer darts shot into the room. Owen took three in the belly and fell soon after. Body-armored soldiers got to their feet and ran at Trish, their gloved hands scrabbling for her.

She forgot about casting spells and fought back the old-fashioned way: with hands and feet and elbows and teeth. One soldier she pulled to the ground. Another she bit on the forearm. Two more flares of pain spiked in her stomach, but she ignored them and barreled toward the bearded sorcerer. *He's the real threat. Once you get past him, you can find a way to Cairo. Find Jacinda. Make sure she's still—*

WHAM! The butt of a rifle slammed into her skull, sending her sideways. Once she was down, getting up proved to be impossible. The tranquilizers combined with the pain in her head made the act of standing akin to climbing a slick, feature-less wall. Her body went slack and her eyes fluttered closed. Her last thought before she slipped into darkness was of Jacinda's ruined, bloody face, her gray eyes glassy and vacant.

CHAPTER 15

RUDE AWAKENING

A metal *thunk* jolted Trish awake. Propellers roared somewhere nearby, which made sense since she was strapped to a seat inside a cargo plane. She lifted her head to take in her surroundings and immediately regretted it. Pain flared like a burning spike in the part of her skull where she'd been struck with the rifle stock. Unlike the head wound she'd received in the Black Forest, this injury had not been healed by magic. Her body was sore too, no doubt due to the Euclidean tranquilizers coursing through her veins.

Trish went to touch the lump on her head, only to discover her hands were encased in a locked metal box. It was roughly the size of a shoebox, made of reinforced steel and chained to a hasp imbedded in the floor. She attempted to move her fingers, but they were surrounded on all sides by immovable metal molds.

Trish had seen such a box only once before, and it had been on the hands of a sorcerer who'd been imprisoned by Euclideans.

So she was a prisoner, then. She turned her head—gingerly this time—to take in the rest of her surroundings. The cargo plane had a line of seats on each side of the hull, with an open space in the middle for storage. Owen and Perry were on the other side of the plane, their hands also encased in metal boxes that were chained to the floor. Both of them were asleep or unconscious. There were no other people in her line of sight. There were a few windows, however, which allowed her a view of the puffy sunlit clouds outside. Since they were flying at least ten thousand meters up, she couldn't tell where in the world they might be.

She turned her eyes to the plane's cargo. Wooden boxes, live animal crates, and even a military-grade Humvee were strapped down in the center of the plane. The floor, she saw, was studded with bolts and clasps so equipment, walls, and seats could be attached as needed. Within the animal crates, she spied a red-and-gold-scaled quetzalcoatl the size of a Great Dane, the unicorn they'd lost in Germany, and a strange serpent with the paws and head of a cat that she recognized as a TATZELWURM. All of them looked like they were being taken to the scariest veterinarian in the world. But worst of all, in a plastic crate about halfway back, she saw Varmint. A leather muzzle had been strapped over his mouth, and no amount of pawing and shaking could get it loose.

TATZELWURM

GERMANY

FRANCE

SWITZERLAND

ITALY

**HABITAT:
BAVARIAN,
SWISS &
ITALIAN ALPS**

THE SLITHERING SURPRISE

(Also Known As:
STOLLENWURM)

WEIGHT:
12 - 15 kg

LENGTH:
100 - 125 cm

HEIGHT:
50 cm

MAGICAL PROPERTIES:

venomous breath,
claws can cut through any substance

A **solitary** cryptid, the tatzelwurm lives in the **forested alpine slopes** of **Europe**. Like many lizards, it will **only attack** as a last resort. It prefers to use a high-pitched **whistling yowl** to **scare off** predators. The wurm has **two powerful forelegs** with which it can **dig burrows** and scale sheer rock faces.

One whiff of its **venomous breath** can **kill an adult human**, which gives a new meaning to the phrase "dragon breath."

DID YOU KNOW?

Because of its deadly breath, the tatzelwurm **convinced** many esteemed **scientists** that it was in fact a **dragon**.

But as we all know, **dragons do not exist.**

"Varmint!" she whisper-called, then followed it up with a whistle. "Over here, boy."

The cryptid turned at her voice and his eyes widened in recognition. "Hmmmee ddrrry!" he called.

"Stay calm," she told him. "I'll find a way to get us out of this."

"Hard to do that with your hands locked up," came a sarcastic but familiar voice directly to her right. Trish swung the hand-box defensively, but there was no one there. The voice had come out of thin air. Once her heartbeat went back down, she thought she knew why.

"Bryan?" she whispered.

"Correctamundo, Big T. You have no idea what a hassle it's been to keep my head WET for the last twenty hours. I had to stick my head in the police station drinking fountain at one point."

"So you've been with us since the temple?" Trish was unable to keep the surprise from her voice.

"Geez, don't act so shocked. I know we're not besties, but that doesn't mean I wanna see my fellow sorcerers kidnapped and tortured."

"You coulda fooled me," she replied testily.

THE CODEX
ARCANUM

Since the Spell for Invisibility uses liquid water as one of its main components, it only lasts as long as the caster stays WET. Once it evaporates, the effects of the spell are negated.

"Look. I . . ." He sighed, and his disembodied voice shifted to her other side. "These last few weeks have been super weird for me. My dad, he . . ." There was a metal *bong* as he kicked the hull of the plane. "He thought everyone was an enemy. Everybody always out to get him. And he beat that into me. Every day, for fourteen years, over and over and over. One time he gave me this dog, a really sweet pit bull. Man, I loved that thing. Then one day, after three months of me feeding it and walking it and caring for it, he made me give it to the pound. All to toughen me up, he said." *Holy crap.* Trish didn't need to see Bryan to visualize his bitter expression. "But now, with you guys . . . I can see it doesn't have to be that way, okay? That there are people you can actually trust. And I'm trying . . . I'm trying to learn to do that. So maybe you could do the same, huh?"

Trish blushed guiltily. She'd spent so much time thinking of Bryan as a bully, she had never stopped to consider him as a human being. "I will," she said, trying to meet his invisible eyes. "So you got a plan to get us outta here?"

His voice shifted as he moved back and forth across the cargo area. "I've been trying, but I couldn't get into the detention room without making a big scene. Then the Euclideans showed up and you guys got tranq'd. I managed to follow you on the plane, but I've been sitting here twiddling my thumbs for the last six hours while you all sawed logs. Last thing I had to eat was some weird Egyptian crackers in the police station."

"I know guys think with their stomachs, but try to focus. Where are we?"

"East of Egypt, way out over the Indian Ocean. I think the Euclideans are taking us to their 'hidden island base in the middle of the sea.'" His disembodied voice came back toward her. "Looks like Cat Lady called it."

Moving as gingerly as she could, Trish craned her head to look out the nearest window. Blue water sparkled far below the plane. "So why don't we blow the door and fly out?"

"The plane's pressurized, genius. We punch a hole in it and all these cryptids will get sucked outside. I say we sit tight until we land."

"Screw that. Get this box off my hands and we can—"

But before she could finish the sentence, a door to the front cabin opened, revealing a much nicer seating area about six rows long. It was filled with Euclideans in comfortable chairs. They were talking and laughing and sharing phone pictures of cryptids with one another. Trish clenched her teeth in anger at the sight of them. She found herself straining against the metal box, fingers striving to cast a spell, but it was like her hands had been encased in concrete. Then Owen's mom stepped through and pulled the door shut.

Meeting With The Enemy

"Stay chill. I've got your back," Bryan whispered in her right ear. His breath was not the freshest after nearly two days without a toothbrush, but she appreciated the sentiment.

Eleanor Macready cracked a gel-filled ice pack and sat in the seat beside Trish. "May I?" she said, holding out the ice pack to Trish's head.

As much as she wanted to pummel the older woman, Trish's skull was throbbing with pain. She nodded, and Eleanor pressed the ice pack to the lump on the teenager's head.

"I'm sorry things ended up this way," she said, looking and sounding truly apologetic. "I was hoping you kids would be allowed to go home. But after your . . . reaction in the police station, my superiors want you kept someplace more secure."

"You mean a prison," Trish said.

"A research facility," Eleanor corrected her. "Someplace we can help you learn to regulate your abilities without hurting others. And you can help us in return."

Trish scoffed. "I gotta hand it to you, lady. Imprisoning your own son to study him in a lab is like, fairy-tale-level evil."

Eleanor looked guiltily over to where Owen and Perry slept. "I know he won't understand what we're trying to do, but maybe you can. I can tell you're . . . practical."

Trish pulled her head away, even though it caused the spike in her skull to start burning again. "The only thing I'm practical about is how long it will take me to mow through your security team once I get this box off my hands."

Eleanor sighed. "I can't force you to believe us, Trisha, but I would ask that you keep an open mind. We're actually after the same things. We both want to preserve these creatures." The plane banked steeply, making Owen's mom brace herself against the wall. Trish's ears popped. She looked out the nearby window to see they were descending to a small green island surrounded by bright-blue water. The island held an airstrip and a large gray building complex, but otherwise appeared UNINHABITED. Spell diagrams glowed on the compound's rooftops. Trish couldn't read them from afar, but she was fairly sure they were SPELLS OF CONCEALMENT. No wonder Whitmore hadn't been able to find the Euclidean base.

Eleanor stood. "We'll be landing in a few minutes. Please, try to keep Owen and Perry calm when they wake up. There are plenty of people on this plane who would be more than happy to sedate you again." She reached into her pocket and held out two red pills.

ENCHANTING
DETAILS

There are dozens of islands around the world that, for one reason or another, are UNINHABITED. But just because a place has no people doesn't mean it is unclaimed. In fact, there are only two landmasses on the entire planet that are not owned by anyone—Marie Byrd Land in Antarctica and the Bir Tawil Triangle in Africa. Both are bleak, featureless deserts, and neither is much worth a visit.

THE CODEX
ARCANUM

SPELLS OF CONCEALMENT, unlike invisibility, work by convincing whoever draws near them that they are urgently needed elsewhere. They also cloak magical energy and stymie Spells of Location.

Trish narrowed her eyes suspiciously. "What are those, sleeping pills? Truth serum? Some kind of nano-controller that lets you take over my body?"

"Ibuprofen," said Eleanor. "For your headache."

Trish desperately wanted to take it, but knew she couldn't swallow a drop of water from the Euclideans even if she was dying of thirst. She faced her eyes forward. "I'm fine."

Eleanor pocketed the pills. She seemed about to say something more, but then turned and went back to the seating area.

EUCLIDEAN HOSPITALITY

The landing woke Perry and Owen. By the time the cargo plane taxied to a stop, an invisible-but-still-smelly Bryan had convinced all of them to wait for his signal until they tried to escape.

"Hopefully they'll take these boxes off your hands at some point," his disembodied voice whispered. "Otherwise this'll be a whole lot harder for our hero."

"You think *you're* the hero?" Owen was indignant. "I'm the one who found the spell book. None of you would be here without—"

"Shhh!" whispered Perry. "We can debate asinine topics at a later time."

"Seriously, boys, get over yourselves," Trish said. "*I'm* clearly the hero here."

The back of the cargo plane opened, letting in a blast of heat and the smell of salt air. Trish squinted in the bright sunlight.

Beyond the airstrip she could see a four-story concrete facility towering above the island's lush jungle greenery. The building was surrounded by two layers of barbed-wire fences with security cameras every ten meters.

"Yeah, that doesn't look anything like a prison," she said sarcastically.

Six armed Euclideans entered the cargo plane. They unlocked the crate holding the unicorn, tugging it out by the ensorcelled silver chains. The noble animal bucked, the restraints burning its red flank as if they were white hot. The unicorn whinnied in distress and the teenagers shouted for them to stop, but none of their efforts could prevent the unicorn from being escorted from the plane.

Several minutes later the guards returned. Three unchained the teenagers' metal boxes from the floor of the plane, while the others kept their weapons pointed at their heads. They were led off the plane at gunpoint. Glancing around, Trish saw the rest of the compound was set up like a makeshift military base—rows of sleeping tents, Quonset huts filled with high-tech equipment, soldiers running training drills. The unicorn, she saw, was being inspected by several excited scientists.

The gates to the facility opened, and each Euclidean had his or her wrist scanned as they entered. The teenagers were taken over a large stone slab carved with a diagram Trish recognized as a removal ward. A few of their clothing items shimmered briefly, returning to their non-enchanted states. Trish hoped Bryan would have the sense to find a way around it.

The sorcerers were escorted into the main building, led down a series of featureless gray hallways, and eventually deposited in a surprisingly ordinary conference room. A wall of windows overlooked the tropical jungle, and a basket of pastries had been left on the table. The guards put out three bottles of something called protein water (with straws, since the teenagers had no way of picking them up with their boxed hands) then left them alone in the room.

"Nice of my mom to make sure I'm okay after her coworkers shot me full of tranquilizers," Owen said bitterly.

"Technically, she accomplished that when she spoke to Trish," Perry said, then quickly changed her tone when she saw Owen's dark expression. "But yes, incredibly rude."

"Dude, I really don't think she knows what's going on here," offered Trish. "She's like a file clerk at the CIA."

Owen slammed the metal box encasing his hands into the polished wooden conference table. "That doesn't make her not guilty. Anyone with eyes can see these guys are a-holes."

"Perhaps she joined us to protect you," said a familiar, accented voice. Samson Kiraz strode into the conference room carrying a tablet computer. The patchwork skin on the left side of his face looked waxy under the fluorescent lights. His glowing blue bionic eye had been replaced, and swiveled to scan each of the teenagers in turn. Two guards shut the door of the conference room, standing at attention on either side. One was a muscled middle-aged man with a thick beard while the other was a broad-shouldered woman even taller than Trish.

Kiraz set down the tablet and smiled at them in the way a jackal smiles at a plump meerkat. "We have been greatly worried for your safety, children. Ever since we heard Whitmore sent you across the world, literally into the jaws of death." He clucked his tongue in what seemed to be legitimate concern. "As tragic as the Sphinx's demise was, you are lucky to have escaped with minimal injuries."

"Minimal?" said Trish, unable to contain her anger. "Jacinda's in critical condition. Your guys cracked my skull. All of us have been kidnapped."

"Kidnapped?" Kiraz managed to look offended. "Our goal is to protect you. From your terrorist mentor, and from yourselves."

"We've been doing just fine without you, Eyeball." Owen attempted to casually lean back, but the heavy metal box on his hands got in the way.

The Euclidean smiled thinly. "I'll admit, you have shown remarkable resourcefulness for three so inexperienced. But each time you cast a spell, you risk injury and death to all around you."

The teenagers bristled. "That's hypocritical, coming from an organization populated with armed mercenaries," replied Perry, glaring at the two Euclideans by the door. The female guard blew her a kiss.

"With such abilities at your fingertips, how else are we to protect ourselves? Euphemia Whitmore and her Council Arcanum began this 'arms race' by granting weapons of mass destruction to unlicensed, unsupervised children."

"She's always made sure we were safe," said Trish dismissively.

"You call being struck by an automobile safe? Being attacked by wild animals? Sent into danger without a legal guardian?" Kiraz clucked his tongue again, making Trish want to yank it out of his mouth and smack him with it. "You might have been killed, Trisha. Any of you might have been. And for a woman you barely know."

THE WISDOM OF WHITMORE

He flipped open the tablet computer and double-tapped a file folder. With a swipe of his hand, the file's contents were sent to a large widescreen television mounted on the wall. Pictures of Euphemia Whitmore filled the screen—blurry security camera footage, screen grabs from newspaper articles with the word *terrorist* in the headlines, and mug shots of a much younger Whitmore, her hair chestnut-brown instead of snowy white.

"This 'librarian' has been distributing spell books to minors for decades. Do you know how many of them have been injured in the process? How much destruction has been caused by her hands-off approach to instruction? How many lives she has ruined?" He flipped through more photos, showing burned-out buildings, traffic accidents, and schools with large holes in them. "Just three months ago, one of her illegal operations resulted in the deaths of several adults and a Peruvian child."

THE CODEX ARCANUM

If you'd like to know more, SELESTINO'S tragic story is recounted in *Seeking the Salamander: A Codex Arcanum Case Study.*

A picture of a smiling brown-skinned boy with round cheeks and dark curly hair appeared on-screen. The word *DECEASED* was emblazoned across his face in red text. His name, Trish saw, was **SELESTINO ESCORZA**. *He must be the sorcerer who died during Jacinda's salamander mission*, she realized.

The teenagers looked at one another uncomfortably. They'd certainly created their own share of destruction while on assignment for the Codex Arcanum. But surely Whitmore wasn't allowing these things to happen because she was evil. Was she?

"It's not her fault that only minors can learn sorcery," said Perry defensively. "She told us herself she wishes it were otherwise."

"And yet she continues to teach her dark, dangerous art to any child who will listen, rather than set up a system of oversight in which only the brightest, the most responsible, are granted access to the secrets of the universe."

Trish snorted. "In other words, you want to control sorcery. Again."

Kiraz spread his hands amiably. "Isn't that what humans do? Make sense of the natural world? Bring order to chaos?" He indicated the photos of destruction. "Whitmore and her ilk kept magic a secret for centuries. They didn't trust people. They certainly don't trust you. Doling out books one at a time, when she possesses a whole library of knowledge."

"That's for our safety," said Owen. "The books are enchanted so we can't see advanced spells without proving we can handle them first."

"Is that why, or is she keeping the information for herself?" He flipped through more pictures on the table, showing scans of spell pages, books, and runes carved into stone. "We have evidence of over a thousand ENCHANTMENTS, far more than the 144 contained in your *Sorcery for Beginners*. Why do you think that is?"

Again, the teenagers shifted uncomfortably. Kiraz answered his own question: "It is because she has not, nor has she ever, told you the full truth. Have you ever considered that Whitmore recruits children not because of their nascent neural architecture, but because they are easier to manipulate?"

This had occurred to them, but Trish refused to admit that to a Euclidean. "Cut to the chase already, dude. You brought us all the way to your Dr. Evil island base, you Photoshopped a bunch of suspicious pictures, so you're obviously trying to sell us on something. Spit it out or stick us in a cell."

BEWARE THE
EUCLIDEANS

The Euclideans are unaware there are over 10,000 unique spells on this planet alone. Spell casting, like language, adapts to fit the times, so many older ENCHANTMENTS have fallen into disuse. Examples include the Spell to Replenish Lamp Oil and the Spell to Improve the Comfort of Saddles.

Kiraz frowned, erasing the pictures from the television screen with a flick of his hand. "Another issue that comes with your mentor's loose teaching methods is the lack of respect it engenders." He shook his head and sighed in a dramatic fashion. "But you're right, there is another reason we brought you here. You are going to help us capture Euphemia Whitmore."

THE GRAND TOUR

As this was the last thing the teenagers were expecting, it took them a moment to recover. When they did, Trish gave a dry laugh. "Not a chance, One Eye. Now take us to whatever torture you've got planned."

Kiraz pursed his lips. "You consistently mistake our intentions. Whitmore is a danger to everyone. Unregulated, unscrupulous, outside the laws of any country. She needs to be brought to heel. Help us do so, and we will share all the knowledge we have, not just that which she deems appropriate for your consumption."

He tapped the tablet computer again, opening a folder of scanned parchment pages and sending them to the television. He flipped through them one by one. The pages were covered in handwritten runes and were in various states of decay, but the look of them was familiar enough: they were spells.

"A thousand enchantments at your fingertips," said Kiraz. "More magic than perhaps even the Codex Arcanum holds. And not just spells, but magical places, artifacts, and creatures as well. All yours to discover, once you join us."

There was a long moment of silence. "Fabrications and falsehoods," Perry finally said defiantly. "That's what you're offering. We've actually walked the aisles of the Codex Arcanum. We've seen what sorcery can do. And 'eye' choose to fight for the side of magic."

"'Eye' see what you did there." Owen pushed away the fancy protein water with his box-covered hands. "And 'eye' agree."

"I guess the 'eyes' have it," said Trish. Then she loudly whispered to her friends, "We're making fun of his robot eyeball, right?"

Kiraz pursed his bloodless lips. "Understand this: we will capture Whitmore, with or without your assistance. In fact, she's very nearly in our grasp. But you wish for more motivation? Very well."

He nodded to the guards, who stepped forward and used their tranquilizer guns to indicate the teenagers should stand. They had little choice but to obey. Kiraz snapped his tablet closed and led the way out of the conference room. He took them to a heavy security door, which opened with a scan of his wrist and revealed a featureless gray hallway. Locked doors lined either side, showing a variety of despondent prisoners behind small viewing windows. One room held the entire European team of teenage sorcerers, though Council member Augustus Stromberg was not among them. Another held an eight-foot-tall hairy creature Trish recognized as a SASQUATCH. The crown of his massive head was bald, and he played a mournful tune on a harmonica. If he had been wear-

CRYPTID CORNER

While there were once several packs of SASQUATCH in the Pacific Northwest, human deforestation has reduced the population to less than five.

ing a pair of overalls, Trish would have mistaken him for a kind old mountain hippie.

A third cell held the bearded sorcerer they had encountered in the Egyptian police station and in the helicopter above the Black Forest. Trish assumed he was also responsible for the enchantments that concealed the Euclidean base from the outside world. His metal walls were covered in thousands of scrawled runes. He stood on his bed, scratching more symbols into one of the few remaining blank spots. As the teenagers passed, the sorcerer turned to stare at them. His wild, unblinking eyes followed them hungrily.

They continued on. Each new cell made Trish hope and fear that she would see Jacinda inside. She didn't want her to be captured, but she also wanted to know she was okay. But there was no sign of her. Hopefully their team leader was still safe in her Cairo hospital.

Finally they reached the end of the hallway. Kiraz punched a code into an elevator panel and held his wrist to another scanner.

There was a confirmation beep and the doors opened. He gestured for them to enter.

Trish hesitated, but she felt Bryan's hand on her shoulder and heard his voice in her ear. "Do it. I got your back."

"What was that?" asked the female guard, turning to glare down at her.

"I said, I'll take the back," Trish replied quickly. Bryan squeezed her shoulder and she stepped into the rear of the elevator. Owen and Perry followed. She could feel Bryan pressing in beside her. She was glad he'd found a way past the magic-removal wards, but it was difficult to resist elbowing him for more room.

They ascended to the top level. The doors opened to reveal Owen's mother. She did a double-take upon seeing her son, but maintained her composure.

"Mr. Kiraz. I, uh, didn't realize our meeting included our new arrivals. Have you all had breakfast?" she asked the teenagers, as if they had come to the secret island base for a sleepover.

Owen scowled. "Like we'd eat any of the poison you psychos try to give us. But thanks for the super comfy sleeping arrangements, Mom. I haven't brushed my teeth or showered in nearly two days now."

Eleanor shifted uncomfortably as they exited the elevator. "I'm sure we can see about getting you fresh clothes and showers. Perhaps after we're finished, sir?"

Kiraz ignored her, leading them into the center of the facility. Unlike the bland hallways and nondescript rooms Trish had seen so far, the top level resembled a Silicon Valley computer company. There were floor-to-ceiling windows and top-of-the-line workstations. Shiny chrome coated every surface. Trish estimated there were around one hundred Euclideans in this one room alone, all scouring the world for traces of sorcery. Whitmore was right about one thing—the members of the Codex Arcanum were greatly outnumbered.

Kiraz led them past the workstations to a security door. He again held up his wrist to an electronic scanner. "Subcutaneous microchips," Owen's mom explained, evidently deciding her role was to function as a tour guide. "Every Euclidean has one, tracking their vitals, location, and security clearance."

"Too bad they don't come with a morality meter," Trish said sarcastically.

Once all the Euclideans were scanned, the security door opened to reveal a massive high-tech laboratory. It was cordoned off into glass-walled examination rooms that contained all manner of cutting-edge medical equipment—electron microscopes, ultrasound scanners, centrifuges, and robot-operated surgical arms. The back wall of the building looked out onto a pristine beach ringed by palm trees. But what caught Trish's attention were the cryptids. There were around twenty of them, which she recognized thanks to *Cryptozoology for Beginners*.

The tatzelwurm she'd seen on the plane was being prodded by several Euclideans in lab coats. Its powerful front claws had been covered in foam gloves, and some kind of muzzle had been fitted over its mouth to prevent it from spewing poison gas. The poor creature swung its reptilian head this way and that, but to no avail.

In another examination room, a great winged KONGAMATO was chained to a table. Its massive bat-like wings kept it airborne, and its huge beak snapped at anyone who came too close. The Euclideans were tossing larger and larger objects at it. Each time, the cryptid caught whatever it was in its magically expanding beak pouch—a toaster, a car tire, a fifty-pound gym weight—and then spat it back out in disgust. The scientists were clearly delighted.

A third room held what Trish knew to be a BLACK SHUCK, a wolf-like creature with dark-gray smoke sputtering from its patchy fur. It had a single red eye, but it was acting more like a scared stray than a terrifying monster. As she watched, the cryptid burst into a cloud of smoke. The Euclideans in the room shielded their faces, but the smoke cloud made for the door, clearly seeking an escape. Realizing the room was airtight, the smoke huddled in a corner and the black shuck reappeared, its tail between its legs.

The rest of the exam rooms were filled with creatures Trish had already encountered, each of them in similar distress. The hissing chupacabra shot its back quills at any Euclidean who approached, three jackalopes were protesting in a variety of voices, and the regal unicorn, its pelt bright red with anger, bucked against the enchanted chains that held it fast. The animal screams in the room were horrifying.

KONGAMATO

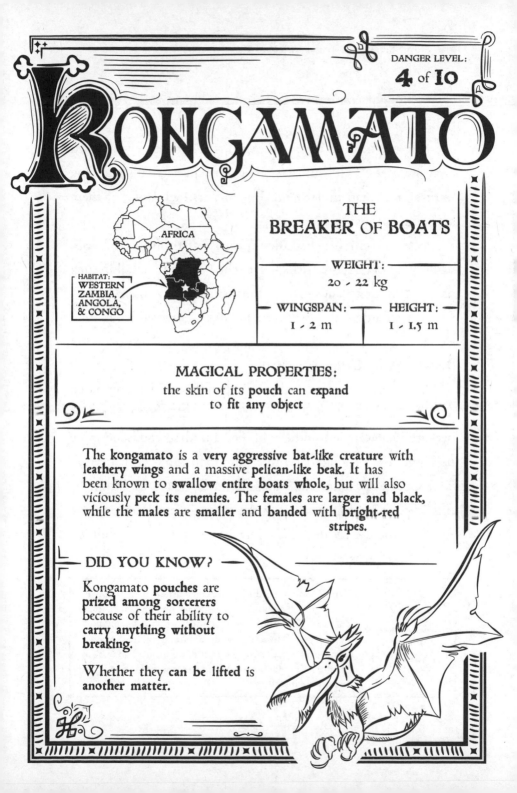

AFRICA

HABITAT:
WESTERN
ZAMBIA,
ANGOLA,
& CONGO

THE
BREAKER OF BOATS

WEIGHT:
20 - 22 kg

WINGSPAN:
1 - 2 m

HEIGHT:
1 - 1.5 m

MAGICAL PROPERTIES:
the skin of its **pouch** can **expand**
to **fit any object**

The **kongamato** is a **very aggressive bat-like creature** with **leathery wings** and a massive **pelican-like beak**. It has been known to **swallow entire boats whole**, but will also viciously **peck its enemies**. The females are **larger and black**, while the males are **smaller** and **banded** with **bright-red stripes.**

DID YOU KNOW?

Kongamato **pouches** are **prized among sorcerers** because of their ability to **carry anything without breaking.**

Whether they **can be lifted** is another matter.

"I thought you wanted to help these creatures," Owen said to his mother accusingly.

"We are helping them," she said, though her eyes looked away guiltily. "Unfortunately, that concept is not something most animals can understand. But rest assured, none of them are being harmed unnecessarily."

As if to contradict her, the unicorn reared on its back legs, whinnying in distress. Trish's heart ached to see them all in such pain. "Why are you doing this? Can't you just leave them alone?"

"If we do that, they will certainly die," answered Kiraz.

TRUTH AND CONSEQUENCES

The Euclidean leader flipped open his tablet computer. "Thirteen hundred animal species went **EXTINCT** last year because they were left in the wild. Five hundred thousand more no longer have enough land to ensure their long-term survival. Your Codex Arcanum and humanity at large can no longer be trusted to protect magical creatures. If we do not intervene, the DNA of these creatures, and more importantly their abilities, will be lost forever."

ENCHANTING DETAILS

These numbers are not an exaggeration. If there are an estimated 2 million animal species on the planet, then between 200 and 2,000 of those species go **EXTINCT** every year. However, because not all animal species have been discovered, the extinction number may be as high as 100,000 per year. It makes one feel worse about squishing insects.

BLACK SHUCK

**HABITAT:
BRITISH ISLES**

COUGH AND YOU'LL MISS HIM

(Also Known As: **OLD SHUCK, OLD SHOCK, SHUCK**)

WEIGHT:
20 - 35 kg

LENGTH:
120 - 150 cm

HEIGHT:
100 - 130 cm

MAGICAL PROPERTIES:
can generate **smoke** from its **fur**,
teleportation

Black shuck sightings go back as far as **the 1500s**. The account of this cryptid **appearing in a church during a violent storm** forever solidified its **dark reputation** as a **harbinger of doom**, though it's more likely the poor beast simply wanted to get out of the rain.

The animal is **quite friendly but easily startled**. If intimidated it will **shroud itself in smoke** and **teleport away**. This happens quite often, thanks to all the screaming that occurs when people spot it.

DID YOU KNOW?

The shuck's single **glowing eye** can **see heat signatures**, which is helpful considering how much time it spends obscured by its own smoke.

"That's why you've been capturing them," said Perry, unable to hide her satisfaction at finally solving the mystery. "You think if you can map their genetic codes, you can replicate their evolutionary adaptations for your own benefit."

Kiraz gave her a small nod of acknowledgment, but Trish laughed. "Seriously? How are you dummies gonna get someone to grow a unicorn horn?"

The Euclidean gave a humorless smile, making the waxy skin grafts on his face wrinkle grotesquely. "Humankind has long sought the abilities of lesser creatures. We wished to fly like birds, so we invented the airplane. We wished to move faster than cheetahs, so we gave birth to the automobile. Genetics grants us the means to identify and appropriate cryptid characteristics that took thousands of years to evolve. And we need those abilities now. Climate change, lack of resources, and overpopulation has set humanity on a path to destruction. If our species cannot adapt, and quickly, we, too will go the way of the Sphinx."

He beckoned the teenagers to a gray-and-black machine the size of a Xerox copier. There was a large square slot in the front and a digital screen. "This is a gene sequencer. Do you know what it does?"

Perry had told them plenty of times about such machines, but Owen chose to play dumb. "Does it sort pants?" he asked innocently.

Kiraz gritted his teeth. "This American humor of yours, it can be so tiresome. 902-Echo," he commanded Eleanor, "explain."

Owen's mom blushed at the use of her Euclidean name. "It—it catalogues the DNA of any living creature," she stammered. "We use DNA sequencing to find the genes that cause an animal's magical traits, and—"

"And once identified, we use CRISPR technology to cre-

BEWARE THE EUCLIDEANS

While modern CRISPR technology was developed to treat genetic diseases, our enemies use it to "improve" already functional DNA.

ate enzymes that will activate those genes in other creatures," Kiraz finished for her. "Even humans. No longer will magical beings be permitted to hoard their gifts. Imagine if anyone could metabolize poisons like a unicorn. Or phase-shift like the Loch Ness Monster." He turned to Trish. "Or imitate any voice like your friend. The jackalope."

He stepped aside to reveal a glass-walled examination room, and Trish's stomach dropped. Inside, strapped to a padded table and flanked by two Euclideans in face masks and white coats, was Varmint. His yellow eyes were wide with fear.

"Things are lookin' bleak, young missy," the cryptid said in his favorite cowboy twang. Then, switching to Owen's voice: "Get out of here, dude. Run!"

Kiraz's left hand fell on Trish's shoulder. Even through the leather glove, his fingers felt skeletal and wrong. She tried to shrug him off, but the Euclideans tugged the three teenagers forward into the glass-walled examination room. "As I said, we have no wish for harm to befall these creatures. But if Whitmore and her organization continue to block our cataloguing efforts, the cryptids will be lost. Sacrifices must be made."

The door to the tiny room was locked behind them. The two armed guards stood just inside, while Eleanor rushed over to check the jackalope's vitals. Trish hoped Bryan had managed to squeeze in with them.

Kiraz tapped his tablet computer and turned it to show Trish, Owen, and Perry a security video feed. On-screen they saw the ten-story Codex Arcanum, each of its levels a different style of architecture, standing in the center of a large, well-tended backyard. It towered over a nearby plantation house, making the expensive four-story building look like a train set model. It would have been an amusing sight if the library were not surrounded by Euclidean soldiers lobbing grenades at it.

"As you are no doubt aware, children, we have operation bases all over the world," said Kiraz as explosions rocked the library. "One of our largest is located here"—he tapped the tablet screen—"on a plantation in Mississippi. Your mentor and her 'repository' appeared in its backyard five hours ago. It is only a matter of time before our soldiers break though her spells of protection."

Indeed, while the Euclideans didn't appear to have damaged the building, the lighted windows of the ten-story structure were flickering off and on as if the entire structure were trembling. Trish couldn't understand why Whitmore didn't just whisk the Codex Arcanum away, as she'd done so many times before. Was it possible she was trapped in some way? Or injured?

"However," Kiraz continued, "you could end this conflict right now. Tell us how to overcome her defenses. Assist us with her capture, and I swear, you and your animal friend shall be freed."

OVERDUE LIBRARIAN

The three teenagers said nothing. *Maybe Whitmore really is losing it,* Trish thought desperately. *It's not like her to appear right in front of the Euclideans and let herself be openly attacked. Unless . . .*

Hope flared in her chest like a match struck in a dark room. *Unless that* is *the plan. Reveal herself to her enemies, knowing they'll come to us for help. What better way to send us a message?*

But what was the message? That was the real question. *Ugh, Bryan's right. Why does everything she's involved with have to be a puzzle?* she thought sourly. *That's Perry's kind of thing, not mine.* She nudged the tiny teenager with her foot, trying to psychically convey her thoughts. It did not work.

"I can see you need some inducement," said Kiraz. He pointed to the female guard, who grinned and pulled a Taser from her belt holster. She approached Varmint, holding the electric device over the jackalope's quickly rising-and-falling chest. She pulled the trigger, demonstrating the blue lightning-bolt arc of electricity that leapt between the two prongs.

"Mom, are you seriously allowing this?" said Owen angrily. "You let 'em zap Varmint, and it could kill him!"

Eleanor stepped to Kiraz's side. "Sir . . . you said we wouldn't resort to these methods."

"And I won't, unless they force me to," said Kiraz. "Three seconds, children." He held up a gloved finger. "One."

Trish looked desperately at Perry and Owen. "I think we get the *message*," she said, looking pointedly at the television screen. The windows of the Codex Arcanum continued to flicker strangely. "Let's just tell them about *Whitmore*."

Perry blinked in confusion. "Such an action is morally reprehensible. We swore an oath."

"Two," announced Samson Kiraz.

"Which is why we should *look at* the bigger *picture*," replied Trish, now jerking her head toward the screen.

Kiraz was amused. "You act as if we cannot see your clear attempts at communication." He nodded to the guard. "Three."

She jammed the Taser into Varmint's chest. Electricity coursed through the jackalope, making it buck and wordlessly scream in a series of human voices. Trish could hear Perry, Jacinda, her mother, and even Bryan, all of them in extreme pain. It was a bizarre, heart-wrenching sound. She tried to shove her way forward, but the burly, bearded guard's hand was like an iron manacle on her upper arm. She could only watch, horrified and sickened, as the cryptid twitched on the table, then lay still.

The female guard removed the Taser. Eleanor rushed to the animal, checking its pulse. She rubbed the cryptid's chest vigorously, and Varmint gasped, shuddering back to life.

"Please," it panted in Perry's voice, "don't do that again. My poor old ticker can't take it."

"This kind of treatment is not what we discussed," Eleanor said severely to Kiraz.

"Treatment?" Owen repeated. "Wake up, Mom. This is torture!"

"You would put this one creature's life above those of dozens, perhaps hundreds, of other humans?" Kiraz asked Owen's mom. "Because those deaths will occur if Euphemia Whitmore is not apprehended." He jabbed a finger at the tablet's news feed. "She's in our backyard. Taunting us. These children—your child—can deliver her. But only if they are properly motivated."

"And how do you plan to motivate my son?" Eleanor replied coldly. "By Tasing me next?"

"I shall take it under consideration." Kiraz nodded to the bearded guard. The big man holding Trish used his left hand to unclip his Taser from his belt and point it at Eleanor. The two scientists in the room were concerned, but at a glance from Kiraz they looked back down at their monitors.

"I feared you never had the real stomach for this work. Pity." The head Euclidean turned to the female guard. "Shock it again. And this time, let the creature stay dead until they tell us how to get inside."

The guard advanced. Trish glanced back at the news feed on Kiraz's tablet. *It's up to me. I'm the only one who can figure out Whitmore's message.* She studied the bombarded building, searching for something that would help her decipher what the librarian was trying to say. Something that would prove her theory was correct. If only she could cast a spell. But with her hands in the lock box she couldn't even form a single rune . . .

Runes.

That was why the flickering windows of the Codex Arcanum had been so puzzling. *They're not flickering randomly. They're doing it in a pattern.* Now she just needed a few more moments to confirm what that pattern was.

"I'll do it," she said right as the Taser was about to touch Varmint. "I'll tell you how to break through her spells. Just don't hurt him."

"What?" said Owen. "You can't be serious, T."

Perry stepped in front of her. "I know he's your friend, but we cannot let emotions impair our—"

"Shut up," Trish said, peering closer at the video feed and counting under her breath.

Kiraz motioned for the guard to wait. "What is it? You see something?"

Trish grinned. Her supposition had been correct: the window lights of the ten-story Codex Arcanum were flickering in a repeated pattern of eleven rune symbols. The problem was, she didn't recognize them all. Some were familiar, as they looked almost exactly like Roman letters, but others were more difficult to DECIPHER. But after a few long moments of muttering under

THE CODEX ARCANUM

An additional element that makes runes difficult to DECIPHER is that some symbols represent Roman letters while others stand for entire concepts such as "wealth," "fire," and specific types of trees.

her breath, she was able to confirm that the sequence was three separate words, repeated over and over:

ᛈᚻᛗᛇᛗ ᚠᛈᛗ ᚼᛙᛏ

Because of her spotty rune knowledge, however, Trish translated this as:

WHEZE OZE YAK?

Whether Whitmore was searching for a wheezing yak or not, Trish knew the time had come to choose. It came down to trust. Did she believe what the Euclideans had said about Whitmore, or did she trust the librarian in spite of her mysterious and frustrating methods? Trish only had to glance around the room to know the right choice. But she had to play her hand just right.

Taking a steadying breath, she turned back to Kiraz. "I'll get her to come out. Someone hand me a phone."

TENSE NEGOTIATIONS

"Trish, no!" wailed Perry. Owen looked stricken by his friend's betrayal.

Kiraz pulled a high-tech satellite phone from his pocket. "Who are we calling?" he asked suspiciously.

Trish nodded at the Euclidean soldiers on the security feed. "Them."

After some negotiation, Kiraz and the commanding Euclidean on the plantation agreed to let Trish speak to Whitmore over a megaphone. Kiraz held his satellite phone to the teenager's mouth so her voice would be transmitted into the backyard. "No tricks," he warned her.

"No tricks," she replied. Then, leaning over the phone: "Ms. Whitmore? Ms. Whitmore, it's Trish Kim."

On the security feed, they saw the flashing windows of the Codex Arcanum go dark. "She hears us," Kiraz breathed. His left hand squeezed the back of Trish's neck. "Now get her to come out."

"We're with the Euclideans," she continued, speaking quickly. "They want you to turn yourself in. They have the unicorn. Go back in time, and track its energy signature—"

Kiraz muted the phone, his eyes narrowing. "That's enough."

The adults and teenagers studied the security feed, waiting for Whitmore's response. When there was no movement from the Codex Arcanum, he pointed at the female guard. "Kill it."

"No!" said Owen. "Mom, stop them. Do something!"

"Sir, please—" Eleanor began, but the burly guard pulled the trigger on his Taser, sending a loud arc of electricity between the leads. The message was clear: if she said another word, she'd be the one electrocuted next. Owen's mother bit her lip.

The female guard grinned, turning back to the jackalope. Trish winced as electricity arced between the prongs of the woman's Taser. Even though she'd manage to figure out Whitmore's message, it had done nothing to save Varmint. It was time to take matters into her own hands.

"Bryan," she whispered between her teeth, "I hope you're nearby."

WHAM! She flung the metal box on her hands upward, striking the burly guard in the face. Blood spurted from his nose and he let go of her arm. The female guard lunged toward Trish, her Taser crackling—

"Stop!" Eleanor suddenly cried, pointing at the tablet screen. "Something's happening."

Everyone froze as they regarded the security feed. Bolts of purple energy crackled along the Codex Arcanum. Suddenly it vanished from the backyard, leaving the Euclideans looking around in confusion.

Kiraz pulled off his left glove, revealing a metal **PROSTHESIS**. He grabbed Trish by the throat, his titanium fingers squeezing her windpipe. "What happened? What did you tell her??"

In spite of the pain, she managed to croak a reply. "I gave you what you wanted, cyborg."

ENCHANTING DETAILS

Modern **PROSTHETICS** can be controlled by the brain and even convey a sense of touch. A shame they don't also come with morality chips.

He released her, pressing a button on his smart watch. "She's coming. Full alert. Defend the cryptids at all—"

But he didn't finish the sentence before a sonic boom rattled the glass walls of the Euclidean laboratory. Everyone in the room looked toward the disturbance to see that a ten-story building had appeared on the beach outside the compound's fence line. Each level was a different style of architecture (one was even a wooden ship), and it looked no worse for wear despite having very recently been under attack by a large contingent of Euclidean soldiers.

Euphemia Whitmore had arrived.

Chapter 17

JUST DESSERTS

The front door of the Codex Arcanum opened. Whitmore stepped out of the building, smartly dressed in an emerald blouse and a long navy skirt. She adjusted her silver spectacles, unruffled by the size of the facility before her or the array of military-grade weapons being aimed in her direction.

"You got what you wanted," Trish said gleefully to Kiraz. "She's out."

"Oh, you guys are about to get spanked," said Owen.

"I knew you wouldn't betray sorcery, I knew it!" Perry exclaimed in relief.

Kiraz shoved the teenagers aside, going to look out the building's front window.

On the beach, Whitmore made a few elegant hand gestures, and her magically magnified voice was transmitted into every nook and cranny on the island. Her words were, as always, calm,

wise, and impeccable: "Greetings, Euclideans. For years, we have been engaged in a zero-sum conflict. You have tried to secure items and beings of magical value, while we have worked to prevent you. But in the last weeks, you have crossed a line, greatly endangering dozens of cryptids and human children. Such behavior will no longer be tolerated."

Whitmore cast her severe gaze across the line of soldiers forming a half circle around the Codex Arcanum. Each of them held a rifle loaded with ammunition far more dangerous than tranquilizer darts. "You will release every sorcerer, cryptid, and any other prisoner you have captured as part of this war. Fail to comply, and each of you will receive your just desserts. You have five minutes."

The librarian removed her gold watch and clicked the timer button. She stood patiently, as if she were merely in line for a latte and not facing a platoon of armed mercenaries.

Back inside the laboratory, a voice issued from Kiraz's watch. "Your orders, sir?"

The Euclidean locked eyes with Trish. The blue glow of his bionic eye was cold and emotionless. "Open fire."

On the beach, fifty automatic rifles were lifted. Trish closed her eyes, wincing in anticipation, but the roar of expected gunfire never came. She cracked one eyelid to see the soldiers' weapons had been replaced by bundles of colorful flowers.

"What happened?" Kiraz demanded. "I told you to shoot her!"

"Uh . . . she replaced our guns with flowers, sir," came the voice from Kiraz's watch. They heard a cautious sniff. "I think they're begonias."

"Then attack her with your hands, idiot!" he shouted into his watch.

But before they could move, Euphemia Whitmore clicked her gold pocket watch and shook her head.

"Time's up," she said in her magically magnified voice. "A bit shorter than five minutes, perhaps, but I see a snake cannot change its scales. I shall release your captives myself, then. Enjoy your just desserts."

She began to form a complicated series of runes, moving her hands elegantly through the air. Trish recognized the SPELL FOR TRANSMUTATION somewhere in there, but it was combined with several other enchantments. The librarian's brow was furrowed in deep concentration. Then she stood upright and spread her fingers wide.

A wave of purple energy radiated outward, passing through every Euclidean soldier, every war machine, every glass pane and metal strut of the high-tech facility. A tremor went through the building. Alarms blared and emergency lights flashed as security systems across the complex failed simultaneously.

THE CODEX ARCANUM

At its most basic, the SPELL FOR TRANSMUTATION transforms one substance into another. But if you desire to transmute multiple substances at the same time, additional enchantments are required.

"Guess that's my cue," came Bryan's voice from a corner of the lab room. *"Fulgur venire!"*

THE CAKE ESCAPE

The guards spun toward his voice, but two bolts of electricity crackled out of thin air, striking both Euclideans in the chest. The female guard fell against the steel table, which cracked as if it were made of papier-mâché, revealing a moist yellow interior. Oddly, the scent of lemon filled the room. At the same time, the bearded guard stumbled backward into the glass wall, which shattered as easily as if it were made of sugar. Both of them lay unconscious.

Kiraz bent to grab the female's Taser, but Trish swung the metal box on her hands into the small of his back. He yelled in pain, but was already turning to attack her. She and Owen used their boxes to keep him at bay until Bryan was able to cast the Spell to Conjure Thunderclaps. The sound exploded through the small room, knocking Kiraz through the table, several machines, and a glass wall. Each obstacle shattered as if it were made of nothing more substantial than toothpicks. The head Euclidean groaned, dazed by the force of the spell.

Bryan cast off his invisibility spell, revealing clothes that were even more rumpled and dirty than the ones worn by the other teenagers. *Guess it's difficult to stay clean when you can't see yourself,* Trish thought wryly.

"Boo," Bryan said to the two Euclidean scientists, who wisely ran out through the broken glass wall.

"Always wanted to do that," he said to the others. "We gotta move, though. Whatever Whitmore did, it's not gonna take these guys long to figure it out."

"Can you get these boxes off?" Owen asked.

Bryan began to cast a spell, but Perry stepped in front of him. "Wait. I think they're warded against magic." She indicated subtle runes stamped into the box's edges.

"She's right," said Eleanor, getting to her feet. "Kiraz had them made especially. You need a regular key to open them." She bent over the unconscious female guard and removed a key ring from her belt. Finding the right one, she quickly unlocked the teenage sorcerers' restraint boxes. They flexed and shook out their cramped fingers.

"Thank you," Perry said with relief.

"Don't thank her," Owen snapped. "Just 'cause she helped one time doesn't mean we're on the same side now."

"Owen, I . . ." Eleanor began. She glanced at Kiraz, who was still struggling to dig his way out of the crumbly pile of debris. Her expression was confused and angry and sad all at once. Finally she seemed to come to a decision. "Let me help you get out of here."

Bryan snorted, and for once Trish was inclined to agree with him. Around them, the other Euclideans were beginning to recover from Whitmore's attack. They only had a few more seconds to decide on an escape plan.

"You'll need me to unlock the detention cells," Eleanor continued. "Those are warded against magic too. Please. I . . ." She looked again at Kiraz. "I don't want anyone else getting hurt."

Trish turned to Owen. "It's your call, dude."

"Fine. You can help, but we are not a team." Owen's eyes stared daggers into Eleanor. Perry tried to put a soothing hand on his arm, but he shook it off. "Not now, not ever."

"Can we do family therapy later?" suggested Bryan.

Trish bent over the examination table to undo the straps on Varmint, and found the leather braces had become brown CAKE FONDANT. Everything broke easily as she scooped the jackalope into her arms. The table crumbled as well, revealing more of the lemon-scented moist yellow interior.

"Sorry you had to go through that, buddy," she said. "You okay?"

The cryptid nuzzled her with the side of its antlered head. "Right as rain, partner," it said in Whitmore's elegant British accent. "Now what say we skedaddle?"

Trish nodded, turning to see Bryan was nibbling on a handful of the table. "Lemon cake," he said in admiration. "Whitmore

ENCHANTING
DETAILS

CAKE FONDANT icing can be made out of sugar or marshmallows and has the consistency of wet clay. It is used in more sturdy cake decorations and while technically edible, it is nowhere near as tasty as traditional buttercream frosting.

changed everything in the building into cake and candy. No wonder everything busted so easily."

Trish looked around to see the rest of the lab was in chaos. Cryptids were breaking through their fondant bonds and kicking down sugar-pane walls. The unicorn knocked aside several scientists while the chupacabra shot back quills at every Euclidean it saw. The kongamato swallowed one of its tormentors whole, then spat him into two guards. The black shuck burst into a cloud of smoke and teleported through the cake-ified gene sequencer, turning the expensive machine into a pile of crumbs. The Euclideans tried to retaliate, but their chocolate tranquilizer guns fired only bolts of licorice. The animals broke through the glass back wall, galloping and flying and just plain running toward the Codex Arcanum.

Trish laughed as the creatures escaped. "Guess Whitmore wasn't kidding when she said 'just desserts.' Come on, let's go free the guys downstairs."

She set down Varmint and karate-kicked the sugar-glass wall of the examination room. Sugar fragments went flying. Since the floor had become lemon cake as well, their sneakers left footprints in the gray icing as they ran through the laboratory.

"Euclideans!" Kiraz yelled, slipping in frosting and becoming stuck to the floor. "Stop them!"

A couple guards tried to follow his orders, but Trish blew a hole in the floor with a thunderclap spell, sending them tumbling to the level below.

When they reached the security doors, rather than bother with another enchantment, Owen and Bryan grinned and simply ran through the thick barrier. Lemon cake and icing exploded outward, coating their shoulders and hair. Trish, Perry, and Eleanor stepped through the hole after them. The jackalope licked icing from his paw.

"That there's a tasty vittle," the creature said in his cowboy voice.

They surveyed the research room. Many of the cubicles and desks had collapsed, coating the Euclidean workers in icing and cake crumbs. The computers were no longer functioning, and the researchers seemed at a loss for how to proceed.

"This way," Eleanor said, leading them toward a stairwell. "I wouldn't trust the elevators right now."

As she pushed open the door, it too crumbled into cake fragments. "Halt!" a voice screamed from across the room. It was Kiraz, stumbling out from the laboratory. His white-blond hair was streaked with frosting, and his bionic eye had become a decorated gumdrop. He yanked off his licorice-rope prosthetic arm. "She's taking the prisoners. Don't let them escape!"

A few more Euclideans moved toward them, but Bryan cast a fire spell, melting a large semicircle into the cake-ified floor. Once one or two pursuers toppled through, the others thought better of following them.

"Wish I had a good cake-related quip for that, but I'm coming up empty," said Bryan. "'Piece of cake' is too obvious, right?"

"'Cake that'?" suggested Trish.

"'Nice to frost you'?" added Owen.

"I suggest we continue this discussion later," said Perry.

The teenagers, Eleanor, and Varmint carefully made their way down the stairs. The going was a bit tricky, as the cake stairs were prone to collapsing and many other people were trying to escape. Thankfully the railings and support beams had been converted to more sturdy candy canes, which helped the stairwell hold its structure.

By the time they reached the detention level, however, much of the building had collapsed into crumbs. To save themselves from being smothered by four levels of cake and frosting, Perry cast a Spell to Conjure Ice in the hallway. The cake floor panels and sugar lights froze solid. The slick ice made walking tricky, but for the moment it held.

At the end of the hall, they saw several rooms had been unaffected by Whitmore's spell—those containing the European sorcerers, the Sasquatch, and the Euclidean sorcerer. A fourth cell held Augustus Stromberg, the Council member they'd briefly seen in Croatia. His skin was even grayer than usual and he could barely stand. Eleanor released the sorcerers first, punching a code into the keypad then holding her wrist over the scanner.

"Head to the beach," Owen told them. "Whitmore's waiting at the Codex Arcanum. Take out anyone in your way."

"Who appointed you team leader?" Bryan asked him.

"Nobody, I'm just trying to move things along."

"Good, 'cause let's not forget I'm the one who made this breakout possible."

"Actually, if it wasn't for Whitmore—" Owen began, but Perry interrupted them.

"Enough!" she said, sounding impressively like Jacinda. "It's not a competition."

"Yeah, glad to see this whole near-death experience has made you boys mellow," Trish said sarcastically. "Besides, *I* was the one who got Whitmore here."

Thankfully, the European teenagers had ignored the bickering and were now finished casting spells of flight on themselves. Carrying Stromberg between them, they zoomed down the corridor and disappeared around the corner. Eleanor went to release the Sasquatch next.

"Much obliged, young'uns," the eight-foot creature said in a deep but warm voice. He flashed them the peace sign, then began leisurely skating down the ice hallway on his huge bare feet. When he reached the end, he leapt out onto the beach in one huge bound.

"What about Creepy McCreepster?" Owen asked, indicating the magically fortified cell that held the Euclidean sorcerer. The bearded man stared at them with his dark unblinking eyes.

"He chose his side," said Trish. "Let his buddies deal with him."

"Then allow me to speed up our egress," said Perry, twisting her arms in an elegant fashion. *"Kasirga!"*

A **CYCLONE** erupted from her hands, opening a circular hole in the ice-coated wall. Frosting and cake spiraled away, creating a round tunnel that led directly to the beach.

"Show-off," said Owen warmly.

THE CODEX ARCANUM

Magical **CYCLONES** are also useful in creating pathways through water, moving heavy objects, and drowning out tedious conversations.

The group jogged out to solid ground to find Euclideans dashing in every direction. An occasional cryptid was still making its way toward the ten-story bookstore, but it seemed most of them had escaped captivity. The giant facility itself was filled with holes and broken windows. Only moments after the teenagers exited, the entire structure collapsed in on itself with a soft *flump*. Dozens of Euclideans were left floundering in frosting, but no one appeared to be injured.

"And that's what you get when you don't read the recipe," quipped Bryan. When none of the others laughed, he threw up his hands. "Nobody? Come on, that was a solid one-liner."

On the other end of the beach, Whitmore stood in the doorway of the Codex Arcanum, waving in cryptids and sorcerers with one hand while holding back Euclidean soldiers with the other. The teenagers and Eleanor began to jog toward the ten-story building.

"Mrs. Macready?" Perry pointed to a large Quonset hut set back from the beach. Its walls were filigreed with runes and familiar diagrams. Unlike the other structures nearby, it still appeared to be made of metal. "Can you identify that structure covered in spells of protection?"

Owen's mother shaded her eyes to peer at it. "I haven't been allowed in there. Kiraz told our resident SORCERER to make sure it was shielded, but I never knew what was inside."

As if it had overheard their conversation, the doors to the spelled structure parted. Inside they could see rows of metal cages, water tanks of various sizes, and scientific equipment of all sorts. But what really drew their attention was the animals.

Like the cages, they were of various sizes. Some of the creatures were water-based, some had four legs, and some had wings, but all of them looked unnatural. They reminded Trish of the experimental potatoes she'd grown in Saturday Science Club—discolored, misshapen things sprouting strange tentacles. Unlike her potatoes, however, these experiments were moving.

Samson Kiraz stood near a particularly large cage, a remote device in his sole remaining hand. With a look of furious satisfaction on his face, he punched in a code and the cage door opened.

BEWARE THE EUCLIDEANS

It should be noted that not every SORCERER in the Euclideans' employ is a prisoner. Some are merely freelance spell casters who have been enticed by easy cash. Once they have performed such work, however, their memories of magic are usually erased by one side or the other.

CHIMERA

Whatever was inside snapped at him, rocking the cage, but he pressed a button on his device. A blue flare of electricity illuminated a large four-legged shape inside the metal box, and an angry yowl echoed across the beach. Kiraz gestured at the teenagers, and the thing inside finally emerged.

It looked wrong. Its body was similar to that of a full-grown lion or a tiger, except for the four purple tentacles sprouting from its back. Its mouth was far too wide for its face, and filled with hundreds of thin needlelike teeth. Its patchy orange and brown-striped hide smoked like that of the black shuck. But worst of all were its eyes—there were four of them, small and beady and blank. They were like snake eyes. Every other cryptid Trish had met, she had been able to see that they had feelings, a personality, a soul. This thing had none of those.

It wasn't an animal. It was a killing machine, built out of muscle and bone and teeth.

"Please tell me that's something you saw in the cryptozoology book," Owen said to Trish.

She shook her head, repulsed to see the creature move. "It's got the traits of a bunch of creatures, but there's no listing for whatever that is."

"Kiraz must have created it," said Eleanor in horrified realization. "It's a **CHIMERA**. A combination of several animals into one." She stared at it in wide-eyed shock. "He talked about doing gene treatments down the line, trying to activate cryptid

CHIMERA

A FEARSOME FOE

WEIGHT:
217 kg

LENGTH:
3 m

HEIGHT:
1 m

MAGICAL PROPERTIES:

teleportation, fire breathing,
unbreakable teeth and claws,
strong resistance to magic

Created in a lab by **Samson Kiraz**, this **unnatural creature**
possesses the **genetic attributes** of the **black shuck, Bear Lake
Monster, bunyip,** and possibly more cryptids.

It is believed the chimera's **core
DNA** is that of a **Bengal tiger.**
Like all Euclidean creations,
the chimera is **fitted with a
behavior-controlling device**
that can be used
for training purposes.

DID YOU KNOW?

The chimera is the **first living
creature** to gain magical powers
through the application of **gene editing.**

One hopes it is also
the last.

According to Greek mythology, the classic CHIMERA had the front half of a lion, a goat's head rising from its back, and a tail made of the front end of a serpent. The word has since come to be used for any strange combination of elements, be they animal, chemical, or sandwich creation.

traits in living specimens, but I thought it was all theoretical. I had no idea he'd been . . . making one." She sounded as if she were going to be sick.

"It appears he's made several," observed Perry grimly. "But how has it already gained cryptid traits? I thought you had only recently identified the cryptid genes."

"We did," she admitted. "He must have used some kind of accelerated growth hormone."

"Or spells to speed up GROWTH," said Owen darkly.

The chimera stretched its paws forward and shook itself. It gave a few hacking coughs, and little bursts of flame issued from its mouth.

"Man, it can breathe fire too?" said Bryan. "If this thing wasn't coming for us, I'd want it as a pet."

Kiraz gave the chimera another jolt with his remote, and they saw a restraint collar had been fitted around the bizarre

While spells to increase GROWTH can be useful, they are not recommended on sentient creatures. The sudden proportion changes can cause strange reactions in the subject's brain.

creature's neck. The animal snapped at the Euclidean, but he pointed at the teenagers and jiggled the remote. Hissing, the creature began to lope toward its prey.

Trish looked back at the Codex Arcanum. Whitmore was still occupied with holding off the attacking Euclideans, her hands a blur of rune shapes and magical energy. She turned back to the chimera.

"We'll have to hold it off ourselves," she said crisply. "Ideas?"

"Well, fire spells don't usually work on fire-breathing cryptids," Bryan recalled as the animal drew closer. Gray smoke poured off its body as it increased its pace. It was only fifty meters away now. "And water or ice spells will just annoy it."

"I propose a **SPELL TO INDUCE SLUMBER**," Perry piped up. "That works on almost any living thing, provided the casting's strong enough."

It was one of the most advanced spells from *Sorcery for Beginners*, but Bryan said he knew it. "It's a tough one, but being on house arrest gave me plenty of time to practice." He fished a few components out of his pocket and began going through the hand movements.

Owen stepped forward. "In the meantime, we gotta slow this thing down. Perry?"

He nodded to her, and they both began moving through the motions for a Spell to Manipulate Earth. They

THE CODEX ARCANUM

Not only is casting a SPELL TO INDUCE SLUMBER difficult, but it also has a tendency to make those casting, listening to, or even reading it fall asleep.

muttered an incantation in Latin, then thrust out their hands at the same time. Pillars of lava rock burst from the sand, forming a dense circle around the chimera. The creature skidded to a stop, narrowing its four unnatural eyes. It was trapped.

"Oh my goodness," Eleanor said with parental pride. Clearly she hadn't seen very many real-world demonstrations of sorcery yet. "I'm still not sure I approve of this underage spell casting, but that is very impressive work."

But as she spoke, the chimera began to twitch. More gray smoke billowed from the animal's patchy fur. Suddenly it burst into a cloud of smoke and vanished. Almost immediately, a burst of smoke appeared on the other side of the stone prison. The chimera stepped out of it, shaking itself all over.

"Oh great, it can teleport," said Trish. "That's fun. Bryan?"

"Workin' on it," he said, stifling a huge yawn as he continued to form runes.

The chimera once more began loping toward them. Seeing it approach, battle-hardened Euclidean soldiers dove out of the way.

"A Spell of Attraction," Owen suggested quickly. "We can attach it to the beach."

He, Perry, and Trish each formed the required runes, then stretched their hands toward the approaching animal. Jets of colored light sizzled across the beach, but they merely bounced off the chimera's mangy hide.

"I—I don't understand," stammered Perry. "Our casting was perfect."

"It must be resistant to magic," Trish said. "Like the bunyip." When Owen looked at her blankly, she quickly explained, "It's an Australian cryptid that recently went extinct. Do you ever read these books?"

He turned to Bryan. "How we doing, Mr. Sandman?"

Bryan yawned, which forced him to break off his spell casting. He sleepily shook his head. "I told you, it's a tough one. I gotta start over."

"We don't have time to start over!" Trish replied. She quickly fired a lightning spell at the approaching animal, but it absorbed the magical energy as simply as inhaling. Sparks crackled along its patches of fur. And still, it kept coming.

"New plan," suggested Owen. "Run."

He, Perry, and Eleanor resumed their sprint to the Codex Arcanum, but Trish could tell the chimera was faster on the sand than they were. It—and more importantly, its many teeth— would catch up to them in moments. Bryan was still going through the movements of the sleep spell, but she had a feeling that any magical attack they tried would be useless. Instead, she kneeled on the beach, scooping up two handfuls of sand.

The chimera was only a few meters away now, close enough that Trish could smell the burned rubber scent of its skin-smoke. She exhaled to calm herself.

The animal coiled its muscles to spring—

And Trish hurled sand into its four beady eyes.

The chimera yelped, curling into a protective ball and tumbling sideways. Its back tentacles pawed at its face and it shook its misshapen head, but it couldn't get the grit free.

"Come on," she said, grabbing Bryan by the wrist and breaking off his spell in the process. He was about to protest, but when he saw what she'd done, he ran along willingly.

They tore across the beach, worried that at any moment the creature might get back to its feet and come after them. But they reached the doorway of the Codex Arcanum in one piece. Whitmore stood several meters away, having just frozen a half dozen soldiers in a time bubble. Trish and Bryan looked back to see the chimera was still trying to shake the sand free of its eyes.

"Nice throw," he said appreciatively.

"Three years of softball," she replied.

Greetings, sorcerers, a voice spoke directly into their minds.

They winced, but turned to see Kyle the kirin sitting calmly in the open doorway. He seemed unruffled by the chaos on the beach before them. *Your intentions are honorable,* the kirin continued. *You may enter.* The teenagers stepped across the threshold, feeling as if they were passing through a fine cool mist—

And the sounds from the island vanished. As did the smell of the nearby ocean, the heat of the tropical sun, and the ever-present fear they might die at any second. They were inside the **AIR-CONDITIONED** Codex Arcanum, and they were safe.

THE CODEX
ARCANUM

You may wonder where an independent teleporting structure like the Codex Arcanum gets its power for lights and AIR-CONDITIONING. The answer is generators, with a bit of magically enhanced fuel.

"Good security system," Owen said. Trish quickly scanned the library to see all the Euclidean prisoners—the European sorcerer team, Stromberg, the twenty cryptids, even the frosting-streaked Sasquatch—had all made it to the enchanted building. Eleanor gaped in amazement at the surroundings.

I see you took my advice, Kyle intoned into Trish's head, walking down the side of a bookshelf. He silently hopped atop a glass display case and fixed her with his piercing multicolored eyes. *You are no longer hiding your true self. It suits you.*

"Oh. Yeah," Trish said, taking care to avoid Bryan's questioning stare. "No big deal."

Not true, the kirin replied. *You forget, I can see how challenging it was.*

Trish gave the cryptid a half-smile of thanks as Euphemia Whitmore strode through the Codex Arcanum entrance.

"Welcome, all," she said to the gathered crowd. "And well done, Ms. Kim. Telling me to track the unicorn's magical signature was clever, indeed."

"Should we not be leaving now?" said one of the European sorcerers, a Swedish girl with close-cropped purple hair. She glanced nervously at the door.

"Not to worry. This building is layered with hundreds of protective enchantments, which no Euclidean technology may—"

A loud *THUMP* at the front door made her break off. Everyone turned toward the sound to see the chimera scratching and biting at the building's entrance doors. Each time its claws or teeth touched the doorway, a golden enchantment shimmered into being and broke apart.

"About that," said Bryan. "I think the Euclideans finally figured out a way around those."

"Impossible," breathed the librarian, studying the attacking animal with a sort of fascinated horror. The chimera clawed and tore its way through layers of spells as if they were no more than cellophane.

"Not impossible," said Eleanor grimly. "Genetics."

Whitmore strode over to a three-dimensional globe. It stood one and a half meters high and was incredibly detailed, with lights illuminating cities on the dark side of the planet. It was encircled by two golden bands representing latitude and longitude, which could be positioned anywhere on the globe.

The librarian moved both golden bands to an empty spot in the Indian Ocean and locked them into place. The point the two bands met glowed green. The globe began to spin of its own accord. Faster and faster it went, until it was a blur of colors.

Outside, Trish saw the chimera react to another jolt from its restraint collar. It shook its head and bounded away from the front door, disappearing around the corner of the Codex Arcanum. But before she could discover where it went, Whitmore called out to the eclectic group.

"Prepare yourselves," she warned everyone. "You may find this a bit jarring."

Then the globe snapped to a stop, and the Codex Arcanum vanished.

The Empty Doorstep

Whatever spell the building used to move through time and space, it was much worse than traveling by portal.

Trish felt as if the ground had suddenly dropped from beneath her feet, but instead of falling, every bone and sinew in her body was being stretched like taffy. She screamed, either out loud or in her mind, but just when it felt like every cell inside her would be ripped in half, her body slammed back together.

Several people collapsed to the floor. A few of the cryptids moaned, but none seemed to be permanently damaged. Trish managed to stay on her feet, but her head was spinning. She put a hand on a bookshelf to steady herself.

"You go through that every time this place teleports?" Bryan said to Whitmore. "You're tougher than you look."

"Let's not ride that bronco again," said Varmint in Perry's voice.

"I know it can feel a bit strange," Whitmore said, though she appeared to be unruffled by their journey. "Take a moment to regain your equilibrium, and if you need to be sick, please do so in a waste receptacle."

Thankfully, no one took her up on that offer. Whitmore flung open the entry doors, revealing a similar climate to the one they'd just left. It was warm, the sun was still shining, and they were surrounded by seawater. The difference was, the island upon which the ten-story bookstore now sat was little more than a sandbar, barely the circumference of the building.

"Where are we?" asked Perry.

"LEMURIA," Whitmore replied. "Completely uncharted by human mapmakers or satellites. Have a look."

Trish and the others stepped outside, inspecting the tiny circle of sand. It was devoid of features—no buildings, no docks, not even a lone palm tree to make it resemble the clichéd image of a cartoon desert island. Lemuria appeared to be nothing more than a mound of sand surrounded by blue water in every direction.

"No wonder it's uncharted," said Owen. "This place is Deadsville."

ENCHANTING
DETAILS

LEMURIA is known to non-magical humans as a mythical lost continent that existed in the Indian Ocean and sank beneath the waves. While this theory was discredited, the myth was based on sightings of this magically hidden island.

Trish took a deep breath. The air around the island was as warm as it had been at the Euclidean compound, though she estimated the time was at least an hour or two later in the day than it had been at that location. Since all she could see was ocean, though, she had no idea where they were.

"We are still in the Indian Ocean," Whitmore said as if she'd somehow heard the unasked question. "Southeast of the Maldives, five hundred nautical miles from anything, and almost exactly on the equator. One of the most remote magical places on this planet."

"I don't get it," Trish said. "Shouldn't a magical island be more . . . magical?"

"I admit, the doorstep is not terribly thrilling." Whitmore strode across the sand to the edge of the water. "But too many other magical places have been ransacked or destroyed because they proclaimed their existence to the world. Lemuria only reveals itself to those who possess the key."

She formed a few runes with her fingers, clicked open an ornate antique lighter, then spoke in Latvian: *"Atklāt visu burvju."* She blew on the flame, which detached and expanded outward in a glowing golden orb.

A transparent stone pillar appeared on the empty isle. It was composed of slats that could be rotated and pushed into different positions. Her hands working quickly, Whitmore spun and locked several slats into place. The pillar dropped into the sand, creating a kind of large stone handle that remained visible when the Spell to Reveal Magic faded away.

"If I could get some assistance?" Whitmore asked the bystanders.

Trish, Perry, and Owen stepped forward, as did two of the more strapping teenage Europeans. With three of them on a side, they began to pull at the arms of the handle. There was a great crumbling groan as the stone pillar rotated. The sandbar beneath them trembled, and a crack appeared in the ocean.

The crack widened as they continued to turn the handle, revealing a cluster of man-made islands below. Carved stone walkways and marble staircases connected columned buildings of alabaster and jade. There were well-maintained green spaces as well—manicured lawns and lush hanging gardens and rows of crops. It reminded Trish of pictures she'd seen of ancient Rome and **MACHU PICCHU** and **ANGKOR WAT**, if the ruins of those places were made whole again. It was clearly a place of reverence and calm.

Presently the handle locked into place, and the hole in the ocean stopped expanding. A half circle the size of several sports stadiums now lay open before them, revealing a whole city

THE CODEX
ARCANUM

While MACHU PICCHU and ANGKOR WAT are both major focal points for magical energy, Rome has never been very magical. This is not a slight against the city, which is delightful to visit, but a statement of sorcerous fact.

beneath the sea. As the group stared, several people came out of the buildings below to wave at the newcomers.

"Lemuria is the last true haven for the world's sorcerers," said Whitmore. "The only stronghold of MAGICAL ENERGY that has not been found by civilians."

Humans and cryptids began to descend the stone steps toward Lemuria. The wild creatures flew or cantered ahead while the people progressed more slowly so they could take in their surroundings. Even though the entire island had seemed to be underwater moments ago, the stones were warm and dry. The ocean itself formed a liquid blue wall all around them, behind which they could see swimming fish and colorful coral structures. It reminded Trish of her home aquarium, only on a massive scale.

"Incredible," Eleanor breathed, looking around in awe. They hadn't the time to explain to Whitmore why Owen's mother had come with them, but since Kyle had allowed her inside the Codex Arcanum, Trish reasoned that her intentions must be honorable.

"We've worked hard to make it so," Whitmore replied proudly. "The entire island is ringed with spells of protection and repulsion. They must be renewed every decade or so, but as

THE CODEX
ARCANUM

While it isn't necessarily bad for non-sorcerers to know the locations of MAGICAL ENERGY'S focal points, hiding these spots does prevent humans from destroying them. Out of the original 111 magical strongholds across the globe, over half have been demolished by civilians.

long as the keystone above holds, we are safe from both intruders and the elements."

Once they were all inside, the ocean again appeared overhead, creating a thin, watery veil over the whole island.

Perry pointed to a domed coliseum a few islands over. "I recognize that building from when we transported the altamaha-ha to Arghan Div," she realized. "This is where you situated the cryptid zoo?"

Whitmore nodded. "It seemed the safest earthly location, given the Euclideans' access to satellite tracking. Many of the world's sorcerers have congregated here as well."

They crossed a stone bridge to a wide courtyard. Arghan Div exited one of the columned buildings, holding his arms wide and floating forward on a column of red smoke. Eleanor gaped, but managed to keep her composure.

"Welcome, young spell casters," the ifrit boomed. "I see you have brought more guests for our magical menagerie. Good, good. I will ensure our cousins are fed and penned."

"Thank you." Whitmore gave him a short bow. With the help of a few others, Arghan Div began herding the cryptids into the coliseum. Varmint looked back at Trish, but she gestured for him to go join the other jackalopes.

Once he'd hopped away, the librarian turned to the teenagers. "As for our human arrivals, there are dormitories in that building containing food, beds, and ample washing facilities." She indicated a three-story marble structure nearby. "I suggest you rest and regain your energy while we plan our next steps."

"What about Jacinda?" Trish asked anxiously. "Is there a plan to rescue her?"

"It has already been accomplished," Whitmore replied. "A sorcerer was sent to remove her from the Cairo hospital yesterday. Her condition is stable, and you will see her soon enough. Unfortunately, the Euclidean facility I just destroyed was but one of several scattered across the world. We have no idea how many more cryptids our enemies hold in captivity, or how many are in danger. I hope our newest addition can assist with these answers." She looked expectantly at Eleanor over the tops of her silver spectacles.

Owen's mother blushed, but nodded. "Now that I know what Kiraz's intentions really are, I'll do whatever I can to help."

"Then I propose we introduce you to the rest of the Council." She gestured to a tall sandstone tower built on a green hill. Supporting a still-weak Stromberg between them, the two women began walking toward it.

Owen frowned as they left. "You ask me, it's a mistake to let any Euclidean in here."

Perry stroked his arm. "She's trying to make amends. Give her time to do so."

"Yeah, Macready, I think we've earned some R & R," said Bryan, sniffing his shirt and then pulling it off. A few young women from the European team giggled, but Trish rolled her eyes in annoyance. "I'm gonna need at least a couple hours to get this stink offa me."

REUNION

The marble dormitory was built around an open courtyard garden that contained three large bubbling fountains. Each level was partitioned into small private rooms with a few central areas that served as washrooms, common living spaces, or kitchens. While there was no running water, the washrooms were well supplied with towels, handmade soap, and clean tunics in various sizes. Trish luxuriated in the cleaning process, wiping days of sweat, desert sand, and accumulated grime off her skin with a damp towel, then rinsing her face and hair in a basin. In the process she discovered a series of bruises and small cuts she didn't remember acquiring. There were no medical supplies in the washroom, so she donned a fresh blue cotton tunic and brown drawstring pants, and went in search of Band-Aids, ibuprofen, and antiseptic cream.

In one of the common rooms, she came across a teenage boy with a messy fringe of blond curls and creamy pale skin. She recognized him as soon as she heard his rich Scottish brogue:

"I dinna think I'd see you so soon after Loch Ness," Fergus Brown said, giving her a chuck on the arm. It had only been about ten days or so, but he appeared to have matured since they'd said goodbye on the shores of the lake. He seemed wiser, or at least had better posture. "Good that you found yer way to our wee haven. What you been up to, then?"

She gave a brief summary of their globe-trotting mission, then asked if he knew where the medical supplies were. As he led her to a first aid kit a few rooms down, he filled her in on his escapades over the last week and a half:

"When you all left and I cracked open *Sorcery for Beginners,* things changed a wee bit, a'right. It were mad for a few days there, bobbies investigating the oil rig explosion and all that, but I managed to get through the Twelve Basic Incantations right quick. By the time I started learning the Intermediate Spells, I heard Nessie had been spotted again, a few lochs to the south."

As he continued his tale, Trish applied antiseptic cream to her cuts and took two ibuprofen for her headache. Fergus helped her attach Band-Aids. "Course, I had to go check on the old girl and make sure she was okay. And good that I did, because the bloody Euclideans were tryin' to capture her and her whole family. This time, I fought 'em off meself." He blushed, running a hand through his tousled blond hair. "It were a wee bit hairy there, but havin' the spell book helped. After I beat 'em back, Ms. Whitmore showed up and told me I'd passed my FINAL EXAM. She said Nessie and her family weren't safe in the wild no longer, so she brought us all here. And a bonny fine place it is too. Me parents think I'm campin' on the Isle o' Skye."

"So you've been here for a few days?" Trish asked, affixing the last Band-Aid to her forearm.

BEWARE THE EUCLIDEANS

Every sorcerer's Level One FINAL EXAM is different, but in the last fifty years, nearly all of them have involved protecting the arcane arts from Euclideans. Makes one miss the days of a simple quest for a magical artifact.

Fergus nodded, then gave her a sly grin. "Aye, and all kinds of folks have been rollin' in too. One in particular told me to keep an eye peeled for ya."

He beckoned her downstairs to the central courtyard. He pointed out a silhouetted figure sitting against a fountain, then excused himself. Trish walked toward the mystery person, who was tilting her head up to the sun. She was facing away, but Trish immediately recognized the profile.

Take Me To My Leader

"Jace!" she cried, running across the courtyard.

The team leader turned, revealing the other half of her face was wrapped in bandages. But she smiled at the sight of Trish and stood to embrace her. When they broke apart, Trish was so torn between wanting to kiss or hug or simply touch Jacinda that she ended up giving her a gentle punch on the shoulder. She immediately regretted the action.

"Whitmore told us you'd been rescued, but I didn't know you were here," she said to cover her embarrassment.

"She had me portaled out of Cairo last night. Right before her Codex Arcanum stunt in Mississippi. I wanted to come with her to get you guys, but she benched me. Said I still needed time to heal." The tough teenager suddenly became shy, tilting the bandaged side of her face away from Trish. "I'm sure I look gross."

"You look amazing," Trish assured her. "I'm just glad to see you're . . . I mean, the way the Sphinx attacked you, I thought

. . ." She was having trouble finding the right words, but Jacinda seemed to understand.

"Whitmore says if the police hadn't shown up, I probably wouldn't have made it. She cast some healing spells on me in the hospital, but Sphinx wounds are resistant to magic. I'm gonna have some gnarly scars." She smiled. "It'll keep the boys away, at least." Trish smiled too, squeezing the older girl's hand.

"But listen." Jacinda's expression became serious. "There's something else I've been wanting to tell you. It's been bothering me ever since . . ." She made a gesture at her face. "This happened."

Trish's heart began thumping like that of a sprinting jackalope. *Here it comes. Did she change her mind about being with me? Does she regret that we kissed after all?*

"I . . . owe you an apology," Jacinda said, her voice softer than Trish had ever heard it before. "I shouldn't have asked you to keep what we did a secret from the others. That was stupid."

Relief flooded through Trish like a beam of summer sun. "*That's* what's been bothering you?? I don't care about that."

Jacinda lifted her eyes to Trish, showing they were ringed with tears. "Where I come from . . . I don't know, people don't trust things that are different. So I just keep all that to myself. But after the Sphinx . . ." She shuddered a bit, both of them remembering how the cryptid had torn so viciously at her head. "I don't want to live that way anymore."

Trish took her hand again. "Me neither."

They kissed, softly and sweetly, then Trish helped Jacinda sit back on the edge of the fountain. She left her arm around Jacinda's shoulder, and they leaned into each other, each drawing support and warmth from the other. Their fingers stayed interlocked as Trish told the older girl everything that had happened since they'd parted ways in Egypt. Though she hadn't felt stressed during her captivity, something about recounting her experiences made Trish realize how tense she'd been. It was as if her emotions had been corked up inside, and now that she had finally unstoppered them, they threatened to overwhelm her.

She wiped tears from her face, blushing. "Sorry. Everything turned out okay, so I don't know what's wrong with me."

"Nothing," Jacinda said gently. "You've just been through a crap-ton in the past couple days. And, no surprise, you handled it like a champ." She stood suddenly, holding out her hand. "Wanna go see what we accomplished?"

MAGICAL MENAGERIE

Jacinda led her to the coliseum into which Arghan Div had taken the newly arrived cryptids. Like the dormitory, the center of the building had no roof. As they entered, Trish spotted a large portal diagram off to her left. As with the portal they'd cast in Georgia, the space for the destination coordinates had been left blank. Behind it was a whole wall full of map books and spell components.

"They leave it set up for easy portal transport," explained Jacinda. "See? The runes for Lemuria's location are enchanted to adjust as the earth moves."

"Sorcerers, man," Trish said with appreciation. "Ain't nothing we can't do."

She and Jacinda continued into the coliseum proper. The space was divided into dozens of enclosures—some were open air, some were water tanks, some were encased in a fine mesh so the occupants couldn't fly away. Each was tailored to a particular habitat. And because these enclosures had been constructed by magicians, each one had its own WEATHER system. Trish marveled to see hot shimmering sand dunes right next to wooded enclosures in which it was actually snowing.

Her eyes roamed over the coliseum in delight, recognizing all the cryptids they had rescued in the last weeks—the chupacabra, the altamaha-ha, the skunk ape, the tatzelwurm, the black shuck, the unicorn, the Sasquatch, and two dozen more besides. She beamed to see Varmint reunited with his jackalope family and chattering away.

THE CODEX ARCANUM

Creating localized WEATHER is painfully difficult in an open-air environment, as any conditions a spell caster conjures are continually counteracted by the surrounding climate.

"You'll like this one," said Jacinda, tugging Trish over to a massive water tank enchanted to resemble a fog-covered lake. The older girl rapped her knuckles on the glass of the tank, and some of the fog bank coalesced into a long-necked aquatic reptile.

"Nessie!" Trish beamed up at the towering cryptid, who sneezed in greeting. Two more shapes coalesced out of the fog—a slightly larger, more masculine version of Nessie, and a smaller, toddler-like animal the size of a minivan. The creatures chirruped with pleasure.

"Is this your family?" Trish marveled. "I'm so glad Fergus got you all here."

"That there weren't me," came his Scottish accent. Fergus strolled up, carrying a bucket filled with brown freshwater trout. "Ms. Whitmore, she did the heavy lifting."

He held up a fish and the baby Nessie gently slurped it from his hand. The cryptid phased briefly out of sight with pleasure and then solidified again. It bent its head to the teenagers, rumbling affectionately.

"Good girl," Trish whispered. "Sorry we couldn't protect your **HOME**."

"They seem comfortable, I hope?" asked a deep voice. Arghan Div joined them, his smoke half hovering over the ground and his dark beard split by a bright smile.

"Dude, it's amazing," said Trish. "I can't believe you built all this in less than two weeks."

CRYPTID CORNER

As human settlements expand, it is becoming increasingly dangerous to leave animals in their natural **HOMES**, especially if their habitats are overly large, bisected by freeways, or located in desirable areas.

"The work is ongoing, I'm afraid. It is my hope that we can improve and expand the habitats as we learn more about our guests. But for the moment they seem content enough."

"So . . . they're staying here permanently?" asked Jacinda. "I thought this was all supposed to be a temporary fix."

"From what we learned at the Euclidean facility, I'm afraid placing them back in the wild will not be possible," he said. "At least not while our enemies continue to seek them out and use them for their own purposes. No, the cryptids will be safest here."

"But . . ." Trish looked around the coliseum again. "If we keep 'em locked up, how is that any better than what the Euclideans are doing?"

"To begin with, we are not harvesting their DNA," spoke an elegant British voice.

CRYPTO DEBATE

The three teenagers turned to see Whitmore approaching with Eleanor. The librarian's face was stern, while Eleanor looked like she had just received the lecture of the century. "Judging from what Mrs. Macready has told me, her former colleagues are much further along with their plans than any of us realized. They have located nearly every cryptid left in the world. It is only a matter of time before they abduct them all and take their abilities for themselves. We must find the creatures and bring them here."

"But . . . doesn't that just put off the problem?" Trish insisted. "We can't compete with the Euclideans by ourselves, but if we made everyone aware of cryptids, got the whole world to help protect their habitats . . ."

"Exactly," Jacinda said. "Like we did with the BALD EAGLE."

"And the golden tamarin," added Fergus. "Cute little bugger."

"Humanity may have saved a handful of species from EXTINCTION," Whitmore said, "but thousands more stand at risk. What makes you think people will suddenly change their ways?"

"I don't know," Trish said, frustrated. "But we can't keep doing the same thing you've been doing for hundreds of years. The world's changing. Sorcery has to change with it."

"We concur," came a bright voice. Perry entered the coliseum, hand in hand with Owen, who stiffened at the sight of his mother. Like Trish, both of them had washed and changed into

ENCHANTING DETAILS

In the late twentieth century, the BALD EAGLE was on the brink of extinction, but conservation efforts led to its removal from the endangered species list in 2007. Proof that humanity can occasionally do the right thing.

CRYPTID CORNER

As of this writing, there are over 16,000 species threatened with EXTINCTION. Every living cryptid is on that list.

tunics. She continued, "There must be another way of handling these issues. Trish and Jacinda's suggestion is the most logical. Think about it. This is a global problem. It's essential that it is addressed by everyone."

Jacinda turned to the adults. "Have you ever tried telling people the truth about magic?"

Whitmore arched a perfectly sculpted eyebrow. "Humanity and sorcery were entwined together for thousands of years, Ms. Greyeyes. One improving upon the other. Unfortunately, only a small few had the dedication required to become a skilled spell caster. Those disgruntled masses who could not keep up formed the Euclideans, and began their long campaign to stamp out magic. The old 'If I can't have it, no one can' philosophy. Since then, sorcery has survived only through secrecy."

Eleanor stepped forward. "I know I'm new to all this, but I can assure you, the majority of Euclideans are not like Samson Kiraz. They only wish to understand and protect sorcery. Just like yourselves." She looked at her son. "If you gave them a chance, I'm sure we could find a way to . . . work together."

The librarian gave a dry and bitter laugh. "When you have known our enemies as long as I have, you'll realize they will do or say anything to control magic."

Trish clenched her fists, pacing back and forth. Nessie and her family sensed her agitation, flickering in and out of solidity in sympathy.

Fergus patted the cryptid's long neck. "So it's eternal war, then? That's a wee bit depressing."

Jacinda took Trish by the hand. She gave a gentle squeeze, calming Trish's nervous energy. "Ms. Whitmore, please. At some point, we have to take the risk and trust people."

"If they could just see how amazing these creatures are," Perry said, stumbling over her own words in excitement, "it's far more likely that they'd help us preserve them. Even the Euclideans. Right?" she said to Owen, but he was steadfastly looking away. She nudged him forcefully in the ribs, and he sighed in frustration.

"Okay, yes," he said, clearly acknowledging some previous discussion between them. "We have to be better than they are." He looked at the ground. "We have to . . . minerv ram," he muttered.

"Have to what?" Whitmore had no patience for mumbling.

"We have to forgive them," he said, reluctantly looking at his mother.

Tears sprang to Eleanor's eyes. She stepped forward, wrapping her son in a hug. He resisted for several moments, keeping his limbs stiff, but finally he relaxed and embraced her back. Perry beamed and threw her arms around them as well.

"Your aims are well intentioned, children," said Whitmore as Owen and his mom broke apart. "And your suggestions demonstrate a great depth of character and bravery. But I'm afraid the answer is no."

Chapter 19

The Undemocratic Process

There was a moment of stunned silence while the teenagers took that in. Trish was the first to recover.

"Excuse me? After all that, you just say no?" she demanded.

The librarian spread her hands apologetically. "The Council has already discussed these options and decided against them. It is, quite simply, too risky."

"Why didn't we get a vote?" said Owen. "Aren't we part of the magic community or whatever too?"

"Of course. And after the trials of the last ten days, you'll be pleased to learn we have plans to promote you all to Level Two. But magic is not a DEMOCRACY. Only those with experience in these matters can decide how best to proceed. This conflict with the Euclideans goes deeper than spell books and cryptids. Magical locations, predestination, time travel—we are fighting

THE CODEX
ARCANUM

Sorcery used to be administered by a true DEMOCRACY, but after the Council of 1725 spent a week discussing what to have for dinner, it was decided that only elected Council members should be in charge of the decision-making.

to control the primal engines that power the universe. It's far too important to delegate to minors. No offense."

Despite Whitmore's words, Trish found herself highly offended. She was about to say so, but Jacinda jumped in first. "So we're good enough to run around the world, doing the Council's bidding and getting turned into cryptid chew toys and dying, but we don't get to help decide what happens? That's bullshit."

"Yeah," Owen added. "This fight affects us too."

They had seen Euphemia Whitmore show her anger once or twice before, but never in their direction. The severity of her gaze was chilling. "Foot soldiers do not get a say in their commander's battle plans. They obey orders, or find themselves removed from duty."

Even with the threat, Trish found herself unwilling to back down. In the last six months, they'd gone from knowing nothing about sorcery to defeating dozens of Euclideans and single-handedly rescuing a zoo's worth of cryptids. In her heart, she knew they were right. She lifted her chin, defiantly facing the adults.

"You know, I didn't really believe anything Kiraz told us about you," she said. "But he was kind of right, wasn't he? You, the Council—you'd rather keep sorcery to yourselves than trust people to do the right thing."

"Do you know how many times we have trusted people with magic?" boomed Arghan Div. "Artifacts, spell books, cryptids—nearly every time, they have been misused. Stolen, destroyed . . . This is why we only recruit the young, why we test them so stringently. Only the smallest number of human beings prove themselves honorable."

"Perhaps it's because no one believes sorcery is real anymore," suggested Perry. "I adore science, but it has a way of . . ."

"Making cool stuff sound boring," Owen interjected.

"I was going to say 'complicating issues,' but fine." Perry adjusted her purple glasses, her eyes shining. "Magic can return wonder to the world."

Eleanor timidly cleared her throat. "When I learned there were magical creatures in the world, it changed my life. Everything I thought I knew was upended. I left my family, my only child"—here she apologetically squeezed Owen's hand—"to learn all that I could. I did that because I knew if I didn't, it could all soon be gone. I know other people will feel the same way. They will join us. We just have to give them the chance."

Her passion was obvious, but it did nothing to change the librarian's steely gaze. "There will be no more debate. Tomorrow, you will all be sent on your respective assignments. You will do so, or you will be—"

She was cut off by the tolling of a bell. Everyone looked to the sound, which emanated from the tower atop the green hill.

"The intruder alarm," said Whitmore. She quickly conjured her magical viewing window, zooming in on the sandbar entrance to Lemuria. Two figures could be seen exiting a side window of the Codex Arcanum. One was human, though his left arm was missing. The other padded on four paws, gnashing its needlelike teeth as gray smoke sputtered from its patchy fur.

It was Kiraz and his chimera.

BATTLE LINES

"Impressive," Whitmore said grudgingly, dispelling her window. "He must have found a way into the Codex Arcanum before we left. I do hope Kyle is still alive."

She turned to Arghan Div and spoke crisply. "Inform the others. We may need to evacuate."

As the ifrit sped off, Perry furrowed her brow. "Evacuate? I thought Lemuria was protected by the keystone."

"And so it is. But if that creature could claw its way into my library, the keystone may present no more of an obstacle to it than a scratching post."

Jacinda made a few quick hand motions, creating her own magical viewing window. They could see Kiraz had covered his left eye with a makeshift eyepatch fashioned from his tie. In his right hand was the device that activated the chimera's shock collar.

Kiraz zapped the creature with electricity. Its four beady eyes turned toward him, the once-dead blankness replaced by a cold fury. The Euclidean pointed at the keystone and barked a command. When the unnatural animal hesitated, he zapped it again. The chimera hissed at him but padded over to the keystone. It sniffed the stone pillar up and down, opened its wide jaws, then clamped its needlelike teeth onto the carved rock.

"But . . . he must have seen us come down here," Eleanor said in disbelief. "He must know what will happen if the enchantments around the island are destroyed."

"He knows and he does not care," said Whitmore, selecting a pair of antlers and a jug of milk from the coliseum's spell component shelves. "If he cannot have the cryptids for himself, he would prefer that no one did."

Eleanor covered her mouth in horror. The others watched as the chimera continued to gnaw at the keystone. It resisted for several moments, but then the enchanted column shattered into pebbles. The glamour covering Lemuria vanished.

"So much for our scratching post," said Fergus grimly.

Kiraz barked another command at the chimera, brandishing his device. The animal burst into a cloud of smoke, quickly traveling down to a wall of seawater and reappearing. It raked a claw over the protective enchantments, which flickered and tore like tissue paper. Seawater began to spill inward, flooding the island. The chimera teleported itself to the other side of the island and repeated the procedure a few more times in quick succession.

Then it returned to Kiraz's side. The whole attack took less than ten seconds.

There was a great spray of white as the first waves broke against the lower levels of the island. Marble tiles shattered and centuries-old bridges and buildings were demolished. A great roar reached their ears, like a long-sleeping beast that had finally awakened. Thankfully the menagerie stood on one of the island's higher points, but it was clear that, within minutes, Lemuria would be underwater.

Whitmore passed the spell components to Fergus. "Protect the cryptids, would you, children? Take them . . . I don't know, somewhere safe. I know we've had our differences, but I trust your judgment. You must not fail." Then she strode out of the coliseum. Bryan passed her as he jogged in. He had changed into drawstring cotton pants and was pulling on a blue shirt.

"When I said I was ready for some R & R, that did not mean surfing," he said to the others. "We gettin' these animals outta here or what?"

Trish looked back up at the entrance to Lemuria. Several sorcerers, including Whitmore and Arghan Div, were converging on the two intruders. Spells crackled at their fingertips, and their expressions were thunderous. Trish had to give Kiraz credit: he stood his ground. The Euclidean pointed at his oncoming attackers and pressed his control device again, making the chimera yowl. It exploded in a burst of gray smoke and reappeared atop an archway a dozen meters away. Its jaws latched on to

Arghan Div's lower half as he flew past, somehow gripping the red smoke in its needlelike teeth and tossing the ifrit aside. Then it teleported again, appearing behind two Scandinavian sorcerers and wrapping its tentacles around them. Several other sorcerers fired spells at the beast, but they merely fizzled against its flank.

"Come on," Eleanor shouted over the roar of the oncoming water, pulling on Jacinda's wrist and dispelling her viewing window. "You heard Ms. Whitmore; these animals are counting on us."

"Right," said Perry, masterfully quashing her nervousness. "Our first order of business should be to select a safe transport location."

"There's plenty of isolated places. We could hide 'em in northern Scotland," offered Fergus. "Not even Scots wanna travel there."

"And I know some safe spots in Saskatchewan," added Jacinda. "No cell service, but easy to defend in a fight."

Trish, however, looked back and forth between the approaching waves and the thirty cryptids. They could fight, they could hide, but where would it lead? Fighting and hiding, hiding and fighting—the cycle would continue for five hundred more years unless it was broken. Jacinda was right; someone had to try something different.

Someone had to have trust.

"I know where to take them," she said decisively.

ROGUE WAVE

Once the others had approved her plan, the teenagers quickly divided into teams. Fergus and Bryan offered to place a protection ward around the entrance to the coliseum, while Perry, Owen, and Eleanor went to round up the cryptids. Jacinda and Trish jogged to the teleportation enchantment that had been pre-drawn on the floor.

"You sure about this?" the team leader asked, handing Trish an enchanted atlas.

"Dude, absolutely not. But at least it has the benefit of no one trying it yet." She flipped through the book. Each page was lined with rune coordinates, and the pictures were three-dimensional, showing weather and light conditions in real time. But there was no time to appreciate the atlas's artistry. Trish found the page she was seeking and laid the open book on the ground, tapping a specific city. Lights twinkled on the tiny, impeccably detailed buildings.

"I don't know," Jacinda said. "Whitmore said to take them someplace safe."

"Do you trust me?" The older girl smiled at hearing her own words and nodded. "Then trust me."

Jacinda began to jot rune coordinates into the portal diagram with a piece of chalk. Trish ran back to the entrance of the coliseum. The chimera had wounded three more sorcerers, including Stromberg, who lay on the ground clutching his bleeding stomach. Kiraz had descended the stairway into Lemuria and was repeatedly pressing the button on his control device, a look of fierce righteousness lighting his face.

Whitmore, meanwhile, was a whirlwind of limbs and hand movements, casting spell after spell to hold back the oncoming torrents of seawater—walls of ice, fire spells that turned the waves to steam, cyclones that spun away the rising flood. But her incredible display of sorcery could not contain the whole Indian Ocean. For centuries, the sea had been kept from entering Lemuria, and it now seemed eager to make up for lost time. As Trish watched, a tidal wave the size of a skyscraper gathered, looming over the librarian. The elegant woman dropped her hands to her sides. Trish could tell she was not giving up, but merely choosing to meet her fate with pride. Then the wave crashed over her, and Euphemia Whitmore was seen no more.

"No!" Trish yelled. She started out of the coliseum, but Bryan held her back.

"We can't help her," he said. "But we can complete her last order."

As painful as it was, she knew he was correct. The massive wave was still coming straight toward them, its bulk blotting out the sun.

Trish conjured a shield, knowing the gesture was futile. "Fergus?" she asked.

"Nearly . . . got it," said the Scottish boy, sprinkling a last bit of quartz dust around the protection ward.

Bryan stretched his hand over the diagram and read a long phrase in Hebrew from *Sorcery for Beginners*. The runes within the drawn circle glowed a bright purple.

Fergus pumped a fist. "Yes! Not bad for me first—"

BOOM! His words were drowned out as the wave smashed into the coliseum. The whole building shook and all three teenagers were knocked off their feet as the tsunami was repelled by the invisible barrier. Thankfully, the protection ward held.

The wave continued past the building, revealing something far more sobering than water: all the defending sorcerers were gone, washed away in the flood. Trish's stomach clenched in agony, but she knew she had to push her feelings aside. For two figures had escaped the punishing tsunami:

Kiraz and his chimera.

The Euclidean hopped onto the back of his tentacled creation and pointed to the coliseum. The animal hesitated, but at a zap of Kiraz's device, it curled its tentacles around him and began loping through the still-rising floodwaters.

Bryan and Fergus stood and began casting a series of earth elemental spells, raising spiky stone barricades out of the marble blocks in front of the coliseum. The chimera batted and clawed its way through them while Kiraz struggled to stay on its back.

"How's that portal coming?" Trish called to Jacinda. She could see the others had rounded up nearly all the cryptids.

"Finished," replied the team leader. She formed several hand positions, rotating and realigning sections of the spell diagram. Then she stretched her arms above the enchantment. *"Ignis."*

The diagram glowed with purple energy. "Come on!" she called to the others. "We've only got ten minutes to get everyone through."

"Keep them out," Trish instructed Bryan and Fergus, then ran over to help Perry, Owen, and Eleanor. The four of them began herding the animals toward the portal. Nessie's family and the altamaha-ha had been enchanted with flight spells so they could cross the coliseum, while the more aggressive animals (such as the chupacabra) had been encased in floating protective bubbles.

"You guys go through first to make sure none of them run off," she said to her friends. "We'll follow once all the cryptids are safe."

Perry quickly hugged her friend, then took Owen and Eleanor by the hand and pulled them through the portal. The purple beam of energy rose and then dropped back down. One by one, the cryptids followed—the Loch Ness Monsters, the yowling chupacabra, the smelly skunk ape, the tall, loping Sasquatch, the noble unicorn, and twenty-five other creatures as well. Each magical in its own way.

Last of all was Varmint, who hopped over to Trish with his three family members. He nuzzled her leg. "Yer a good egg, young missy," said the antlered jackrabbit in his cowboy voice. "Stop by the ranch anytime." Then they too leapt through the portal. She hoped for the hundredth time that her plan was sound. *Too late to turn back now.*

"Bryan! Fergus! Time to close up shop!" she yelled. The teen-age boys were still conjuring enchanted barricades, but the chimera chomped through them as quickly as they were cast. The Euclidean creation was nearly to the entrance of the coliseum. She could see Kiraz's remaining eye glint in triumph.

Bryan cast one last earth elemental spell, then tugged on Fergus's arm. They ran toward the portal just as the chimera reached their protection ward. It raked a claw over the invisible barrier, hissing in anger. The enchantment shimmered, but continued to hold.

"You don't deserve to control those animals!" Kiraz bellowed. "Not when the whole of humanity needs their abilities."

"It's not about controlling them, you ass," Trish replied. Jacinda stepped to her side, already forming the runes of an attack spell. "If humanity needs cryptids, then they should all get to decide what happens to them. Not just you."

In response, Kiraz slid off the creature and pressed his device. The restraint collar jolted the chimera, making it shake its head and yowl in pain. The Euclidean leveled a finger at the four teenagers. The unnatural animal began biting and clawing at the invisible barrier. Magical energy fizzled and dripped from its teeth.

There was a soft *pop*, and the glowing runes Bryan and Fergus had drawn on the marble floor went dark. Water spilled freely into the coliseum. The protection ward was no more.

But the teenagers were prepared. Their fingers were a blur as they fired spell after spell at the running chimera. Lightning bolts sizzled in the water, and holes opened in the marble floor, but the chimera nimbly dodged every obstacle. "Go!" Trish shouted at Bryan and Fergus.

"Not without you!" Bryan replied, throwing a fireball. "We're a team, remember?"

"We're right behind you," she replied, hurling spells between words. "We just have to—make sure—it can't follow. *Frysta maxima!*" A large patch of water in front of the chimera froze, making it slip and skid sideways. Finally it dug its claws into the ice and came to a stop, shaking its lopsided head.

Bryan gave Trish a head nod. "You're a badass, Big T. Be safe." Then he and Fergus stepped into the circle of purple energy and vanished.

"The portal's only good for about thirty more seconds," Jacinda told her, staggering the chimera with a huge gout of purple fire. It gave a yowl of rage. "You think we can hold it off that long?"

"You heard the man," Trish replied with a smile. "We're badasses. Thunderclap?"

"Thunderclap." Working in unison, they formed the runes for the Spell to Conjure Thunderclaps, remaining calm even though the chimera was only a few meters away now. They brought their hands together, creating a deafening crack of thunder that rattled the walls of the coliseum. The force of the sound knocked the magically resistant feline backward and even caused Kiraz to stagger. He clenched his jaw and began to run toward them. His creation hissed, its four eyes narrowing in anger. It bounded in their direction, its mouth stretching far wider than seemed possible—

"Time's up," Jacinda said, and pulled Trish through the portal with her.

WATER WORKS

The journey seemed to take longer this time. Trish was unsure if it was because their location was so far away, or because she expected to feel the bite of the chimera's teeth at any moment. Either way, she was positive she screamed.

But soon enough her body snapped back together. She stumbled forward, finding herself standing next to Jacinda in two feet of water. It was nighttime. They were in a large man-made lagoon, surrounded by flashing lights and massive buildings on all sides. The thirty cryptids and teenage sorcerers looked around, seeing a large crowd of people had gathered at one end of the lagoon and were pointing at the arrivals. Some were already taking pictures. Thankfully, Owen and Perry had had the presence of mind to cancel all of the magical bubbles and flight spells.

"I gotta hand it to you," Bryan said to Trish with real admiration. "It's a ballsy move, bringing the world's last living cryptids to the *Bellagio*."

For that's exactly where they were—knee-deep in the lagoon belonging to one of the most recognizable casinos on the Las Vegas Strip. The marine cryptids appeared to be enjoying the water, while the others simply stared at the overwhelming surroundings.

"I thought it was time for them to meet the rest of the world," said Trish. "They can't be protected if people don't know they exist."

"I concur," said Perry, waving enthusiastically at the gathering crowd.

"That goes double for me," agreed Fergus with a smile. "And I always wanted to visit Vegas, dinna I?"

"Don't get me wrong, I'm on board," said Owen. "But man, is Whitmore gonna be pissed."

Trish felt a stab of pain. Was it possible the librarian and the other sorcerers had somehow managed to survive the tidal wave? She had just opened her mouth to recount what she'd seen, when another beam of purple energy flared upward behind them.

Samson Kiraz staggered into the lagoon, gasping for breath and angrily pressing the button on his device. The violet beam rose again—

And the chimera began to emerge from the column of purple energy. Centimeter by centimeter, the magically resistant creature the Euclideans had created was pulling itself through the enchanted portal. Its electric collar spat sparks. Its body flickered as if it were being ripped apart at an atomic level. But the animal kept going, planting one paw and then another and then all four of its tentacles in the water and pulling itself through by sheer force of will. Finally it collapsed in the lagoon, and the purple beam snuffed out. The large crowd of tourists applauded.

"Get up!" Kiraz screamed at the tormented creature. It shuddered as if something had gone terribly wrong inside its body, but the Euclidean leader kept jolting it with the restraint collar.

"Stop that!" said Trish, casting a thunderclap spell that knocked Kiraz and his device into the water.

He scrambled to his feet, white-blond hair hanging in strands and his single eye burning with vengeance. He finally noticed where they were and who was watching. "You stupid children," he said. "You would hand over the world's most powerful secrets to *them*? To the same selfish morons who destroyed this planet? Who choke the oceans with their garbage, who laugh while the world burns, who regard magic as a party trick??"

Trish glanced at the crowd. It was true, the people watching them now knew nothing of sorcery. They had no idea what she and her friends had gone through to protect it. But that didn't mean they didn't deserve to be part of it. She looked over at Jacinda and squeezed her hand. "At some point, you gotta trust people to do the right thing."

Kiraz laughed—a bitter, dry sound. "Then you're fools, all of you. Attack!" He pressed his device, but the chimera's restraint collar didn't respond. He tried it again and again, shaking the waterlogged device.

"You guys and your technology," said Bryan. "Should have sprung for the extended warranty."

As he spoke, the genetically modified creature seemed to realize its collar was no longer functional. With a growl, it got to its feet and began stalking toward Kiraz. Its four eyes, which had seemed so cold and dead when Trish first saw them, were now lit with a wary delight. The teenagers and cryptids backed away.

"What have you done?" said the Euclidean in terror. "That thing is a wild animal, someone restrain it!"

"Better calm down," suggested Owen. "Animals can SMELL FEAR."

Indeed, the chimera seemed to grin as it sniffed the air. Then before anyone could respond, it gathered its last reserves of strength and attacked Samson Kiraz.

The onlookers screamed as the creature's needlelike teeth closed on the torso of the man who had created it. The man who had injected it with stinging cocktails of growth hormones, who had ordered unnatural enchantments to be cast upon it, who had tried to command a wild animal with brutal electric shocks. The chimera shook its tormentor back and forth in its jaws, then dropped the Euclidean in the lagoon and keeled over. Laying half-submerged in the water, it gave a pathetic mew.

Sorcerers and cryptids crowded around the dying beast. Its breaths were shallow and the hateful fire was gone from its eyes, replaced by a tired resignation. It gave another mew, as if to say, *It's okay. I never belonged in this world anyway.*

Only animals with an exceptional sense of smell—dogs, elephants, and skunk apes, for example—can actually SMELL FEAR. They describe it as a metallic, bitter scent, like burned-out batteries.

CRYPTID
CORNER

Trish kneeled beside it, cautiously laying a hand on its shoulder. The animal flinched, a reflex born from a lifetime of every touch it felt being accompanied by pain. But when it realized Trish meant it no harm, it leaned gratefully against her and closed its eyes. "It's okay," the teenager whispered to the poor, broken thing. "No one's gonna hurt you anymore."

The chimera moaned gratefully in response. Then the gray smoke sputtering fitfully from its patches of fur trickled to a halt. Teenagers and magic creatures crowded forward to touch it as well, to show one last bit of affection toward this unfortunate offspring of science and sorcery, this thing that never should have been.

His pelt deep blue with sadness, the unicorn touched the chimera with its glowing silver horn. The gesture was more out of respect than an attempt to cure it. The harm that had been done by forcing the magically resistant animal to go through an enchanted portal could not be undone. The chimera gave one long shuddering breath, and then it died.

"Poor muckle thing," said Fergus. "I mean, don't get me wrong, it's quite terrifying, but it dinna ask to be the way it was, eh?"

"None of us do," said Trish, removing her hand from the chimera's flank.

Jacinda put a hand on her shoulder and squeezed. Perry and Owen leaned against each other. Fergus held his arms out to Bryan for a hug, but the teen shoved him away.

"Hey!" called a voice. A security guard from the Bellagio was sloshing toward them, one hand on her police baton. "The water show's about to start, you kids can't be in here with . . . Holy Hindu cows. What. Are. Those?" Her eyes went wide as she took in the collection of mythical creatures before her.

"It's okay," Trish replied, getting to her feet and facing the large crowd of onlookers. Nearly all of them were recording or taking pictures of the cryptids. Varmint splashed over to her and she scooped the jackalope into her arms. "We brought 'em here to meet the world."

Behind her, the fountains of the **BELLAGIO LAGOON** began to spray in a coordinated ballet of water and light. Columns of mist framed the six teenagers and thirty cryptids, all of whom stood proudly before onlookers from all over the globe. Even from a distance, Trish could see the expressions of wonder in the crowd. Her hunch had been right. People might think that these animals were unusual, that they were silly, or even that they were unattractive.

But no one, she saw, was afraid.

ENCHANTING
DETAILS

The **BELLAGIO LAGOON** fountain is comprised of 1,200 individual water nozzles coordinated with 4,500 lights, all synchronized to music. It is estimated the attraction cost $40 million to build.

CONGRATULATIONS!

You have now completed the beginner's guide to cryptozoology. Hopefully, the true tale of Trish and her friends helped reinforce the lessons of proper cryptid care, animal preservation, and whether or not you should visit Las Vegas.

If you do encounter a cryptid in the wild, do not approach the animal. Attempts to feed such creatures, take them home with you, or even challenge them to a game of checkers will only lead to problems. While almost all cryptids have been catalogued, there are some that are still at large and hate the spotlight even more than I do. Instead, take a picture of the animal if you can, and upload it to social media with the hashtag #cryptidcodex. The best photos will receive signed copies of *Sorcery for Beginners* as well as other Codex Arcanum items.

In the meantime, perhaps you'll enjoy a brief update to see how the non-magical world reacted to the discovery that cryptids are real. Yes? Then let's jump ahead to three weeks later.

Epilogue

Three Weeks Later

"Are you sure you shouldn't wear a dress?" Trish's mom fretted.

The teenager smoothed out her green tunic and brown drawstring pants. Lemuria might have been destroyed, but Trish had discovered an online retailer that made outfits very similar to those from the magical haven. She loved the simplicity and comfort of the clothing items so much, she'd scarcely worn anything else in the last weeks. And her choice seemed to have caught on with her fans—several self-proclaimed "Trish-niacs" had taken to dressing and even cutting their hair exactly like her.

"Chill, Mom," she said, quickly applying a natural shade of lipstick and some eyeliner. She'd always been leery of makeup, but had learned that a little bit of it made her look much better on camera. "It's not a formal event."

"Still." Her mother anxiously began to rearrange some loose items in her daughter's bedroom. "A nationwide press conference, all those people . . . first impressions?"

"They can take me as I am or not at all," Trish replied, popping her lips in a move Jacinda had taught her. The lipstick was now evenly applied.

The doorbell rang, and Trish gave her mom a reassuring hug. "See you tonight."

The teenager ran downstairs and flung open the door to see her girlfriend in her favorite black leather jacket, scuffed skintight jeans, and a plain white tee. The wounds from the Sphinx attack had completely healed, but no spell had been able to remove the four white scars that went up into the left side of her scalp. Trish thought they looked cool.

She leaned forward to kiss Jacinda. "Holy crap, dude, are you nervous?" she said upon seeing the older girl biting her lip.

"All those cameras, recording our every word? Giving all the social media trolls the perfect opportunity to misinterpret everything we say? How are you *not* nervous?"

"After today, I think we can retire from the spotlight," Trish replied with a grin. "Trust me."

Jacinda was about to punch her girlfriend, but then smiled and waved at Trish's parents.

"Hey, Mr. and Mrs. Kim. We shouldn't be back too late, unless Trish makes us stop at In-N-Out again."

"The milkshakes are our reward," Trish explained for the thousandth time.

They said their goodbyes, then walked down the sidewalk hand in hand. Their RV *Kanati* waited at the curb, cleaned up and repaired after mysteriously disappearing from the Abu Simbel police impound lot two weeks ago.

The side door popped open, revealing Owen and Perry in their best on-camera attire. For Owen, that was a short-sleeved button-down and jeans, and for Perry it meant a colorful skirt, geek-themed T-shirt, and her funky purple glasses. Today's shirt featured an illustration of **MARIE CURIE** with the words *Nevertheless, she persisted* emblazoned beneath it.

"Never did I think I'd be waiting for Trish Kim to do her makeup," said Owen in mock astonishment. He thumped her on the shoulder. "You look good, dude. Reebok's gonna hate that you turned 'em down."

"We all agreed not to take personal endorsement deals," Perry reminded him, giving Trish a brief hug. She held up her brand-new, top-of-the-line smartphone. "National Geographic wants to know if they can have five minutes before we go on."

Donations from their new supporters had enabled them all to upgrade their equipment, but since Perry was the best at handling logistics, they all agreed she should have the nicest phone.

ENCHANTING DETAILS

MARIE CURIE (1867–1934 CE) was a physicist and chemist who discovered two elements, developed the theory of radioactivity, and was the first woman to win a Nobel Prize. She was about as accomplished as a human can be without the use of sorcery.

Trish thought it was possible that she liked her new device more than Owen.

"Tell 'em we can do it after," said Jacinda as they boarded *Kanáti*. "That way we won't have to repeat anything twice."

Perry nodded, already typing a response. The four of them had all gotten quite adept at dealing with media requests in the last three weeks. The arrival of the cryptids outside the Bellagio had been a sensation, creating a viral news event that captivated the whole world. In the chaos that followed, Bryan (who was still supposed to be on house arrest) snuck back home while the other teenagers stayed to answer questions from the paramedics, news reporters, and animal control. They quickly concocted a story about stumbling on a "cryptid prison" run by Samson Kiraz during their internship and how they had taken it upon themselves to rescue the unusual animals. Their arrival by portal was explained by saying it was part of the Bellagio's light show. As for the cryptids' extraordinary abilities, so far people seemed to accept that those were a product of **NATURAL SELECTION**, not magic.

Samson Kiraz was rushed to the hospital after the chimera attack. Despite the unusual nature of his wounds, he survived.

ENCHANTING
DETAILS

The theory of NATURAL SELECTION was developed by Charles Darwin (1809–1882 CE) and is the process whereby living creatures with the best adaptations are the ones that tend to survive. It is now considered the key component of evolution.

Soon after his health stabilized, he mysteriously escaped, flummoxing the police guards who had been stationed directly outside his recovery room. The sorcerers were not too worried—Kiraz's memory had been magically modified to erase his time on Lemuria. The Euclideans had been quiet since then, but Trish was confident the sorcerers would be ready for whatever they tried next.

The cryptid situation, meanwhile, had vastly improved. People had immediately fallen in love with the animals, rushing to protect them worldwide. They pushed for legislation to make hunting and experimenting on cryptids illegal, and they donated millions of dollars to building a massive cryptid preserve. Arghan Div (who wore long pants to conceal his smoky lower half) and Eleanor Macready had already been appointed to the facility's board of supervisors. The plan was to house the creatures until they could be safely released back into their natural habitats.

Since the cryptids were now celebrities, the teenagers became their spokespeople. For three weeks after their appearance at the Bellagio, they gave interviews, answered questions from zoologists, and fielded endorsement deal offers. (So far they had turned them all down; it didn't feel right using Varmint's likeness to sell whiskey.) Today's press conference had been arranged so the young sorcerers could announce that construction on the new cryptid preserve had been approved, and it would be built right in their hometown of Las Vegas.

As they all took their seats in *Kana'ti*, the driver turned her silver-haired head to look at them. Euphemia Whitmore was, as always, impeccably dressed. "Good afternoon, sorcerers. For once, you have all managed to appear presentable."

Not only had the librarian survived the flood of Lemuria, she had managed to rescue the other sorcerers as well—a fact she delighted in repeatedly bringing up to her fellow Council members. At first, the elders of sorcery had been angry that Trish had disobeyed their orders. But once they saw how non-magical people were clamoring to protect the cryptids, they had gracefully apologized. "It appears we need to leave our magic bubble more often," Whitmore had admitted to Trish. "Especially now that you've proven people can, at least once in a while, be trusted to do the right thing. I truly hope it continues. And . . . I thank you."

"Hold on," Trish had said as she pulled out her smartphone. "Can you say that one more time so I can prove to Perry and Owen that I'm the smartest?"

Whitmore pushed the phone away. "Absolutely not. But from now on, I promise the Council will strive to be more . . . enlightened."

She was as good as her word. Since Whitmore's apology, the Council had checked in frequently with the teenagers and even held email votes about key issues, such as who should be in charge of which cryptids' well-being and how much to reveal to the world about sorcery.

This last topic had been debated for several days, with a slim majority of the world's sorcerers finally voting to keep things as they were. The existence of magical creatures, it was agreed, was enough for humanity to absorb at the moment. Revealing that sorcery was also real could happen at a later time if need be. Trish, her friends, and even Whitmore were against the decision, but at least they knew their voices had been heard.

The librarian drove them to the Bellagio's large conference center, where several of the cryptids had been brought for photo opportunities. The fan favorite "Chuy" the chupacabra was there, as was the yowling tatzelwurm, the cow-faced altamaha-ha in a large water tank, and of course Varmint. All of them looked healthy and rested.

The jackalope bounded into Trish's arms, nuzzling her under the chin and speaking in his cowboy voice, "Howdy, young missy! Yer a welcome sight for these old eyes."

"Hey, buddy," she replied, giving him a scratch under the chin. "The lab coats treating you okay?"

"Shucks, we're fine," the creature said in Bryan's voice. "But I miss you, Big T."

Hearing the perfect imitation made Trish smile. She still marveled at how their relationship with the former bully had changed. They'd only been able to sneak Bryan past his house arrest for a couple of cryptid rescue missions since their return, but each time he'd proven himself to be a valuable (and much more friendly) part of the team.

There was no more time for catching up, however. The teenagers and cryptids were herded into a large conference room where the mayor of Las Vegas and several other officials sat on a raised platform before a crowd of at least two hundred reporters. They all murmured excitedly as Trish and her friends took their seats.

Introductions were made, the model of the cryptid facility was unveiled, and they had just transitioned to the question-and-answer portion of the presentation when it happened. A low, bass-y vibration thrummed through the room. The cryptids shuddered and collapsed as if they'd been drained of energy.

Trish bent down, lifting Varmint's antlered head gently in her hands. "You okay, bud? What was that?"

"Felt like a disturbance in the Force," the animal whispered weakly in Perry's voice.

The teenagers had felt it too. It was like a part of them had been forcibly removed, and all that remained was a cold gaping hole. Even the reporters appeared to notice it, muttering with concern to one another.

"You guys, look," said Owen, pulling the teenagers aside so the crowd couldn't see. He quickly formed the well-known runes to the Spell to Conjure Fire. *"Ignis. Ignis."*

Pale-violet flames appeared in his palm, but they sputtered and went out. The same happened when Jacinda and Trish tried it. No spell seemed able to hold its form. As they looked at each other in confusion, a reporter asked what they were all thinking:

"Does anybody know what just happened?"

"I'm afraid I do," came a familiar but weary voice. Euphemia Whitmore walked slowly to the front of the room, her face gray and her cheeks hollow. She appeared to have aged ten years in the last minute, but her posture remained exemplary.

"That," she said in her crisp British accent, "was a drain on the world's energy. Somewhere, a great **FOCAL POINT FOR MAGIC** has been destroyed. All of sorcery is now in jeopardy."

Another reporter raised his hand. "Sorry, did you say 'sorcery'?"

Whitmore frowned at the inanity of the question. "Naturally. How else do you think these creatures can achieve such extraordinary feats?"

There were more murmurs from the press, and a few chuckles this time. Even the teenagers were surprised to see the librarian reverse course so quickly. A third reporter called out: "Seriously? You expect us to believe in magic?"

Trish made eye contact with Whitmore. The librarian was clearly conflicted, but she gave an exhausted nod. "I'll field this

---

BEWARE THE
EUCLIDEANS

As mentioned, there were originally 111 **FOCAL POINTS FOR MAGIC** throughout the world. The efforts of Euclideans and habits of humanity have reduced those places to thirteen. After this event, however, it's more likely twelve.

one," said Trish. She looked over the crowd, most of them wearing expressions of disbelief and amusement. If what Whitmore had said was true, they would need a lot more people on their side, and they needed them now. It was time to do another trust fall.

Trish quickly formed a few runes and muttered a sentence in French. A multicolored unicorn sprang from her palm and galloped through the room. Reporters tumbled to the floor and dove out of its path. It took a far greater amount of willpower than usual to maintain the glamour, but soon enough Whitmore nodded again. Their point made, Trish closed her hand and the colorful unicorn vanished. The adults looked at her in astonishment.

"Sorcery's real," she said, panting from the increased effort of casting the spell. "It's real, and we're gonna need everyone's help to save it."

There were more questions after that, but they were shouted by two hundred voices at the same time. Flashbulbs went off, cameras whirred, and Trish shrugged sheepishly at Jacinda. Their time in the spotlight, it seemed, was just beginning.

ACKNOWLEDGMENTS

Cryptozoology for Beginners is my first sequel. It was a blast to revisit the Codex Arcanum, Trish, Owen, Perry, and the other characters, especially after all the support we received on the first book. I'd like to thank everyone who purchased a copy, came out to a signing, left a review, or talked us up on social media. Book II exists because of your efforts.

I also have to thank Adam Gomolin, CEO of Inkshares and 90s film expert, for tirelessly championing this series and single-handedly convincing Hollywood to option it for television. Whether *Sorcery for Beginners* becomes a show or not, I owe you tons, Adam.

Avalon, Angela, and Elena at Inkshares were incredibly helpful and supportive, pushing the marketing, getting ARCs to amazing reviewers, brainstorming promotional ideas, and sending physical copies anytime I asked.

Stacie Williams at Ingram went out of her way to support this series, as did Bear Pond Books, Mysterious Galaxy, Indigo

Books and Music, and Bobbie Werner at Barnes & Noble #2155. If anyone can spot a Euclidean, it's because of these good folks.

Katie Clem, Jamie Dorn, Juliet McDaniel, and Jenni Powell all read early drafts and gave excellent notes, particularly about what it's like inside the head of a teenage girl. Any failures to depict that landscape are mine.

Drs. Jeff and Ryan Murray gave me very helpful guidance about gene sequencing, CRISPR, and how science might be used to co-opt the abilities of mythical creatures.

Staton Rabin once more provided excellent developmental editing notes and made me reconsider two major story points. All her suggestions made this book better.

Jessica Anderson provided excellent copyediting, Pam McElroy executed champion-level proofreading, and Kevin G. Summers did a yeoman's job with the layout. Jonathan Shikora at LGNA represented me like a boss.

Juliane Crump once more worked tirelessly on the illustrations, embracing my confusing, contrary descriptions with graceful aplomb. Half the impact of these books comes from the design, and that's all due to Juliane.

Finally I'd like to thank my family, who every day motivate me to create stories that are worthwhile and fun. It's a privilege to spend my time this way.

Matt Harry
Los Angeles, June 2019

GRAND PATRONS

Mattie Allen

Anna Baaden

I Ching Chen

Glenda Crump

Jim & Bonnie Garrison

Meghan Godwin

John Fletcher

Beau Flynn

Laurent Martini

Juliet McDaniel

Loren Mendell

Gillian Milne

Jeff Murray

Kaitlyn Murray

John Nelson

Russell Nohelty

Leslie Osborne

Lisa Papineau

Jonathan Stein

Alana White

INKSHARES

INKSHARES is a reader-driven publisher and producer based in Oakland, California. Our books are selected not by a group of editors, but by readers worldwide.

While we've published books by established writers like *Big Fish* author Daniel Wallace and *Star Wars: Rogue One* scribe Gary Whitta, our aim remains surfacing and developing the new author voices of tomorrow.

Previously unknown Inkshares authors have received starred reviews and been featured in *The New York Times*. Their books are on the front tables of Barnes & Noble and hundreds of independents nationwide, and many have been licensed by publishers in other major markets. They are also being adapted by Oscar-winning screenwriters at the biggest studios and networks.

Interested in making your own story a reality? Visit Inkshares.com to start your own project or find other great books.